'SHE WAS ▮▮▮▮▮▮▮▮▮▮ IA
TODAY.' H▮ ▮▮▮▮▮▮▮▮▮ 'I
TOOK THE ▮▮▮▮▮▮▮▮ HE
OFFICE, AND WE WENT FOR A WALK.

'She doesn't want to come out and do a
season but she doesn't want to hurt Loelia
either. She thinks Loelia is motivated only
by love for Diana and a desire to do right
by her dead friend's daughter. All very
touching.'

'And you can't tell Pammy the truth?'
Esther said.

'I can't be sure it's the right thing to do.
Lately, I've thought about it constantly,
Esther. Should I or shouldn't I? Have I the
right to tell? Or the right not to tell? What
do you think? Help me, darling.'

Esther groaned softly. 'Howard, I'm no
more sure than you. But, if you push me,
I'd say Pammy has a right to know.'

'A right to know what?' Pamela was
standing in the doorway. 'Whatever it is, I
think you should tell me now.'

DENISE ROBERTSON

TOWARDS JERUSALEM

THE THIRD VOLUME IN
THE BELOVED PEOPLE TRILOGY

A SIGNET BOOK

SIGNET

Published by the Penguin Group
Penguin Books Ltd, 27 Wrights Lane, London W8 5TZ, England
Penguin Books USA Inc., 375 Hudson Street, New York, New York 10014, USA
Penguin Books Australia Ltd, Ringwood, Victoria, Australia
Penguin Books Canada Ltd, 10 Alcorn Avenue, Toronto, Ontario,
Canada M4V 3B2
Penguin Books (NZ) Ltd, 182–190 Wairau Road, Auckland 10, New Zealand

Penguin Books Ltd, Registered Offices: Harmondsworth, Middlesex, England

First published by Constable and Co. 1993
Published in Signet 1994
1 3 5 7 9 10 8 6 4 2

Printed in England by Clays Ltd, St Ives plc

BOOK ONE

1

June 1946

'Stand still!' Anne said, through teeth clenched on a half-dozen pins. She was threading the hem of her sister's dress through her fingers, lifting it here, dropping it there, pinning it as she went. Esther eased her weight to her other leg and tried to be a statue, but her fingers itched to get at Anne's cluttered mantelshelf, the uncleared table, the rim of dust along the top of the wireless set. Through the window, beyond the long garden, she could see the roofs of Belgate. If only the kitchen were as neat as the rows of vegetables.

All the same, however slack a housewife Anne had become, she still had magic in her fingers. The blue cloque dress fitted snugly over Esther's breast and flowed from her hips – a masterpiece of dressmaking, in spite of the shortage of material and petty rules of clothes rationing.

The war had been over for almost a year but Britain was still in the grip of shortage and austerity. A world food-shortage had brought about a reduction in rations and there seemed little hope of easement in the near future. Even bread was rationed now, something that had not happened in the darkest days of the war. The British people had been promised milk and honey with peace. Nowadays they were lucky to get bread and scrape.

Esther felt a tug at her skirt and moved obediently to the left. Anne was putting her heart and soul into this dress, so the least she could do was be co-operative. Besides, it was nice to stand still for a moment, to be away from the telephone and the constant stream of callers to the office she shared with her partner, Sammy Lansky. Normally she enjoyed the demands of their retail business but lately, as her wedding-day loomed, she had felt pressured by them.

'I am marrying Howard Brenton,' she thought. 'I will be Mrs Howard Brenton.' And she would be mistress of two homes, the rambling house on the Scar, the hill above Belgate; and Mount Street, the elegant town-house in Mayfair. 'Am I up to it?' she had asked Sammy, when the full implications of marriage to a rich man dawned upon her. She had said yes to Howard Brenton in the euphoria of VJ night, but in the cold light of morning she grew scared.

'Up to it?' Sammy's eyebrows had almost disappeared into his dark curls. 'Esther – the tycoon who built my business for me while I scrubbed the barrack square – not up to being a wife? Feh! Besides, this Howard of yours is a great man; he knows what he's doing. He thinks you're a pearl, and he's right. So – no more doubt! Enjoy it, that's my advice.'

The first time Esther had seen Howard Brenton up close, she had thought him the handsomest man she had ever imagined. That had been thirty years ago, when she was a child living in Belgate and he was a man, the son of Charles Brenton who owned the Belgate coal-mines. He had roared through the village in his motor-car like a giant of the silver screen, and never, in her wildest moments, had Esther dreamed he would speak to her, let alone ask her to be his wife. So much had happened in those intervening years. 'Too much,' she thought, as she responded once more to Anne's impatient tug.

Howard Brenton had been married in those days, to the beautiful wilful Diana; Esther, little more than a child, had gone to work at the Scar as a maid. 'And who are you?' Diana had enquired on their first meeting. 'I was fifteen, then,' Esther thought, remembering how her mouth had dried at the sight of her new employer. She had tried to stammer out an answer and Howard had come to her rescue.

'I'm Howard Brenton and this is my wife. You call her Mrs Howard, or madam.' Diana had taken pity on her then and held out a welcoming hand.

'Do you sew, Esther? Good. Then you shall be my

personal maid. No, don't look so scared, I'll teach you all you need to know.'

'She was beautiful,' Esther thought now, remembering Diana that day, her dark hair cut short and curling over her cheek, her hand resting on a belly swollen with her first child. And now that child was dead in the war; and Diana was dead too; and the fifteen-year-old maid had become Sammy Lansky's business partner with a home and a bank-account whose contents sometimes scared her.

'That's it,' Anne said, breaking into Esther's reverie. 'Well, almost. Just turn slightly to the left again . . .'

'You're going to look the part, our Esther,' Anne had said, once she had come to terms with the fact that her only sister was marrying out of her class – and marrying a hated coal-owner, to boot. 'I was done out of a white wedding myself, and our Stella got married behind my back. I'm making sure you have the trimmings, and there's no power on earth that'll stop me. It can't be white, with a war on . . . or as good as . . . but it's going to be posh.'

So the blue dress, with ruched pockets and a cowl neck, had been planned, and with it a matching hat, a round confection of rouleaux and net to perch over Esther's eye, and tan court shoes, brought all the way from London. There was a drawerful of nightgowns and petticoats, cut from the white parachute silk that abounded now, and lovingly faggoted and embroidered by Anne until her fingers were sore and her eyes ached.

'She loves me,' Esther thought, and was filled with warmth for her sister, so that her eyes pricked uncomfortably. Life had been hard when they were young, and Anne never off her back, or so it seemed. It was only now, as they grew older, that they were becoming close.

Esther closed her eyes, remembering her father behind the polished counter of their drapery shop, in the days before her mother had died and he had taken to drink. The shop had smelled of new fabrics, and Anne had had hair like a raven's wing and hands that looked as though they'd never seen hard work. Impulsively Esther reached out to stroke her sister's brow. 'How's Stella?' she asked. 'Any news yet?'

Stella, Anne's eldest daughter, had married a GI during

the war, and she was now awaiting transportation to the United States for herself and her baby son, much to her mother's dismay.

Anne removed the last pin from her mouth and set it in place before she replied. 'You can take it off now. Mind the pins! No, she's had no orders yet . . . just to be ready when she gets the word.'

'They say the GI brides will all be gone by the end of next month,' Esther said, her voice muffled as she pulled the dress carefully over her head.

'Stella's got a passport. They told her to get that, and be ready to leave at a moment's notice. Yanks always think they're doing you a favour – them and their bubble gum, getting British girls into trouble, and whisking them off just like that.'

All over Britain brides were waiting patiently. At the end of 1945 Congress had agreed 'to expedite the admission to the United States of alien spouses and alien minor children of citizen members of the United States Army Forces.' Immigration to the States was severely limited and eagerly sought: Congress was making a concession to the GI brides, but few of them appreciated it. They read the booklet, *A Bride's Guide to the USA*, with its warnings that all America was not Hollywood, but few of them heeded. They waded through the piles of official forms with their eyes fixed on that golden country where there was no rationing, no austerity, and where nylons grew on trees.

Stella's own goals were more specific: tinned peaches every day, a wardrobe like Joan Crawford's, and a large white car with tail-fins.

'It'll never work,' Anne said gloomily, as she set about making a pot of tea for herself and Esther. 'There's marriages breaking up every day right here in Britain . . . a tidal wave of divorce, it says in today's paper. Thirty-five legal teams have been set up to get them through the courts. And our Stella, who's never been farther than Blackpool, is expected to work it out on the other side of the world.' For months Anne had agonized over Stella's impending departure. She would not be entirely sorry to wave her turbulent daughter goodbye – but her grandson was a different matter. 'How I'll part with that bairn I do not know,' she said now, spooning sugar into her cup.

'Cheer up,' Esther said. 'The world's shrunk since the war, Anne. Everything's changed. Stella'll visit, and you can go there . . .'

'Oh yes,' Anne said sarcastically, 'I can just see me and Frank visiting America on a pitman's wage. Easy! Shall I book the *Queen Mary*, or shall we fly? I've got a broomstick somewhere.' As usual an opportunity for sarcasm restored her spirits. 'Still, like Frank says, I'm living a day at a time, our Stella being our Stella. I'll believe she's gone when she's on the water . . . and even then she has a chance to be on the first boat home once she finds she hasn't married a Rockefeller. Mario's an Eye-tie, when it comes down to it, American or not. And they expect women to pull their weight. Remember the Pastorelli girls in the ice cream parlour in Sunderland? They scrubbed those tables down twice a day, and worked behind the counter till they dropped. If our Stella gets within a smell of a bit of hard work, she'll be home in a flash.'

Esther shook her head tactfully, but privately she agreed with everything Anne had said. There was no disguising the fact that Stella had always been a headache. The shot-gun war-time wedding to Mario, when Stella was already pregnant, had not exactly been a shock – but there was still a mystery about it somewhere, Esther always thought. There was nervousness on Anne's part when the subject came up; and unease in Frank's expression when he dandled his grandson on his knee. Still, the American boy was nice; plump, and sweet-natured, and a good Catholic, which had pleased Anne. Perhaps it would be all right.

Sipping her tea, Esther thought ahead again to her own wedding. It was taking place in Bishopwearmouth, the church in the very centre of Sunderland. She would have liked her dearly loved partner Sammy, or his father, Emmanuel, to give her away, but they were Jews. Frank, Anne's husband, was a Catholic. So she would be walking down the aisle on the arm of Edward Burton, her future husband's friend. And Howard would be waiting there for her, smiling reassurance . . . at least, Esther hoped he would. And suddenly the thought of his face swept away

11

her doubts. 'We will be happy,' she thought. 'Of course we will be happy.'

Anne picked up the dress and held it at arm's length. 'When I get this done I can get on with the bridesmaids' dresses.' Howard's daughter, Pamela, would be the chief bridesmaid, assisted by Anne's daughters, all of them in white parachute silk with blue smocking at the shoulders and blue sashes. Howard's daughter – who was also Diana's daughter! 'Will it work?' Esther thought again. 'Am I cut out to be an instant mother to three?' For in addition to Pamela, there were two sons, Ralph and Noel. Howard's eldest son, Rupert, had been shot down over the Channel just before the end of the war.

'Well . . .' Anne sounded justly proud. 'I can't have – er – Howard . . .' She hesitated over the name and Esther put up a hand to hide her smile. For years Anne had referred to her future brother-in-law as 'that bugger Brenton', or words to that effect. The transition to familial terms would be hard. 'I can't have Howard and his fancy friends thinking we don't know how to dress. If it hadn't been for coupons, I'd have sent you down that aisle like a fashion-plate.'

'I will be a fashion-plate,' Esther said, looking down at her dress and then up to the mirror. The clear blue matched her eyes and set off her fair hair. 'I'll look nice,' she thought and felt a thrill of anticipation at the thought of Howard's face as she came down the aisle towards him. He loved her. What did it matter that she was not of his class, that his friends looked down on her, that his first wife had been a beauty. 'We love one another,' she thought, 'and that's all that counts.'

'It's a nice enough dress,' Anne said, 'but it's not *bridal*. Not white . . . and it's short.' She sighed. 'I used to think I'd have white lace when I married. Yards and yards of white lace, with a train and everything. And arum lilies and a Mary Queen of Scots head-dress. And what did I get? A washed-out frock and a bunch of raggy chrysanths – and not even a mattress on the floor for me wedding night.' Anne had married Frank, a young miner, hard on the heels of her father's bankruptcy and death – to avoid having to go, like Esther, into service at the Scar. 'Still,' she said, 'we've been happy – and we were lucky with our bairns except . . .' She faltered then and Esther knew she was thinking of Joe, her eldest son, who had died on a Normandy beach-head.

'If Howard and I', she said, anxious to divert her sister, 'are as happy as you and Frank, I won't grumble.'

'Are you *sure* you're doing the right thing?' Anne said suddenly. 'Not that I'm criticizing Howard. He means well . . . even Frank says that. But he's been wed once, Es, and there's his children . . .' She hesitated, and Esther finished for her.

'. . . and he's a different class. That's what you mean, isn't it?' Anne was shaking her head, but Esther was not to be gainsaid. 'I don't think about that, Anne, and neither does he. Do you think I'd love him if he was a snob?'

'He's a coal-owner,' Anne said dourly.

'Yes, he was born to a coal-owner, Anne. Like you and I were born to a draper, and Frank was born to a collier. We can't be blamed for that. Howard followed in his father's footsteps: he's not a coal-owner from choice.'

'Well, he won't be one for much longer,' Anne said, suddenly triumphant. 'He's going to lose his pits, and the men'll own them: Clem Attlee's seeing to that.' But then she remembered that she was gloating over the man who was soon to be her brother-in-law, and her words dried up. Esther saw her expression and chuckled aloud.

'Don't worry, our Anne. Howard can't wait to lay the burden down. He'll have his financial compensation, and the men'll have the headaches. Now, have you finished with me for today? Because I can't sit here as though I had corn growing – not with Sammy away.'

She hoped she sounded confident but inside her unease was growing again. Was she doing the right thing? Was love enough? Could she cope with life in London when the time came, with the Hon. Loelia Colville, Diana Brenton's dearest friend, breathing down her neck?

It was warm on the hill without a breeze to ruffle the grass. Frank Maguire plucked at a blade, placed it carefully between his thumbs, and blew. He had been able to whistle out of grass when he had been a boy but now he could not produce the reedy note.

He looked down on Belgate. There was a bright new roof on the end house in Edith Street where two incendiaries had gone clean through one night in 1943. It had been empty for nearly three years, but tenants were in there now . . . a lad who had lost a leg at El Alamein, and his wife and baby. If only his son, Joe, had come back: Frank felt he wouldn't have minded anything if Joe had come home, safe and sound. But Joe was only a name on the raw, white war memorial – 'Joseph Maguire, aged 21. Died 6. 6. 44'. And above, the other name: 'Charles Rupert Neville Brenton, aged 21. Died 14. 7. 44.' Howard Brenton's son and his son, Joe, had been born on the same day, in the same village; one to a collier, one to a coal-owner; they had died in the same war . . . and yet, to the best of Frank's knowledge they had never exchanged a word. That was class for you; an invisible wall that was yet made of steel. Not that it had stopped Stella. She had climbed the wall to conceive Rupert Brenton's child, and then palmed it off on a gullible GI. As far as the world knew, the child was a Yankee. Only he and Annie and Stella herself knew the truth. And now Esther, his sister-in-law, was marrying a Brenton. It couldn't have happened without a war!

Frank began to descend the hill, moving from tussock to tussock, humming gently under his breath, wondering what Annie would have conjured up for his meal. Rations were down to the bone now. The peace-time loaf he had looked forward to throughout the war was already darker than the 'victory bread' they had tolerated for so long. He got a bigger ration than most because he was a manual worker, but if the bloody stuff was uneatable where was the satisfaction? All in all, life was a bugger, he thought, for his loss of the nomination to be Labour's candidate at the next election still rankled.

He had been sure of being chosen, proud of the respect he had gained by being a crack hewer down the pit and a trade-union activist up above. He had ridden the men hard in the war to keep up production, and he didn't regret it – but it had made him enemies. And then there had been the matter of the war memorial. As a parish councillor, he had

14

drawn up the list of names of Belgate's war-dead, among them Rupert Brenton, who had died in a dog-fight over the Channel.

It had been Stanley Gallagher who had raised the first objection: Rupert Brenton was a coal-owner's son, and had been born just outside the parish line into the bargain. Frank had defended the boy's right to be included, and he had won, but not everyone had been pleased with the decision; the smirk on Gallagher's face as they left the meeting had boded ill. When the nomination was made, it was Gallagher's name which went forward. Frank's dream of a seat in Parliament was gone. But he did not regret his stand: even a coal-owner loved his children, and Brenton's pain had been no less than his own. If seeing his son's name carved on marble had helped that pain even a bit, he was entitled to it.

Reaching the foot of the hill they called the Scar Frank turned to look back at the house that crowned it. It was Howard Brenton's house, a home of privilege and power. Little Esther had been a maid there when she was knee-high to a grasshopper and wore her hair in braids. Now she was to be its mistress. It was nice to think she was going up in the world: she was a hard worker, even Annie admitted that, and had no fancy airs about her, for all her success. But how would she cope with the London nobs who were Howard Brenton's friends?

As Frank pushed open the yard door he sniffed the air. Leeks! A nice leek pudding boiled in a clout, and a good Oxo gravy to dip it in. His mouth filled with saliva and his spirits lifted. If he *had* got the nomination he might have been bound for Westminster, and Annie's leek puddings a thing of the past. There were compensations to everything.

Howard Brenton leaned back in his chair and tried to look attentive as the man on the other side of the desk made out his case for a share of Brenton business. Long ago Howard had employed Edward Fox as his chauffeur, and had dismissed him for dishonesty and offensive behaviour. But Fox had grown fat in the war. He was a haulage magnate now, with a fleet of lorries and a long, sleek car that was nearly as shiny as the black hair that crowned his arrogant head.

'So you see,' Fox was saying persuasively, 'I could cut your transport costs by a fifth at least. Probably more.'

'I'd have to lay men off, in that case,' Howard said.

'Yes.' Fox was trying to look concerned but failing dismally. 'A few men. But they'd find other work easily enough. I might take on one or two of them myself.'

'I can't lay them off now, with some of them just returned from war-service.' Howard spoke sharply, seeing the slight jowl on the other man, the whiteness of his hands, folded now across his waistcoat front. Was it for men like this that Rupert had given his life? While so many young men had fought and died, men like Fox and that other scoundrel, Gallagher, had milked the situation for all it was worth. 'I believe you employ Stanley Gallagher?' he said.

Fox nodded. 'Yes, he's my book-keeper. He was never suited to teaching and . . .' He met Howard's eye squarely. 'I don't see why he should be penalized for his old man's shortcomings.' Stanley Gallagher's father had been sentenced to prison for war-time corruption, and many people thought Edward Fox should've been in the dock alongside him.

'No,' Howard said, 'I wouldn't want that. I never liked Gallagher. The man was a scoundrel, as he's proved, and I've no room for men who seek to profit from war, Mr Fox. But I wouldn't want another generation to suffer for it.'

He expected to see his shot go home, but Fox merely smiled. 'Someone has to profit. Wars must be serviced, like anything else. I made money from the war, I don't deny it . . . but I provided a service, too. Just like the Brentons did in the Great War, if I'm not misinformed?'

'Yes,' Howard said, 'we did expand during the 14–18 war. Still . . . I can't countenance sacking men at the moment. You can leave your figures with Norman Stretton, and if the situation changes . . . we'll see.'

He got to his feet to indicate that the interview was over. Fox followed suit, but in a leisurely fashion. 'By God, he's sure of himself,' Howard thought.

'I believe congratulations are in order?' Fox said as he

reached for his hat. 'You're marrying Esther Gulliver, I hear. I remember Esther when she worked for your wife.'

'Yes,' Howard said, 'Esther worked for us at the Scar. A long time ago.'

'Times change,' Fox said, grinning.

'I'd like to land a jab to his jaw,' Howard thought but aloud he said: 'Everything changes, Mr Fox. Thank you for coming.'

Back at his desk, Howard looked at the triple frame that held photographs of his children flanking a picture of his dead wife. Perhaps he should remove Diana's photograph now, and replace it with a picture of Esther? But that would be somehow disloyal. He leaned forward, gazing at the picture. He had been married to Diana for twenty-two years, she had borne him three sons, and yet he had never truly come close to her – not until the very end when she had been blinded. They had grown together, then, but more as comrades than lovers. Now that he made love with Esther he understood what union between a man and woman could be: a blend of spiritual love and physical passion that surpassed any other emotion.

But he had loved Diana, too, in a way – even when she had betrayed him. Pamela had been born as a result of Diana's affair with Max Dunane, her friend Loelia's brother. Howard had not only forgiven his wife, he had accepted her daughter as his own . . . and Pamela had unwittingly repaid him a thousand times over by the depths of her love for him – the man she believed to be her father.

Thinking of Pamela reminded him that one day he must tell Esther the truth about Pamela's birth. And perhaps Pamela, too, would need to know?

He was relieved when the telephone's shrill cut across his thoughts, until he heard the voice on the other end of the line.

'Loelia? How nice to hear from you.'

The Hon. Loelia Dunane, now Mrs Henry Colville, had mothered his children when they were evacuated to her home in the country during the war. She was twittering away on the other end of the line, now. 'It's so lovely to have servants again, Howard, although I can't say their

17

attitude is all it might be. Still, things will settle down eventually, if we're all patient. One fears a dreadful element is creeping in; things are not as they were. Cynthia Cheevers says you can pay someone to present your daughter at Court nowadays. I can hardly believe it, but with those dreadful socialists in Downing Street, anything could happen. Still, I mustn't take up your time. I know you're fearfully busy, with the wedding in the offing and all these stupid controls Attlee's bent on imposing on businessmen. I'm telephoning about the wedding, actually, Pamela insists she's a bridesmaid . . .?' There was a pause and then: 'Oh well, of course, if that's what Esther wants . . . Anyway, the child wants to have her hair properly cut. Henry and I took her out from school on Sunday – it's aeons since we saw her, and I do miss her so. She was looking absolutely splendid. Max was with us, and she was so full of high spirits he said how she reminded him of Diana at that age . . .'

Howard listened to the flow of words, his mind in a ferment. Damn Max Dunane! Would he forever cast a shadow over Brenton lives?

Esther turned out the warehouse lights and began to lock the doors. Sammy usually performed this ritual, but he was in London inspecting freezing equipment for the new cold-store. She tested the locks one last time and walked to her car. She would need a new car as soon as they were available again, but Heaven only knew when that would be.

She took off her hat in the car and laid it on the passenger seat. It would be nice to get home and out of her sticky work suit. She was going to the Scar tonight, to cook for Howard and talk over the final wedding arrangements, but first she must call in on the Lanskys and make sure all was well there.

As always, thinking of Howard made her go moony, and she allowed herself a mental picture of him, tall and handsome still at forty-nine, tipping his hat to passers-by for all the world like Anthony Eden. She hugged the thought of their coming happiness all the way to the tree-lined street where the Lanskys lived, in the house that had been a second home to her for more than twenty years.

She had gone there to be the Lanskys' fire-*goyah*, performing for orthodox Jews the tasks they were not allowed to perform for themselves on the Sabbath. She had been sixteen then, living alone in one room Lansky had helped her to find in Hendon. What had the rent been? Three shillings a week? A tiny fraction, anyway, of what she now earned.

'It's me,' she called as she let herself into the Lanskys' hall. She loved this house, with its sense of peace and the warm smells of cooking.

'In here, Esther.' Naomi was in the kitchen, stirring a pan on the stove.

'What's in it? It smells good,' Esther said, bending to sniff the steam rising from the pan.

'It's chicken soup. For Sammy, when he gets home. Tonight, he said on the telephone.'

'Has it gone well in London?'

Naomi nodded and turned out the gas. 'Sit down, and I'll tell you. But first, try the soup, and see if there's too much salt . . . I always worry about salt.' Naomi's German accent seemed to dwindle daily. Soon she would be a proper Sunderland housewife, and her old home in Hamburg only a memory. As Esther reached for a spoon she was remembering Naomi and her sister Ruth when they had arrived at the Lansky home, weeping refugees from Hitler's Germany. They had been children then. Now Naomi was a wife and mother, and Ruth almost a doctor.

'It's delicious,' she said, sipping the hot soup. 'Honestly. I'd say if it wasn't, wouldn't I?'

Naomi grimaced. 'I'm not sure. You used to praise my biscuits in the old days, before Sammy and I were married.'

'*Oy vey*, the biscuits,' Esther said, rolling her eyes. 'But that was then. Now you're a chef, a genius. Sammy is a lucky man . . . and he knows it.'

They went through to the living-room, to find Papa Lansky asleep in his chair, his grandson cooing on a rug at his feet.

'Don't wake him,' Esther said.

'No.' Naomi's voice was sombre. 'It's better he sleeps,

19

Esther. He is sad today, about Palestine. We Jews need a home now, a place to build new lives.' Hundreds of thousands of Jews wanted to go to Israel, but, fearful of reaction from the Arabs, the British government was seeking to curtail immigration. Esther's face must have shown concern, for the girl reached out suddenly and patted her arm. 'Don't worry, I know there's no hope for my parents. Sammy has tried so hard to find them that I now accept they are gone. But there are others, who need a homeland. They say Palestine can never be purely Jewish because it lies in the heart of Arabia – but if not Palestine, where? And Papa Lansky takes it all to heart.'

'Sammy will cheer him up,' Esther said confidently. 'What time will he be home?'

'Midnight, if all goes well. If not, tomorrow morning.'

Esther bent to tickle the baby and click her tongue against her teeth.

'Who's a good boy? Who's a little pet?'

'You like children,' Naomi said, watching her. 'Will you . . .?' She stopped, suddenly embarrassed.

'Will I have children? Well, of course I will: three of them, ready-made. Howard's children. We'll need time to adjust to one another, but eventually, I hope we'll be at least friends.'

'Yes,' Naomi said, 'of course, you have a ready-made family. Still, a baby is a godsend.'

'Yes,' Esther said carefully. 'Yes, babies are lovely.'

As she walked back to her car she thought of her baby, Philip's baby, the baby she had given away when Philip, until recently the love of her life, had died. She could not marry Howard with such a secret untold – and yet the thought of telling him terrified her. Howard had said the past did not matter, and she knew he meant what he said; but sometimes the past had a life of its own. Howard had a ghost in his – the beautiful Diana; but Esther's ghost was a living one: a child somewhere, growing, changing, perhaps wondering about the woman who had borne him.

'Make room there,' Anne said. 'Stella, pass those plates.' The family was assembled around the table for the five-o'clock meal. As she prepared to dole out mince and dumplings, she looked around the table. Frank at the head; Stella and her baby; Angela; Theresa; David and Bernard. Only Gerard, her eldest surviving son, was absent. Soon he would be Father Gerard, a priest and destined to be a monsignor at the very least.

'Stella, will you pass those plates! America? If you don't pull your socks up you won't get as far as Southampton. Put them in front of me, here . . . no, not on the cloth, on the mat. My God, how that bairn'll survive without me I do not know.'

Anne went on grumbling, well aware that no one was taking a bit of notice of her . . . especially not Stella, whose eyes had that peculiar glazed look that meant she was thinking of her imminent passage to New York. She was expecting milk and honey there, and it would be God help Mario if she didn't find it waiting, Anne thought.

As she pushed her own mince and dumplings around her plate she acknowledged that seeing the back of Stella would be a relief. She had always been a headache, right from the pram. As long as she visited them now and then, her loss could be borne. But Tony, the baby . . . that was a different thing. He would be irreplaceable. 'Maybe something'll happen to stop them going,' she told herself again. Anything could happen where Stella was concerned. Chances were she would soon meet another man who would drive the thought of America clean out of her head.

'What is this?' Stella said suddenly, poking at the food on her plate.

'What does it look like?' Anne said. 'Mince and dumplings.'

'Gravy and dumplings,' Stella said. 'I don't see much mince.'

'Now then, our Stella.' Frank sprang to his wife's defence. 'Your mother does her best. In case you don't . . .'

'. . .realize, there's a war on,' Stella finished for him. 'The sooner I get to the States and send you back some food parcels, the better.'

'To the States.' Theresa was mimicking her sister's drawl. 'Wait till she gets to the States.'

'You shut your gob, our Terry,' Stella said, but there was no venom in her tone.

From the other end of the table her father waved his fork. 'Less of that, if you please.'

'Let them go at it,' Anne said sweetly. 'It's only the joys of family life. I'm used to it now. Any more dumpling, Frank?'

'I will,' David said, pushing forward his plate as Frank shook his head.

'And me,' said Bernard, who always echoed his brother.

'Me too.' Angela and Theresa spoke as one.

'That settles it,' Anne said. 'I'll finish it meself.'

The sky was streaked red in the west as Esther drove up to the Scar. Howard came out on to the step, holding out his arms to embrace her. 'I was getting worried about you. I was almost ready to telephone.'

They walked through the hall, past the wide staircase and down the passage to the kitchen.

'What sort of a day have you had?' Howard was pouring gin into glasses. 'No lime, I'm afraid. How glorious it will be to have limes again. Say when . . .'

Esther watched him pour a generous measure of lemonade into the gin until he winced. 'You're drowning it,' he protested, ceasing to pour.

'Yes,' she said. 'I can't sip like you do . . . I drink my drinks. That's why I like them weak. If I'm going to make something of this lot . . .' She gestured at the odds and ends of food she had brought with her. 'I'll need a clear head.'

'What is it?'

'It's stewed scrag-end, Howard. I bet you've never heard of scrag-end.'

'No,' he said carefully. 'On the other hand, I've eaten some pretty peculiar stuff in the last six years.'

'How *was* your day?' he repeated when he had perched on a corner of the huge table and Esther was chopping vegetables.

'Fraught! A fitting with Anne, the SS dressmaker. My dress is a dream, so it's worth the suffering. But I am not allowed to question a dart or a tuck. Then, when I escaped Anne I went to the office. There I had to deal with shortages. We've got about half of what our customers need . . . and Sammy's away still.'

'What's he going to do with his grandparents' house in Paris?' Howard said.

'I think he wants to use it for refugees. He's talked to the French Red Cross. It's complicated, because he won't give them the house. He loves it, and his grandparents' memory, too much. He wants the Red Cross to use it while there's a need, but for it then to come back to him.'

'Strange to think of his being there during the occupation. And never saying a word until his medal was gazetted.'

'Medals!' Esther said proudly. 'He's proud of his French award.'

'Europe is one vast refugee camp now,' Howard said sombrely. 'People milling around, looking for their families. No sign of the Guttman *père et mère*?'

'No. Sammy's tried everywhere, but there's no record of them. But then, there's no record of their deaths either, so I suppose Ruth and Naomi still hope. They say they don't, but I think they must do.'

'The SS were fearfully efficient. That's what will hang some of them. They kept records, so there may be news eventually but it must be awful for the girls, not knowing.'

'I saw Naomi today. Sammy's due home tonight, so she's beaming. Anyway, how's your day gone?'

'Oh, work . . . getting ready to hand my collieries to friend Attlee when his Nationalization Bill comes into force. Does your sister still think they'll have to wrest the pits from me by brute strength?'

'No. And don't tease her next time you see her. I've told her you'll be glad to be relieved of them, but I don't think she believes me.' There was silence for a moment and then, when Howard spoke, Esther sensed a strain in his words.

'I heard from Loelia Dunane today.'

Esther looked up. 'About the wedding?'

'No. Of course she mentioned it, sent her regards, et cetera. She was actually ringing about Pammy. They took her out from school last weekend.'

'That's kind,' Esther said carefully.

'The thing is,' Howard said. 'The point is . . .'

'Come on,' Esther said. 'The thing and the point is . . .?'

'I can't very well say no to Loelia, or keep her at arm's length. There are . . . reasons. I know she's been difficult, and unpleasant to you since she heard we were getting married . . .'

'Since the moment she laid eyes on me,' Esther said dryly. 'She didn't wait until we were actually engaged.'

'There are reasons why she feels proprietary about Pamela,' Howard said miserably. 'Things you ought to know.'

'Secrets,' Esther said lightly but a void had opened up in her, a black hole of fear. So he had a secret, too . . . and either secret, if it were told, could break the other's heart.

'Tell you what,' she said. 'Let me get this in the oven to heat up, and then we'll talk.'

2

June 1946

Esther was awake long before dawn, reliving every moment of her conversation with Howard the evening before. She had not told him her own secret, for he had shocked her into silence with his own revelation.

He had begun falteringly: 'I think you should know . . .' Esther had wondered what on earth he might be going to say and then, when she could bear his hesitation no longer, she had leaned forward and put a hand on his arm.

'Tell me, Howard. It can't be as bad as all that.'

She had meant to reassure him but her anxiety showed through and spurred him on.

'It's Pammy. You know how much I love her. She means the world to me, but the fact is . . . there is no tie of blood between us.'

You mean, she's not your child?' Esther had not expected this.

'Oh, in every sense of the word but one, I *am* her father. But she was born out of an affair Diana had with Max Dunane, Loelia's brother. So you see why I have to accept Loelia's interest in the child?'

Hugging her knees to her chin, blankets pulled around her, Esther sat now and remembered seeing Diana, years before, sightless in a hospital bed, and a pad lying beside her with its scrawled handwriting. '*My darling Max, I am so lost without you . . .*' And then at Rupert's memorial service, the whispered asides between Loelia and Max; and Loelia's hostility towards Esther when Pamela had talked sweetly to her. 'Max Dunane her father,' Esther thought and was amazed, comparing the dark-haired child, her quiet demeanour so like Howard's, and the flame-haired, hoity-toity Dunanes.

'Does Pamela know?' she had asked Howard, and received a vehement shake of the head.

'No! She has no idea. Diana would have hated her to know. I've wondered, in the past, whether she's a right to be told, and whether Max has some parental right to be consulted? But I don't know.'

'Has he ever attempted to play the father to her?'

'Oh no, friend Max is very careful. It's Loelia who is sometimes proprietorial. I hope all this won't make difficulties in the future . . . for you, I mean.'

'Don't worry about me! I can hold my own with Loelia if I have to. But I'm not sure whether you can keep the truth from Pamela. Not forever.'

Esther had spoken confidently of her own ability to stand up to Loelia Colville, but now, as she cleaned her teeth and got ready for the day ahead, she wondered. She had seldom, if ever, been out of Durham. She knew nothing of high life, of the world to which Diana Brenton had belonged, the world her daughter had a right to inherit if she wished. Could she, Esther Gulliver, daughter of a draper, help Pamela through the vital years of growing up into a world she, Esther, did not completely understand?

'I want to love Pamela,' Esther thought. 'Perhaps I already do love them all. But am I up to mothering them?'

Anne carried the letter up to Stella, along with a pot of tea. She knew it contained bad news; the official US government stamp told her that, together with the bulkiness of the contents. She shook Stella awake and watched her struggle up from the bed, rubbing sleep from her eyes.

'She's a bonny lass,' Anne thought, seeing the sooty lashes around the blue eyes, the perfect bow of the mouth, the fair hair tumbling on to rounded shoulders. 'But if she's twelve pence to the shilling, I'll eat my hat.'

Stella was about to protest at a rude awakening when she saw the letter and squealed in anticipation. 'It's come . . . give it here! I hope they'll give me time to get some things ready; I don't want to look like a poor relation. Hang on to the cup, I'll get it in a minute. Let's see what this says first.'

Her instructions from the US authorities were explicit, even down to bringing two dozen 'diapers' for the baby, and two cork stoppers for each feeding bottle. She was to hold herself ready to leave at twenty-four hours' notice, and a railway ticket was enclosed, together with four labels: 'Three for baggage, one for coat.'

'I'll be gone by the end of July,' Stella said happily, skimming the pages, uncaring that her words were a knife to her mother's heart.

'Have you thought what you're doing?' Anne said desperately. 'Taking a bairn to a foreign country? He's only a baby . . .'

'It's America, mam, not Timbuctoo. They've got running water there, and electric and gas. And at least I'm getting him out of this dump.'

It was useless to speak of birthright or family ties. As Anne made her way downstairs she cursed her own folly. When Stella had first confessed her pregnancy, Anne had forbidden her to tell Howard Brenton that she was carrying his airman-son's child. And then young Brenton had died in the war, and Stella had palmed the bairn off on a daft young American with candyfloss where his brains should be.

'You brought it on yourself,' Anne told herself sternly, knowing that was what Frank would say if she moaned aloud. He had wanted to be honest about the child's parentage, but she had feared and hated the Brentons, for their pride and their power and their dominance over lesser people's lives. She had feared they would claim their grandson and take *her* grandson from her. But now her sister was marrying the very same coal-owner, and Tony was to be whisked off to America. It was a topsy-turvy world, thanks to Hitler.

Frank Maguire drew his hand across his brow to wipe away the sweat that was carrying coal dust down into his eyes. They were nearing the top of the shaft now, the cage rattling to a halt and the gate opening. His marrer fell into step beside him as they checked off and bathed and began the weary trudge home.

'I could get depressed about this world, Billy.' Frank spat a stream of black-tinged saliva into the gutter. 'We got rid of one dictator, but now we've got Joe Stalin acting himself up.' It was three months since Churchill had warned of an Iron Curtain descending across Europe, and catastrophe in the making. President Truman had been cool, even hostile to the speech, and Britain's Labour leaders had expressed horror, but Frank was not so sure.

'There's nowt wrong with old Joe,' the other man said equably. 'Not unless you listen to Churchill . . . and I haven't forgotten that bastard before the war. He was OK in war-time, but he's still a Tory.'

Frank grunted non-committally and moved his snap tin to his other arm.

'It won't be long now till your lass's sister weds Brenton,' the man said. Frank had endured some stick about his family's alliance with the Brentons, and was not about to go through any more.

'June the 27th, Billy . . . and it's nowt to do with me.'

'I know that, marrer. Besides, what Brenton does won't matter much longer. Another six months and he'll be gone, and we'll have the pits.'

'Aye, Attlee's got it all in hand,' Frank said.

They had reached the corner of Trenchard Street now and Frank quickened his pace at the sight of his grandson's pram at the door. 'I'll see you tomorrow, Billy . . . unless you're down the Half Moon tonight?'

They parted at his gate, and Frank went in to chuck the baby under the chin. 'Who's a good boy then? Who's granda's pet lamb?'

'Never mind the sweet talk,' Anne said from the doorstep. 'Stella's had word. We're losing the bairn next week . . . and not a blind thing we can do about it.'

'It'll be strange not to see all this any more,' Howard said. He was standing in his office, looking out over the pit yard, seeing the men emerge from the cage, blackened and weary.

In its first year in office, the Attlee government had nationalized the Bank of England, civil aviation, Cable and Wireless and coal. The railways, electricity and long-distance transport were to follow but coal was the most important of the nationalization measures. For most miners, it meant an unbelievable improvement in working and living conditions. The Brenton collieries had pithead baths, but many collieries throughout Britain lacked the most basic amenities.

Beside Howard his manager, Norman Stretton, was also regarding the scene below. 'You did your best for them,' he said to Howard. 'They're for nationalization, every manjack of them, but some of them will remember the Brentons quite kindly, I think.'

Howard chuckled. 'I hope you're right, Norman, but I fear you're wrong. As a *bête noire* I rank slightly above Beelzebub.'

'Nonsense.' Stretton's voice was firm and Howard looked at him with affection. Norman Stretton had come to him as manager in 1937, when England had been in crisis and Howard torn between management of his business interests and his duties as a Member of Parliament. From the moment of his coming Stretton had eased things for Howard, building good relationships with the men and keeping peace in the pits.

'What will you do when you leave here?' Howard asked, now.

'I don't know,' Stretton said. 'I did think of going back to India, but the situation out there has changed, and I don't think we're going to be as welcome as once we were.'

Howard grimaced. 'I sometimes feel as though we lost the war. Churchill was cast aside once it was over, and I don't think Europe sees us as a saviour. There's not a lot of gratitude around, is there?'

'There is, on a personal level,' Stretton said. He had moved to stand at Howard's side, looking out on the yard but not seeing it. Both were remembering the dark days of the war. 'Individuals are grateful. I talked to a Pole the other day, who pumped my hand up and down until I thought he'd have it off at the elbow. But other governments resent us: we remind them of their own failings. We stood alone in '40, when they fell. However, I don't know why we're sifting the ashes of war. You're a bridegroom . . . well, almost . . . and I'm a best man with a speech to write. Now that is a worry!'

They laughed and moved back towards the desk. 'How's the bride bearing up?' Stretton asked.

'Esther is . . . just Esther. She seems to take it all in her stride.'

Howard turned away, afraid Stretton might see his face. He was remembering Esther last night, eyes fixed on him as he told her about Pamela. She had smiled to reassure him, and brushed aside his apologies for keeping her in the dark.

'You couldn't tell me before, Howard: it was none of my business. But I'm glad you've told me now. We can share it. We all have some secrets, Howard.'

But looking into her lovely, open face, Howard had known there were no secrets there.

'Is it good?' Naomi asked anxiously. Sammy wiped his mouth with his napkin and pursed his lips.

'Well . . .' he said and then, seeing his wife's mouth form into an O of apprehension, 'It was wonderful!'

'There's more,' Naomi said, but Sammy held up a hand.

'One bowl of that soup put life into me, *liebchen*. Now I want to hear the news.'

Across the table his father nodded. 'Ruth is well, and so excited about Esther's wedding. She will be home for Shabbos, too.' The wedding was to take place on a Thursday so as not to fall on the Jewish Sabbath, and all the Lansky household would be there. 'As for Esther, she goes about her preparations as though she gets married every day. She's a wonder.'

Naomi had left the room, and Sammy bent to his father and lowered his voice. 'Has Esther told Howard, do you think? About her *boy t'shikl*?'

The old Jew shrugged. 'I don't know. Should she tell him? I ask myself this, but I see no answers.'

'Better to keep it a secret always, perhaps? We would

never tell, and . . .' He stopped as Naomi came back with a tray.

'Tell what?' she asked, and he moved to kiss her brow, and then clutch his chest.

'Secrets,' he said in sepulchral tones. 'Dark, dark secrets.'

Naomi tut-tutted. 'You don't improve, Sammy Lansky. Now, I have honey-cake or tea-bread or . . .'

'I want all of them,' Sammy said, holding out his plate. 'Pile them up. You know I can't resist your cooking, my *oytser*. Tell me what else has been happening, Papa?'

'More unrest in Palestine. When will it cease?'

'I don't know, but things are getting better. I saw that in Paris, last month. It will all settle down eventually. In the meantime we have the boy, and Ruth is coming home, and Esther is marrying a *mentsh*. And your daughter-in-law is an angel who cooks like a seraph. Don't be greedy, Papa: we have good things enough.'

But as he ate his tea-bread, spread with watery turnip jam, Sammy was remembering the haunted faces he had seen in France a few weeks ago, the confusion of people wandering across Europe trying to find some semblance of the life they had known before the war. In a café a man had recognized him as a Jew and shown him a photo: *'You have seen her, my wife?'* Sammy had shaken his head and pressed the man's arm, and then walked out into the Rue de Rivoli, to see a plaque on a wall proclaiming that Martine Desbeau, who had fed him in a Paris tenement while he hid from the Germans, had died on that spot in the liberation of Paris on 25 August 1944.

Esther wrote the address at the top of the page and then the date. 'Dear Pamela,' she began and sucked the top of her fountain-pen.

The time is really rushing by now. Your father looks paler by the day. Will he last, I ask myself. Worse still, will I be left at the church? Seriously, I *am* looking forward to seeing you, and having you to help me, and getting your approval of the dresses. Your final fitting is arranged for the afternoon you get home, just in case, but Anne will work all night if she has to. She's managed to get enough material to make you a rather nice hat, like a tam-o'-shanter set on a band. Angela and Theresa are thrilled, and I think you'll like it but if you don't, we'll think of something else. The boys will be home the same day, so it will be a full house once more and good for your father's morale.

Esther sucked her pen again, thinking of Pamela, so like her mother, so devoted to a man who was not in fact her father.

I hope we're going to have a happy day but I expect we'll all have a few tremors. I hope you know how much your father loves you; and I do, too, if that's OK with you. But I don't expect to take your mother's place. She was very special, beautiful and brave, and none of us will forget her.

Esther closed her eyes, suddenly remembering Diana long ago, paused on the stairs at the Scar, dressed in red for Christmas. *'This is my house, Esther, and it's right, isn't it? Just right!'* Beautiful, imperious, foolish Diana, who had left behind a time-bomb for her daughter. Howard could keep the secret forever, and so could Esther . . . but who could trust the Dunanes to keep quiet any longer than it suited them? Loelia was coming north for the wedding, and already Esther could feel the chill of her presence.

'I expect I'll have a cabin of my own on the ship,' Stella said confidently. She was sitting on the floor, her bare legs sprawling from her short nightgown.

'Sit up, our Stella, before your dad gets in,' Anne said irritably. One more word about the bloody US of A and she might well murder Stella. She had been contemplating it for long enough.

Stella moved a fraction, and then continued. 'Mario says his family is decorating our room specially. Pink and white, and a wall-to-wall carpet in blue.'

Anne sniffed. 'Living in with the family never works. You'd be better off with your own place.'

'We'll have our own place, once I get over there. But I don't want him choosing somewhere on his own. I want to pick the place myself.'

'It's up to who's paying for it,' her mother said. 'He can't have anything saved out of army pay.'

'I keep on telling you – they're rich, mam. Family money. They don't scrat over there. Four ice-cream parlours they have, right across New York.'

'There's not that much money in ice-cream,' Anne said. 'And cover your legs, girl. We have Eye-tie ice-cream parlours here, and by God the families who own them work. Well, they did before they were all interned. I doubt they'll come back. Why doesn't Mario come here and start up, if he's that keen?'

'He'd stay here,' Stella said, sweetly, 'but I wouldn't. I've got plans. You needn't worry – I know he'll have to work . . .'

'It won't just be him,' Anne interrupted. 'You'll have to pitch in too, no doubt.'

'Not when I have the bairn to look after,' Stella said smugly. 'I can't be in two places at once.'

Anne leaned forward to poke the fire, her eyes pricking at the thought of the baby thousands of miles away in some foreign woman's home. At the sound of the back gate opening, she straightened up.

'*Will* you cover those legs, madam? Here's your dad.'

But it was not Frank who appeared in the doorway. It was Gerard, her son from the seminary, putting down his case and taking up a determined stance.

'I'm sorry to shock you, mam, but I'll come straight out with it. It's over. I've come home because I've got no vocation for the priesthood. And there's no good ranting and raving, because I've made up my mind.'

3

June 1946

Emmanuel Lansky could hear excited chatter from the room along the landing, where Naomi and her sister Ruth were getting ready for Esther's wedding. Last night Ruth, his scholar, had come home from her Edinburgh medical school. At first she was a new Ruth, taller and slimmer, her hair fashionably cut, holding her head high and not immediately rushing to greet him. He had felt a pang of disappointment. But then she was throwing her bag and tripping over furniture to hug him. 'Oh Papa Lansky, it's so good to be home.'

While Sammy had gone to carouse with the bridegroom, Emmanuel had sat by the fire with both his girls, the baby asleep in the crib beside them, and listened delightedly as they swopped news of college life and babies and every single detail of tomorrow's wedding. And to think he had once wanted boy-children to foster! Truly, God was wise.

Now, this morning, he looked anxiously out, fearful of even one cloud to spoil Esther's day. But the sky was an even blue, and he sighed with relief. Downstairs, Sammy was feeding his son, spooning in nutritious pulp and all the while exulting aloud that this was the best, the most special baby ever. 'Aaron Emmanuel Lansky: I can see that name becoming famous. We are going to go places, little Aaron. Your papa is thinking big. All these new towns they are planning, with homes for a million people, will need furniture, carpets, electricals. We will have a shop in Fawcett Street, in the centre of the town: *Lanver, the home of good furniture*. Or perhaps *Lansky and Son*? *Lansky, Son and Gulliver*? Esther will know. Now you eat up, so your mama can get you ready to be admired.'

'What are you saying to that baby?' Ruth said as she came into the room. Sammy cleaned the baby's mouth with the spoon and turned. What he saw brought a whistle of appreciation to his lips. 'Is this the scholar I see, or the Oomph girl? Ruthie, you look wonderful.'

'Are you sure?' She was suddenly the old Ruth again, uncertain and awkward. Sammy put down spoon and dish, and went to take her by the shoulders.

'I'm sure, Ruth. I've always thought Naomi was the beauty; now all of a sudden I'm not so sure. Her sister is something!' He was kissing her brow as Naomi came into the room. 'See,' he said, 'you've lost me. I've fallen for a woman of the world, a glamour girl.'

Behind him the baby let out a yell of delight as he upturned the dish containing the remnants of breakfast on his dark hair and let the contents trickle down his forehead.

Sammy looked stricken. 'I forgot he likes to do that.'

'You let yourself get carried away,' Naomi said sweetly. 'I'm used to it by now. Give him here and I'll take him to get cleaned up.'

'There,' Anne said, moving back to get a better picture. 'I might as well say it . . . I made a good job of that dress. *And* the hat.'

'They're lovely,' Esther said. 'I feel like a queen. And I'm grateful, Anne – you know that, don't you?'

'Oh, hush,' Anne said. 'We're sisters, aren't we? What am I supposed to do, let you go down the aisle like a scarecrow?'

'You do like Howard, don't you?' Esther could not bear to meet her sister's eyes, fearing what she might see there. Anne turned to the mirror and stroked her hair into place.

'I like him,' she said at last. 'He's a good man, according to his lights. But the Brentons have always used the likes of us. Frank works his guts out in a Brenton pit, and so did Joe, till the war took him. You were once in service to them, and I would've been too if I hadn't been fly. They own us, Esther, and that's what I've always resented: that they have the power of life and death over this area. Their area. Their kingdom. He's all right, and you'll even say

35

he's different . . . but birth is birth, Esther. You're marrying into it, but you won't really belong. You'll have your work cut out surviving in that lot. Still, me and Frank'll be here, whatever happens.'

Esther smiled her gratitude, but somehow the joy she had felt while dressing was diminished. She thought of the pews in church; of Howard's sister and her husband, who were unknown quantities as yet; and of Loelia Colville and her husband, outwardly so pleasant, inwardly so resentful of her. And then there was a tap on the door.

'It's Mary,' Anne said, and Mary Hardman, Frank's sister, was there, embracing her, smiling reassurance, admiring the dress, bringing calm. Years ago, when the girls' father had died, Mary had been a tower of strength. She had worked in the Brenton house, too, as housekeeper, until she married Patrick Quinnell, who was now the Belgate doctor. She stood back and regarded Esther. 'You've come a long way,' she said. 'I never doubted you would, but I never thought you'd land a Brenton! Still, he's all right, is Mr Howard, and I should know: I worked for him long enough. And as for that toffee-nosed bunch from London, I don't think he gives twopence for them, so neither should you. Now, why don't I go downstairs and get three glasses of something strong? Our Frank's sipping away, and Pat won't be far behind. Why should we be T T?'

And then they were raising their glasses, and bubbles were tickling Esther's nose, and somehow things were righted again, and all she knew was that she was going to live happily ever after.

A hush was falling on the church, the faint twitter of the congregation dying away. Had it really been twenty-five years since he last waited like this, Howard wondered. '*Do you, Diana Elizabeth, take this man . . .?*' He abandoned memory and turned to look at his sons, Ralph and Noel, in the pew behind. They were enjoying themselves, in spite of the faint air of embarrassment they wore. He looked at Loelia, staring straight ahead from under the brim of her pale grey hat, and Henry beside her, in morning dress, studying the architecture of the church for all the world as though it was an abbey. How Diana would have laughed at this meeting of two camps. Across the aisle from Loelia, Frank Maguire was easing his unaccustomed stiff collar, until Anne tugged at his elbow and whispered that he should desist.

'We will be family now,' Howard thought, 'Maguire and I.' He remembered a day in the pit yard, when young Maguire's eyes had been angrily fixed on him, the body of a man killed in the pit lying between them. And champagne in the kitchen at the Scar, the night they had toasted the birth of sons born to each of them. Both these boys were wasted in war. But mostly he thought of the message Maguire had sent him after Diana had killed herself, when everything was dark: 'Tell the gaffer to hold on.' 'He understands me,' Howard thought. 'He is closer to me than he knows.' Last night, over dinner, Loelia had conveyed her sympathy that Howard was 'taking on quite something' . . . as though he were marrying into some savage tribe.

At that moment Maguire looked up and their eyes met. For a second the man stared at Howard, and then his left eye drooped in a wink.

The organ halted suddenly, and then the Mendelssohn began. Howard turned to see his bride coming towards him, for once looking a little unsure of herself.

'All right?' he whispered, as she arrived at his side. There was a nod of the head beneath the blue hat, and then the familiar words were sounding in the silent church: 'Dearly beloved, we are gathered here . . .'

'By gum, Frank, I could get a taste for this.' Anne was sluicing champagne around her mouth and holding up the glass to see the bubbles.

'Well, don't,' Frank said. 'It's five quid a bottle, according to our Stella.'

'And she'd know!' Anne said. 'Where is she, by the way?'

'Over there, somewhere . . . she had two lads in uniform laughing and joking earlier on.'

'What is it with her?' Anne said, still searching the crowd

37

for the sight of her daughter's blond head. 'She's like a jam-pot where men are concerned.'

Frank shook his head. 'Jam sticks, Anne, which is more than she does.'

'I'll miss that baby, Frank.' Suddenly the champagne had gone flat, and Anne's wedding euphoria evaporated. 'You'll never understand how I love that bairn. He saved me after Joe was killed . . . but then you never took that to heart either, not like I did.'

'Don't say that, Annie. I don't want a scene here, but don't say I didn't care about Joe.'

Anne had gone too far and she knew it, but she couldn't turn back. 'It's the same with our Gerard. He's on the verge of a mortal sin, and do you speak up? Oh no. "Please yourself" – that's all he gets from his father.'

'Just hush, Annie, before I lose my rag. It's our Gerard's life . . . and at least he'll have a life now.'

Across the room Frank could see his eldest son smiling shyly as he listened to a tall girl who was waving her hands about and telling what looked like a funny story. Anne had seen it too, and pursed her lips in disapproval of someone who had so nearly been a priest enjoying himself in such a fashion.

Frank gazed around, hoping to find something to divert his wife. 'Look,' he said, 'there's that woman . . . the one Esther's scared of, over there in the big grey hat.'

'Our Esther's not scared of her,' Anne said, a gleam returning to her eye. 'She's a Gulliver, Frank, like me: she's frightened of nothing.'

'Howard's girl's bonny,' Frank said, watching Pamela moving about with a basket of cake. 'Like her mam.'

Anne had grown fond of Pamela during the fittings for the bridesmaid's dress. 'Yes,' she said. 'Like her in looks, but not in ways. She's a good bairn.'

'I never believed all the stories about her mam,' Frank said. 'We all liked to pick at the Brentons, and the tales grew. But I dare say it was all gossip.' His eye fell on Stella again, flushed and animated as she always was with men around, and he sighed, thinking of the tearful parting to come. He exchanged his empty glass for a full one. At least

Esther was settled now, and Brenton would have someone at his side when he lost his pits.

'Will you do something about that?' Anne said in scandalized tones. In the corner the youngest Maguire, eight-year-old Bernard, was expertly filching icing from the base of the cake and cramming it into his mouth. 'I crawled for that icing,' Anne said. 'To a woman I cannot stand. Go and tell that little sod I'll swing for him if he doesn't give over.'

Frank smiled as he went on his mission. That was the good thing about family life: it stopped for nothing, not weddings or funerals. There would still be a bairn misbehaving at the Second Coming. 'Your mam's got it in for you,' he said to Bernard when he reached him and saw greed replaced by fear in the round blue eyes. After all, bairns had little enough sweet nowadays. 'Get that big bit there,' he whispered hurriedly, 'and then get off out of it before you get me shot.'

Howard and Esther settled back in the Daimler as it sped down the drive. Behind them their guests ran, throwing confetti and calling goodbyes, the adults dropping out soonest, the children running on as long as hearts and legs would carry them.

'Happy?' Howard asked, reaching for her hand. But suddenly Esther felt afraid. They were alone together, man and wife. She had promised to honour and obey him. She was no longer her own mistress.

As if he sensed her mood, Howard drew her hand through his arm. 'Make me a promise, Esther: that you will always tell me if anything troubles you, or if you feel I've been . . . reticent. That's a failing of mine, that I don't always say what I feel. I shy away from expressing myself – or I have done in the past. For some reason, I've been better since I met you, and I mean to go on like that; but if I fail you, you must tell me. And, in case you're worrying about it, I know you will want to honour your partnership with Sam Lansky, and work as hard with him as you always have.'

A week ago Esther had tried to make Sammy revoke

their partnership and had met with a spirited refusal. 'Firstly, I don't go back on agreements, Esther. Secondly, I wouldn't have this business now if it weren't for the way you carried it on during the war. Thirdly, and most important, I should let go of the best businesswoman this side of London? Am I *meshugge*?'

She smiled now, remembering Sammy's words, comforted that Howard understood. She put up a hand and pulled out the pin that held her hat in place. 'Let me get rid of this,' she said, 'and then kiss me. Properly.' Howard's hesitation was only momentary, a glance towards the chauffeur's back, a flicker to the world outside the car . . . and then his lips were on hers, warm and vulnerable at first, and then more than satisfactorily demanding.

The following morning they left for Paris from Heathrow, the new airport to the west of London. It was little more than a vast plain with rows of huts and tents and some telephone boxes, but there were signs of building work in progress, and a spattering of planes stood on the tarmac.

'We're taking one of the first flights from here,' Howard said. 'They're going to spend £20 million on developing it into a major airport – I had to pull a few strings to get seats.'

Seen from a distance across the tarmac, their Paris-bound plane looked tiny. It was a little more comforting close up, but Esther's stomach churned as she strapped herself into the seat and the engines began to throb. *'No good'll come of it,'* Anne had said. *'God made birds for flying. We have legs.'* Esther shut her eyes tight, as Howard squeezed her hand, and then they were rushing down the runway, and were airborne, and bits of cloud were floating past the window for all the world like cotton-wool. She turned to see Howard was laughing at her.

'It's not funny,' she said and then, as the plane dipped suddenly, she clutched his arm. 'Oh God, we should've gone to Blackpool!'

But Paris was a revelation to her: the boulevards, the trees, the mighty buildings, so different in style from London. And at night, in their bedroom at the George V they lay together, sometimes making love but more often talking and making plans for their children. Once or twice

40

Esther almost confided to Howard the secret of her own child by Philip Broderick, but in the end she stayed silent. Why complicate a relationship that was so wonderfully, gloriously simple?

She had long since abandoned the messy contraceptives she had used with David Gilfillan. Now she had a Dutch cap. Howard never questioned her about it, and she assumed he was used to a woman who attended to such things as a matter of course.

One night, as they lay together on the feather pillows, Esther raised herself on her elbow to look down at his face.

'Penny for them?' Howard said. She put out a finger and traced the tiny scar on his cheek, a relic of the First World War.

'I was wondering if you got this in a duel.'

'No. Much more mundane: at Ypres. I was blown from a trench. I have this and a gammy knee as souvenirs.'

Esther pulled a face of mock disappointment. 'Only the war? Tame!' He pretended to savage her in protest and then they subsided on to the pillows.

'I love you, Esther.' He looked suddenly so serious that she pulled a face.

'You don't sound very cheerful about it.' She put up a hand to touch his shoulder, feeling the strength of bone and muscle. Philip's shoulder had been fragile, the bones like a bird's. She closed her eyes momentarily, embarrassed that she should remember one lover in the arms of another. Did Howard have memories too, of making love with Diana? Had Diana been the only woman in his life? They were married, and yet they knew so little about one another.

He put his face close to hers and she felt the faint bristle of his chin. 'My love for you is too important to be light-hearted about, Esther. I'm afraid that I may lose all this . . .' His hand was on her breast, his lips upon her brow, her eyelid, the corner of her mouth.

'Just try losing me,' she said, folding him into her arms. And then they were moving together, and their knowledge of one another was enough for the moment.

*

'It was a nice wedding,' Gerard said. He was perched on a rocky outcrop on the Scar, below the Brenton house, his father seated on the grass at his side.

'Aye,' Frank said. 'It made your mother happy for five minutes, so it must've been.'

Below them Belgate shimmered in the June heat, smoke rising from all the chimneys in an orgy of Sunday-dinner-making.

'The old place hasn't changed much, has it?' Gerard said.

'No, we got off lightly in the war. A few incendiaries, that's all. There's great gaping holes in Sunderland, and a few hundred dead there.'

'Fifty-five million people killed in six years, they say.' The boy was sombre. 'There can't be a God, if that happens.' Frank plucked a blade of grass and sucked the sweet base of it before he answered, for his son had posed it as a question, not a statement.

'It's not as simple as that, lad. Oh, we're all tempted to see it black and white sometimes, but it's not. Was that why you came home from the seminary – because of the war? Those concentration camps were hard to stomach.'

'No.' The boy's eyes had filled and he wiped them angrily on his sleeve. 'No, if I'm honest it wasn't that. It was fear, dad. I got scared of what I was taking on, and scared of what I was giving up.' He began to recite suddenly, a litany obviously well-studied: '*I hereby testify and swear, after diligent consideration and in the sight of God. I declare I am fully aware of all that is implied by the law of celibacy. I am determined to fulfil this obligation and to keep it totally with God's assistance to the very end. This I promise. This I vow. This I swear. May God assist me and these His holy gospels, which I touch with my hand.*'

Gerard put out a hand to touch a dog daisy rising from the short grass, and then looked at his father anxiously, hoping to see understanding on his face. 'In a way it was you and me mam, dad. Seeing you two together, and all the spooning. Me and our Joe, we used to laugh about it when we were kids. But we liked it, really.'

'Yes,' Frank said, remembering Joe's letter, written on the eve of D-Day, in which he'd said the same kind of thing. 'I know what you mean.'

'What am I going to do, dad? Me mam's so upset . . .'

Frank got to his feet and brushed the dried grass from his Sunday trousers.

'She's usually upset, Gerard. It's what you might call a chronic condition in your mother. But at the bottom of her, she wants her bairns to be happy. She'll come round. In the mean time, we are going to go down there and have a pint in the Half Moon, and then we will polish off a good Sunday dinner, or the best you can come to nowadays with nowt but veg about. And then we will have a nice snooze, and when we wake up there'll be bubble-and-squeak for tea, and another evening of hearing your sister getting ready to astonish America. God help anybody that spoils my Sunday. We have to work thin seams nowadays on account of the war, so I need my day off.'

They started down the hill together, and then Frank spoke again. 'As for the bigger question, lad – let it lie a bit. When the good Lord's ready, you'll get your instructions. And there'll be precious little your ma can do about it then.'

The Sunday papers were strewn about the Lansky parlour, and Ruth and Emmanuel were engaged in a heated discussion of the news about university grants to poor students. Children of families earning less than £600 a year would receive a grant sufficient to cover maintenance during their course; those of families with higher earnings would get a lesser sum; and those whose parents earned more than £1500 a year would get nothing.

'It's good, Papa Lansky. It means everyone will have a chance.' Ruth's face was earnest, behind her glasses. 'I have fellow students who starve, almost. Not everyone is as lucky as I am. You spoil me.'

'Hush,' Lansky said. '*Ni to far vus.*'

But Ruth was not to be hushed. 'No, it's time I told you "thank you". Without you, where would we be, Naomi and I?'

'Happy young women,' Lansky said, 'not tied to a madman, like your poor sister. Have you heard the latest scheme? Furniture! One minute a market stall, the next

43

minute Marshall and Snelgrove. Never moderation for my Sammy: that's too simple. After furniture, what then? Motor cars? Crocodiles?'

'Sammy knows what he's doing,' Ruth said firmly. 'And Esther keeps his feet on the ground.'

'But will she always?' Lansky said. 'She has married a rich man. Will she come to the warehouse every day now, watch a *meshuggener* and keep the books, like a wage-slave?'

'She won't let Sammy down,' Ruth said. 'Not Esther. And she's too old . . .' She blushed a little, suddenly. 'Well, if she had been younger there might've been – complications.'

Lansky's eyes twinkled. 'Complications? What could you mean by that? My Aaron's a complication? Shame on you, his aunt. But of course Esther is *very* old . . . in her thirties. At the altar I heard her arteries hardening, her bones creaking.'

'You are a terrible man,' Ruth said, shaking out her paper. 'Now, pay attention! It says here that Morris cars are going to be dearer: £270 for a two-door saloon. Aie, aie, aie.'

'You will need a car when you have a practice. A Morris is nice, but a Rover would be better. Black for a doctor, more professional. Sammy will fix it, when the time comes.'

'There's one small snag,' Ruth said dryly. 'I can't drive.'

'So?' Lansky said, raising his hands, palm upwards. 'This will be difficult, for someone who can perform operations? You will drive like an angel.' He leaned forward. 'Did you hear about Naomi's driving lesson? Three times on the kerb . . . even Sammy was white when they got back! What a cook, what a wife, what a mother. But not a driver!'

The looked up as Sammy came into the room. He went to the clock on the mantelpiece and tapped the case. 'Three minutes slow.'

'It's Sunday,' Lansky said. 'Who counts minutes?'

'Esther will be in Paris by now,' Sammy said. He sounded a little wistful.

'You will miss her,' Lansky said and Sammy nodded.

'I'll miss her, but I'm really worried that she won't come back at all. She says she will, but it will be just my luck if she takes to marriage like a duck to water . . . and me poised to expand.'

Emmanuel tut-tutted. 'Selfish. Get your priorities right, Samuel. If she doesn't want to come back, take it as a sign that you should moderate your ambitions.'

'This is a new world, Papa.' Sammy sat down on a stool and wound his arms round his knees. 'We can't stand still any more. People won't be content with little or nothing in the future. British servicemen have had their eyes opened: in Germany and Holland, they saw destruction – but they also saw better houses than they'd left behind. They've come back to a country exhausted by war, and they'll make allowances for that – but only for a while. They've put in a Labour government, and they'll expect to be repaid for it.'

Emmanuel Lansky shook his head. 'I pity the government, whatever its complexion. They've inherited a poverty-stricken, wounded country, never mind an exhausted one.'

'But it's a disciplined country, Papa.' Sammy's voice was earnest. 'People are used to obeying orders. They'll pull their weight, all those men out there in their identical demob suits and their trilby hats and the women who made ends meet in the war. They'll make it work, you'll see. But they'll want their just rewards – nice things for their homes and good food. And I mean to supply them.'

'And Esther will help you,' Naomi said from the doorway. 'Now, if the big tycoon could go and fetch his son, who is crying in the nursery, we can all have tea and discuss this expanding world.'

Emmanuel leaned conspiratorially towards Ruth. 'See, she is changing, this little one. She bosses us all. Poor Sammy, he married a kitten and winds up with a tiger.'

Stella stuck out a leg and turned it from side to side. 'How did we live without nylons?' she said.

'Easily,' Anne answered from the sink. The dishes from the Sunday dinner were piled on the draining-board and she swished the sieve containing remnants of soap in the sink to bring up a lather.

'Want a hand?' Frank said, from behind his paper.

'Yes,' Anne said, but she did not expect him to move and he did not disappoint her.

'The first thing I'm going to buy when I get there is a chinchilla coat.' Stella had raised her other leg and was contemplating her nyloned limbs and the neat wedge-heeled sandals that covered her feet.

'Chinchilla? You'll have a few things to buy before you get round to chinchilla. Whatever that may be.'

'Like what? Mario says they've got everything. They've got a big house and two cars. I'll have to learn to drive.' She sounded so complacent that her mother's nerve snapped.

'For God's sake, is your only topic self, self, self? What about taking that bairn to a foreign country? Why not worry about that for a change?'

'Tony'll be better off there,' Stella said. 'He's well off out of a dump like Belgate.' She looked around the kitchen with a scornful eye.

'Now then,' Frank said from his chair. 'There's nowt wrong with Belgate.'

'Hah!' Stella said.

Anne was drying her hands, and now she lifted the towel to her lips. When she took it away her mouth was set in a line that meant trouble. 'Never mind "hah", miss, it's time we had this out. That bairn hasn't got a drop of American blood in him. He's a Maguire and a Brenton. He belongs here.'

'That what you say, but he's my bairn. And Mario knows he's not Tony's father. It doesn't matter to him.'

'I don't think you've told Mario the truth,' Anne said. 'He knows Tony's not his, but he doesn't know the father was young Brenton.' She was guessing, but the flush on her daughter's cheek told her she was right. 'I thought so! Mario thinks it's a Yankee baby, doesn't he? One of his GI friends'? He only married you because you lied to him. What a scandal!'

The minute the words were out, Anne knew she had made a mistake. A year ago she had confessed to Stella that she had inveigled Frank into marrying her by pretending to be carrying his child, and in telling her she had put a weapon into her daughter's hand.

46

'Well, you'd know all about lying!' Stella's tone was a sneer.

'That's enough cheek,' Anne said, but it sounded lame. Frank lowered his paper.

'No,' Stella said. 'You can dish it out, but you don't like getting it back. You lied to me dad about being pregnant, because you wanted to get married instead of going into service. You hooked him with a cheap trick. At least what I did wasn't deliberate.' Her eyes flickered slightly at the size of her own lie.

Anne came to life and stepped forward to bring her hand across her daughter's face, leaving a red weal to show where it had landed.

But it was too late. When she turned she found her husband looking at her with incredulity. 'What's she talking about?' he said in a tone that meant he intended to get an answer.

4

July 1946

'Come back inside now, Anne.' Frank tugged gently at his wife's sleeve but she stood, gazing after the taxi which was carrying Stella and the baby to the railway station, with Gerard in attendance to see to the luggage. 'Come on now, it's no good carrying on.'

Since Stella had dropped the bombshell of Anne's long-ago falsehood there had been strain between Frank and Anne. She had tried to bluster and accuse Stella of lying, but her own flaming cheeks had betrayed her, and when she had met her husband's open gaze her own eyes had dropped. That night he had climbed into bed and turned on his side, his back to her. Anne had moved gingerly under the covers and then attempted an explanation.

'I was young, then, Frank. I didn't know a bee from a bull's foot. I thought I *had* fallen wrong at first, and then, when I found I hadn't, I didn't dare say . . .' But they both knew that even in those days she had dared say anything.

Frank didn't move, and when he spoke his voice was flat. 'It's all a long time ago, so it's matterless now.' But there had been no forgiving kiss, no familiar movement of his arm across her to gently squeeze her breast before he fell asleep. Since then there had been a state of armed neutrality between them, for as soon as Anne had recovered, she convinced herself she was in the right and adopted an air of martyred piety.

But as the day of Stella's departure drew near, the two of them were drawn together by a sense of loss. The last time one of the children had gone right away from them, he had not returned. You couldn't count Gerard, for he had never really left the family.

'I don't know why you're doing this to me,' Anne told God, threading her rosary with indignant fingers. 'Losing our Joe was enough; then Gerard throwing his life's vocation away. Don't take that bairn, you know he belongs here. He needs me.'

But for once God was unresponsive. Stella had revelled in the carefully planned details of her departure, had made her farewells cheerfully, and now she was nothing but a hand waving through the rear window of a taxi, Tony's little head just visible over her shoulder.

When the cab was lost to sight Anne let Frank lead her indoors, tears erupting again from her swollen eyes. 'She won't look after him, Frank. Not like I did.'

'Mebbe not, but she has her own row to hoe now, pet, and that's all there is to it. Besides, Mario will be there. He's got sense. And his mother . . .'

It was the wrong thing to say, but too late to take it back. At the thought of another woman – a foreigner – laying hands on her precious grandson, Anne's wails redoubled.

Frank's patience snapped. 'Now that's enough. You couldn't leave well alone, you couldn't be truthful, you encouraged Stella to lie about the bairn. You've made your bed, now lie on it.'

He had stung Anne, and, as ever, it did the trick. 'If you utter one more bloody platitude, Frank Maguire, I'll kill you.'

They put the kettle on, then, and drank tea, and were moist-eyed together for a baby grandson gone from them to the other side of the world.

The Parisian honeymoon had been a romantic dream for both Howard and Esther. To Howard it meant, for the first time, complete companionship with a woman. It also meant a depth of physical pleasure he had never expected. He felt safe with Esther, at liberty to explore, to express, to experiment . . . and at the same time he felt more protective towards her than he had ever felt to anyone, except his children. For Esther, Paris was a strange, enchanting revelation, and when it was time to leave all she could dream of was how soon they could return. But as they set off from the Gare de l'Est, for they were returning by the Golden Arrow, she began to think again of home.

'I wonder how Anne's getting on? Stella'll be gone to America by now, I should think, or on her way.'

'He seemed a nice young chap, the father?' Howard raised inquisitive eyebrows and Esther nodded.

'He is . . . good-natured. Too soft for Stella, but a perfect father.'

'That's an Italian trait,' Howard said, smiling. 'They're dreadful soldiers but good papas.'

'According to Anne, he's a gangster. All Italian Americans are in what they call the Mafia, she thinks. But I'd back our Stella against gangsters any day!' She laughed when Howard laughed but inwardly she was annoyed with herself for saying 'our Stella'. It was one of the speech patterns she had dropped, or almost dropped, along with 'them roses, them houses'. Tonight, in London, they would be dining with the Dunanes at their house in Chester Square, and she would have to watch her Ps and Qs.

'What are you thinking about?' Howard said, leaning across the carriage to touch her hand.

'Oh, things.'

'What things? Come on, Mrs Brenton, I want an answer.'

'Say that again.'

'Say what?'

'Mrs Brenton. I like the sound of it.'

He crossed to sit beside her then and put his arm around her shoulder. Outside the railway carriage stretched the French royal forest of Chantilly, but he only had eyes for his wife.

'We're going to be happy,' he said.

'Yes,' she said, 'I think we are.'

The train was standing in Amiens station when they looked out and saw a newspaper stand, and the headline on a billboard. 'Bomb in Jerusalem,' Howard translated. 'I'll get a copy.' He leaped from the carriage.

When he returned they scanned the report together. Jewish terrorists had blown up the King David Hotel, the headquarters of the British Army in Palestine. There were reported to be many casualties.

'Poor Papa Lansky,' Esther said, at last. 'He'll hate this. Unrest in Palestine always makes him unhappy.'

'And it's going to get worse,' Howard said. 'I rather fear there'll be more bloodshed before we're finished.'

'This won't be the end of it,' Sammy said. 'All those lives lost: there'll be retaliation, you can depend on it.'

'But who has done this?' Emmanuel was genuinely puzzled. The Jewish Agency had expressed horror at the outrage. Haganah, the illegal Jewish army, did not commit acts of terrorism on this scale.

'The Stern Gang,' Sammy said. 'That's who it will be.'

The plot had been well planned. A lorry, guarded by two armed men, had drawn up at the basement entrance to the hotel, and milk churns packed with explosives had been taken to the kitchens of the Regency Restaurant, which was under the offices of the Secretariat. Two minutes beforehand, a woman telephoned a warning to a newspaper office: *This is a movement of Jewish resistance. We are about to blow up the government offices. We have warned them.* Now there were forty-two dead, fifty-two missing and fifty-three injured; and alleged terrorists were being arrested all over Jerusalem.

'Was it for this we endured a war?' Emmanuel said, not particularly to Sammy, more to himself. 'That now people are killed in dozens instead of thousands?'

Patrick Quinnell read the reports of the outrage with a heart full of sympathy for his friend, Lansky. He was fond of the old Jew for many reasons. When he had come back from France in 1917, a doctor who was a drunkard and a failure, it was Emmanuel Lansky who had helped him to settle in the Durham coalfield and begin to practise. It was Lansky who had fetched him to Belgate to deliver Anne Maguire's first child, and there he had met Mary, the woman who had transformed his life.

So now, as Patrick played cricket in the July sunshine with young Ben, his son, he grieved for Lansky, who had so looked forward to the end of the war and the fall of the

Nazi régime. The victory was being soured, even before the Nazi war criminals had been executed for their crimes.

He was raising his arm to bowl another ball to his son when he saw young Ruth Guttman at the gate. She was to accompany him on his rounds today, to get her first taste of medical practice.

'Ruth, it's good to see you. Come in, Mary's waiting.' He smiled as Ruth greeted young Ben, solemnly shaking the child's hand.

'I wonder what this is?' she said, producing a small parcel from her handbag. The child's eyes shone.

'For me?'

'Well,' she said, looking puzzled. 'I think it must be.' He removed the paper with eager, fumbling fingers, to reveal a small bar of chocolate.

'Chocolate!' Patrick said. 'He'll be your friend for life.' They walked across the grass towards the house, the child running ahead to show his prize to his mother.

'I remember chocolate in Munich before the war,' Ruth said suddenly. 'Chocolate with a sugar inside, holding . . .'

'Liqueurs,' Patrick said. 'Kirsch and brandy.'

'And rum,' Ruth said.

'In wonderful boxes.' Patrick was smiling ruefully.

'It's a long time since I let myself remember things about home.' There was amazement in Ruth's tone.

'I know.' Patrick halted and took her elbow to turn her to face him. 'Believe me, I know how we can blank out what is not easy to bear. I did it for years. But it eats away at you. Let it out, Ruth . . . to me and Mary. Esther will understand, I promise you.'

Ruth smiled at him, and he thought what an attractive woman she had become, so different from the diffident, reserved child he had first known.

'The trouble is, if you start to let it out will you be able to stop it?' She was still smiling but her eyes were wary.

And then Mary was in the doorway, holding out a hand in welcome; and a few moments later they were out in Patrick's ancient motor-car and beginning the evening rounds.

*

Anne had spent an hour on her knees in the cool church, her eyes fixed on the Virgin in her niche, the scent of smoking candles in her nostrils, her mind filled with thoughts of little Tony. 'Take care of him, Holy Mother. He's not strong . . . well, you know what I mean. He's parky with food, and he needs his silky. Stella never remembers.' She had had to run down the stairs with the 'silky', an old rayon petticoat the child liked to rub between thumb and forefinger as he went to sleep.

'I'm not taking that old rag,' Stella had said, but Anne had put her foot down.

'Tony's going to a strange place, you daft ha'porth. He'll need all the comfort he can get.' So it had been packed, but only God knew if the child would get it.

'Bring him back to me,' she ended her prayers, before hauling herself to her feet and emerging into the startlingly bright July afternoon.

On the way home she bought a twopenny pamphlet issued by the Health Education Council. '*Homely savoury dishes adapted to war conditions for families and canteens,*' it said on the cover.

'Someone should tell those buggers the war's over,' she muttered to the woman next to her. When she got home she leafed through it, before deciding she had wasted her money because she had better recipes in her head than ever came out of a pamphlet. As she beat a batter and cut potatoes for fritters, she looked around her kitchen. It was shabby and careworn: 'Like me,' she thought, and sighed.

But there was a comforting smell in the kitchen when Frank arrived, weary from a hard shift but jubilant.

Anne put his plate in front of him, and cut thick slices of greyish bread to sop up the gravy.

'Champion,' he said. 'Where's yours?'

'I'll get mine with the rest,' she said. She couldn't raise much interest in food at the moment. There was an uncomfortable lump in her throat all the time, and a dull ache in the pit of her stomach.

Frank laid down his knife and fork. 'Look,' he said. 'I know you miss the bairn . . . and our Stella, too, for all her shenanigans. But in case you've forgotten, you've got five other bairns to think about. Stella isn't dead, Anne.'

'She might as well be, for all we'll see of her.'

There was such a note of tragedy in Anne's voice that Frank realized how serious things were. He stood up and went to take her in his arms.

'You're a terrible woman, Anne Maguire. As broody as a Rhode Island Red. Well, if it's a bairn you want . . .'

He had meant to be suggestively funny, but when Anne looked up at him her face was deadly serious. 'I've thought of that, Frank, don't think I haven't. But we're just working our way out of the muck now, with most of them nearly up. And I'm forty-three; I'm no spring chicken.'

'Get away.' He put up a hand to stroke the hair from her brow. 'I don't think you've changed a jot since the first time I laid eyes on you . . .'

'I was a bairn then, Frank, for God's sake.' But she was pleased all the same.

'I might have a bite with you now, just to keep the peace,' she said, and Frank kissed her fondly before he went back to demolish his fritters. Watching him chomp, Anne's resentment rose again.

'Look around this house,' she said, gesturing towards the dingy walls. 'No wonder I'm depressed, the state of this place. And don't say, "There's a war on," because there isn't. Not any more.'

Howard and Esther went straight to the London house in Mount Street from the boat-train. 'Now don't get into a state,' Howard said, as Esther flapped between her navy crêpe and her cream cloque. 'Loelia only appears the *grande dame*. Underneath it all, she's very sensible, and straight as a die. And her clothes have been rationed, too, you know. We've all had to make do.'

But there was very little 'make do' about the vision that greeted them in the hall at Chester Square. Loelia was wearing a new Frederick Starke creation in grey, with a draped peplum and padded shoulders.

'My dears,' she said, holding out her hands first to Esther and then to Howard, and kissing both of them on the cheek. 'How was Paris? I'm longing to see it again. Is it much changed?' She bustled them through to the drawing-room where a man-servant waited with drinks.

'Sit down, do, and tell me all the news. Henry sends his apologies. He's just returned from the Ministry and he's still dressing.'

Esther looked around at the wall hangings, the porcelain, the giltwood furniture, the framed photographs of men and women who looked suspiciously like crowned heads. Was it the done thing to praise a room? There were so many rules.

'You're staying at Mount Street?' Loelia said. 'It's so convenient to have a house in town, isn't it? Where else would one change for the theatre, quite apart from anything else? Hotels are so seedy nowadays, even the Ritz.'

Esther smiled in what she hoped was a non-committal fashion as Loelia rattled on.

'How is Max?' Howard asked at last, when Loelia paused for breath.

'He's in America, visiting Laura and the boys.' She turned to Esther. 'You've never met my sister-in-law, have you? She's American. Henry says he can forgive Americans anything but their tinned lobster. Laura is old America, which is far more snobbish and rigid than anything we have here. That's what soured that odious man, Joe Kennedy: he tried to get into American society but they simply won't have provincial outsiders thrust upon them. I shall never forgive President Roosevelt for inflicting a bootlegger on us as ambassador in the face of impending war. Ah, here's Henry . . .'

As another round of kissing and hand-shaking and drinks-pouring went on, Howard whispered to Esther: 'How do you feel?'

'Like a provincial outsider,' she mouthed, and they grinned at each other conspiratorially.

'This is nice,' Loelia said when they were settled again. 'I'm so enjoying peace-time. Just to have servants again . . . I shall never ever take them for granted, as long as I live. And all the old institutions restored, or almost restored. We must make time to talk about Pamela's début. The boys have been so isolated at Valesworth, during the war, and now at Durham, that they deserve some fun. We must give a huge party for them all.'

'How are your sons?' Esther said desperately, anxious to contribute something to the conversation.

'They're very well,' Loelia said. 'Greville is out of the army now, and going up to Oxford this term. Hugh takes his Highers next year. And the girls, both of whom adore Pamela, are still at school, of course. They go on to Switzerland next year. I do wish Pamela was going to a finishing school, but if she refuses I suppose we can't make her.'

'You're in business, I believe, Esther?' Henry asked politely, as silence fell.

'I'm a partner in a retail business,' Esther said. 'We're a reasonably large firm, for the north.'

'Why did I say that?' she thought to herself. 'As though the north was a far-flung outpost.'

'That must have been a difficult business to keep going in war-time?' Henry was trying to help make conversation.

'It's worse now, with the staff shortages and, of course, the lack of goods. Everyone grumbles about the queues. My partner is enthusiastic about self-service shops, without counters. It's an American idea that he thinks would make life easier for shopper and retailer alike.'

'Self-service?' Loelia said.

By now Esther was wishing she hadn't ventured into the realms of trading, but Loelia's eyes were fixed on her, awaiting answer.

'The goods are all out on display. You help yourself, and take the goods to a till to pay for them.'

'I don't think I'd like that,' Loelia said firmly. 'It's so much nicer to be helped.'

5

August 1946

There was a twitter of excitement in the warehouse as Esther entered, and then the workers were clustering round to wish her well and ooh and aah about the wedding. 'A picture, that's what you looked.' 'I saw it in the *Echo* – what a lovely write-up.' 'It's *Mrs* Brenton now, then – no more Miss Gulliver?' 'What's it like being wed? Wish I was.'

Sammy was waiting for her on the stairs that led up to the office. 'Am I glad to see you, partner! A desert, the last month – a wasteland. Welcome back!'

Esther felt her eyes fill with tears. Sammy saw them and consternation showed on his face.

'It's all right,' Esther said quickly, putting out a hand. 'I'm just so happy . . . it's daft, but I am.'

'Hush.' He was holding up a hand. 'No need to explain to me, the *shlemil* who fills up at the mention of puppy-dogs. Now, get rid of that hat and sit down here. I've got plans to tell you.'

Esther settled herself at her desk with a sigh of pleasure and a surge of wary interest. 'What are these plans of yours, Sammy Lansky? No pie in the sky, mind. Times are hard.'

'*Now* they are, Esther, with no food, no clothes and no fun! But I can see ahead. What's the biggest shortage at present?'

Esther knitted her brow. 'I don't know. Everything, that's what's short. There's hardly anything in the shops and what is there is rubbish – sewing cotton that snaps, needles that break, saucepans that burn through in weeks, shoes that come apart at the seams when it rains. What else have I missed?'

'Homes – that's what's needed most. And what do homes need? Furniture!' Sammy stood back like a magician who has produced a dove from a silk handkerchief.

It was true, Esther thought. People could not understand why a government machine which had provided for the needs of war, as though by magic, could not cope with the demands of peace. Some 40,000 people were squatting in disused service-camps up and down the country. The 300,000 new houses that had been promised by the end of the second year of peace would only touch the edge of the shortage. In her maiden speech, Bessie Braddock, the formidable Labour MP, had thundered: 'Our people are living in flea-ridden, bug-ridden, rat-ridden, lousy hell-holes,' and that was only a mild exaggeration.

Sammy was rushing on, his hands waving, his face alight. 'What have we got plenty of? Workers. Men needing jobs. I want you to get in the car, Esther, and find me a factory.'

'Is that all?' Esther said.

'To start with. Then I'll need benches, lathes, band-saws. Master carpenters, french polishers, metal-workers . . .'

'Excuse me,' Esther said. 'I can condense all this. I'll just pop out and find a fairy godmother. Then you can have anything you want.'

'OK, OK, I'm leaping ahead . . . but I can see it, Esther! I don't know how I contained myself till you got back. Now, here's my outline plan, with cost projections and sales potential. *You* go through them and find the holes and then . . . we'll be in business.'

'I should have stayed at home,' Esther said. 'Cleaned my windows, hoovered my floors, seen to my husband . . . Instead, I come back to a madhouse. I'm *meshugge*!'

'You're a pearl. Now, no more *plaplen*: get reading.'

Esther sat at her desk, sipping a cup of coffee brought to her by an office junior, and worked her way through the papers.

'Well,' she said at last, putting them down and stretching to ease her neck and shoulders. 'I can see it might work . . .'

*

Anne let herself into the kitchen and flopped into a chair. Tears of vexation were still pricking her eyes, and she clouted her empty oilcloth bag on to the table. Things were getting worse, no doubt about it. In the war she had queued like everybody else for what the shops had available. Now women were so desperate they joined any queue they saw, regardless of what it was for, just in the hope of getting *something*! She had done that at the butcher's opposite the Half Moon, and had discovered, when she got to the counter, that the queue was for animal lights for dog or cat food. And the worst thing was, she had stood looking at the evil-smelling mess and seriously contemplated taking it home and cooking it for the family meal.

She couldn't feed a family on what she was getting now. She couldn't even keep them clean, with soap on the ration. She was tired of queuing, tired of making do, tired of trying to turn pig-swill into palatable meals. 'We won the bloody war,' she said aloud. 'When's the victory coming?'

For each adult she was allowed one-and-twopence-worth of meat – but only if the butcher had any. Three ounces of bacon, two-and-a-half ounces of tea, two ounces each of butter and cheese – lumps no bigger than dominoes – four ounces of marge, and one egg a fortnight. If it hadn't been for her hens and the odd gift from Esther they'd've starved by now. Wearily she got to her feet and set about making the hens' mash, aware as she did so that it was getting harder to provide even that nowadays.

She still had points on her ration books, but the goods they covered – things like corned meat and fish, dried fruit and biscuits – were frequently unobtainable. Sighing, she resolved to get out to the shops earlier tomorrow. Better still, she would keep Theresa off school and they could both join queues. That should produce something. And when all this was over, she would buy herself a block . . . a half-pound block . . . of milk chocolate, and eat it herself, every bloody piece. And if she sicked it up, she would scoop it up and eat it again!

Anne was lifting the mash from the range when Frank came in at the door. One look at his dispirited face told her something had happened.

'Gaffney's dead,' he said.

Anne let go of the mash pan and sat down on a kitchen chair.

'Gaffney? The MP?'

'How many Gaffneys do we know?' Frank said. 'Of course, it's the MP. That means a by-election.'

'And now that little shit Gallagher's got the nomination, it's him that'll get your seat in Westminster,' Anne said, bitterly. 'That's all I needed to hear.'

'So Gaffney's dead,' Howard Brenton said as Norman Stretton, his manager, came into the room.

'Yes,' Stretton said. 'Of course he's been ailing for a long time. Heart, I'm told.' He smiled at Howard. 'Will you stand again at the by-election?'

'I will not,' Howard said fervently. 'Fourteen years as Tory MP for Belgate were quite enough. It almost killed me . . . and I was a fitter man than Gaffney.'

'So Stanley Gallagher will inherit the seat,' Stretton said. 'It's quite amazing, the way he's managed to bamboozle the men.'

'Yes, it should've been Maguire . . . and I'm not saying that because he's my brother-in-law. The man has integrity.'

Stretton's normally frank gaze shifted slightly. He would have disguised it, but Howard had already noticed.

'You're wondering how we get on? Well, I wondered myself how it would be. That was before I really understood my wife and her sister, who are two determined women. If there had been any awkwardness, it would have been dealt with, I assure you. In fact, we get on rather well, within the family. Here, at the pit, on the odd occasion our paths cross, it's as it always has been. And in a way nationalization has made it easier: Frank knows he'll be free of me as his boss soon. Besides, Norman, the world has changed. War is a great leveller. We both lost sons, Maguire and I. It's a bond of sorts.'

'I can see that the future is different now. The men will be the masters, or so they say.' Stretton was smiling wryly. 'You don't see it as being their salvation?'

'Perhaps,' Stretton said. 'But I'd tell them to beware the dead hand of the bureaucrat. We shall have to see.'

'What will you do when the pits are nationalized?' Howard asked. 'It's possible they may offer you a place here but if not – or if you'd prefer – you can come over to one of my other interests. The foundry, if you like, or the works?'

'That's good of you,' Stretton said. 'And it's reassuring to know you'd have something for me. The economic climate is far from rosy.'

It was true: the war had been won, but now the price was being paid. There was a massive deficit in Britain's balance of payments with the dollar area. Export markets were non-existent, for the industries that had once served them had long since turned over to war-production. Overseas investments had been plundered to pay for imports; and the American lend-lease scheme, which had been so generous to a war-time ally, had been axed immediately after VJ day. America was prosperous, but Europe and the Empire were a desert of want. If Britain were ever to regain economic independence, it had to restore its industrial output; but without raw materials from the United States this would be impossible.

'The dollar rules,' Howard said. 'We must begin to export again, but that means holding back on the import of food . . . and the nation is hungry.'

'Not only for food, either,' Stretton said. 'My sister is setting up home, and she tells me that all coloured or patterned china goes for export. She has to make do with utility white. And furniture is impossible to come by.'

'Young Lansky is setting up a furniture manufacturers,' Howard said. 'I heard about it at the club, and Esther says it's true.'

'He'll be a millionaire yet.' Stretton was grinning. 'We ought to take shares.'

'I think he will quite probably make my wife so rich that I can retire . . . though, come to think of it, friend Attlee has made sure I'll retire.' Howard was smiling, but a small knot of anxiety formed inside him. Esther's going off each day to run a business had seemed such a good idea when he, too, had a busy schedule. Nationalization would bring

61

financial compensation, but his life would be much emptier. How would it work out then?

'And I'll have the fish-cakes,' Esther said. Across the table Pamela was gazing round at the other diners in the Grand Hotel dining-room.

'Did daddy tell you about that London club?' Esther asked.

Pamela grimaced. 'You mean Boodles? Where they served roast beaver? Horrid!'

'Apparently no one would eat it, although they'd stuffed it and larded it up.'

'I should think not, poor creature.'

'There's a shortage of meat, darling. Perhaps they were desperate.'

'Not them,' Pamela said with feeling. 'When we were living at Valesworth during the war Uncle Henry used to take great hampers back for his club: pheasants, hares, rabbits, grouse – even venison sometimes. Everyone did it, especially Scots members. He said they were sick of salmon.'

'Oh dear,' Esther said. 'That *is* deprivation.' They both grinned and then their first course was arriving: a strange, grey-looking concoction that purported to be pâté.

'You enjoyed living at Valesworth, didn't you?' Esther asked tentatively as they ate.

'I missed home, and never coming north, but Aunt Lee was kind, and Uncle Henry, too. And the Dunane boys were amusing . . . most of the time. You know boys.'

'Worse than alligators?' Esther said.

'Much. I liked it when Rupert came down, though. I miss him, Esther.'

'I know. I had a nephew . . .'

'Joe? Daddy told me about him. He was born on the same day as Rupert, and you tried champagne for the first time and the bubbles went up your nose.'

'They did not!' Esther said indignantly. 'That was the kitchen maid. I was at least two rungs above her, and I drank my champagne like a veteran.'

'I remember all the maids we had when I was growing

up,' Pamela said, suddenly thoughtful. 'And I can't ever remember thinking about their lives, except in relation to ours – to our convenience. That's dreadful, isn't it?'

'You can't judge what happened then by the standards of today. There's been an upheaval, since, and expectations have changed . . . on both sides.' Esther paused. 'And lots of barriers have come down. I'm not sure that your father and I . . . well, it wouldn't have been accepted quite so easily before the war.'

Pamela looked down at her plate, aligning her knife and fork carefully. 'What's coming?' Esther wondered.

'Aunt Lee says second marriage is . . .' She was obviously seeking the right words.

'Is what?'

'Well, for different reasons. I mean, well, in the beginning . . . the first time . . . you marry for . . . for silly reasons sometimes.'

'Like love?' Esther asked, wondering what exactly Loelia Dunane had said to puzzle Pamela so. The girl was sixteen: she must understand about relationships. She leaned towards her step-daughter and squeezed her hand. 'Believe me, darling, second marriage is just as foolish . . . and just as wonderful. I married your father for the same reasons as I expect your mother married him: love and companionship.'

Impossible to mention lust to a sixteen-year-old, but that obtained too. 'I want to be with him: it's as simple as that – and I hope he wants to be with me. But that doesn't take away from what he felt for your mother. If she'd been alive still, he and I would never even have been aware of one another. But now I love him . . . and you and the boys.'

'Will you have babies?' Pamela said.

Esther was suddenly floored. 'I honestly don't know. I'm fearfully old, you know, almost forty. So probably not.' She tried to sound as reassuring as she could, but she had misjudged Pamela's mood.

'I hope you do,' Pamela said fervently. 'That would be the most gorgeous thing.'

'Yes,' Esther said faintly. 'Well, we'll see. Now, if you want to do some shopping, we'd better eat up.'

*

Stella had left Southampton clutching a *'Welcome'* pamphlet in one hand and carrying Tony in her other arm. Aboard, she shared a cabin with two other girls with babies. 'Lucky us,' one of them said. 'The girls without babies are on F Deck, below water-level. They've just got mattresses in hammocks, and no lockers.' Some of the girls stayed at the rail until England faded from sight, but Stella couldn't wait to get below.

As the voyage wore on, though, the cabin became a prison full of squalling infants. She had never before had to care for her son single-handed. Now she realized just how much of the work her mother had done.

She was scarcely troubled with seasickness, though some of the girls suffered terribly. There was a big box of lemons in the cafeteria to suck to stave off nausea, but Stella was too busy stuffing herself to bother with lemons. For the first time in her life she ate salmon; and there was fruit and eggs and milk and meat in a never-ending stream, served by black crew members with soft voices and pink-palmed hands.

The ritual examinations for lice continued, and there was a last-minute health check which consisted of yet another scared young doctor going over their naked bodies with a torch. To cheer themselves up they had sing-songs – 'Deep in the Heart of Texas' and 'The White Cliffs of Dover' were favourites – but most of the time they gossiped and boasted about their glowing future. And then they were steaming up the Hudson River, the sun emerging to form a halo around the head of the Statue of Liberty, which appeared to be a peculiar shade of green, and the towers and skyscrapers of the city silhouetted against the sky.

The ship docked at Pier 84 to the strains of 'Sentimental Journey' from a military band. 'God bless America,' one girl said fervently. Another was less sanguine: 'And God help us,' she said.

The brides lined the rails of the liner, dressed in their best, some wearing hats and gloves in spite of the sunshine, all of them anxious for the first glimpse of their new homeland. Stella had put on her best dress, made by her mother from black-market cotton lawn, sprigged with anemone-like flowers. She had pearls at her neck and in her ears, and plain court shoes on her nyloned legs. She felt she looked like a lady, and at least as good as, or better than, most of the girls lining the rails of the liner, anxious to pick out that one special face on the dock. It was so long since she had seen Mario that his face had become blurred in her memory. She screwed up her eyes now in an effort to 'see' him. He had been dark-haired and olive-skinned, with deep, soulful eyes. And his kisses had been nice . . . a bit undemanding, but that could change with time. She shifted Tony to her other arm and scanned the dockside for a glimpse of the upright figure in the lovely uniform that was now imprinted on her mind's eye. He had been a bit like Dana Andrews, if she remembered aright, only darker.

But there was such a mass of people, such a waving of banners and handkerchiefs, such a cacophony of noise, that she had to be shepherded, bewildered, down the gang plank and ushered to an enclosure where unclaimed brides stood nervously, looking for all the world like lots in a saleroom. Until, suddenly, Mario was there, clutching her and the baby, planting wet kisses on whatever area of uncovered flesh he could find.

'Stella! *Cara* Stella! And Tony, my little Tony . . .!'

Stella looked at her husband, trying not to let her disappointment show in her face. In the months they had been apart she had forgotten that he was short and fat. But in uniform he had at least looked something. Now he looked like a nobody: a greasy, perspiring little man with eyes like a spaniel and a mouth that constantly cooed and clucked at either her or the baby.

She allowed herself to be half-carried towards the exit, Mario's left arm about her waist, Tony cradled in his right. An obliging young seaman came behind, her baggage on a trolley. Where she had expected a limousine, there was instead a garish yellow taxi-cab that had seen better days.

'Everyone's at home,' Mario said. 'The whole family's waiting for you and the *bambino* . . . but I wanted to meet you by myself.'

Stella shuffled along the cab seat, wrinkling her nose at a strange smell, a strong spicy odour that seemed to ooze from Mario's pores. He leaned back from giving the address to the driver and patted her hand with his own, soft, damp palm. 'Oh Stella,' he said, 'we're going to be so happy.'

She smiled and tugged the skirt of her dress from under his pudgy thighs. His navy trousers were shiny at the knees, and the cuffs of his jacket were frayed. She tried to tell herself that rich people were often shabby, having nothing to prove, but as the cab ground its way through the congested streets her unease deepened.

'Here we are,' Mario said at last, as the cab pulled up, and he opened the door.

Stella had often imagined the house she would live in: white stucco, set back from the road, with a mailbox on a pole and a curving drive, just like in the movies. But they were about to enter an ordinary city house, tall and narrow, its ground floor occupied by a café whose windows bore the legend 'Tony's'.

She turned back to the street, as Mario fished in his pockets for change for the cab-driver. She was suddenly aware of the noise, the bustle, the heat, the stench of exhaust fumes, the brilliantly coloured blue, green, yellow and orange cars and taxis, dashing here and there, hooting madly. At home all the cars were black or blue, much smaller and somehow more dignified. Stella felt a lump of disappointment form in her throat. But then she noticed the pedestrians moving past her on the pavement. The men were big and bronzed, and walked with a loping stride; and the women . . . the women looked like fashion-plates, teetering along on the most divine high wedges Stella had ever seen.

She was still smiling as Mario shepherded her through a side door and up a narrow staircase to the room where his family were waiting.

Her first impression of the room was of darkness. Heavy curtains were at the window; there was deep-hued wall-paper; religious pictures were everywhere, and family photographs on every flat surface, all of them in heavy, ornate frames that looked like gold. But it was the women who frightened Stella most. They stood, waiting to greet her, row on row of dark-browed, dark-haired women, the older ones fat and dressed in black, the young ones pretty

66

and slender but – as she later wrote to Anne – 'everyone of them with a moustache'.

The executive of the Belgate Labour Party had met in the back room of the Half Moon to plan a by-election strategy. They had with them their chosen candidate, Stanley Gallagher. Now, after an hour or two of discussion, they had split into groups for a last drink.

'So you'll work for Gallagher?' Frank Maguire's companion asked him quietly.

'No.' Frank was stoical. 'But I'll work for the party, marrer. Till I drop. And if Gallagher's Labour's man, so be it.'

'Aye, well, there's that in it. Many a one wouldn't, though, in your place.'

Frank shrugged and the man continued: 'You know why it wasn't you that got the nomination? You kept the lads' noses to the grindstone in the war, and you wouldn't criticize Brenton or Stretton. Now Gallagher, he'd badmouth his grandmother if there was owt in it for him. Men has short memories, Frank: they forget who argued their case before the war. All they think of now is your lass being Brenton's sister-in-law.'

'That happened *after* I lost the nomination, Billy,' Frank said.

'Aye, but it's the same thing. Hold on a while – give that little shitehawk enough rope, he'll hang hisself. I've seen his type before.'

As Frank walked home alone, he could see no prospect of Gallagher ever relinquishing the seat. The Conservatives would never get back in, in Belgate, that was sure; and Gallagher was thirty-one years old, younger by fourteen years than Frank. He would be in the seat for life.

Frank was passing the war memorial now, a tribute to the dead of two world wars. There, etched in the stone, were the names of his son and of the father of his grandson: *Joseph Maguire* and *Charles Rupert Neville Brenton*. The night he had stood firm against the others and ensured that the coal-owner's son was also named on the memorial had been the night he really lost the nomination, whatever Billy said. Still, it had only been justice by young Brenton. He turned as a large car roared up behind him and on towards the Durham road. At the wheel was Fox, once the Brenton chauffeur and now a bloody tycoon with his fleet of lorries and cars.

Frank walked on, thinking of the tales about Fox . . . his double-dealing, his corruption, his profiteering. Other men had gone to gaol for less, but Fox prospered. And lads like Joe had died to make it possible. It was difficult to understand.

The War Crimes trials at Nuremberg had rumbled on since November, the men who had spread terror throughout Europe sitting ashen-faced in the dock at the Palace of Justice in Nuremberg which had been the scene of Hitler's rallies. Emmanuel Lansky had wanted vengeance; now he longed for it to be over, and the dreadful litany of evidence ended. It was a catalogue of infamy, taken from books and records which, according to the accusers, had been kept with a 'Teutonic passion for thoroughness'.

Lansky turned from reports of Nuremberg to read of unrest between Jews and Arabs and the growing reluctance of the British Government to bear responsibility for it. 'There will be war in Palestine, Sammy, mark my words,' Lansky said. 'War in a holy land . . . as if enough misery has not engulfed the world.'

But Sammy had spent the day talking to men who wanted to work in his new factory, and they had been telling him of the difficulties of peace. Men who had held commissions in the services were desperate now for a job at a bench. 'Anything, Mr Lansky, as long as I don't have to walk the streets. You can't even go for a drink without some wag saying, "Oh, here's a lad with demob money," as though we were bloody lucky to have it. The war took six years out of my life, and I've come back to find resentment.'

Each demobbed serviceman received 146 clothing coupons and a gratuity: a single private with three years' service received £83, a married man £99. They emerged from the demob centres to find spivs with wads of notes clamouring to buy their coupons, and even the new suits off their backs, such were the shortages. It was not much of a homecoming.

One man had returned to find his wife's loving letters had been covering up an affair with a shopkeeper who had not gone to fight. 'I've got nowt now, not even the sight of me bairns. And if I did see them, they'd still call *him* dad.' But most of the men used the same phrase: 'We thought it would be different.' Some of them wore an article of military clothing, as though they clung to their war-time status . . . a flying jacket, a naval scarf, a regimental tie or pin. 'God help them all,' Sammy had thought as he left the factory, and had given thanks for his own good fortune.

Now he dandled his son on his knee and tried to soothe his father. 'You can't have a new state born without teething troubles, Papa. Give them time.' But Lansky was not to be pacified. Homeless Jews were being forcibly prevented from entering Palestine: how could that be justified?

'We should have learned, Samuel, from all the pain. If knowledge had grown, it would have made sense of it. But everywhere, everywhere there is discord . . .'

He was still shaking his head when Naomi entered with a tray.

'Such long faces,' she said as she began to pour the tea.

'We're just moaning,' Sammy said. 'Come and cheer us up.'

He looked quizzically at his son, as he seated him in his high chair. 'Shall we keep her, the mama? Or trade her in for a new one?' The baby chuckled and bounced up and down energetically.

'He'll walk soon,' Emmanuel said.

'He'll have to,' Naomi said sweetly, sitting down with her cup. 'I can't carry two at once.'

There was silence for a moment, while she nibbled a biscuit with eyes downbent.

'You mean . . .?' Sammy asked. Then, as she nodded, he turned to his father. 'Don't dare to cry, Papa. Don't you dare.'

But the old Jew had taken out his silk handkerchief to wipe his eyes, and all the admonitions in the world would not have stopped him.

'It will be a girl,' Naomi said. 'I need some support in this house. And before anyone argues, it will be born here, where I am happiest, not in hospital. And let no one dare say different.'

'If I had known,' Lansky said wonderingly. 'If I had known what a dragon she was, I would have chased Eli Cohen away when he brought her to my door.'

'Go on, Papa Lansky, perjure yourself!' giggled Naomi. 'We both know you couldn't do without me, but only one of us is prepared to admit it.'

And Sammy, seeing people he loved locked in good-natured banter, looked from them to his son and thought that surely his cup was overflowing.

'Are you sure you like this house?' Howard said suddenly. He and Esther were in their bedroom at the Scar, the curtains drawn back to reveal the late evening landscape, which was a blend of charcoal and black, with only a tiny chain of lights on the horizon to mark the road to Durham.

'Why do you ask that now?' Esther said, in mild astonishment. 'I've never even thought about it. It's a lovely house, it's where you live, and where I live now. The children are happy here. Oh, I miss my old home; I loved it. But we couldn't have lived there. Why did you ask that, Howard?' She moved close enough to look up into his face.

'I don't know. It suddenly occurred to me that we assumed you'd live here. And I just wonder if that was fair?'

Esther was reaching for the buttons at the back of her dress and he moved round to unfasten them for her. 'Thank you. I don't think "fair" comes into it, my love. And anyway, these last few weeks have been so hectic I couldn't have coped with a move as well.'

'But you'd tell me if you wanted to?'

She turned suddenly to take his face in her hands. 'If I ever want to move I'll trumpet it from the roof-top. I'll take a page in the *Sunderland Echo*. Better still, I'll tell our Anne. She'll get the point home.'

'Not a word against your sister. She is beginning to realize I don't have horns and a tail.'

'At the moment she thinks you'll be on the breadline when the pits are nationalized,' Esther said ruefully. 'When she hears about the level of owners' compensation, it'll all change.'

'What am I going to do, then?' Howard said as Esther moved to pick her wrapper from the bed. 'All my adult life I've had responsibility for other people's lives. A pit – several pits, in fact, with all their moods and viciousness, and trickery. I've longed to be free of them, but now . . .'

'Don't think about it,' Esther said. 'Not tonight anyway. One day at a time. An answer always turns up when you're not trying to nose one out. And you still have other business interests. Perhaps they'll expand.'

Howard caught her hand as she passed him, moving towards the bathroom. 'That's what I love about you, Esther. Your calm.'

'Thank you! That makes me sound like a stagnant pool.'

He kissed her to punish her for mocking him, and she knew then that they would make love tonight. 'I love him,' she thought. 'In every possible way, I love him.'

Alone in the bathroom she took her Dutch cap from its hiding place behind her toiletries and prepared to insert it. But something made her turn to the mirror. Her own face, staring back, shocked her. 'I'm growing old,' she thought. 'I'm forty, and I look it. Inside I may still feel fifteen, but outside life is catching up with me.' She stood tense for a moment and then her shoulders drooped and her head fell. After a moment she put the Dutch cap back in the cupboard and began her bedtime ritual. Russian roulette, that was what they called it. Clicking the chambers of a gun. Click . . . you're safe; click, click . . . you're dead. Or pregnant. 'Have I the right?' she thought, and then remembered her own words: 'One day at a time.'

6

September 1946

It was not a good time to hold a by-election and Frank Maguire knew it. The war was over and with it the threat of death by enemy action but, as Anne informed him hourly, they would probably all die of cold or starvation anyway, and at least Hitler would've made their end quick. The new Labour government had not solved the problems of peace. In particular, Anne resented the tyranny of shopkeepers. Some of them would not open until they saw a queue long enough to absorb available supplies. Then the shopkeeper would open up, do all his work in half an hour, and bang down the shutters with a muttered, 'That's it,' leaving those at the end of the queue with nothing to show for perhaps an hour's wait. The result of shortages and controls was an ever-flourishing black market.

There were rumblings in the press about 'a permanent socialist dictatorship dedicated to rationing and other controls', and even down the pit men were becoming restive. Only the dream of nationalization, so soon to be realized, lured them on. So, Frank thought, Labour would almost certainly hold the Belgate seat in today's elections, and Gallagher would take his place in Parliament. 'You're mad,' Anne told Frank bitterly, 'working your feet off for that little sod.' But even she baulked at seeing the seat fall to Howard Brenton's successor as Conservative candidate – a foppish ex-lieutenant from the Scots Guards who had lily-white hands and a retreating chin. 'He's never put a shovelful of coal on a fire, let alone mined one. What does he know about us?' was everyone's cry. Some even mourned the passing of Howard Brenton as MP on the grounds that 'the bugger might be a Conservative but at least he was born and bred here'.

On election morning Frank was up with day-break, making the best breakfast he could muster and trying to get five minutes peace before Anne came downstairs to nag him, and polling began. Soccer had begun again in Britain that month, and in the quiet kitchen Frank studied reports about his team, Sunderland, and their chances in Saturday's match. They were one of the big six, teams that attracted crowds of over 50,000, and he fancied their chances in the League. If they were champions this year, it would be a good omen for the area.

He had managed to get through the paper and was refolding it when Anne came downstairs.

'Any tea?'

'In the pot. I'll pour it for you.' As he handed her the tea he saw there were new lines around her mouth and shadows beneath her eyes. She was still missing Stella and the baby.

'Cheer up,' he said. 'It might never happen.'

'Oh it will, Frank . . . whatever you're on about, if it's bad it will happen. That's the story of my life.'

'Things aren't that bad,' he said. 'You've got our Gerard back home again.'

'Oh yes, I forgot that. I clean forgot I had a failed priest for a son.' She slapped her own wrist. 'Ooh, naughty Anne. Didn't count her blessings, did she? What's he going to do with himself, Frank – go down the hole? That's nice for a lad with exams. Seven children I've reared, Frank, and only our Terry likely to make something of herself.'

'Listen,' Frank said, feeling a surge of both irritation and affection for the turbulent woman who shared his bed. 'Let's get today over, and then we'll sit down and sort out our Gerard and . . .' He cast around for something, anything to cheer her. 'And I'll have a surprise for you. Something nice. Something to bring a smile to your gob.'

'It'll need to be something big,' Anne warned, but her face softened a little. As Frank left the house he reflected uneasily that he had put his head in a noose now, all right.

Twelve hours to get Gallagher into Parliament and himself off the hook. It was going to be a hell of a day.

'They'll be going to the polls in Belgate now,' Howard said. Esther was sitting up in bed, a tea-tray in front of her. Outside, in the London street, the noise of traffic was beginning to mount.

'Yes,' Esther said. 'Do you miss it – the cut and thrust, or whatever they call it?'

'No.' Howard's tones were heartfelt. 'I was never at ease in politics. Fourteen years in the House of Commons and I only spoke a handful of times. I did my bit on committees and in the constituency, but I never even came close to changing the face of Britain . . . thank God!'

'Frank will be working his head off for the Labour Party, no doubt, and Anne calling him a fool for his efforts,' Esther said, cutting her toast into fingers.

'She has a point, Esther. He ought to have had the nomination: he's a natural leader, and he's straight. He defended the men. I often had cause to wish he worked in another pit, I can tell you. And Gallagher . . . young Gallagher, I'll never think of him as anything else . . . is a bandwagon-jumper. He smelled the success of socialism in a post-war world, and he jumped that way. But he's got no real convictions. In different circumstances he'd be out there today calling for capitalism and more capitalism.'

Howard went to the window as he spoke and looked down on the street. 'Before the war this street used to be full of horses. Now you seldom see one. More change!'

Esther was throwing back the coverlet and getting out of bed. 'Hey! Why so gloomy? I have three days in London to enjoy myself, to have fun. Don't you dare spoil it.' The white nightdress, so lovingly cut on the bias from parachute silk by Anne, clung to her limbs as she moved towards him. He put down his cup and held out his arms.

'Tell me what you want to do and we'll do it.' As his arms closed around her Howard felt the comfort she always brought flooding through him. Her lips were warm on his cheek, and then she whispered against his ear.

'I want to be with you. That's enough.'

Outside London was gearing itself for a busy day. Howard had a dozen things he ought to do, but suddenly they counted for little. He scooped his wife into his arms and carried her back to bed.

'This is nice,' Emmanuel Lansky said. For once Sammy was home from work early, seated opposite his father. On the settee, Ruth and Naomi were winding wool, or rather Naomi was winding and Ruth was holding the skein of wool between her outstretched hands, turning them this way and that. On the floor at their feet Aaron was building a tower of blocks, only to knock it down when it was finished and start again.

Naomi looked at the clock. 'What time shall we eat?'

'Not yet,' Ruth protested. 'I still feel full from the last meal.'

'What's the food like in Edinburgh?' Sammy asked.

'It's just food. When I qualify, I will never eat an oatcake again as long as I live.' In Edinburgh Ruth lodged with a good Jewish family, but kosher food was no more plentiful than any other and they too were forced to plug gaps with whatever came to hand.

'Well, today we have chicken,' Naomi said. 'I got it from a friend of a friend, so no questions.'

'Not on the black market?' Emmanuel said, disapprovingly.

'No, Papa, not the black market. I saved our sugar ration – we don't use as much as other people – and some tea. I exchanged them. So we sacrificed for it. You can enjoy.'

'Not another,' Ruth protested, as more skeins for winding were produced.

'One more,' Naomi pleaded, and they set to work again. The firelight flickered on the walls, and even Sammy stopped thinking about tomorrow's business.

'Two more years,' Naomi said at last, 'and then you'll be a proper doctor, Ruth. You'll need a surgery and a car.'

She sounded awed by the magnitude of these requirements, but Emmanuel tut-tutted. 'These are trifles. Already I have them in hand.'

'I thought I might practise with Patrick Quinnell in Belgate,' Ruth said. 'Just at first, to gain experience.'

'Yes,' Emmanuel nodded, 'that makes good sense. Then, a little later, you can come to Sunderland and be the best doctor in town.'

'Only the best?' Sammy said. 'Such small ambitions for your scholar, Papa. Is that what you want to do, Ruthie? Practise here, on your doorstep?'

'Yes,' Ruth said firmly, 'that's what I'll do.' But she didn't say 'What I want to do,' and Sammy noticed.

'Then of course you will,' he said easily. 'But if you didn't choose to do that? What else might you do then?'

'If I didn't want to stay here, beside you and Naomi and Papa, I think I would go to Israel. They need doctors there. One of the boys in my year is going – not forever, just for a year or two.'

'For boys, that is good,' the old Jew said. 'To give a year or two to Israel is right and proper.'

'Women are equal to men in Israel,' Ruth said. 'They work side by side there, building the kibbutzim.'

At her side Naomi shuddered. 'Don't speak of the kibbutzim to me. They take the children from their parents when they are only a few months old!'

Ruth laughed at her sister's look of horror. 'They don't *take* them, silly; they just look after them while the parents work. In a crèche. The children play together, and are happy and safe, and their parents take them back at five o'clock.'

'It's not natural,' Naomi said stubbornly.

'Well, we're not a kibbutz, so we needn't argue,' Sammy said. 'And things are different there, my *oytser*. Israelis live in a perpetual state of war.'

'But they have comradeship,' Ruth said, 'and a pride in their achievement. They are making the desert bloom with trees, and exotic flowers like bougainvilleas and hibiscus and poinsettias and acacia. It's like Paradise. And all of it surrounded by hills and rivers and groves of date-palms . . .'

Sammy, watching her flushed face, saw how her eyes shone behind her glasses. This was a new Ruth. Whoever had been telling his sister-in-law about Israel had certainly sold his product well.

Anne had not expected Frank to return home when the polling booths shut, but to stick with his party colleagues, downing a well-earned pint and then get ready to watch the count. She had met him in the street in the afternoon, and heard that all was going well for Labour. So it was a surprise when he appeared at a quarter to ten, beer on his breath and a smile on his face.

'I promised you a surprise, didn't I? Well, here it is.' He gestured around the room. 'How would you like this house done up? All of it, every room?'

'I can smell the beer, Frank, but I didn't realize you were that drunk. In case you've forgotten, there's no paint in the shops except for war damage . . . and if there was, who has time for decorating? You're working, and I'm queuing. If you're thinking of our Gerard, he's never been able to use his hands. Well, take that grin off your face, Frank, because it's irritating me. If you've just discovered a magic word, trot it out!'

'Not a magic word, Anne: a tradesman. Demobbed, and at a loose end. He was a painter before the war – not a decorator, a proper artist. But he can't go back to that, on account of no one has any money for portraits. So he's house-painting in the mean time, till things pick up. And . . . and . . .' He paused for effect. 'He supplies the paint!'

Anne would have poured scorn on this too-perfect, set-up if she had been given the chance, but at that moment Gerard came in from the yard, his face serious. 'Mam, dad! I've just made a decision.'

Anne clasped her hands to her breast. He was going back to the seminary. Her prayers had been answered. But she was wrong.

'I'm going to be a teacher, mam. That's what I want to do. I'll likely get a grant for studying, Father Lavery says, but if I don't the Church will help me. I can start this month, if I pass the entrance exam.' He looked from one face to the other. 'I hope you're pleased?'

'We are,' Frank said hastily, not daring to look at his

wife. She had sat down on a kitchen chair and was watching the door.

'Well?' Gerard said at last.

'Don't distract me,' she said grimly. 'They say everything comes in threes. I've just been spun two fairy-tales, so the third one's bound to be along shortly.'

Howard and Esther were dining with the Dunanes at Chester Square; a cold consommé, a bird and a concoction of cream laced with a liqueur.

'Things are so much easier now,' Loelia said as she and Esther went through to the drawing-room, leaving the men to their port. 'Hartnell is making me a suit . . . quite divine. And he says we can lower the hem a little and have just a tiny bit of detail. I can't wait.' She looked at Esther's delphinium-blue crêpe dress with its draped basque. 'You always look so smart, Esther. How do you manage it? Diana used to moan about the lack of style in Durham.'

'My sister makes a lot of my clothes,' Esther said. 'She's very clever. And we do have magazines, you know. We can keep up with fashion trends.'

'Yes,' Loelia said doubtfully. 'I remember your sister at the wedding. Still . . . let me pour you coffee. You're sure you won't have a liqueur? Some armagnac, perhaps?'

'No, thank you,' Esther said. 'But the coffee smells wonderful.'

'Well, it *is* coffee,' Loelia said. 'Max gets it from someone at his club. They're vaguely South American, some dago ancestor, I think. So that's the connection.'

They supped appreciatively for a moment and then Loelia spoke again. 'You must miss Pamela, now she's back at school.'

'Yes,' Esther said. 'I love her being at home.'

'I sympathize. I miss her still. Of course, I'd have kept them all with us if Howard would've let me . . . after all, Diana was my closest and dearest friend. But I miss Pamela especially. Actually, I hoped we'd get a chance to talk about Pamela tonight, and about her coming out in a year or two. In her mother's absence, I'll be happy to present her. You do understand about the débutante thing?'

'Yes.' Esther leaned forward to set her cup on the sofa table. 'And of course if Pamela wants to be a deb, she will be. But I think we should ask her first.'

'No.' Loelia's voice was firm. 'No girl ever wants her first season, not if she's in her right mind. The strain is horrendous. But Pamela must do it. How will she meet the right young men if she doesn't come out? And we'll give her a party, of course . . .'

'I rather think Howard would want to do that himself, Loelia.'

'Oh, pish and tush to Howard. He must appreciate that I feel close to the girl . . .'

'Does she know?' Esther wondered. 'Am I listening to the devoted friend – or the aunt? I wish I knew.' For a moment she was tempted to speak out: '*I know Pamela is Max's child.*' But what if Howard was wrong when he said he was sure Loelia already knew too? What if horror passed over Loelia's face at the revelation? 'It's not my place to speak,' Esther thought, 'but I'm beginning to see the impossibility of living with lies and evasions.'

When she and Howard were home in Mount Street and going through the comfortable routine of preparing for bed, she summoned up her courage.

'Howard, when we first spoke of marriage I said we both had too much in our past for a union. I think I mentioned secrets. If I didn't I should've done.'

'You did, and if I remember my reply: I said I didn't care about your past or your secrets. I haven't changed my mind.'

'No, I know you haven't, but I have. Tonight, talking to Loelia . . . and of course she wanted to talk about Pammy . . . I thought what webs we weave for one another and ourselves – especially ourselves – when we keep things hidden. I haven't many secrets, but those I have are big ones. And I don't want to keep them to myself any longer.'

Howard crossed the room to take her hands in his. He was in his shirt-sleeves now, his collar stud unfastened, his hair falling on his brow. 'I love him,' she thought, 'but I have to go on now, whatever the consequences.'

'Are you sure, Esther? There's no need to tell me anything. I genuinely don't care. I don't want to know, unless sharing will help you?'

'I have two secrets, Howard. There was a man called David Gilfillan, who died in the war. I never loved him, but I did sleep with him, as often as he could get leave.'

'So?' Howard was half smiling. 'You were thirty-nine when we married, Esther. I knew you would have had men in your life.'

'But there was another man. You and I have spoken of him: Philip Broderick, the man I worked for. We were real lovers, Howard. Philip was an invalid, a cripple, people said. That's why he wouldn't marry me – but it wasn't sordid, it was splendid; and I don't regret it. He died when we had only been together a few months. I had his child. Because Philip was already dead, I gave it up for adoption. I've never seen or heard of it since.'

Howard did not speak, and Esther held her breath. What would be his reaction?

'Boy or girl?'

It was not the question Esther had expected.

'A boy. He'd be a man, now – well, sixteen.'

'So you were twenty-three when he was born?'

'Yes. I can't plead that I was a child, or that I was led astray. I wanted to love Philip, and I'd never have given it up, not voluntarily.'

Suddenly he reached out and drew her closer. 'As I'd never have left Diana. I understand, and I'm glad you told me. We'll have no secrets between us from now on. Do you think about the boy? Or want to see him?'

'Sometimes. In the long watches of the night, that sort of thing. I often wondered, in the war, whether or not he was safe.'

'We could look for him. These things can be done, whatever they say.'

'No, I wouldn't want that. It would be nice to know he was well and happy, but I wouldn't want to see him, and I hope he doesn't ever think about me.'

Howard put up his hands and cupped Esther's head between them, her ears resting lightly on the web between his thumb and forefinger.

'That's that, then. It's done. Now . . .' He bent to kiss

her brow. 'Can we go to bed? And if a single amorous twitch escapes me, please ignore it. Your husband is a happy man, but he's full of Colville port and very sleepy.'

'Come, then,' Esther said. 'Confession is pretty tiring too. Let's sleep.'

But he caught her as she would have moved away. 'You didn't confess. Confession implies guilt, and there is none. So sleep soundly, my darling. And in case I haven't convinced you, here's another kiss for absolution.'

7

October 1946

Esther sat in the car for a long time, plucking up the courage to go in to the surgery. Patrick Quinnell would laugh at her. Nearly forty years old. It was crazy. She checked her nose in the driving-mirror to make sure it wasn't shiny, settled her hat firmly on her head, and went in search of the doctor. She found Patrick Quinnell in his bottle-lined surgery, the smell of antiseptic in the air.

'Esther! This is a pleasure. I hope it's a social call? You certainly look healthy.'

Esther smiled. 'Half social. I brought these tins for Mary, I thought they might come in handy.'

'Spam! Luxury. And peas! They'll be more than welcome. How much do I owe you?'

'Nothing,' Esther said. 'Just a minute of your time.'

'You shall have as many minutes as you like. As old Lansky would say, what's a little time for a friend?'

'I'm not getting my periods,' Esther said, when they were settled, her cheeks flushing. But the area around her mouth was an oval of pallor in her pink face.

'How many?'

'Only one. It's two weeks late.'

'And you could be pregnant? Yes, of course you could. Do you want to be?'

'I don't know. Partly . . .'

'There's no such thing as a partial pregnancy, I'm afraid. Still, hop on the couch and we'll have a look. It's too early to do an examination but . . .'

He examined her breasts, and probed her abdomen with gentle fingers.

'My guess is that you *are* pregnant. Probably six weeks. We can arrange a test a bit later, but in the mean time . . .'

'. . . in the mean time, I don't want anyone to know. Especially not Howard.'

'I think you're wise, at this stage . . . and at your age. Let's give it a week or two.'

When Esther came out into the street again, she felt strange. Seventeen years ago she had felt like this, half in awe, half afraid. Then she had been alone in the world, with Philip, the father of her baby, already dead, and no one to depend on except the Lanskys. Now she was a loved wife, and she had security. Why was she so afraid?

Sammy read the report a third time. It came from the International Red Cross, and informed him that Chaim and Golda Guttman had perished in Sachsenhausen concentration camp on or about 14 August 1941. How was he to tell that to his pregnant wife, or to her sister who was up to her eyes in study? He put the letter in a drawer of his desk and locked it. Tonight he might tell his father. Then again, he might not. The old man was reasonably content at the moment. Why spoil it?

His secretary came in, carrying his morning coffee.

'No biscuits?'

'Only arrowroot, and you said you'd rather eat cardboard.'

'*Oy vey*, a giant in the food trade and even *I* can't get a decent biscuit.'

Sammy shook out his paper as he supped coffee and perused the headlines, skipping details of the executions of German war criminals in Nuremberg. He'd had enough of that already. Doctors were muttering about the link between smoking and cancer . . . it was a good thing that he'd given it up. A father of children couldn't afford to jeopardize his health.

On an inside page, the row between Truman and Attlee rumbled on. On Yom Kippur, the Jewish Day of Atonement, the President had urged Britain to let 100,000 displaced European Jews into Palestine and to establish a Jewish state in an 'adequate' area.

This was the usual vague language that everyone had used since 1917, when the British Foreign Minister, grateful for Jewish help during the First World War, had issued the Balfour declaration that 'HM Government views with favour the establishment in Palestine of a national home for the Jewish people.'

It was a recipe for discord. The Jews wanted to see the promise made good; the Arabs regarded it as the wilful disposal by Britain of territory over which she had no control or rights, and done without the slightest attempt to consult the 92 per cent non-Jewish part of that territory's population. It had taken Hitler and the gas-ovens to bring matters to a head – and now the President wanted immediate action.

Clement Attlee had fired off a sharp rejoinder to the President, accusing him of sabotaging delicate British negotiations with the Jews and Arabs, which were now at a critical stage. Truman was obviously counting the Jewish vote in America, but Arabia was a volatile area. The British were just managing to keep order there. Too much interference could cause a cataclysm.

Sammy was draining his cup as Esther returned. 'Want some coffee?'

'Thanks,' she said wearily, unpinning her hat and combing her hair with her fingers. 'I could do with some.'

'Were you held up at home?'

'No.'

Immediately Sammy sensed a mystery. Esther was not given to monosyllabic answers. 'Well, what then? Don't leave me guessing.'

'Shopping,' she said. 'I've been shopping.'

'So where are the parcels? The carrier bags? This is Sammy Lansky you're speaking to, he's no *shlemil*.'

Esther smiled wryly.

'I've been to the doctor's, if you must know. Nothing serious. Just run down.'

'Sure?'

'Very sure. Now, you wanted to discuss the furniture designs. I liked the outlines for the bedroom stuff for prefabricated houses, but some of the drawers are very small, more like trinket drawers than the real thing. I know the rooms are tiny, but people will still need to put clothes away.'

'Prefabs are small, Esther, and that's a fact. But they're the only way Bevin can fulfil his election promise: "*Five million homes in quick time.*" Throwing them up overnight is the only way. I'm told he calls prefabs "rabbit hutches".'

'That's nice for the people who have to live in them.' Esther's coffee had arrived and she took a sip. 'Ugh!' A sudden wave of nausea swept over her, and Sammy saw it.

'Are you pregnant, Esther? I've seen that face before . . . on Naomi.'

He had meant to make a joke, but Esther's rejoinder was too quick.

'I'm not. Don't be ridiculous.'

Sammy recovered his composure and smiled. 'OK, fob me off. Here I am, ready to give you sympathy, mix the peppermint and water, rub your back – I know all the touches. But shut me out! *Oy vey!*'

'It is *oy vey*, Sammy,' Esther said, slumping back in her chair. 'I don't know why I let myself get into this situation . . .'

'So you *are* pregnant!' Sammy leaped to his feet and hurried to put an arm around her. 'Well, there's a nice kettle of fish.'

'Don't mention fish,' Esther implored, leaning against his shoulder.

'Sit still. I'll go out for some soda water. Drink it, and eat a water biscuit. It works like a charm.'

'I'll try anything, if it takes this sick feeling away. But Sammy, not a word to *anyone* . . . on your life?'

'On my life, on my Naomi's life, on the life even of the *boy t'shikl*. Until you tell me I may, not a word!'

Anne was making Theresa a skirt from black-out material, stitching bands of green and red binding at the hem and the high waist. Theresa was fourteen now, and clever, blond, and attractive – but not quite as beautiful as Stella, which Anne considered a blessing in the circumstances. One man-trap in the family was enough; and if her teachers were right, Theresa had the brains to make something of herself without depending on getting a man. She sighed with satisfaction. On the dresser two real bananas were resting and Anne was beginning . . . just beginning . . . to believe in the return of peace, especially now that the hated gas-masks had been put into the rubbish bin. And she had had a letter from Mario, that morning, written before Stella arrived, which had lifted her spirits a little.

I have always known the boy was not mine, mom: Stella was honest from the start. But his father was my best friend, and after he was killed it seemed right to me that I should give a father's protection to his son. After all, Ricky would've done the same if it had been me who went and him who survived. I love Stella with all my heart and know my family will love her, too. We are going to be happy and I want you to be happy. Once Stella and I settle down to work together in the family business, we'll be able to save. England is not so far away, and I miss the Yorkshire puddings and gravy. So we'll all be back as soon as we can. In the mean time my mom is sending you some goodies, tins and dried goods, because I know things are still tough over there. I am longing to see Stella and the boy. Give my love to everyone in the family, and my best regards to friends and neighbours.

Your loving son, Mario.

Anne reread the sentence about Stella settling down to the business. At least the boy was an optimist. But if her only chance of seeing the bairn depended on Stella working, that would be that. Well, she would be there by now – the letter was two weeks old – so it wouldn't be long before the balloon went up.

She tried to find comfort in Gerard's new direction in life. Angela was earning, too, and that was a help. All in all, she had a family to be proud of, but she wanted the feel of a baby in her arms again, and that was a fact. She was roused from her reverie by a knock at the back door.

The caller was wearing an old army greatcoat and the

red tie of a wounded soldier, and Anne's face softened. That garb was passport enough for anyone.

'Maguire?' he said. 'I'm your painter.'

'Come in,' Anne said, standing aside to let him pass. 'I see you've brought your tools.' Behind him a barrow was piled high with planks, ladders and buckets.

'Let's review the battlefield,' he said grandly, stooping through the doorway. He was handsome, Anne decided, and there was an air about him of one who had suffered.

'It's not much,' she said lamely, looking at her peeling walls and at the greying whitewashed ceiling where the marks of Frank's brush-strokes still showed.

'There's been a war,' he said. 'Besides, I like a challenge.' He smiled at Anne and she felt a warm glow inside her chest.

'Sit down,' she said. 'I've got the kettle on.'

'You're Anne,' he said, 'if you'll forgive the familiarity. Your husband mentioned your name. I'm Victor Devine.' He held out his hand and Anne allowed her own to be shaken.

'I've got some rock-cakes put by, if you're hungry,' she said, when her fingers were restored to her and she could wipe the faint sweat from her upper lip. Victor nodded graciously. He was already unbuttoning his greatcoat.

'I thought you might like the rooms stippled,' he said grandly, when the tea and rock-cakes were done.

Anne had never heard of stippling but she wasn't about to let on. 'Well . . .' she said doubtfully.

'It's all the rage,' he said. 'You could have peach on buttercup, or rose on eau-de-Nil.' It sounded wonderful.

Within minutes the furniture was shrouded in dust-sheets so that the ceiling could be whitewashed. As Victor waved the brush back and forth, spattering whitewash like rain, he talked, and Anne listened, open-mouthed. He had come down in the world, he said, from artist to artisan. That was Hitler's fault – but then, being Russian and of high birth, he was used to adversity. When he announced that he had to come down from the ladder to rest his war-wound, Anne helped him alight in a welter of sympathy, and then gave him the mince she'd cooked for Frank, hanging on to his description of the Normandy beaches while he ate.

When Frank came home he found a half-painted ceiling and some black-pudding sandwiches, which was all that was left.

The next day Victor progressed to North Africa. He'd been sent there, he told a spellbound Anne, because he couldn't be allowed anywhere near the Russian front. When she asked why, he heaved a sigh and changed the subject.

That night Frank pointed out that progress was slow. Also he was tired of black-pudding sandwiches and wanted his meat ration. Anne asked if he begrudged a wounded war-hero 1s 2d-worth of meat, and he hastily assured her that black pudding would be fine.

The next day the painter was devastated to hear Frank thought him slow. For twenty minutes he dashed from wall to wall at high speed, sloshing buckets of peach distemper left and right. After that he had to sit down for the pain to subside, and to eat the wee piece of ham-and-egg pie Anne pressed on him. He apologized for his slow progress. He was, he sighed, used to better things. Anne moved nearer, lips parted in anticipation. Had she heard of the White Russians he asked. Indeed she had! They were the opposite of Bolsheviks and were all related to the Tsar of Russia.

Victor asked her to contemplate the exquisite pain of being royal and reduced to stippling for a living, and she gave him the rest of the ham-and-egg pie. He stood there, munching, hawk-nosed and handsome against the dripping peach walls, while Anne tried to think what else she could feed him. When he went home early to recover from the trauma of revealing his true identity, Anne tidied the distemper buckets into a corner before she went off to rake up something for Frank's evening meal.

Frank was more interested in where the ham-and-egg pie had gone than in Imperial Russia. He was paying for 'stippling', he said, and it was a long time coming! He stayed at home the next morning until the arrival of the Grand Duke, as he referred to Victor. If 'stippling' had not begun by 5 that evening, he said, the deal was off.

The rest of the day was perpetual motion. The Grand Duke went off and returned with a partner who made no claim to royal blood but could distemper fast. More peach distemper in the living-room, lemon in the bedrooms, beige in the kitchen. By lunchtime they were ready for 'stippling' to begin, and Anne retreated to a corner, wide-eyed.

Two huge sponges; one bucket of brown distemper; two men with all the appearance of dementia. They dipped their sponges in the brown sludge and flung them higgledy piggledy against the walls. Brown squidges appeared, some of them running at the edges. They were three-dimensional, alive and bombarding you from every angle. When the men moved upstairs to disfigure the lemon walls there, Anne let out her breath in a long, slow sigh and turned to Theresa. 'There'll be hell on when your dad gets home.'

Once Frank had recovered from the visual and aesthetic shock, he paid up without a word. Anything to get the Grand Duke out of the door. It took four coats of whitewash to diminish the brown squidges to a state where you didn't keep wanting to duck, but Anne's loyalty to Victor did not waver. 'You couldn't really expect him to be handy – not coming from where he did.' Frank's snort implied that where the Russian painter came from wasn't nearly as important as where and how far he'd gone.

Once, when Anne wondered aloud what might have become of him, Frank painted a graphic picture of furious householders, driven mad by stippling, chasing the Grand Duke off the point of Land's End. He even suggested that the fall of the Russian monarchy might have been due to an excess of stipplers within their ranks.

But Anne was secretly glad his handiwork could still be seen faintly through the whitewash. It was the nearest she would ever get to Imperial splendour, and she fingered it fondly from time to time.

'It's a grisly business, these Nazi executions,' Howard said, looking up from his paper as Norman Stretton entered his office.

'Bizarre,' Stretton agreed. 'It may be justice, but it still turns the stomach.' In Nuremberg they were now hanging the Nazis. Only Martin Bormann, who was tried in absentia and believed to be dead, and Hermann Goering, who had taken his own life, had escaped the gallows. The others, lead by Joachim von Ribbentrop, had mounted one of three black-painted scaffolds, submitted to a black hood, and fallen into eternity.

'I remember von Ribbentrop in London in the old days. He seemed invincible – and yet in the pictures I've seen of him lately he looked like just one more tired old man. It says here that he wished peace to the world: those were his last words.'

'It's a pity he didn't practise them sooner,' Stretton replied. He cleared his throat. 'Have you got a moment? I'd like your advice.'

'Of course.' Howard laid aside the paper. 'Fire away.'

'I've been thinking about the future. When the pit goes, in January, I'll be at a loose end. You said you'd still have a place for me, but we both know that you're fully staffed at the factory and the foundry. I appreciate the thought, but I want something to stretch me.'

'I understand. I simply wanted you to know the opening was there.'

'Thank you. I've been making some enquiries, anyway, but it's not easy, with the market flooded with demob men . . . quite highly qualified in man-management, some of them. Anyway, as I say I've been looking. And then yesterday Edward Fox approached me.'

'Fox, the haulage man?'

'Yes. The one who once worked for you at the Scar. His business mushroomed during the war, with demolition and site-clearance, and now he's expanding. He wants a partner. He says I'd be ideal.'

'I don't doubt it,' Howard said carefully.

Stretton looked at him narrowly. 'Why the reserve, then? I need you to be frank.'

Howard pursed his lips, weighing his words. 'I think perhaps, I'd better tell you everything. Fox was my father's chauffeur, originally – he was with him from a boy. When Diana came into the family, she was forever borrowing him to drive her, so eventually I took him on, and my father got someone else. Fox was good at his job. I valued him. But then Mary Quinnell – she was Mary Hardman then, our housekeeper at the Scar – told Diana that Fox was robbing us. Small sums, but he was doing it regularly . . . too regularly to be overlooked. When Diana took it up with him, he threatened her.'

'Threatened?' Stretton was shocked.

'Not physically. No, he threatened to talk about her to me . . . her friends, places she'd been, that sort of thing. It was blackmail, not to put too fine a point on it. So I told him to do his damnedest, gave him a month's wages, and sacked him.'

'I should think so. That settles it, then: I'll tell him I'm not interested.'

'Wait a moment. All this was years ago. People change . . . and to be fair, Fox wasn't highly paid, so perhaps I was partly to blame. If I were you, I'd look into his proposal before I turned it down.'

'I suppose so. If I put money into the business, as Fox suggests, I'd be an equal partner, and I could keep my eye on things. But I'm glad to know what you've told me. I'll talk to him, and we'll see how it goes.'

Ruth slid into a seat on the top deck of the bus and put up a hand to wipe rain from her forehead. Sitting next to her, a soldier was reading the paper, and a headline leaped out at her: 'Goering cheats hangman'. There was a picture of the Field-Marshal, grosser than ever in death, and underneath was an account of the executions in Nuremberg. She craned her neck to see the names: Kaltenbrunner, Rosenberg – the man who had propounded the idea of a master race – Hans Frank and Wilhelm Frick, Streicher and Jodl . . .

'Would you like to have a look?'

Ruth felt colour flood her face as the man with the paper proffered it to her. His voice was accented, but when she looked at him she saw that he was wearing British army uniform.

'I'm so sorry!' she said. 'It was rude of me. It's just that I saw . . .' She hesitated then, not knowing how to describe the article.

'Nuremberg? It serves them right, but it doesn't make for pleasant reading. You're not a Scot?'

'No. I came over here in 1939. I'm . . . I'm a Jew.'

The soldier was smiling. 'So am I. I'm Czech . . . I used to live in Prague. I was a student there before the war, although my home was in Bratislava.'

'I'm at medical school here in Edinburgh. I live in Sunderland now, but I was born in Munich.'

'A student! I thought you looked clever.'

Ruth too smiled, but really she didn't want him to think her clever. Mysterious – that would do. Or charming. Or helpless. But preferably beautiful . . . for this was the handsomest young man she had ever seen.

'Look, don't think me impertinent,' he said suddenly, 'but would you care for a cup of coffee somewhere? Or rather, a cup of chicory, or dandelion, or whatever they're using?'

Ruth was on her way to a seminar on venereal diseases, but what did that matter now?

'I'd love some coffee,' she said. 'If we get off at the next stop . . .'

8

November 1946

'That was a big sigh,' Esther said, as Howard shook out his newspaper at the breakfast table and turned the page.

He looked up at her and smiled. 'Sorry. But there's not much cheer in it today: eight servicemen killed in Jerusalem; and the House of Lords debating a "tidal wave" of divorce.'

'Cheer up.' Esther put out a hand and felt the tea-pot. 'Another cup?'

'No, thank you, I'm full. Such a treat to have an egg . . . but you haven't eaten much.'

Mention of food made Esther's stomach heave, and she tried not to let it show in her face. 'I wasn't hungry, I never am in the morning. Anyway, I must hurry.'

'It's today you visit the factory, isn't it?'

'Yes. Sammy is full of it – but I wonder. We're just beginning to rebuild the food and drapery side, and God knows that's difficult enough. Should we be diversifying now? And I'm still not sure furniture is right for us.'

'I'm cautious, you know that,' Howard said encouragingly. 'But Sammy hasn't done badly so far. I'd trust him.'

Esther grinned. 'You've been got at . . . I can hear it in your voice.' She threw up her hands in a Sammy gesture: 'Can't stand still, Esther. Got to keep moving . . . expand, expand!'

'He did tell me about his plans,' Howard said, sheepishly, 'but I really do think he's on to something. People need homes now.'

'What's going to happen to all these people, Howard? They're flooding out of the forces, full of hopes. Can we meet their expectations?'

'We must, somehow. But what I fear is a boom . . . rebuilding, refurbishment, factories tooling up for peace . . . followed by a slump. It happened last time, in the '20s and '30s. It mustn't happen again.'

Esther got to her feet and went to kiss his cheek. 'I'll leave the national economy to you, darling. My role is to stop my partner from ruining our business. Every time he says, "I'm going to make things hum, Esther," my blood runs cold.' She paused, wondering if this was the moment to tell him about the baby, but in the end the fear that her pregnancy might fail overcame her and she stayed silent.

'I forgot to tell you,' Howard said, looking up at her. 'Loelia rang yesterday – just to chat. Max's wife is coming back from America next month.'

'Is she sure it's safe?' Esther had meant to sound mocking but in fact she sounded bitter. 'Sorry. I ought to be glad they're going to be a family again.'

'I'm not sure how she'll take to austerity,' Howard said drily.

'What's she like?'

'Laura? She's a hypochondriac,' Howard answered. 'And a snob. And she runs away from trouble. Otherwise . . .' He grinned. 'Otherwise, she's fine.'

'It's lovely to have you home again,' Mary said. It was a crisp winter day but the sky above was blue and leaves rustled on the pavement as she walked. In front of her, Ben was pedalling furiously on a three-wheeler bike. Her daughter, Catherine, on leave from her nursing post in the WRNS, walked at her side. 'She's bonny,' Mary thought proudly, looking up at the tall, slender, fair-haired girl.

'It's nice to be back,' Catherine said, but there was a note of uncertainty in her tone that made Mary look at her sharply.

'What's the matter, love? You sound a bit down.'

'No, I'm not. I *am* glad to be home. And I'm *damn* glad the war's over: you can't nurse young lads who are maimed and dying, and want war to go on a day more than it has to. But all this time I've had a cause, a challenge. Now what?'

'Oh, talk to your stepfather,' Mary said. 'Pat'll give you plenty of things worth working to cure: VD, and now this scare about smoking and cancer.'

'I expect I'll feel better when I get back to hospital nursing, but . . . well, friends have moved on. A lot of them have married. I feel a bit of a fish out of water, to be honest. I loved the Wrens but that episode is over now. The service hospitals are emptying, and I want work to get my teeth into.'

'Would you like to be married?' Mary asking daringly. She had never talked to Catherine like this, but it seemed right now.

'To the right man, yes. I don't want it for marriage's sake, but it would be nice to have someone . . .' She sounded wistful, no mistake about it.

'Was there never anyone while you were away?'

'Plenty, mam . . . but not lasting. Ships that pass in the night, mostly. They came into the wards, fell in love with their nurse, got better, and went home and forgot her.'

'Is that what happened to you?'

'A couple of times . . . but I got over it. Anyway, don't worry about me, watch out for that lad there. He's coming to a kerb.'

They ran up to Ben and took a grip on the saddle of the bike.

'You're a little terror,' Catherine told her brother in indulgent tones and then, to her mother, 'Remind me not to have children. I couldn't stand the wear and tear.'

'You'll change your mind when the right man comes along,' Mary replied.

'If.' Catherine sounded a little doleful. 'It's "if" in my case, mam. The ones I want I can't have, and the ones who want me don't appeal.' She noticed her mother's anxious expression, and threw back her head to laugh. 'It's not that tragic. I haven't given up altogether.'

They were into the churchyard now. Ben was safe between grassy borders and Mary could concentrate on her daughter. 'Sit down here a minute,' she said and perched on a wooden seat. 'Not too long, or we'll freeze – but a minute won't hurt. Who are they, these men you can't have?'

Catherine pursed her lips. 'Well, Pat Quinnell for one – he's already taken.'

'No, seriously,' Mary persisted.

'I do like older men, mam. Authority figures, I suppose. Lads are all right, but they mostly talk about nothing. I like a good conversation.'

'I wonder if you and Rupert Brenton . . . well, when you were little you were never apart. But I don't suppose Miss Diana would've stood for it.'

'She was a tartar, wasn't she?' Catherine mused. 'Still, it must've been awful for Mr Howard when she killed herself. I saw him just afterwards in London, you know. On VE night. He looked so lonely. We didn't talk much . . . I said I was sorry Rupert had been killed, I think. But all the time I was afraid of upsetting him.'

'He's happy with Esther now, that's one good thing. And you'll be happy one day, pet. Leave it to fate.'

Stella lay back on the pillows, waiting impatiently for Mario to come to bed. While she waited, she tried to work out what time it would be in England now. Five hours' difference, or was it six? And forwards or backwards? Forwards. She glanced at the clock: ten-thirty. It would be half-past four in the morning in England now, and everyone asleep after a good night out. She sighed and punched up her pillows. America was supposed to be the most exciting place on earth, but inside this house she felt as though she were buried alive.

Today Mario had taken her to see the Empire State Building. It had all been very impressive but somehow she had felt diminished, an ordinary little person walking along wide-eyed among hundreds of others, not striding giant-like across the landscape with everyone applauding.

She smoothed the sheet, and told herself it would all come right with time. She was here, at last, and there was bound to be a need for time to adjust. The main thing was to keep Mario sweet, so that when the clash with his mother came . . . as come it would . . . he would be firmly on her side.

When he entered the bedroom, Stella smiled warmly.

'Come on, pet. I've been waiting for you.' She invested the smile and the words with every ounce of seduction she could muster.

Mario smiled back and began to loosen his shirt. 'I had to talk to Pops about the parlour in Fountain Street. He says it doesn't do so good lately, but once we take it over things will pick up.' He moved across to the curtained alcove where Tony slept and she heard him murmur something soft. Her brow had furrowed at his use of the word 'we'. She wasn't going to serve ice-cream in the Fountain Street parlour. There was a perfectly good manager there already, so they didn't really need Mario, let alone her.

'It'll be nice working together, won't it?' he said, moving back towards the bed.

'Hurry up,' she said sweetly, not answering his question. 'I'm waiting.'

Mario finished undressing, turning his back on her to step into his pyjama trousers. He had lovely olive skin, but his body was pudgy. Rupert had been fair as a lily and muscular; it was a pity he had died. On the other hand, she would never have got to America if Rupert had survived, and America was the land of opportunity ... everyone said so. She smoothed the sheet again, and arranged herself seductively on the pillows while Mario cleaned his teeth in the bathroom along the landing, and looked suggestively at him from under her lashes as he came back to the bedroom.

But instead of leaping into bed, he kneeled down and went through a long series of muttered prayers, his eyes screwed up and his brow furrowed with intensity. Stella hadn't realized he did this *every* night. Surely once a week would be enough?

By the time Mario put out the light and climbed into bed, she felt thoroughly irritated. But it wouldn't do to show it. She snuggled down and accepted his warm goodnight kiss; but instead of it leading to the lovemaking she both expected and wanted, he settled back on his pillow, put out a hand to pat her arm and, in an instant, was breathing the rhythmic breath of a hard-working man of easy conscience.

'Mario?' she said. Then louder, '*Mario*?'
The only answer was a gentle little snore.

Gallagher was there, on the front of the morning paper, smirking like an idiot: '*Belgate MP makes maiden speech*'. Anne felt bile rise in her throat. It should have been Frank standing up in Parliament to stick up for Belgate, which was more than Gallagher would do. Self first, self last, and, anything over, self in the middle – that was him. His speech had been about nationalizing railways – as if that mattered.

Anne threw the paper aside and got on with making the meal. She was wiping her brow, hot from the flames, when there was a tap at the door and Mary, her sister-in-law, came in, wearing a blue silk scarf in the neck of her coat which brought out the blue of her eyes.

'I can't stop long,' she said, settling into a chair. 'The bairn'll be out of school at four, but I haven't seen you all week. Frank all right, and the bairns?'

'They should be,' Anne said, 'the way I have to run after them.'

They sat by the fire and drank tea, exchanging their worries. Mary was concerned for Catherine, soon to leave the Wrens and go back to Sunderland's Royal Infirmary.

'It'll be lovely to have her here, Anne, don't misunderstand. But I worry that she'll miss the life, the comradeship . . . the excitement, come to that. Can any of them settle back into their old lives after the hurly-burly of war?'

'They did after the last war,' Anne said. 'And at least Catherine won't be having to nurse gas cases from this one.'

They were silent for a moment, then, remembering the ashen-faced men who had coughed and gasped their way along the streets of Belgate in the years between the wars.

'How is Gerard doing?' Mary asked at last.

'Well, according to his letters he's loving every minute of his teacher-training. God knows – I've given up on my family, Mary. Once you've dealt with our Stella you've got no gumption left. There's only our Terry going to do something with her life. Oh, Angela'll be happy enough, but she'll wind up with a houseful of bairns like me. As for the lads: down the hole, probably – or the army, God forbid. Everything I hope for comes to nothing, Mary, and that's a fact.'

'They're all healthy,' Mary said, trying to inject a note of cheer.

Anne's mouth threatened a satisfied smile, but she controlled it. 'Well, they've got good limbs on them, and they don't ail, I'll give you that. And I managed to feed them, in spite of Hitler.'

'How *did* you manage?' Mary said, shaking her head. 'I used to live in hopes of a grateful patient giving Pat a jar of paste or some jam. They were our treats, and there weren't many of them. Still – it's over.'

'There'll be shortages for a long time yet.' Anne was determined not to seem sanguine. 'I think I was born to struggle, Mary. Or else I'm being punished. It's hard to bear . . . a man cheated of his place in Parliament and a bairn in America that by rights should be up at the . . .' She stopped suddenly, her eyes widening. '. . . up in the bedroom,' she finished lamely. If she had not looked so distracted Mary might have pushed her. There was something about Stella's baby. But what? Whatever was bothering Anne, it was a secret too important to be shared, even with a sister-in-law.

Howard was packing his briefcase to take home when Norman Stretton came in. He paused, hesitant, seeing Howard with his coat on. 'I can wait, if you're in a hurry to get home?'

'No,' Howard said, 'there's no hurry. Have you made up your mind about Fox's offer yet?' He gestured Stretton to a chair and sat down himself.

'Yes, I think so. I've thought it over very carefully, particularly in view of what you told me about Fox in earlier years. But I've been through his books, and so has an accountant chum. They're OK. And Fox's plans for expansion are good, Howard. Good, viable plans.'

'Fox is no fool,' Howard said. 'He's proved that. And if you've checked things out . . .'

'You still sound dubious?'

'I don't like the man, but . . .' Howard stood up and moved to the window to look down on the lamplit pityard. 'The one certainty is that there's no place for us here any longer. We must both move on.'

'What will you do? The foundry and the works won't occupy all your time, and the pits were always the part of your business empire you cared most about. Or am I wrong?'

'No, Norman, you're right – and I'm not even certain I want to stay in industry at all. I'd be tempted to sell up and sail to Tahiti or something equally wild, except that my lovely wife is wedded to her career. And as I couldn't live without her . . .'

'You're very lucky,' Stretton said, with such feeling that Howard turned to look closely at him, seeing suddenly how tired his friend looked. There was a button hanging by a thread from his jacket, something Esther would have pounced on in a second.

'Yes, I am lucky and I know it. You must come and have dinner one night, and we'll talk more about your plans. These are turbulent times, but they're exciting too, Norman.'

'Yes, you can feel the buzz. And the traffic these days. Every time I go to Sunderland now I'm stuck in a jam behind a tramcar. But they'll go next, I suppose – they're outdated, like me.'

'Hush,' Howard said. 'You sound defeatist, and that's not allowed in our brave post-war world.'

'I suppose not. Don't you wish you were still in Westminster, with a hand on the tiller?'

'I do not!' Howard said fervently. 'I pity Attlee. He has to humour the United States to wheedle the loans he needs. He won't be able to raise living standards as he's pledged to do . . . and I know him well enough to know that will trouble him.'

'He's promised an awful lot,' Stretton said doubtfully.

Howard nodded. 'All good, but perhaps a little idealistic. Still, the impulse to be good is in all of us, isn't it? Now it's to be institutionalized, that's all.'

Stretton moved to the door. 'Let's hope it all works out. See you in the morning.'

As Howard switched off the lights and made his way down to the yard he tried to convince himself that Stretton had made a wise decision. But the picture of Fox that day at the Scar remained in his mind: the insolent expression, the venom in his eyes. 'I don't like you or trust you, Brer Fox,' Howard said to himself as he unlocked the door of his Daimler. 'And I don't intend to let you harm my friend, not if I can help it.'

Nathan was waiting in a doorway when Ruth turned the corner into Princes Street. He took her arm with a welcoming smile, and they began to walk together towards the little tea-room where they spent most evenings now. It was dusk and the castle's bulk loomed high above them against the lavender sky. He ushered her into the brightly lit room with its checked tablecloths, and to a corner table, set a little apart from the rest. They called it 'our table' now, and felt affronted if they arrived to find it occupied by someone else.

'How did the studying go?' he asked, pulling out her chair, and Ruth smiled into his thin young face.

'Badly. I kept wanting to close the books and come to meet you.'

She dropped her eyes, afraid she had let her feelings show too clearly, but Nathan only smiled and put out a hand to cover hers.

'Let me get the coffee, and then we'll talk.'

'Tell me about your home,' Ruth said, when Nathan was settled back at the table, the coffee steaming in blue cups between them.

'Bratislava? Or Czechoslovakia? It's a beautiful country, mostly forested, with mountain spruce and beech. And we have wild horses, what do you think of that? And stag, and roebuck, and other deer . . .' Ruth's eyes had widened and Nathan laughed aloud. 'And a few bears, and wild cats, and wolves . . . *oowll*!'

'Sh,' Ruth said, 'everyone's looking.' But her tone was indulgent, and he continued.

'Bratislava has a castle.' His face darkened suddenly. 'And I lived in a house with leaded windows, and my mother grew roses.' Before Ruth could speak he shook his head: 'All dead, Ruth, so don't ask. Now, what else, Napoleon said the Danube, which flows through the country, was the king of the rivers of Europe. And Czech beer is the *best* . . . most towns have their own brewery. Have you ever tasted slivovic?' Ruth shook her head. 'It's plum brandy.' He closed his eyes, remembering. 'Nectar! Czechs have a sweet tooth, so you can buy ice-cream almost everywhere. It's called *zmrzlina*. And strudels drenched in cream . . . Well, that's how it was, before Hitler.'

'Will you go back there?' Ruth asked quietly.

'No, Ruth, I won't go back. None of us can go back. I want to go to Israel, that's the future for Jews. Tel Aviv, a city risen from an empty sea-shore, that's where I'll go.'

'And marry a nice Israeli girl?' Ruth teased.

'A *sabra*,' he said grandly. 'A native-born Israeli. Do you know what *sabra* really means?'

Ruth nodded. 'Fruit of the cactus.'

'That's right. Fruit of the cactus – outwardly tough, inwardly tender. But I don't want to marry a *sabra*, Ruth. I'd sooner marry a nice girl from Edinburgh with eyes like pools and her mouth hanging open like a fish!'

'Beast,' Ruth said, slapping his arm.

'Seriously,' he said, looking down into his cup. 'Would you come with me if I went? To Israel?' Around them the tea-room hummed with laughter and chatter, but for Ruth and Nathan it was a dome of silence, hanging in space, until at last she answered.

'No,' she said slowly and painfully. 'I dream of Israel, like every other Jew, but I could never leave my family: Naomi, and Papa Lansky, and Sammy, and little Aaron. I owe them too much.'

Nathan was silent for a while and then he bent across to kiss her cheek, clear of the dark, curling hair. 'Well, perhaps I'll stay here, after all. Drink your coffee, it's getting cold, and then I'll get you another.'

'I mustn't be too late tonight. I'm tired,' she said.

'Me too. It's been a long day. We'll drink it quickly and then we'll go.'

Ruth was fishing in her handbag for her purse, but Nathan frowned and stood up. She watched him as he moved to the counter, his back straight, his head noble. 'I love him,' she thought and marvelled that a man from far-off Bratislava could meet a girl from Munich in a place like Edinburgh, and they could fit together, heart and mind, as if they had been one from birth.

9

December 1946

Patrick Quinnell put the cap back on his fountain pen, and smiled at Esther as she entered his surgery. 'How are you?' he said, getting up and gesturing towards the chair opposite him.

'Quite good. Not so sick in the mornings any more. Tired sometimes, but otherwise I'm fine.'

Patrick fastened a sphygmomanometer around her arm and pumped at the band. 'Blood pressure up a little, but nothing to alarm. You're . . . what? Thirteen or fourteen weeks now?'

'Yes,' Esther said.

'And you still haven't told Howard?'

'No. I want to be sure it's safe . . .'

'He'll notice soon. He's been through this before, remember.'

Esther's chin came up and she held his eye. 'So have I, Pat. I had a child many years ago that no one knew about. I gave it up for adoption. I don't want it broadcast, but I felt you should know that this is not my first.'

If Patrick was surprised, he didn't show it. 'Yes,' he said, making a careful note on her card. 'Thank you for telling me. As for telling Howard about your baby now, I think you could make him a Christmas present of the news. He will be pleased, I take it?'

'I think so. A little scared, like me, but pleased. That's why I don't want to tell him, only to have it go wrong.'

'OK, I'll be honest. You're forty, which is not so good, but you're very fit, and you haven't abused your body in any way. All the indications are that you'll have a successful pregnancy. The first three months are over, so that's a danger past. I think we're OK. But it's up to you.'

'I'll wait a *little* longer, I think. Just a week or two. You haven't told Mary?'

'No. I'm longing to, but I won't say anything until you give me permission. She'll be delighted, and so will Anne.'

Esther smiled. 'Anne'll be off to St Benedict's to invoke the saints, and then she'll come back and plan the layette, all the while telling me what a grim time I'm in for and what a trial children are.'

'Yes,' Patrick said drily. 'I think that's a fair summing up.'

Esther was still smiling to herself when she parked outside the warehouse and went in to her office. Sammy was perched on her desk, his hat on the back of his head, a sheaf of stock records in his hands.

'I wondered where you were?' he said. His eyes were twinkling. 'I wish I had a partner who pulled her weight.'

'Heaven forgive you, Sammy Lansky. I toil for you.'

He seized her round the waist and swung her off her feet. 'I know it, my *oytser*, and I'm grateful, so grateful I'll make you a millionairess one day.'

Anne hung the last wet garment on the pulley and then hauled it up to the ceiling again. The heat rising from the fire would dry most of it by night fall, which was just as well because otherwise the mass of clothes would obscure the light when Theresa was doing her homework at the kitchen table. Theresa was hardworking and clever, never needing to be forced to her books. David was at the big school now, and only Bernard, her 'Munich' baby, left in the Juniors. They were turning out all right. Not as she had expected, or even wanted – especially Stella and Gerard – but not too badly. And Angela had an office job at the Co-op, and went out every day neat as a new pin. Anne sighed, thinking of Joe: thank God none of the rest would ever need to go to war.

She was preparing leeks for a pudding when David entered the kitchen. She looked up at him and nodded towards the fire. 'Kettle's on.' He nodded back, but he made no move to mast tea.

'Mam?'

Anne knew at once that he had something to tell her. 'What's the matter?' Her tone was sharp and she felt her cheeks flush. Dear God, let it not be trouble. David was twelve now, big for his age, and the image of Frank.

'Nothing's the matter, mam. It's just that I've been thinking, and I know what I want to do when I leave school.'

'Oh?' If that was all it was, it couldn't be trouble.

'I'm going to join the army, mam . . . be a regular soldier.'

'*For God's sake!*' Anne put up a floury hand to cover her eyes. 'I'll have a seizure in a minute!'

'I'm sorry if it upsets you, mam, but that's what I want to do.'

Well, at least he was only twelve and could still feel the back of her hand. Anne pursued him as far as the yard door, and then went back inside to ask God why he had given her the most intractable and uncaring children in the world.

Fox led Stratton into the Grand Hotel's dining-room, waiters deferring to him all the way. Obviously he was a regular customer, from the smiles and greetings as they were settled at their table.

'Now,' he said, rubbing his hands together and then taking the proffered menu. 'What shall we have today?'

By law, meals were limited to three courses and a total cost of five shillings, excluding coffee; but this did not prevent 'luxury feeding'. The menu offered game pie and Cumberland sausages in rich gravy. 'I'll have the salmon, I think,' Fox said and then, with a chuckle, 'Not bad for five bob, is it?'

Stretton merely raised his eyebrows, knowing that though the meal would be charged at five shillings, the extra cost would be accommodated as 'wine' or 'coffee' or 'et ceteras'. The rich would eat well, as they always had done in times of crisis. It was the way of the world.

He and Fox talked of the future as they ate, and of Fox's plans for expansion. 'I'm a bit of a buccaneer, Stretton. No, don't shake your head – it's true. I'll go out and win the business, and it'll be up to you to keep the whole thing ticking over smoothly. It's been frustrating these last few years, with all the petty restrictions – although, God knows, I found a way round most of them. But now we can really do business, and I want you at my side.' He raised his glass of armagnac. 'To "*Fox, Stretton*",' he said, 'and the company's success.' Smiling, Stretton joined the toast, trying to blot out his faint dislike of Fox's obviously manicured nails, the width of his lapels, the very newness of everything he wore. People were scrimping and scraping nowadays, even to look respectable. Fox was obviously unhampered by such restrictions.

'Don't look so worried, Norman.' Fox was grinning, and Stretton realized his own face had fallen into a frown.

He smiled again and shook his head. 'I was thinking of the future for a moment, of all the opportunities – and the challenges. That's all.'

They parted outside, Fox to his waiting car, Stretton to stroll along Fawcett Street in search of a tobacconist. He was almost level with the town hall as the clock in the tower above began to strike the hour. Two o'clock: he would have to get a move on.

The last note of the clock was dying away when he heard a voice saying, 'Hallo, Mr Stretton.' It was Dr Quinnell's wife, a pleasant woman whom he had met several times.

He raised his hat. 'Mrs Quinnell, how nice.' His eyes turned to the young woman at her side.

'This is my daughter, Mr Stretton. Catherine . . . Catherine Hardman. She's just come out of the Wrens.'

'Ah. Is it good to be home?' The girl had short, neatly curled brown hair, and her eyes were grey and serious and thickly lashed.

She smiled at his words. 'In most respects . . . but it's a big adjustment.'

'I bet it is. Well, I hope you'll be very happy here.' He raised his hat again and held it in the air briefly as they walked on. A pretty girl, and self-possessed. Dimly he remembered mention of her being a nurse. If she was, that should make the transition to civilian life easier.

He replaced his hat and hurried into the tobacconist in

the hope that there might be a few cigarettes on sale for once. But as he awaited his turn to be served, the girl's steady gaze stayed in his memory. She had lived at the Scar as a child, Howard Brenton had told him that. Her mother had been housekeeper, and the child . . . or children, for there was also a boy somewhere . . . had played with the young Rupert Brenton. So she was back in Sunderland now.

'Only Woodbines, sir, I'm afraid.' The shopkeeper's voice interrupted his reverie.

'Woodbines?' Stretton said despairingly.

'Well . . .' The shopkeeper hesitated and then ducked beneath the counter. 'Perhaps I could let you have ten Capstan.'

They took a cab back to Chester Square and tumbled their parcels in at the door. 'Thank goodness,' Loelia said. 'I never want to go shopping again . . . not while everything's so difficult.'

'I enjoyed it,' Pamela said. 'Especially seeing the tree in Trafalgar Square.' The magnificent spruce set up between the fountains was a gift from the people of Norway.

'Yes,' Loelia said, 'at least we've got that.'

They carried the shopping upstairs and parted on the landing. 'Your last night here,' Loelia said ruefully. 'I wish you were staying for Christmas. The twins will miss you dreadfully, and so will Greville and Hugh. It's not too late to change your mind.'

'Thank you, Aunt Lee. I wish I could be in two places at once, but I'm looking forward to Christmas at the Scar. It's the first time for yonks, and . . .' She hesitated, not wanting to refer to Esther because it always made Aunt Lee prickly. '. . . And I love the north, especially in winter.'

She saw her aunt's lips tighten and then relax into a wintry smile. 'Of course you do. But it's not really your place, darling – not what your mama would have wanted. She adored London, and she'd want you to have the advantages of life here and in Berkshire. I'm not criticizing the north, but it is an awfully long way away. It's bound to be less . . . well, yes, less civilized than here. This is the centre of everything. I'm not being prejudiced about it: it's a fact.'

Pamela had already decided against argument. 'I know,' she said. 'It does have some advantages. Is there anything I can do for you before I have my bath?'

'No, thank you, darling. Dinner's at the usual time. And do wear that pretty blue georgette – it makes you look so like your mother.'

As Pamela took the blue dress from the wardrobe and slipped it from its hanger, she counted the hours to going home. Her train left before lunch, at eleven. It was six now, so there were only seventeen hours more, and then she would be heading north.

Frank finished stacking the logs he had chopped, and then eased his aching back. 'That ought to keep you going till the New Year.'

The woman standing watching him on the back doorstep nodded. 'Aye, that's grand. Thank you. I've got a pot of tea in-bye?'

A month ago she had been a gaunt wreck of a woman, standing by the newly dug grave in which they were burying her husband, who had been killed in a roof fall on the Red Star face. Today, although her face was pale, her eyes were no longer swollen with weeping and her voice was firm. She would survive. Which was just as well for the five little bairns who depended on her.

'Are you all right for money?' Frank asked as he followed her into the kitchen.

'Aye. With what you brought from the union, and the PAC money, I'll manage.'

'We'll get your compen. settled as soon as we can. In the mean time, let me know if you can't manage.'

She had poured his tea and pushed the mug towards him. Now she put out a hand and patted his arm. 'I know. Everyone's been good. I'll manage, and I'll make a Christmas for the bairns. Eddy always made a big thing of Christmas, so I can't let it go. But it's not easy. I see him everywhere, Frank. He was never without a smile on his face . . . well, you knew him. Have they settled what caused the fall?'

'They've given preliminary findings, but the union won't let it go at that, you can depend on it. We'll get the truth in the end, we always do. And once we hold the purse-strings, there'll be no accidents . . . well, hardly any. That's no consolation to you, Elsie, but Eddy wanted nationalization as much as I did. He'll be pleased when it comes.'

He spoke in the present tense and the woman looked surprised. Frank saw it and smiled. 'Oh, he knows, wherever he is – I've got faith in that.'

Elsie sighed and shook her head. 'You're a good man, Frankie Maguire. Eddy always wanted you for MP. He never liked Gallagher, don't think he did.'

Frank smiled, but inwardly he asked himself for the hundredth time why, since all the population of Belgate assured him they had wanted him to get the nomination, it had in fact been denied him.

'Aye,' he said at last, 'it's a funny old world, Elsie. Now you mind on . . . if there's owt you want, just shout.'

Ruth's eyes were shining as she unpacked her case and stowed her possessions neatly in the drawers or cupboards of her old room.

'Well?' Naomi said. 'Would we like him?'

'I think so. How can I tell?'

'Is he good enough for you?' Esther asked from her seat on the edge of the bed. 'And what would Papa Lansky make of him? What is he doing with himself.'

'He's in the army still, Esther; I told you. But he has plans.'

Naomi's eyes shot heavenwards. 'Not another one with big ideas . . . not two Sammys in one family. It's too much.'

'No,' Ruth said carefully. 'He doesn't want to be a businessman.' She flushed. 'Besides, I never said he'd be in the family.' She looked to Esther for support. 'He's just a friend.'

'Such a friend,' Naomi said. 'Her skin glows, her eyes

shine, her tongue stumbles over words: such a friend we all should have.'

'Well, I think we should stop teasing Ruth,' Esther said. 'She didn't tease us when we fell in love.' A hesitancy in Ruth's manner had alerted Esther to the fact that all was not perfect for the girl.

'I'm not in love,' Ruth protested, but she couldn't quite suppress a smile. 'Anyway, enough *plaplen*. What's for supper? I'm starving.'

'Wait and see.' Naomi heaved herself to her feet and made for the door. 'I've made a special supper to celebrate your coming home. Now I'm going to start saving dried fruit, to make a wedding cake like the Taj Mahal.'

'Get out,' Ruth said, and lunged at her sister's departing back.

'Seriously,' Esther said when the door was shut and they were alone, 'we're not taking anything for granted – but you have mentioned Nathan a lot.'

'Serves me right, then,' Ruth said. 'Anyway, I'm here, and he's in Scotland. So what's the news? I see a change in Papa Lansky – but perhaps that's because I've been away?'

Esther, too, had thought the old Jew was failing, but she covered it up now. 'He's a little tired, that's all. And he's looking forward to having you at home for a while.'

Ruth smiled. 'That's nice. But I've noticed something else, Esther – something about you.'

'What?' Esther's heart started to thump uncomfortably.

'I'm a doctor – well, almost a doctor. I think you're pregnant.' Her eyes were on her friend's face and Esther felt her cheeks flushing. She stood up, smoothing her skirt, wondering how she could wriggle out of the situation, but in the end she acknowledged defeat.

'It's true,' she said, 'but no one else knows. Well, hardly anyone . . . not even Howard.'

'Are you pleased about it?'

'Yes, very.'

Ruth grinned and held out her arms. 'Then I'm glad for you,' she said. 'Now let's go down and see what that sister of mine has managed to produce.'

They ate soup, made from something Naomi declined to name but which tasted delicious, and then gefilte fish, and a pudding of barley kernels, topped off with coffee and something sweet and sticky called, according to Naomi, Polish cake.

'It's been like the old days,' Esther said, kissing them all round when it was time to go.

'But nicer,' Naomi said, looking at her husband.

Emmanuel and Ruth went to the door with Esther, while Naomi moved her seat so as to sit closer to Sammy.

'Ruth seems happy,' she said, smiling at the thought. 'It must be love.'

Sammy grunted. 'A pity she couldn't love someone we know. That Cohen boy's been sweet on her for years. But no, it has to be a foreigner.'

'I was a foreigner,' Naomi said, 'and that didn't stop you.'

'You know what I mean,' Sammy said, abashed.

'Nathan can't help being a Czech,' Naomi persisted.

'So Nathan's a Czech,' Sammy said. 'Do I hold that against him? Not me. He's a Jew, that's all that matters. But for Ruth I want a *toveh*, not some *shmuck* in a uniform who happens to look like Charles Boyer.'

'He sounds really nice,' Naomi protested. 'Kind and clever . . . and she says he always gives up his seat on the bus.'

Sammy put back his head and whistled. 'Why did no one tell me this before? Why should I ask how he'll provide for her, who his family is, whether or not he's a good Jew? He gives up his seat on the bus – what else matters?'

'Now you're being awkward, Sammy.'

'Me?' His tone was outraged. 'I am doing what I'm supposed to do, little one: I'm looking out for the family. Do you want me shot for it?'

'Not shot,' Naomi said, refusing to be silenced, 'but probably imprisoned for a month or two. You're being a beast, Sammy, and if you're not careful you'll spoil it for Ruth. It's her first love. And who are *you* to criticize – you were a Casanova when you were young.'

'When I was young? What am I now, over and done with?'

'Come here,' Naomi said, holding out her arms. 'Come here and shush all the *plaplen*. And let Ruth run her own life . . . just like you and I do.'

10

New Year's Eve 1946

It was already dark by the time the Daimler reached the gates of the Scar. Howard slowed to turn into the drive and then brought the car to a halt. Tomorrow, the first day of 1947, Belgate, like the rest of the nation's coal-mines, would pass to the newly formed National Coal Board. It was New Year's Eve and he was feeling sentimental: he wanted to look down on the pit his family had owned and managed for one last time before it was lost to him forever.

There had been barely concealed glee on men's faces today, and triumph in their eyes. *'We are the masters now,'* was the catch-phrase, and Howard could scarcely blame them for their jubilation. For generations the Brenton family had controlled not only their working lives but their living conditions and the future of their children. Now, at last, they were free. And so was he. As Howard looked down on the pit, blazing with lights like a doorway to hell, he let out his breath in a sigh of both regret and relief. It was going to be a New Year in every sense of the word. As for the future of Belgate, coal had been there for millions of years, solid and apparently in never-ending supply. Men's lives were brief. Whoever was the master in name, it was coal which was the master in fact.

It was a bitter night, the road sparkling with frost and the air keen. The papers were forecasting a bad winter, and stocks of coal were almost non-existent. Twelve cotton mills had already closed and a four-day week was planned in the Midlands because of lack of coal – and the real winter was not yet begun. The problem of organizing enough fuel for the country was enormous, and Howard hoped the new Coal Board would be up to it: if coal production faltered there would be chaos. A workforce of 700,000 manned pits from Fife in the north to Kent in the south, from Selby in the east to Llanelli in the west. There were coke-ovens, and brickworks, and rows upon rows of tied housing, but the industry was run down by the war, and by decades of under-investment. What did the politicians in Westminster know of coal? Thirty-four MPs were sponsored by the mining union, but for every MP who could be described as a horny-handed son of toil there were three or four in the horn-rims of the academic. 'Windbags,' Frank Maguire called them, and Howard thought the nickname not inappropriate.

When he entered the house he saw Esther standing with her sister, Anne, at the hall table, Frank Maguire in attendance. Of course – he had forgotten about Esther's surprise for the Maguires: a phone call to Stella in America.

'Is it time?' he asked. It would be lunch-time in America now.

'It should come through any moment,' Esther said and, as if on cue, the phone shrilled. Esther grabbed the receiver.

'Hello. Yes. Thank you.' She smiled encouragingly at Anne and mouthed, 'It's coming through.' The next moment she was speaking into the receiver. 'Stella? Lovely to hear you. Yes. Yes, fine. She's here . . . and your Dad.' And then she was handing the phone to a moist-eyed Anne, and Frank was gazing at the phone, goggle-eyed, as though he expected Stella to materialize out of its black bulk.

Esther went over to Howard's side and slipped her arm through his. 'Nice, isn't it?' she said, squeezing him.

'It'll end in tears,' he said under his breath, and already the tears were coursing down Anne's cheeks. She handed the phone to Frank and dabbed at her eyes, shaking her head all the while. 'There's pips going,' she said anxiously. 'Does that mean money's running up?'

'Never mind that,' Howard said. 'What did Stella have to say?' But before Anne could answer, Frank was motioning her back to the phone. When the call had ended in a welter of goodbyes, they all walked together from the hall to the living-room.

114

'I hope she sounded happy?' Esther smiled, while Howard went to the tantalus to dispense drinks. But Anne, seating herself on the edge of the sofa, plucked at her cardigan nervously before she answered, in words that Esther did not expect.

'There's something wrong,' she said. 'I know our Stella, and she can say she's fine till she's blue, but whatever's going on over there, something's wrong, you mark my words.'

The Dunanes and the Colvilles assembled in the great hall at Valesworth for aperitifs. The young people congregated on the long window seat, near to the glittering Christmas tree. Henry Colville stood by the fireplace, one foot on the gleaming fender, one arm on the mantel, a glass in his other hand. His American sister-in-law, Laura Dunane, a pale, dark-haired woman now with the lines of the permanent invalid on her face, sat on a chair beside him, her panne velvet dress falling to the floor in folds, her heavily ringed fingers clasped around her glass.

Loelia put a hand on her brother's arm and drew him towards the love-seat that occupied an alcove. 'Sit beside me, Max darling. I want to ask your advice.' Brother and sister sat down together, their two shining red heads inclined to one another.

'Is everything all right?' Loelia asked softly.

Max nodded. 'As right as they'll ever be. We co-exist.'

'Oh, darling, you make it sound so grim.'

He reached to pat his sister's hand. 'It's not, I promise you. I'm at the club more often than not when we're in town, and Laura seldom comes to Valesworth, as you know. Now that I have the boys back in England I'm . . . well, quite content.' There was a pause. 'Did she get away on time?' There was no need to mention a name: they both knew he meant Pamela.

'Yes. She was so sweet when we were shopping together. She's completely unspoilt, Max . . . which darling Diana never was, although I miss her so dreadfully.'

'Yes,' Max said, staring all the while at a portrait of some long-dead Dunane on the opposite wall.

'I tried to draw Pammy out about the new mama . . . she calls her "Esther" by the way. She seems happy enough with her. All the same . . .'

'It's not perfect is it? A housemaid for a stepmother. Granted the woman's done well for herself, but it's hardly what Diana would have chosen.'

'What do we do about it, Max? I lobby Howard every time I see him, relentlessly. He never denies me, but neither does he acknowledge my right to intervene. It's terribly difficult.'

'Well, let's forget it for today. Laura is beginning to look bleak.' They rose and moved towards their spouses. 'We'll manage something, old girl, when the time is right. Blood is blood, after all.'

In the window more red heads were clustered together: Greville and Hugh Colville, men now, or imagining themselves to be men, and their twin sisters, Cicely and Emma, in their first grown-up party-frocks. Max's boys were redheads, too, and their sojourn in America had made their manner more flamboyant than their cousins'.

'It's nice to see them all together again,' Loelia said fondly, but as she and Max joined Henry and Laura they were both aware that another child belonged in that group, and was not there.

For half an hour the Lansky men had talked of world and national affairs, lolling contentedly in their chairs. Now the conversation turned to home.

'This friend of Ruth's – Nathan,' Emmanuel said at last. 'How do you like the sound of him?'

Sammy snorted. 'A no-good. She met him on an omnibus. What kind of friendship begins like that?'

'He was a student,' Lansky said mildly, 'in Prague, until the upheaval. So he winds up in a foreign country on a bus? Hardly his fault, Samuel.'

'Ha, Papa, that's not what you would have said in the old days. Ruth is a prize. We have to be careful . . .'

'So we'll be careful. But Ruth is shrewd. She will not be easily deceived.'

'Ruth is a dreamer, Papa. Always thinking good of

people. I want him down here, as soon as possible, so I can see for myself.'

Emmanuel shook his head, his teeth gleaming in his beard. 'My son is becoming a hard man. He wants to interrogate a poor *boy t'shikl* for falling in love with a nice young woman.'

'You can laugh, but we have a responsibility. Does Nathan talk of going back to his studies? Does he say how he would support a wife? Does he plan for the future? According to Naomi, they talk about politics and music! Do I need to say more?'

Outside, in the hall, the phone rang. 'I'll get it,' Ruth called from the kitchen, and Sammy shook a rueful head. 'See, Papa. She's hoping it's him.'

But Ruth was oblivious of anything except Nathan's voice on the other end of the line.

'I wish I was there, Ruth.'

'I wish you were, too,' she said softly.

'We'll be together soon . . . and one day we'll be together for ever, somewhere where the sun shines every day. Won't we?'

But Ruth stood silent as Nathan spoke. She could not say she would break the promise she had made so long ago: to stay a part of the Lansky family for as long as it existed.

'Happy New Year, love.' Frank kissed Anne on each cheek and then on the mouth for good measure, before turning to the younger children, Theresa and David and Bernard, ranged on the settee in anticipation of a New Year drink.

'I hope the lads and our Angela are all right out there,' Anne said anxiously as she helped him dole out the shandies and the hot sweet mince-pies lifted from the range less than ten minutes ago.

'Of course they are,' Frank said. 'You have to let them spread their wings, Anne.'

'I don't mind them spreading their wings, Frank, as long as . . . no, I won't say it with bairns present.'

'They're all right,' he said, biting into the rare treat of a mince-pie. 'We've got good young'uns, Anne. Trust them.'

117

'I trusted our Stella, Frank, and look where that got us.'

He handed her a small sweet sherry, but her eyes had misted at mention of her distant daughter. 'There's something not right there, Frank. Ever since the phone call I've felt it in my water.'

'It's imagination,' Frank said, trying to pass off his wife's fears. But Anne was not to be deflected.

'No, it's not. It's part intuition, and part working it out, and part bitter bloody experience.' She looked sideways to see if the swear word had been overheard, but the children were still intent on their unaccustomed glasses and mince-pies. 'I know that girl, Frank. I've always known her, more's the pity. She went over there to break eggs with sticks, and where has she got to? She's stuck with his folks, she has no friends, he works all hours God sends – and we both know what she's capable of if she's left to her own devices. I've combed her letters for signs that she was settling down, and there's none. She's stopped boasting and talking big, but what does that mean?'

'I expect it means she's growing up,' Frank said firmly. 'Pass your glass and I'll give you a refill, and we'll drink to nationalization.'

For a week now Stella had alternately prayed and cursed, but the longed-for period failed to arrive. How could it have happened when they had scarcely done it? A few fumbled encounters beneath the sheets, with both of them all too aware of the army of aunts and sisters beyond the bedroom wall, couldn't result in pregnancy.

Stella had still not managed to work out her husband's family. All she knew was that there were too many of them by far, looking like pictures from an old Bible, whispering and watching. Except at mealtimes, when they laughed and chattered and stuffed themselves with pasta and sauce.

Now, sitting up in bed where she had retired after pleading a headache, she thought about home. In a few hours the American New Year would begin, but at home they would already have seen it in with salt and bread and silver and a lump of coal. They would have eaten mince-pies in the warm kitchen, all the family together. Stella wept, then, for the comfort of her family lost to her forever; for her mother's loving ways that she had mistaken for strictness; and for all the fun of Belgate which she had never appreciated when she had it but which she would die for now.

For a while she gave way to crazy thoughts of creeping from the house, heavy with prayers and cooking-smells and everlasting talk of work which seemed to come second only in importance to God, and hitching a lift to the nearest port. But not even she could cajole her way without money across an ocean. In the end she cried into her pillow, until it was wringing wet and she had to move her cheek to a dry patch.

At nine o'clock Mario came to call her down to supper, but Stella sent him away with a flea in his ear. One more night of spaghetti and the price of buttermilk fat, and she would not be responsible for her actions.

A few moments later she heard the lumbering tread of her mother-in-law on the stairs. 'Estella? How your head-ache? I bring you a nice bowl of minestrone . . .'

Stella was hungry by now, but not yet ready to relinquish the role of tragic heroine. 'I don't fancy it,' she said. 'I don't fancy anything.'

She heard the sound of the bowl being deposited on the chest of drawers, and then the bed creaked and sagged as Mario's mother sat down on it.

'Poor Estella, I know what's wrong. I think you're going to have a *bambino* . . . a sister for Tony.'

It was too much. The pleasure in Mario's mother's voice at the thought of Stella's being consigned to purgatory for nine months was unbearable. Stella sat up in the bed and, remembering her own mother at her best, threw out an arm in a gesture of defiance.

'I am not having a baby, a *bambino*, or any other bloody name you care to mention. And I want you to bugger off out of this bedroom *pronto! Va' via!* And don't send your pudgy fat son up here to soothe me down . . .' This as the woman backed, wide-eyed, to the door . . . 'because the only person I want to see right now is my mam!'

Stella cried and howled, then, with a vehemence that

set the whole house trembling, and caused Mario's Aunt Raffaela to mutter darkly of heathens from beyond the sea.

Frank was there at daybreak to see Belgate pit pass into public ownership. The bunting they had put up the night before fluttered in the breeze as jubilant miners thronged the pithead, tearing down every last board bearing the Brenton name, raising a blue-and-white banner of their own, and affixing a notice to the pit gates: *'This colliery is now managed by the National Coal Board on behalf of the people.'* The official vesting day would be the first working day, but this moment of triumph could not go unmarked.

Above, on the Scar hillside, the Brentons looked down on a village *en fête*, at the steaming bulk of the pit-heap, the wheel and the headstock, and the tiny matchstick figures of the men.

'Will they make a success of it?' Esther asked, her breath a cloud in the January air.

'Yes,' Howard said, 'I think so. But the pit will have her way with them first.'

They turned to follow the children, Pamela and Ralph and Noel, who were walking ahead of them, bundled up in coats and scarves, their laughter floating back on the wind. Inside Esther the child stirred and quickened, so that she put a sudden hand to her belly and gasped a little.

Howard turned at the sound. 'All right?' he asked.

She slipped her gloved hand into the crook of his arm and matched her stride to his.

'I've never felt better,' she said, 'but you'd better sit down on that rock. I've got something to tell you. I hope you're not looking forward to an easy life in the next few years, Howard. If you are, you're in for a bit of a shock.'

BOOK TWO

11

March 1951

Esther snuggled down in the bed to savour a few precious moments of peace before getting up to face the day. Howard had just carried Beb from the room, the three-year-old perched high on his father's shoulders, squealing with delight. She could hear Sarah, Beb's nanny, chuckling as she took over her charge. The girl was a godsend and that was a fact.

Beb had been born in June 1947, in the private wing of the Sunderland Royal Infirmary, and named Charles Sidney after his grandfathers. Howard had simply gazed in awe at the tiny fair-haired creature, but Pamela, when she was allowed to visit, had scooped him up in maternal seventeen-year-old arms and pronounced him the 'best-ever baby'. The name, shortened now to B.E.B., had stuck. He had chuckled throughout his infancy, and spent the toddler years hoisted on the shoulders of his half-brothers.

'They'll ruin that bairn,' Anne said from time to time, but not even she could resist Beb's charm, turning into a doting aunt whenever she had charge of him. He was five months old when Esther went back to work on two afternoons a week.

'Thank God,' Sammy had said fervently, and had given her a new office decorated in blue and grey.

Six months later Esther was doing five half-days a week, and Sarah, a pleasant woman who had been in the Wrens with Catherine Hardman, had been engaged to care for Beb, for Howard still spent most days at his office in Sunderland, running what remained of the Brenton industries.

Esther smiled now, hearing him still joking with his son.

He had certainly taken to late-fatherhood. It was a joy to see him with Beb, two heads bent to the study of clockwork trains, or pop-up books, or, favourite of all, wooden jigsaws.

'I'm lucky,' Esther thought, shifting on her pillows. Not everyone was as lucky. Anne's David was soon to join the army, in spite of his mother's protestations, and there was a war in Korea. The Maguires had lost one son; surely that was enough?

Anne shifted her weight to her other knee and tried to concentrate on God. If ever there was a need for prayer it was now. She squeezed her eyes shut and threaded her rosary beads through her fingers. Please God, let it work out all right. Sometimes, though, when she looked at the world, she wondered if even God could sort things out.

She felt her eyes smart and sniffed fiercely. There was no point in crying. David would be gone in a few weeks, and that was all there was to it. Ever since he announced he wanted to join the regular army, not even waiting to be called up for his National Service, she had prayed. Six years of pleading with God – and nothing to show for it. There was a war raging in Korea, a God-forsaken place near China that no one had ever heard of, but Frank swore down it would be over before David finished his training. No one had believed Britain would fight in Korea, but Attlee had given them no alternative. 'If the aggressor gets away with it . . . the same results which led to the Second World War will follow . . . the fire that has been started in distant Korea may burn down your house.' But she couldn't bear to think of losing David. Joe had been dead for seven years and still she kept thinking she caught sight of him in the street, coming towards her, turning a corner.

Opening her eyes, Anne looked at the lights flickering at the altar. How did you manage if you didn't have faith? She believed, but she was still frightened sometimes. The Americans were testing bombs in Nevada, as though blasting Japan hadn't been enough for them, and there was a war in some other unknown place called Vietnam. All the slitty-eyed places were causing trouble, now she came to think of it. And the meat ration had gone down by twopence, thanks to the Argentinians being awkward. You needed three ration books to buy a pound of meat nowadays, and the war had been over for six years! If it weren't for Esther and her 'goodie-bags' now and then, life would be bleak and no mistake. 'We were going to be the masters,' she thought suddenly, 'but it's the Brentons who are still on top, after all.'

There was no sound in the church except for the spluttering of candles at the feet of the saints, and the occasional soft footfall of worshippers. She bowed her head again and prayed that life would take a turn for the better. 'Because I'm fair worn out, God,' she said under her breath and was taken aback at her own vehemence. It didn't do to cheek the Almighty. She said a special prayer and bowed deeply to the altar before leaving the church. The sky overhead was dark and lowering. It would rain soon. Still, she was going to see an Anna Neagle film tonight, so it wasn't all bad.

'We've got to expand again, Esther.' Sammy was seated on a corner of the desk, swinging a leg to and fro. 'Where's the fun in running shops stocked on allocation from the Ministry of Food? And rationing is the death of salesmanship: you can't persuade people to buy goods when they have no points left.'

'We're doing all right,' Esther said, tapping the file that held details of their various properties. 'Why a new shop? Why can't we use existing outlets?'

'Because we can't grow fast enough without space. And if we don't grow, we'll be like the dinosaurs – dead! When I get this off the ground I'll want a fleet of vans to move stock.'

'Is that all?' Esther asked faintly. 'Why not a fleet of charabancs? We could go into the holiday business . . .'

'And don't think that hasn't crossed my mind,' Sammy said. 'I can't be constrained and hemmed in, Esther. I'm still pondering self-service, in spite of the fact that our first try was a failure. Aisles of goods and a basket . . . most women's idea of heaven.'

'It won't take off in Britain,' Esther said firmly. 'We like personal service, here, and a chat with the shopkeeper. And that attempt at self-service wasn't a failure, Sammy – it was a disaster.'

'What's big in America today will be big here tomorrow. We just didn't do it properly.' Sammy's eyes lit up suddenly. 'Let's write to Stella and get an eye-witness report. We could even cut prices, Esther. Now tell me that wouldn't go down well.' He stood up suddenly and came to grasp her shoulders. 'Come on, tell me why self-service won't work in Britain.'

'Rationing,' Esther said. 'Shortages, building restrictions, no labelling materials . . . all your aisles would be full of goods in brown paper bags, Sammy. It's the assistant who makes shopping bearable nowadays, and don't you forget it.'

As soon as Loelia Dunane heard that Pamela was to be in London for three days she posted an invitation to her to stay at Chester Square. *'I know you could stay at Mount Street, but with only daily staff there you'd be alone at night. Besides, I'm longing to see you! It's lonely, with Hugh away doing his National Service and the girls in Switzerland.'*

Pamela was fond of Loelia, remembering the war years when she had been evacuated and Loelia had played mother to her. *'Of course I'll come to you,'* she wrote, and planned accordingly. Now they sat in the stately surrounds of the Ritz Hotel and drank tea from fine china cups.

'This dreadful government can't hang on much longer.' Loelia pursed her lips. 'That odious man, Attlee . . . *The Times* keeps on about the King's prerogative with regard to a dissolution, but your Uncle Henry says the King should send them all to the Tower. Labour only scraped in last year, just scraped in! The poor King! It must worry him – and everyone says he's far from well.'

Pamela was longing to defend the Labour Party but the King was a safer topic. 'He's supposed to open the Festival of Britain, isn't he? Will he be well enough?'

'I don't know – one hears such things. He's been a heavy smoker and apparently he won't give up cigarettes. Still,

126

let's not be gloomy. Have you heard the Noël Coward song about the Festival? I mean, it's such a socialist mish-mash. Herbert Morrison says it's a "pat on the head" for the people. What for, one asks? But the Coward thing is delicious.' She leaned closer to sing softly:

> 'Take a nip from your brandy flask,
> Scream and caper and shout.
> Don't give anyone time to ask
> What the hell it's about.'

Pamela smiled politely but stuck to her guns. 'Well, I'm longing to go to it all the same.'

Across the table Loelia's eyes went misty. 'I remember the Empire Exhibition, the week I got married! Your darling mama went, and your papa too. She told me all about it, because I was too busy with the wedding. She was so happy.' She leaned to pat Pamela's hand. 'You're so like her, Pammy. It's almost painful sometimes . . .' She sniffed and then collected herself. 'But your brains must come from your father. Your mother would never have aspired to be a barrister. Are you sure you're brave enough to stand up in court and harangue people? I'm awestruck.'

Pamela grinned. 'I'm quite good at sticking up for myself, Aunt Lee. You can't grow up with brothers, and not learn to stand on your own two feet. And I want to stand up for other women, too. The female sex is at a disadvantage when it comes to law. I was arguing with Daddy the other night – "Be honest," I said, "you always think a woman is at fault when a marriage goes wrong." He wouldn't have it, but it's true.'

'I'm not sure you should say such things to your papa,' Loelia said faintly.

'Why not? He knows I don't mean it. Daddy's the fairest of men – but I've got to develop my adversarial skills somewhere. Why do you think I shouldn't tease him?'

'Well . . .' Loelia looked down at her cup and moved her sandwich fractionally around her plate. 'If you're only teasing, I suppose it's all right.' But her tone was reluctant and Pamela, watching her, felt that she had struck a nerve with her talk of broken marriage. Surely not Aunt Lee and Uncle Henry? She sought a change of conversation.

'I think I'd like to specialize in union law, eventually. I shall apply to chambers in Gray's Inn, so cross your fingers for me. And then it'll be years and years of hard grind and all those horrid dinners to eat in Hall!'

'But lovely balls, darling, and cocktail parties . . .'

'Oh, yes, I'll have to submit to them. The whole thing runs on patronage, and it's no good my kicking against it at first. I'll have to be a good girl and accept all their weird customs. Do you know barristers don't shake hands on meeting because they consider themselves part of a brotherhood? It's medieval! But I shall have a good degree, and shall toe the line until I'm terribly eminent and then I shall drag it all into the twentieth century.'

'Yes, dear,' Loelia said. 'I'm sure you will.'

They talked of family, then, and ordered more tea, before Loelia returned to a subject she had raised earlier.

'You *must* let me present you this year, darling. You're going to be fearfully old if we don't do it soon, and the whole thing is becoming so commercial and *déclassé* it won't be worth while shortly.'

'Why do I need to do it at all?' Pamela asked desperately.

'Because you can't get engaged until you're out, darling. And I do so want to get you a *simply magical* husband.'

Howard poured tea and pushed a cup toward Norman Stretton. 'Drink that while it's hot, and then you can tell me what's wrong.'

They were seated on either side of a table in Meng's, the table set for afternoon tea and ornamented with a vase of flowers.

Stretton looked startled. 'How do you know there's something wrong? I never said.'

'It's written on your face, my friend. We worked together for a long time, remember? When you telephoned to suggest a meeting, I wondered; when you came in and I saw your face, I knew. What is it?'

'That's half the trouble – I don't know. I don't even know if there *is* anything wrong.'

'But you have your suspicions?' Howard's tone was sombre.

'Yes. It's all too easy, Howard. When I went in with Fox, in '47, we were going to expand his haulage business. Then, two years ago, he suggested we go in for building. A man called Geldart, a good man who'd been with Wimpey, got the workers for us and Fox found the sites. I organized the capital and applied for licences . . . you know the red tape that's attached to everything nowadays. I came up against a blank wall. We had a site for forty houses, but they gave me a licence for only eight! We couldn't get permits for materials, especially timber: we were limited to 1.6 standards per house of 1000 square feet . . . not enough even for a timber floor. I went to Fox, and said we wouldn't be able to go ahead. He asked a few questions, smiled, and said, "Leave it to me."

'The next moment we had licences, permits, lorry-loads of everything we might need. Fittings, furnishings . . . you name it, it was there.'

'And you weren't sure about the origins?'

'That's right. I think he was fiddling those licences and permits, Howard. And the people we were selling the houses to were not the people who were entitled to them. We were selling to speculators, men who were going to squeeze desperate people for money they couldn't afford. If Fox was giving backhanders for permits and materials, he *had* to sell at inflated prices, to make it worthwhile.'

Howard understood the gravity of what Stretton was saying. Expectations had been raised during the war by years of promises; but with peace the shortage of decent housing had become all too apparent. People were so desperate for a home of their own that they had begun to take over unoccupied property. Families with their worldly possessions stacked on a pram would walk into a disused army camp or unoccupied house, and make it their own. Despite the absence of electricity or gas, or even running water, they would settle down to a semblance of family life. 'At least it's a place of our own,' was the cry; more than 46,000 people occupied army camps, and even the newspapers were sympathetic to them. '*In a country so law-abiding as Great Britain,*' *The Economist* remarked, '*it is always refreshing when the people take the law into their own hands on an issue on which the spirit of justice, if not its letter, is so eminently on their side.'* When the Communist Party organized the occupation of blocks of luxury flats in the West End, the squatters were treated leniently by the courts. Pressure to build houses more quickly increased, but they were not built quickly enough to stop the speculators.

'Things are a bit better now,' Howard said. 'Almost a million houses have been completed since '44. There won't be the opportunities for him to behave so badly in future.'

'Fox will find them,' Stretton said gloomily. 'That's why I've decided I've got to get out. He's buying up land all along the North Road – not under his own name: for dummy companies, mostly. He's buying to a pattern, only it's not his name on the documents, it's mine.'

'You think he has inside knowledge?'

'Yes. And I think I know where he's getting it: from George Gedge, who's Chairman of the Council, and from Stanley Gallagher, our upright MP. And that's not all, Howard. Now we tender for council estates, but when we get the contract – and we always do – it's at a different price from the original tender. I think Fox bribes someone to fix it for him.'

The two men sat in silence for a moment, and then Howard signalled to the waitress for the bill. 'Let's sleep on it,' he said. 'I need to think about the best thing to do.'

They parted in front of the restaurant, and Howard had almost reached his car when he heard a screech of brakes, and then a hub-bub broke out behind him. He turned to see Stretton sprawled across the kerb and a crowd gathering around him.

'It's my leg,' Stretton said, when Howard reached him. 'My own fault . . . I wasn't thinking . . . I stepped out into the road. Tell them it wasn't the driver's fault, Howard.' His face went suddenly white and his eyes closed.

'There's an ambulance coming,' someone said, and a woman appeared with a blanket.

On the way to the Infirmary, Howard's eyes were fixed on Stretton's face. 'He means a lot to me,' he thought. 'Let him be all right.' But Stretton's pallor was more noticeable, and when Howard took his hand the fingers were icy.

Suddenly he remembered the dark days after Diana's suicide. Stretton had come to him in London, not saying much, just being there, a source of comfort. He leaned closer to the inert figure on the stretcher.

'Don't worry about anything, Norman. I'll see to the matter we discussed, and I'll let your housekeeper know. I'll be here all the time.'

Stretton smiled, without opening his eyes. 'I'm OK. Don't worry too much. It's my own stupid fault. I can't even negotiate a main road competently.' Looking at him, Howard saw that he had aged lately. There were lines on his brow and silver at his temples.

'Hold on, old chap,' he said. 'We're almost there.' And then the ambulance was clanging through the gates of the Infirmary, and its doors were thrown open, and Howard stepped aside for the professionals to take over.

He was waiting outside the casualty ward when he felt a hand on his arm and turned to see Catherine Hardman. She was smart in her dark-blue uniform, a white starched cap upon her head, a quivering bow beneath her chin.

'Catherine, thank goodness it's you. My friend Norman Stretton's here, with a damaged leg.'

'The tib and fib?' she said. 'He's OK. A little shaken up, and two nasty fractures, but he'll live. He'll be leaping about in plaster tomorrow.'

'Will you look after him?'

'I look after all my patients, Mr Brenton. But if he's a friend of yours, I promise he'll get the de luxe treatment.'

Patrick Quinnell turned on the engine and put the car into gear, as Ruth climbed into the passenger seat. They had just visited their third wheelchair-bound patient, and the girl's expression was grave.

'I never realized there were so many,' Ruth said. 'I saw paraplegics in Edinburgh, but they were rare.'

'It's called the price of coal,' Patrick said, keeping his eyes on the road ahead as the car gathered speed. 'And the people around here have been paying it for centuries.'

'Things are better in the pits now, surely?'

'With nationalization?' They had left the narrow street,

and the Half Moon was in sight. 'Accidents still happen, Ruth. The men thought it would be a New Age, but the conditions and the work are still much the same – too much so, perhaps. But the National Health Scheme is making a difference. If you're injured, you now have access to many more facilities. Before the war we had a patchwork of treatment centres that was so complicated few people knew what was available, or how to get it. There were terrible gaps, and of course people were anxious about money all the time. And doctors didn't work so closely with hospitals. All manual workers are covered by health insurance now, so things are getting better in that way.'

'But men still lose the use of their limbs in the pit?'

'Sadly, yes: I doubt that will ever change. And now, Dr Guttman,' Patrick said, steering round a corner, 'we are going home to discuss our new partnership. Will you miss working at the hospital? And what about the Edinburgh boy-friend of yours? What's to become of him?'

'I expect he'll find what he's looking for eventually,' Ruth said. 'He's finding it a little hard to settle down. But he's coming tonight, to stay for two whole days.'

'Ruth's late.' Sammy moved his son to his other arm. Saul was a year old now, a dark-eyed tranquil version of his father. Cecelie Ruth, who was almost four, sat with seven-year old Aaron, throwing dice for Ludo.

Naomi looked at the clock. 'Not really, *liebchen*. She was going to have a big talk with Pat Quinnell today, about their partnership. She'll be here before Nathan arrives.'

'I hope so,' Sammy said. 'I can't talk to that boy. He doesn't listen.'

'You mean he doesn't agree with everything you say,' Naomi teased.

All heads turned as Emmanuel Lansky entered the room. The children smiled and Naomi plumped up a cushion and patted her father-in-law's favourite chair.

'Come, Papa, come and defend me from your son.'

Lansky settled in the chair and reached to ruffle his grand-daughter's hair. 'Of course, I'll defend you.'

Sammy grinned but in his heart he was thinking that his

father looked suddenly shrunken. 'He is growing old,' Sammy thought. 'And I cannot bear it.' He looked round his family, marvelling at how love could grow. The bigger his family grew, the more he loved each one of them. To lose any of them, old or young, would be unthinkable.

As if he sensed Sammy's distress, Saul put up a fat little hand and caressed his father's cheek.

'Dada,' he said. Sammy caught his son's hand and kissed it and then looked around triumphantly.

'See,' he said. 'An ally, no less. Only a little one as yet but he will grow!'

There was the sound of the front door opening and closing, and then voices in the hall.

'Look who I found on the step,' Ruth said, her face aglow as she ushered Nathan into the room. Naomi rose to kiss him, but Sammy merely nodded his head in greeting.

'Come and sit down,' old Lansky said, but Naomi intervened.

'Not yet, Papa. Take Nathan up to his room, Ruth, and let him get rid of his things. And then we'll all have a splendid tea.'

Nathan smiled as he followed Ruth into the hall, but on the hall landing he put down his bags and reached for Ruth's hand.

'Ruth . . . I have some news. My passage to Israel is fixed. I go in three weeks' time. Come with me – or say you'll come as soon as you can. I need you. Israel needs you. Say yes, Ruthie . . . say yes?'

'You don't see, do you?' Stella said desperately. 'Why I've got to get out of this house sometimes . . . away from this family, those two kids? Do you even begin to see? *Mi sono annoiata . . . mi da sui nervi . . .* it gets on my nerves. Understand?'

'I try.' Mario's face, plumper than ever now, was creased in perplexity. 'I do try, Stella. But you are so . . .'

'*Difficile*? If you think I'm being difficult now, just wait. I am sick, *marito mio*. Bloody sick! Sick of this house, this family, this life! Five years of work and pregnancy, that's been my life. America the Golden? Don't make me laugh.

133

Work and sleep and wipe snotty little noses – that's America to me! Bloody misery!'

'Sh . . . *non possiamo andare avanti cosi*, Stella. We can't go on like this.' He was looking anxiously at the walls.

'What's wrong, Mario?' She had raised her voice. '*Troppo rumore*? Well, I'll shout louder. There is too much bloody *lavoro* around here and *non abbastanza divertimento. Capisci*? Too much work, not enough fun. And don't wave your hand at me and whisper "*basta.*" It's *not* enough, not enough by half. God gave me a mouth . . . a *bocca* . . . and I intend to use it. Can you hear, Raffaela? Anna? Sophia? Shall I shout up? *Sono stufo. Molto stufo!* I am fed up! *Non contento!* I want a house of my own; I want a life of my own. *Velocemente!* And what I do *not* want is the lot of you watching me, hoping I am *incinta*. If I can help it, I will never be pregnant again. *Mai! Mai! Mai!* Not that I'm likely to be, because *sesso* is in short supply around here. Your blue-eyed bloody charm-boy is not very sexy. *Non molto caldo*, if you know what I mean, *a barboncino!*'

To be accused of being cold, less man than poodle, was too much even for the placid Mario. He hurried from the room, leaving his turbulent wife to hurl cushions at the religious pictures that, shaken by her outburst, looked down from every wall. Then she lay down on the bed again and folded her arms behind her head, while the aunts gathered to whisper words like *abusiva* and *disgraziata*.

In Stella's first weeks in America the country had seemed to promise undreamed-of delights. Everything was big, bright, fast and more furious than anything she had seen before and her new family was anxious to show her around. She had gawped at Grand Central Station, the huge department stores on Fifth Avenue, and the George Washington Bridge, second longest in the world. She put nickels into slots in Manhattan and got out wedges of lemon meringue pie, or coffee from dolphin-head spouts. She had her photo taken in an unmanned booth and sent a telegram in her own handwriting, courtesy of Western Union. She saw a silver nightingale sing in the RCA building, and felt sea-sick in the Empire State lift. She bought kiss-proof lipstick and deodorized sanitary towels, and drooled over cars so long and chromium-plated they looked like huge silver snakes.

But Mario's car was a squat black saloon; and in between sight-seeing trips she returned to the Dimambro house, which was dark and stuffy and had never heard of air-conditioning. Her in-laws seemed to think only of work and food and prayer; once they had shown her the wonders of her new city they expected her to be like them and work till she dropped. And she was sick of it, *molto, molto* sick.

Frank lay in bed, waiting for Anne to finish her prayers, admiring the new wallpaper with its green trellis and pink rose-buds. She was a canny hand with wallpaper now, and it had been a relief to see the last of the stippling.

At the side of the bed, Anne sighed and shifted on her knees. Frank flexed his own knees, hearing them creak. He had been working in a wet seam for two weeks and it was telling, but at least he was making canny money since their pay rise: seven shillings extra. What had he earned before the war? For the life of him, he couldn't remember – but it had been a sight less than now. And they'd had nowhere near as much holiday.

'Have you heard what's happening at the Gala yet?' Anne asked, as she rose from her knees.

'What put that into your mind?' Frank asked curiously.

'I don't know. It came in my mind about the end of the war, when I was praying for our Joe, and I thought about that first Gala, the Victory one. A quarter of a million people there, and Attlee and Nye Bevan. There was precious little eats, and you kept moaning about the lack of beer or baccy, but it was a grand day.'

'Aye. There was a canny number of banners that day.'

'It was a canny number, Frank. There's a few closed since then. Remember the rain that year?' Her voice had softened. 'The heavens opened. Manny Shinwell and Nye Bevan scuttling for cover. And the balloons going up and vanishing off, left, right and centre, and they played "Gresford" in the cathedral.'

'This year'll be even better.'

'But do you remember 1947?' Anne asked wistfully.

'Couldn't forget it, Annie, what a year!' Frank put his hands behind his head and interlaced his fingers. 'Only one programme on the wireless, so as to save the electricity. We had to work an extra half-hour a day – '

'And people living by candlelight – we never had to do that in the war.' Her tone was reproachful, as though Frank personally had brought about the fuel shortage.

'It was a terrible winter, Annie – you can't deny that.'

'I know. I've never seen snow like it, and I don't want to again!'

'Twenty-foot drifts – that's what stopped the coal trains.'

'And you couldn't use the lifts in Dunn's, I remember that. What made it all worse was, we'd expected it to be bloody marvellous – the war over and everything. And there we were with nothing, not even electric light. And still rationed – and we're *still* rationed now. It beats me.'

'It hasn't turned out the way we really expected, I'll give you that.'

'Why not, Frank? I mean, Labour had the whole country behind them in '45. Why couldn't it work?'

'Thing *are* better, Annie,' Frank said uneasily. 'Like Sam Watson said at last year's party conference: poverty's abolished, we treat the sick, cherish the old, children get their opportunity – and hunger's unknown now,' he finished triumphantly.

'Well, that's a lie for a start,' Anne said. 'If I wasn't a good manager, we'd starve on what's available round here – and the Germans glutting themselves on the fat of the land.' She snuggled down in the bed. 'There's something wrong somewhere. It's not so long since we were giving up our rations to feed them. Now they're laughing at us.'

Frank, too, had eased himself down into the warmth of the bed. 'Maybe they should send for Dick Barton, Special Agent. Let him sort it.' He put out a tentative foot and when their toes met there was no immediate withdrawal. So far so good.

Anne smoothed the sheets. 'Put the light out, Frank.'

'Why me?'

'Because you're the man.'

'Well, if I'm the man, thou should do it. Woman was made to serve man.'

'Who says that? He'll be a man, whoever he is. Get the light out.'

Frank leaped to obey and back into the bed, only to find she had pinched the place he had warmed. 'Thou's a bugger, Annie Maguire.'

'Yes,' she said meekly, but she took him into her arms to warm him. 'I saw that Ruth today.'

'The doctor?'

'Yes, she was with Pat Quinnell. She's turned bonny. She was a plain little thing when she came, wasn't she?'

'It seems like yesterday, all that. Refugees and gas masks. Didn't she have a boyfriend in the army?' Frank asked.

'Yes. Well, he was. He came out, I think. I don't know what he's done since then. He's due up here, according to our Esther, so maybe there's a wedding coming up.'

Frank was kissing her, drowsily at first, and then more passionately.

'What are you doing, Frank?'

'Giving you a kiss.'

'Why?'

There was a pause while he sought an answer. 'Because I'm a man, Annie, you said so just now. And if I have to do the chores, I might as well have the perks.'

'Comfortable?' Howard asked. Esther snuggled further into the crook of his arm, her head just visible above the paisley-patterned eiderdown.

'Very. Did you ring up about Norman?'

'Just before I came upstairs: he'd doing all right. I wonder, can he come and stay here when he leaves hospital? That house of his is far from ideal.'

'Of course. I'd already assumed he would. You're fond of him, aren't you?'

'Yes. I didn't realize how fond until today. When he told me about Fox and Gallagher, I felt like committing murder. Not a word to Anne about all that, by the way: not until we're sure of the facts.'

'As if I would. She'd go straight to the nearest soap-box and tell the world. If it's true, does it mean Gallagher will have to resign as MP?'

'I don't know. He won't give up unless something is proved against him: friend Gallagher is not thin-skinned, and I think he'll stand any amount of innuendo. The reaction of a political party is always to rally round its members, so they won't ask him to go unless something is proven. And my priority is to extricate Norman, not to bring down Brer Fox and his cronies – much as I'd like to. Still, you never know – it could be Gallagher's downfall.'

'What would happen then? Would it be Frank . . .?'

Howard stretched out a hand to the bedside lamp.

'Not automatically – he'd have to stand for nomination. Is he still interested in a political career, do you think?'

'I don't know. He simply accepted that Gallagher had won and that as he was the younger man, he'd be at Westminster for good. Since then, Frank has just worked hard for Labour, as a cause he believes in.'

'Well, we could be in for interesting times. Let's get some sleep now. Goodnight, my darling.'

'Have you switched out the lamp?' Esther asked drowsily, eyes closed.

'Yes, sleepy. Go to sleep and dream of your business empire. I can almost hear it expanding.'

'That reminds me, I have to tell Sammy . . .'

'Hush.' Howard interrupted her with a kiss. 'No more talking. I'm older than you. I need my sleep.' As his eyes grew accustomed to the darkness he looked down on his wife's face, loving each familiar line.

She turned in his arms, then, and kissed him back. 'If you're so old, I'd better take advantage of you while I have the chance.'

Howard was chuckling now, smoothing hair from her brow with one hand, pretending to take her by the throat with another. 'You, Esther Brenton, are a dreadful woman. There's no dealing with you . . . and I don't know how I ever lived without you.'

12

May 1951

'So we extend the factory out at the back, and move in the new machinery as soon as we can,' Sammy said.

Esther nodded as she led the way towards the office. 'I suppose so. It'll be easier than trying to find new premises. I'll put it in hand tomorrow.' She put down the plans she was carrying and lifted a phone. 'Could we have some tea, Maisie? For two? Thank you.'

Sammy was shuffling through the papers on his desk with one hand, drumming the fingers of his other hand.

'Something up?' Esther asked.

'No,' he said. 'Well, not really. It's Ruth. Since that Nathan, that *shmuck*, went off and left her, she's not the same girl. Too serious for a girl in her twenties. Now that she's back home with us, I notice it.'

'She always was serious, Sammy.'

'Serious, yes, but now she's sad. When I think of that bum . . . that *ley di geyer*. Twice I offered him money to go back to college but no – he didn't want to go to college. He wanted to go and make the desert bloom. "Leave that to others," I told him. "You see to your studies." But I might as well have addressed the walls.'

There was a knock at the door, and a tray of tea was delivered.

'What did Ruth say?' Esther asked as she began to pour.

'Ruth didn't use the brains God gave her, Esther. Ruth was "*in love*", and when love comes in at the window, sense goes out at the door. This *shlemil* wanted to be a labourer.'

'Why didn't she go with him?'

'Don't ask me, but I'm glad she didn't. Instead she pines

for him. And I feel guilty that I didn't fix it for her. I should have kept him here by force and marched him back to college.' Sammy reached for his tea and took a gloomy sip.

Esther was shaking with laughter now, unable to raise the cup to her lips. 'How dare you, Sammy Lansky? How dare you sit there advocating another man should study, when you fought against your poor father about studying, tooth and nail? You hypocrite!'

'I want the best for Ruth, that's all.' But he was looking shamefaced.

'Thank heaven you still have the grace to blush, Sammy. There's hope for you. I do understand you want the best for Ruth, but you forget that she's a doctor, now. *She's* the scholar, Sammy. Maybe one in a family is enough. She'll find another man some day.'

'I hope so, Esther.' His sigh was heartfelt.

'Howard and I have our troubles too, if it's any consolation,' Esther said.

'What's the matter? Maybe I can help?'

'No, it's family business: Pamela and her Aunt Lee, and all this argument about whether or not she's presented at Court. Pammy thinks it's an outmoded ritual, but Loelia says it's what Diana would've wanted. I try to keep out of it.'

'I remember Diana Brenton: a beauty. Pamela is like her, in looks, and in some ways. She was a headstrong lady.' He paused. 'Do you find it easy, following in her footsteps?'

Esther smiled. 'I remember Diana, too, Sammy. No, it's not always easy, but nothing worth having is easy, is it. "Life is hard," as Anne keeps telling me.'

'Ha, that reminds me.' Sammy had taken out a pocket notebook and was riffling through it. 'I cut this from *The Times*. A tiny snippet . . . there it is: it suggests your sister's MP, Gallagher, may soon be under investigation.'

'There,' Howard said, holding out a hand to Pamela. 'How about that for a view?' The county of Durham stretched before them, fields and hillocks, winding roads and pit wheels. The spring air was balmy, and there were daisies beneath their feet.

'It's lovely, daddy. I can't wait to be back to live here for good.'

'I thought you'd want to stay in London when you're called to the Bar?'

'No, I want to work in the provinces, so this will be as good a base as any. And I want to be here, with you and Esther, and be able to ride, and stride out with the dogs, and see Aunt Anne occasionally. I didn't know what laughter was until I met her. I like Frank, too – we have super talks about politics. He's awfully knowledgeable, daddy.' She hesitated. 'Actually . . . would it upset you terribly if I voted Labour at the next election?'

Howard threw a stick for the dog before he replied, laughing. 'Don't think I'm hesitating because I disapprove: I'm just thinking of my father turning in his grave! No, darling, if that's how you feel I approve completely. I'm what I think they call a pale-blue Conservative, myself, and the world is changing.'

'That's one of the reasons I've resisted Aunt Lee and the Court thing: it's an anachronism, daddy. I'm not even sure I believe in the monarchy. Why is someone a king? Because his ancestors fought better than mine is the real reason, but we all talk as though it's divine right. I'd feel a hypocrite if I went through a ritual like presentation, not believing in it.'

'It would make Aunt Lee happy.'

'I know, and at times I think that's a good enough reason. But at other times . . . well, I've hung on in the hope she'd finally decide I was too old, but she doesn't give up.'

Howard smiled sympathetically, but as he turned and pretended to enjoy the view, his heart was heavy. 'I must tell her soon,' he thought. 'She is almost of age, and she has a right to know. Besides, I can't be sure that Loelia won't tell her. If she thinks it will serve her ends, or Max's, she will. And if Pamela has to hear it, I want her to hear it from me.'

*

'Wasn't it lovely?' Anne said as they left the cinema. They had seen *The Mudlark*, with Irene Dunne double-chinned as Queen Victoria and an enchanting little boy called Andrew Ray as the waif.

'I like British pictures,' Mary said. 'He's Ted Ray's son, you know. The comedian.'

'I know,' Anne said. 'Talent comes out in the end. Do you want a cooked tea?' They settled for tea and tea-cakes in Meng's, with pastries to follow, and, having found a table there, took off their hats and coats.

'Is Gerard still liking his new school?' Mary asked.

'Yes. He's a born teacher, I see that now. It's just as well he *is* happy, Mary, with this Korean war still going on and our David in the army. I can't worry about everything.'

'There's not much to be cheerful about, is there?' Mary said, ruefully, selecting a piece of tea-cake.

Anne sniffed. 'That's what they're having this Festival for: to cheer everyone up. Waste of money, if you ask me. There's Aneurin Bevan had to resign, because they're going to charge for false teeth and spectacles, but they can still waste money on a festival.'

'Do you ever think about what would've happened if our Frank'd got the nomination? Your life would've changed, along with his.'

Anne wiped a trickle of melted butter from her chin before she replied.

'I daren't let meself think about it, Mary. Every time I read about that little shit Gallagher lording it in Westminster, I could murder someone.'

'Why *did* Frank stick up for the Brentons then? Pat says that's what did for him. And it was long before Esther married Howard.' Mary was curious now, and Anne dropped her eyes lest her sister-in-law should spot her unease.

'Don't ask me, Mary. Because he's daft, I suppose. But then I wouldn't have him any other way.'

'They don't make politicians like they used to,' Mary said wistfully, dabbing her mouth with her napkin. Around them other women, almost all wearing hats, were chattering busily over tea and cakes.

'Be careful . . . you're showing your age,' Anne said. 'You'll be saying policemen are bairns next.'

'No, I mean it, Anne. Him dying . . . Ernie Bevin, I mean . . . was a loss. He hung on too long as Foreign Secretary, according to Pat, but he was straight as a die.'

'He called a spade a spade, I'll give you that.' They both fell silent then, remembering the fat man with the blunt speech who had served his country well. It was Mary who broke the pause.

'It'll be Attlee dying shortly . . . or Churchill.'

'For God's sake, give over, Mary. I'll be crying next. Do you want another cup of tea?'

Frank came in at the back door and if Anne had not been so excited she would have seen from his face that something was wrong.

'Wait till I get you told, Frank! You're not going to believe it. I bumped into Esther in the town, while I was out with your Mary, and she gave me this. It's happened, Frank – what I always said: the mills of God, that's what it is!'

Frank had slumped into a chair at the table. Now he looked at her, and when he spoke his voice was choked with irritation. 'What is, Annie? You keep on saying it's this and it's that. What *is* it?'

'It's a cutting, Frank, from a newspaper. Sammy Lansky cut it out for us. It says Gallagher's in trouble. He's "under investigation".'

'Is that all?' There was contempt in Frank's voice now. 'A bloody newspaper cutting about Gallagher. I wouldn't give it house-room. There's been an explosion at Easington: fifty men or more dead already, and that's only the start. I thought we'd leave disasters like that behind, once we ran the pits. It seems I was wrong.'

Her last period had been satisfactory and on time, so Stella was feeling chirpy. Aloud, she agreed with her mother-in-law that it was sad that another month had gone by without conception. Privately she reinserted her cap and, at family prayers, blessed whoever had invented birth-control.

She had always thought her own mother a religious fanatic but now she knew just how moderate Anne had been. There were seven other women in the Dimambro household: Mario's mother, his two maiden aunts, and his four sisters. On the whole they were a convenience for Stella, the older women fussing over her children, doing the cooking and cleaning and laundering, while the younger women toiled, unlike Stella, all day and most of the evening in one or other of the *gelaterias*.

Occasionally one of them would appeal to Stella for help, but she had quickly learned that *'non ancora'* meant 'not yet', and would buy her more time to read her wonderful movie magazines or the paperback novels she bought at the newsagent's on the next block. She heard her in-laws mutter darkly, *'molto difficile'* or *'non simpatica'*, but she had been brought up to dodge blows. Words did not hurt her.

After the first few months she had plotted constantly to get away; to Hollywood, to San Francisco, to Chicago, which sounded as though it had a bit of life in it. To anywhere except the brownstone house where she lived in conditions that would've made a convent seem a den of iniquity.

And then she had met Chuck. She was still recovering from the birth of Anna-Maria, but he had given her the glad eye and she had tossed her head and curled her lip. 'You'll know me next time you see me,' she'd said aggressively and he had smiled and said, 'I sure hope so.' He had carried her shopping as far as her corner, and that night they had gone to a movie, and afterwards made love in an alley behind the cinema.

Tonight Mario thought she was going to the movies to see Ann Blyth and Farley Granger in *Our Very Own*, which everyone said was a nice film. In reality, she was seeing Chuck, and every little part of her was itching for the meeting.

Esther took a tray of coffee through to the sitting-room when they finished dessert, while Pamela carried a drooping Beb upstairs to put him to bed.

'She adores that child,' Howard said.

'She adores pretty much everyone, Howard. The whole human race . . . and the animal kingdom.'

'She was talking about Loelia today.' Howard was frowning. 'I took the morning off from the office, and we went for a walk. She doesn't want to come out and do a season, but she doesn't want to hurt Loelia either. She thinks Loelia is motivated only by love for Diana and a desire to do right by her dead friend's daughter. All very touching.'

'And you can't tell Pammy the truth?' Esther said.

'I can't be sure it's the right thing to do. Lately, I've thought about it constantly, Esther. Should I or shouldn't I? Have I the right to tell? Or the right not to tell? What do you think? Help me, darling.'

Esther groaned softly. 'Howard, I'm no more sure than you. But, if you push me, I'd say Pammy has a right to know.'

'A right to know what?' Pamela was standing in the doorway. 'Whatever it is, I think you should tell me now.'

13

June 1951

'There now,' the assistant said, drawing the dryer down over Pamela's head. 'Comfortable? Have you plenty of magazines? Don't let your coffee go cold.' She smiled winningly and sailed through the pink voile curtains, leaving Pamela to gaze at her reflection in the mirror and wonder once more how she had come to this day. She took a sip of coffee and then closed her eyes, seeing her father's face that night at the Scar. For Howard Brenton *was* her father – no revelation in the world could alter that.

'A right to know what?' she had said, and had known, from the glance that passed between her father and step-mother, that something dreadful was there to be revealed. 'What?' she had repeated, rather desperately. 'Come on, it can't be *so* terrible!'

But it had been. In the second that Howard had revealed he was not her father, Pamela had gone through the gamut of emotions; disbelief, amusement, rejection, rage and disbelief again. But the expression on the faces of Howard and Esther had confirmed that it was Max Dunane, not Howard, who had given her life.

'But I don't even like him,' she had said simply, and had seen a flicker of relief spring up in her father's eye.

'Are you sure it's true?' she'd urged, and, without waiting for an answer, she had gone to Howard and hugged him with all her might.

They had talked, then, while Esther quietly poured drinks and added coal to the fire; talked of Diana and her love for Max. 'But she loved you too, daddy, I know she did.'

'Yes,' Howard said, 'I'm sure she loved me – but in a

146

different way. Max was part of her upbringing. They were
. . .' He sought for the right word. 'They were comrades as
well as lovers, I suppose. And you were born out of that
closeness.'

'Why didn't they marry? You could have divorced her?'
But Howard's eyes had dropped at that, and Pamela had
seen the truth: Max Dunane had deserted Diana and her
unborn baby and Howard . . . her father . . . had picked
up the pieces.

Now Pamela looked at herself in the hairdresser's mirror
and thought how much older she had grown in the weeks
since that disclosure. She had agreed to be presented, in
order to please Loelia. 'She loves you, darling, that much
is certain,' Howard had said. 'And it's so important to her.'
Pamela had sat dutifully through a clutch of discussions on
slipper satin as opposed to watered silk, on gold earrings
as opposed to pearl, had agreed that, though *Vogue* could
write articles on 'The Rise of the Ready to Wear' till its
pages turned blue, the only gown worth wearing was one
that had been custom-made; and had stood for fittings till
her legs ached. Still, by tonight it would all be over, and
duty done.

At that moment the curtains parted and Loelia Colville's
face peered through. 'All right, Pammy darling? I'm just in
the next cubicle, so if anything occurs to you, call out.' Her
face was full of auntly concern, and Pamela smiled as
warmly as she could.

'I'm fine, Aunt Lee – almost finished, I think. I'll come to
collect you as soon as I'm free.'

Frank opened the packet and fished for the little twist of
blue waxed paper containing salt. He unscrewed it, and
showered its contents over the crisps in the packet. He was
eating his bait in a refuge, and for once he was alone, for
he had been hewing in an awkward seam with space only
for one. He crunched the crisps and contemplated his
surroundings. On Vesting Day in 1947, a wag had
remarked: 'The pits belongs to us now, so what about
selling them and making a profit?' They had had such high
hopes that day, and here he was, still squatting on his

hunkers in a wet cranny, to the accompaniment of the same old drips and cracks that had been background music in the old days.

If things had been different, he might have been above ground now, standing up in Parliament to have his say about the Burgess and McLean scandal or the Korean cease-fire plan. Instead he was eating Smith's crisps in the pit, with nothing but a polony sandwich and a bottle of Tizer to look forward to.

He shifted his position and tried to look on the bright side: he had the best wife and family in the world, as long as he didn't think about Stella, whose US communiqués were frightening the life out of Anne. They had a few bob now; in fact, Anne was planning a holiday for next year, to a Butlin's camp where there was everything under the sun for youngsters to do and Anne would have her meals made. On top of that he was a Parish Councillor, leader of the Labour Group, and a 'crack' hewer, much prized by the manager. But there was the nub: for the life of him, Frank couldn't see the difference between life in the pits pre-1947 and now, except that the Coal Board got away with murder.

He pursed his lips, thinking of the cost of nationalization. £164 million had gone to the coal-owners for a start, and most of it undeserved. And now money was swallowed up by bureaucracy. In most pits men still answered to the same manager as before, but they had to get through twenty clerks to see him – twenty clerks, where before there had been a secretary, a store-keeper and a couple of girls. The manager was hardly seen down the mine, now – or above it, come to that. Brenton or Stretton had been familiar sights around the yard, but the manager, when not buried in paperwork, now had to see financial experts, welfare officers, safety experts, and visitors from Hobart House, the Coal Board headquarters. 'I've forgotten where the cage is,' he had burst out in his office when Frank had led a delegation to talk about a grievance, and there had been a murmur of sympathy all around.

Still, Frank thought, he had his health – no miner's asthma, the dreaded pneumoconiosis or dust on the lung. No nystagmus, the twitching eye or damaged sight that poor lighting in the pit had brought to some men. And most of all, no loss of limb or paralysis from a fall of stone. He was pursing his lips to whistle when he remembered the eighty-three men lost at Easington only weeks before. Better not tempt fate.

Frank had settled back to work and had struck a few blows when the putter came up behind him.

'Aye aye, Frank. I thowt I'd catch thee slacking.'

Frank leaned his bare back against the weeping wall and grinned, his teeth white in a black face.

'Nee chance, bonny lad. I'm perpetual motion.'

'Well, slack off while I tell you something. Our friend Gallagher's just put out a statement.'

In the last few weeks, the story of Gallagher's possible involvement in corruption had gone quiet, and Frank had thought the incident had blown over. 'What's he said?'

'It's all lies, he's never had a hand in the till, he's whiter than bloody driven snow, and his conscience is clear.'

'I never knew he had a conscience. Still, that should keep everybody happy.'

'Why, man, it'll all come out now! His sort never issue denials till their back's to the wall. Something'll break in the next two weeks, you mark my words. And tell your lass to get her glad rags ready: thou's as good as shaking Clem Attlee's hand.'

'There now,' Ruth said, looking down at the blood- and mucus-stained baby she had just cut free of the umbilical cord. 'You've got another girl, Mrs Cornish. A big, beautiful, baby girl.'

The woman tried to smile but her face was creased with sweat and exhaustion, and all she could manage was a grimace. The midwife was scooping up the baby to be cleaned and weighed. 'Let her hold it,' Ruth said. 'Just a moment.'

The baby was laid in the crook of its mother's arm, and Ruth straightened her aching back and put her hands on her aproned hips. 'Was it worth it?' she asked. The tiny bedroom was sparsely furnished and only linoleum

149

covered the floor, but the look on the mother's face was bliss.

The midwife retrieved the baby and Ruth began to wash her hands in the enamel bowl on the dressing-table.

'Doctor?' She turned back to the bed at the sound of the woman's voice. 'Doctor, you'll likely be getting married soon.'

Ruth laughed aloud as she slipped the pinafore halter over her head. 'I don't think so. And if I do, I'll still be practising, so you won't notice any change.'

'No, it's not that. I'd be glad to see you getting wed, a nice lass like you. But there's something for you in the chest there. Something for your bottom drawer. It's not much, but it's from us, me and Jimmy and the bairns.'

Ruth went on drying her hands on the thin towel, trying not to let her lips tremble. 'You shouldn't have bothered, Mrs Cornish . . .' The husband was only a datal hand: his wage would be £5 or £6 a week. She opened the drawer the woman had indicated, and removed the gift: a pair of white Turkish towels done up in cellophane.

'They're lovely, the nicest present I could have.' She bent to kiss the woman's damp brow. 'Thank you.' She straightened up and moved away from the bed. 'And take care of that baby. Now, get some rest.'

She was putting her bag in the car when Patrick Quinnell drove up. 'All well?'

'Yes. A nice big girl, no complications.'

'Why the tears, then?'

'Don't ask me, Pat, not now. It's nothing to do with the delivery – that was fine. I'm just full today. I . . . I was remembering home . . . and thinking that I really belong here now. And that's fine. So don't ask me why it made me cry.'

'So,' Sammy said, 'what I want is a report on how we can make self-service work. If necessary, I'll have to go to the States and see how it's done. There are manufacturers there, good people like Swifts, who pre-pack foods of all kinds for easy handling. In the shops, you see, you choose, you buy. The customer takes what *she* wants, not what *we* hand her. There's meat, fish, dry goods, drapery, greengrocery, books, chemist's goods, housewares . . . all under one roof.'

Esther had heard all this before but it was useless to argue. Self-service was the future of retailing, of that Sammy was certain.

The world's biggest food chain, Atlantic and Pacific, had around 3,500 branches. Krogers of Ohio, the third largest, had increased its trade to 700 million dollars in 1947, three times its 1928 level, all because of a vigorous self-service programme. Down south, Jack Cohen was blazing a trail. But it was not easy to convert small British retail premises. If Sammy wanted to break into self-service properly, he would have to build. That meant he must acquire land; which was not easy to do unless you knew the right people. But if the jungle drums were to be believed, the reign of Gallagher and his ilk might be coming to an end and competition for scarce resources might be fair. Sammy looked up and smiled. 'We're going to bring about a revolution, you and me, Esther. And not a drop of blood to be shed.'

'Stella?' Mario's voice was both conciliatory and enquiring.

'What?' Stella lay back in the scented water and contemplated her ten red-tipped toes resting now on the bath taps.

'*Cara*, we need you. Anna-Maria is feeling sick.'

Stella groaned and slid further under the water. They were his children, too: why couldn't he manage them?

'*Cara*? Stella?'

She hated it when his voice was pleading. 'Ask your mother. Ask Aunt Raffaela. Give her some seltzers.'

'I don't think you should give a baby seltzers.' Mario was sounding firmer.

'She's not a baby, Mario, she's four. She's a big girl and she's a *rompiscatole*!'

'She's not a pest, she's crying for her mama, Stella. And I'm desperate!'

'*Stai bene*, Mario.' She felt the water touch her hair, and sat up. Well, it did serve him right. He was always fussing.

'She never cries for me, we both know that. She's crying for her grandmother, or for her brother Tony. Ask Tony to see to her. He's her big hero.'

'She wants you; come out now, please!'

'I'm not coming.'

'Why not? You have been in there since you got out of bed. You say you want your own house, but how would I dare risk leaving my children alone with you? You tell me that.'

He was wearing her down now, the way he always did. If she had known how persistent he could be, she would have run a mile. She raised herself, dripping, from the bath and put on her wrapper and mules.

'And *buono mattino* to you, too,' she said. She stormed past him to take up the onerous chores of motherhood, sustained only by the thought that tonight, with Chuck, things would be different.

In the end they had gone to Hardy Amies for Pamela's débutante gown, choosing him in preference to Hartnell, Balmain or Worth. The dress was white slipper satin, simply cut with an underskirt of cambric and dolman sleeves that covered the tops of her long white gloves.

'Clothes are enjoyable once more,' Loelia said. 'At first I wasn't happy with the New Look. It was such a contrast after war-time fashion – what there was of it. We hadn't realized it, but women had begun to dress like men; no chic, just big padded shoulders, and everything quite bare and sparse. So of course the Dior line – unpadded shoulders, a waist once more and the huge skirts – felt grotesque at the beginning. Now it's toned down a little and I've become used to it – I like it.'

'Is it true the Government was opposed to it?' Pamela asked. 'Daddy said they denounced it, but I think he was pulling my leg.'

'No, darling, it was true. Harold Wilson was President of the Board of Trade, and he disapproved because there was still a shortage of cloth. And of course Cripps, who disapproved of almost everything, joined in. But the Royals loved it – they had private viewings. Oh, it was wonderful to have nice fabrics and furs in the shops again – and scent. I was almost down to the last of my Worth. But I never wore Dior clothes myself. By the time I'd come round to it the line was better from Hartnell – more restrained. Now Hardy Amies is almost *de rigueur*.'

'Yes,' Pamela said, looking down at her gown, 'he is awfully good.'

'I think the New Look was a gesture really,' Loelia said reflectively. 'We had so many controls – more than 25 000, according to Henry – and the government was always preaching austerity and saving and asceticism.'

'So you just went mad?'

'Yes. Frilly petticoats, pencil-thin umbrellas, top coats like tents – ' She sighed nostalgically and lapsed into silence.

'I don't want to hurry you,' Pamela said at last. 'But it is getting late.'

Loelia smiled. 'You look lovely, darling.' Pamela stood while Loelia clasped Diana's pearls around her throat; and then Esther, whose presence Pamela had insisted on, came in to hand her a long flat shagreen case. It contained a simple bracelet of pearls with a diamond clasp. 'This is from daddy and me, to celebrate a special day.'

'How nice,' Loelia said and began to fuss with Pamela's hair. But Pamela held Esther's gaze for a moment and smiled her thanks, before they began the descent to the drawing-room, where everyone was waiting.

Howard was the first to her side, bending to kiss her as her arms twined about his neck in a hug. Henry Colville was next, then the Colville boys. 'You look splendid,' Greville said with all the aplomb of the twenty-six-year-old. And then her own brothers, who teased her. And finally, Max Dunane and his wife. She held out her cheek to Max but her white-clad arms stayed at her side.

Only the Colvilles could accompany her to the palace, for the presentation parties were always over-subscribed and the rules were strict. Loelia had applied to the Lord Chamberlain at St James's Palace for permission to present Pamela, along with the 200 or so other débutantes. The rest of the family were ineligible, either because they had not been presented, as in Esther's case, or because they had no one to present and no connection with a girl being presented, as with the Dunanes. 'So Max has lost out,' Howard thought, and derived a quiet satisfaction from the fact.

But all thought of who had won or lost was gone as he watched Pamela walk down the steps, her head erect, looking every inch a lady, turning before she climbed into the car to blow a kiss to him and Esther, as they stood in the doorway.

'Wish me luck, daddy. And pray I don't fall flat on my face and disgrace us all.'

Anne shook out the paper. 'It says here that the average housewife works a seventy-five-hour week, with overtime on Saturdays and Sundays.' They were seated on either side of the kitchen range, their feet on the fender, their bellies full of good food.

'So?' Frank said.

'Seventy-five hours, Frank, plus overtime. How long d'you work?'

'You can't compare going down the pit with a lady's life like you have.'

'No, Frank, I don't know any pitman who could stand my pace. Anyway, this is one of those Mass Observation Studies, so it must be right. They studied 700 working-class homes in the London region – so that means our rate up here must be 150 hours a week! It says the housewife's tyrannized by meal-times and child-minding, and spends a quarter of the day in the kitchen. That's wrong for a start: I spend *three*-quarters of my day there. And it says they do their shopping on Fridays, and spend between ten shillings and £2. Not for a family this size! And it says she spends her leisure reading, listening to the radio, watching television or the cinema. What leisure, that's what I want to know? The cinema's right, but who's got a television set? You read a lot of rubbish in the paper.'

'Our Theresa's late,' Frank said, looking at the clock.

'She *is* on her holidays, Frank. She has to have some pleasure. Besides, you don't need to worry about her – or our Angela now she's engaged. I'm proud of our Terry.

We've never had anybody go to university in this family, Frank. Any university, never mind a London one.'

'Our Gerald went to college.'

'Yes, but you know what I mean. She's at the LSE. She'll have letters after her name.'

'If she passes.' Frank looked meaningfully at the clock.

'Oh, give over, Frank. Speaking of clocks, I wonder how our Esther got on?'

'What's that to do with clocks?'

'You know what I mean, Frank. She's in London today, with that Loelia. What a name. Pamela's being presented to the King and Queen. Our family by marriage – Howard's bairns are my niece and nephews! Well, step-niece and nephews.'

'I thought you didn't agree with royalty?' Frank said, straightfaced.

Anne leaned to poke the fire, desperate to get her answer right. When she sat back, her face flushed from the flame, she looked shifty.

'I don't. Or the class system, either. But while they're here, we might as well make use of them. Not even you could argue with that.'

14

October 1951

Frank carried a rattling cup and saucer up the stairs and set it down by his wife's bed. 'Time to get up, love.' She was going to an autumn fair at the church today, and mustn't be late or the bargains would be gone.

'Is it a nice day?' Anne was struggling on to her elbow and reaching for the tea. 'Did you sugar it?'

'Yes, love, like I always do. Two spoons. And it's a real nice day. Let's hope it stays like that.'

'Anything in the paper?' Anne had settled back on her pillows to enjoy her tea, and Frank turned from the window to watch her.

'A nice picture of Princess Elizabeth with her bairns and Prince Philip. Nothing much else. Just Churchill grinning from ear to ear.'

It was five weeks since George VI had had a lung removed, and the country had held its breath until the operation was pronounced a success. But increasingly the press was focusing on the girl who would one day be Queen.

'Your dress looks nice,' Frank said, nodding towards the navy-and-white confection that hung on the front of the oak wardrobe.

'It'll do. What was Churchill grinning about?'

'Being back in Downing Street, Annie. You don't have to look far for a reason, do you: seventy-seven, and he's PM again.'

'Only by seventeen seats, Frank. It won't last.' She raised her cup to her lips and sipped appreciatively.

'One seat's enough, Anne.'

She was frowning now. 'Did you have to bring that up, Frank? Just when I was enjoying meself?'

'I didn't bring it up, pet, you asked. Any road, it's got to be faced: the Tories are in for the next five years, and we'd better get used to it.' He turned back to the window, to look out on the autumnal garden.

'And that little shit Gallagher's back in an' all. It beats me, Frank. With all the rumours you wouldn't think a soul would have voted for him.'

'They didn't. They voted the only way they could vote, given our history: they voted Labour. I did, and I bet you did – because your hand would drop off if you put your cross against a Tory, now wouldn't it?'

As usual, when caught out, Anne did not argue. 'Get out of here and let me get up, Frank. You'd think we had corn growing.'

He began to move towards the door. 'Anyway, the way things are going we might need old Winnie. There's going to be trouble in the Suez Canal Zone.' It was a week since British troops had seized key points on the Canal, and four British warships were now in Port Said.

'Our David won't have to go there, will he?' Anne had put up a hand to her throat and Frank saw his mistake.

'Why, no – it'll fizzle out. The Egyptians'll never fight. Now come on, you've got a bazaar to go to.'

Esther and Howard sat on either side of the kitchen table, papers spread among the breakfast dishes.

'So,' Esther said, 'is this the nation's apology to Churchill for its ingratitude in '45?'

'I think it's more to do with the collapse of the Liberals,' Howard said mildly. 'They got two million fewer votes than last year. I knew they'd done badly, but it's only now the analysis is coming through that you realize the extent of it.'

'Churchill wants a Liberal in his cabinet, doesn't he?' Esther was turning pages as she spoke.

'Yes, but Clement Davies has turned him down. The knives are out for Attlee, which is a pity, because I like the man, but the left-wingers like Nye Bevan consider he betrayed socialism. Now, what are you going to do until it's time to go in to Sunderland?'

Esther grimaced. 'I'm going to catch up on some chores. This vast house doesn't run itself, and in case you haven't noticed we don't have the trillions of servants you had in the old days.'

'Why not? We can afford them.'

'It's not lack of money, Howard, it's because no one wants to go into domestic service now. They did it before the war because they had to, but times have changed.'

Esther stood up and began to gather up the debris of their breakfast. She was transferring the dishes to the draining board when he came up behind and put his arms around her. 'Esther, we could leave this house, you know. I told you that ages ago. There are other houses. It made sense to live here when I was involved with the pit – but now we could live anywhere.'

'Leave the Scar?' She turned, astounded at his words. 'I've never even thought of it. I thought you adored this place?'

Howard smiled. 'I've never cared for it, my darling, if I'm truthful. Oh, it's a nice enough house, I suppose, but for me it holds too many sad memories.'

'Diana?' Esther's face was apprehensive and he took her in his arms.

'Diana, and Rupert, and my parents, and the war . . . a dozen ups and downs. I could quite look forward to moving.'

'But where to?'

'We'll get a road-map and stick in a pin. Or perhaps we'll build. Whatever you want, my darling. Now put down that tea-towel and let's go and see what Beb is up to with Nanny.'

'I can't believe it,' Esther thought as they went upstairs. 'Our own house . . . a fresh start.' It seemed too good to be true.

A customer had come into the *gelateria*, but Stella did not move from her stool at the counter. If he wanted serving he could come to her, and if the flavour he wanted wasn't within her reach, he could lump it.

'*Ciao*,' she said. The boy was looking along the tubs of brightly coloured ice-cream, deliberating. Stella had eaten avidly of all of them at first. Now she loathed them.

'Neapolitan,' he said at last. Fortunately that was the flavour nearest to Stella's hand, so she gave him a double helping, and slipped the coins he gave her into the pocket of her overall. She did that with every fourth purchase, and the resultant cache of money was mounting nicely. She needed her independence, and the Dimambros seemed never to have heard of wages. At least the Co-op drapery had paid her something, even though she'd been forced to purloin the odd item to bring her wages up to standard. But to her in-laws she was just a maid-of-all-work, a *tuttofare*.

The boy was watching her from the table where he had carried his Neapolitan ice-cream. She pretended not to notice, but she turned her best side to him just the same. Let him see what he was missing. For a moment she enjoyed her pose, but then gloom repossessed her. She had finished with Chuck and now had a man-friend called Pete who worked in the stockroom of Saks on Fifth Avenue but never seemed to have anything special to bestow on her, however hard she hinted. His idea of a good night out was popcorn and a park-bench. But he was handsome as a film-star.

She fell into a daydream, then, thinking about Pete and their next date, and was still in a reverie when Mario came into the shop, carrying two steel containers of ice-cream. That morning he had forced her out of bed. Well, driven her out with his constant complaining.

'*Ciao, cara*,' he said now. 'Tutti-frutti and chocolate.'

'Leave it there,' she said shortly, but he was coming round the back of the counter to stand beside her. She felt his pudgy hand on her back and shrugged it off. '*Basta*,' she said, and heard his breath come out in a sigh – but she didn't regret it. Last week she had overheard a girl customer call him a 'dream'. Bloody nightmare was nearer the mark, with his soft hands and his big brown eyes like well-sucked 'black bullets'.

'What d'you want to do this weekend?' he said coaxingly. 'We have time off. We could go anywhere.'

'There's only one place I want to go, Mario – dear old Blighty, and the sooner the better.'

It wasn't strictly true, but it kept Mario in his place, and that was what mattered.

'This is nice,' Catherine Hardman said, snuggling close to Norman Stretton in the double seat in the back row of the cinema. On the screen in front of them Vivien Leigh was being brutalized by Marlon Brando in *A Streetcar named Desire*. Stretton felt Catherine's cool fingers on his hand and then she was intertwining them with his. He wanted to return the pressure, but a voice in his head was reminding him of how little he had to offer her. Not even security, if all his fears about Fox were well-grounded. For the first time in his life he was in love. He had fallen for women before but now he realized they had simply been infatuations. Catherine, with her courage and determination, had shown him the difference between love and infatuation. And it had come too late.

'She's lovely, isn't she?' Catherine whispered, 'but I can't understand a word he says. He mumbles.' In the darkness Stretton smiled, and gave himself up to the pleasure of her shoulder against his, the scent of her perfume and the gentle pressure of her hand.

15

February 1952

It was the morning Anne had been waiting for for years, but now that it was here she couldn't bring herself to get out of bed. What if Frank lost? What if she saw him humiliated, beaten? Today the people of Belgate were going to the polls in a by-election, to fill the seat left vacant after Gallagher's resignation. It had come overnight – the MP's arrest on corruption charges, and then swiftly the news that he had resigned. The nomination had gone unanimously to Frank, and the Party was behind him, but . . . She struggled up on to her elbow, shivering in the cold room. 'I'll believe it when I see it,' she told herself. 'With our luck, anything could happen.' What if voters blamed the Labour Party for Gallagher's crimes? The Tories would get in, then, and Frank would never get over it.

At that moment she heard Frank's tread on the stair and the chink of cup on saucer. He was bringing her a cup of tea, even on election morning! What a jewel. But all the more reason for her to get out of bed and make bloody sure he got elected.

'Put it down, Frank, and then let me get on. You should be away by now.'

'I'm going in a minute, but I'm not busting a gut. Let's face it: I'm in or I'm out, by now. People's made up their minds whether or not they want me, and all the capering about, and all the bowing and scraping in the world, won't change it. So let's have a nice day, pet, and take what comes. The world won't end if Francis Maguire doesn't win.'

'You speak for yourself, Frank. If the Tories get back in in Belgate, I'll very likely cut my throat. And then you'll be left with the bairns and the house, and a funeral to pay for.'

Shaking his head ruefully, Frank leaned over to take her in his arms. 'By gum, you're a stormy petrel and no mistake, Anne Maguire. Well, if it means that much to you, I'd better get out and shake a few hands. Drink your tea.'

When he had left the bedroom Anne drank her tea and then lay back, contemplating the ceiling. It was here, the moment she had prayed for for more than twenty years. Justice was about to be done, and a good man rewarded. For Frank was a good man: in all the years, she had never seen him contemplate a mean action, let alone carry one out. She it was who had done all the scheming. A sense of her own shortcomings overwhelmed her, causing her to leap from the bed and get down on her knees. No time today for formal prayers, it had to be straight from her lips to God's ears, as Sammy Lansky often said.

'Please God, let Frank win. And if you can make it a thumping big majority, I'd be very grateful.'

Ruth took Nathan's last letter from the papier-mâché box where she stored them all. She knew it almost by heart, but it would bear reading again. His letters were shorter now, the lapses in between letters longer. Sooner or later they would cease, for he was sure to find someone to love, someone with whom to build a life and a home. And when that time came, he would have neither time nor inclination to write to a woman in a far-off country whose face he must now have difficulty in remembering.

'Dear Ruth,' she read. 'How is your flock? In your last letter you made it seem mumps would carry them all away.' Ruth smiled at that, remembering her terror at three cases of mumps in one day when she had known it only as a textbook disease. She read on, through the pleasantries and the teasing, to the place where he wrote from his heart.

Oh Ruth, how often I think of you and wish you were here, to see what we are achieving. Once upon a time the dream was of Jerusalem – next year in Jerusalem.

Now we work towards making the desert bloom and I
see it, Ruth, I see it happening, I am even part of it. Life
is hard here, and hectic, with so much to be done. It's a
million miles away from the old ways, the *Yishuv*, pious
Jews spending their lives in devotions with no time for
toil. Now we work, towards the day when we will need
no hand-outs – from America or anywhere else.

My only sorrow is that our coming here has driven so
many Arabs away. There are new refugee camps now: I
never envisaged that. Still, we must all accept change.

I am not going to try to change your mind, I have
learned the futility of that particular task – but you belong
here, in this melting pot of Herr Doktors and Herr
Professors, artists, and lawyers and musicians and scientists and businessmen and the odd *shlemil* – all different, all united in their determination to build this state.
It is survival or nothing, Ruth. If we learned anything
from the Holocaust, we learned that. Still, I am waxing
serious and that is bad. It is not all work here. Sometimes
we sing and dance and drink a little wine. Some think of
the old days, and so do I – but mostly I think of you,
beavering away in your practice, the good Dr Ruth, and
I hope you find time to remember me.

She folded the letter and put it back in its hiding-place
before brushing the tears from her cheeks and composing
herself to go out and face the world.

Sammy's eyes were bright with enthusiasm as he talked.

'There's 600 square feet in that shop, Esther, and it takes
about £350 a week. It could take more, with better management. I suggest we buy it, and put in wall-shelves, a central
island for display, and a turnstile at the door. We give
every customer a wire basket, have bins of cut-price goods
everywhere, and money-off vouchers for regular shoppers,
maybe.'

'What about advice?' Esther said. 'Customers like to feel
cherished.'

'Floaters, Esther! Two assistants – maybe more – floating,
moving around, smiling, chatting, answering questions.'

'Well,' Esther said dubiously, 'we could try it.'

'That's settled, then,' Sammy said. 'Now before we get down to this paperwork, how's your husband?'

'Worried,' Esther replied. 'He thinks Edward Fox may get away with what he's done to Norman Stretton.'

'I wouldn't be surprised: Fox is *drek*. But he's clever, so I hope Howard doesn't underestimate him. What's going to happen at the by-election today, do you think?'

'Frank's going to win, of course. Pamela has come up to Durham specially to help.'

'Pamela? Howard's Pamela working for the Labour Party? That's a turn-up!'

'Howard says she's just going through the socialist phase, but he's lent her his Rover so she can drive good socialists to the polling-booths. I wish you'd seen Anne's face. Help from a Brenton! It's wormwood and gall to my sister. She said a nice thank-you, but it took it out of her.'

They were still chuckling when Esther glanced through the glass partition to the office below.

'What's up?' Sammy asked, seeing her expression change.

'I don't know, but something is.'

It was a wide-eyed accounts clerk who brought them the news: the King, George VI, had died in the night. The nation had a Queen.

'It's quite a mess, isn't it?' Stretton said, looking down at the documents on Howard's desk and the long history of chicanery they revealed, in which Stretton, unaware, had become implicated. There were counsel's reports, too; none of them hopeful.

'It's not pretty,' Howard said, 'but it could be worse. When you confront him, be careful with your words. Fox twists things.'

'I can't trust myself to speak to him, if I'm honest. But at the same time, I've been naïve . . . and I should be too old for naïvety.'

'We're never too old for that, Norman. If we are, it means we've become cynical, and that's even worse.'

It had begun to snow outside and Stretton shivered as he moved to a chair.

'I know you're trying to cheer me, Howard, and I appreciate it. But the truth is that I've made an abysmal mess of this . . . of everything.' He was looking into the fire now, an expression of abject misery on his face.

'Have you seen Catherine Hardman since you left the hospital?' Howard was seeking a more cheerful subject, but Stretton's air of gloom only deepened.

'Yes, I see her quite often. She was . . . kind to me when I broke my leg, and we've grown quite close since then. Silly really, when I'm old enough to be her father.'

'Hardly,' Howard said. 'She must be thirty-two. She was older than Rupert.'

'And I'm fifty-two, Howard.' He nodded towards the table. 'And probably bankrupt . . . or in the dock.'

There was a tap at the door and Fox's arrival was announced. He had come in answer to an invitation from Howard, and his brows twitched now at the sight of Stretton.

'Norman, I didn't expect to see you here.'

'Sit down, Mr Fox,' Howard said politely. 'Mr Stretton is here at my suggestion. I may as well come straight to the point. We've had counsel's advice on some aspects of your firm's dealings, and that advice is that you've sailed close to the wind in every instance. On a number of occasions, you have broken the law.'

Fox was smiling. '*We* have broken the law, *Mr* Brenton. I have a partner: your friend, Norman.'

'Who was not involved in your dealings.'

'That's true,' Norman Stretton said bitterly. 'But I've been more of a dupe than a partner, haven't I?'

'Not at all,' Fox said smoothly. 'I consider we got on well, you and I. Co-operating, making decisions together. After all, you put your name to the documentation readily enough.'

'You're efficient, Mr Fox,' Howard said coldly. 'No one is denying that. And going over what's done is futile. We must think of the future. Stretton wants to dissolve his partnership with you and he wants the return of his capital.'

Fox was smiling broadly now and shaking his head. 'Out of the question. As far as I'm concerned, the partnership works well. Why break it?'

'Because if you don't, Fox, we'll break you.'

'Words, Mr Brenton, simply fine words. You can leave the partnership, Norman, if that's what you want. But you go without a penny.'

'You can't afford publicity, Fox.' Howard's tone was ominous. 'You know what happened to Gallagher – and in my opinion, you've been a greater villain.'

Fox's smile grew wider. 'Prove it,' he said. 'Prove it! I'm no fool, Mr Brenton – I'm not another Stanley Gallagher. I cover my tracks. Now if you've anything *really* interesting to say . . . No? Then I'd better take my leave.'

He turned at the door. 'In case you haven't heard, the King's dead, poor man. The old order changes, doesn't it? All the time!'

'They say a footman found him when he took in early morning tea. Awful for the Queen . . . and old Queen Mary. Two of her sons dead and one run off.'

Mary Quinnell was pouring tea as she spoke. Her husband accepted a cup and sank back into his chair. In the background the radio played solemn music, all that had been put out by the BBC since the announcement. Tonight theatres would stay dark and many cinemas remained closed in tribute to a King who had led his people through a terrifying war.

'He had a good end, just the same. If I'm right about the diagnosis, it could've been much worse. They say he smoked sixty cigarettes a day, and it seems highly likely that he had lung cancer, poor devil. I suppose there'll be tremendous ceremonial for the funeral . . .'

'. . . and a Coronation. "Queen Elizabeth": "God Save the Queen" – it doesn't sound right, somehow. And she was so happy with her husband and her babies.' Mary shook her head sadly as she stirred her tea.

'She knew it had to come, Mary.'

'But not yet. Still, I'm worried about something else,

Pat.' She rose to her feet as she spoke and went across to switch off the wireless.

'Catherine?' Pat enquired.

'Yes, how did you guess?' She sounded startled and he threw back his head in laughter.

'Because you're as transparent as water, my love. I watch your face and I know precisely what you're thinking. You're thinking Stretton's too old for her . . . and perhaps that he's in partnership with the wrong man?'

'I like Norman, Pat, and everyone speaks well of him – but he must be fifty.'

'And Catherine is thirty-two. But I'm much older than you are, remember, and as far as I know, our marriage is working.'

'Of course it is. It's just that she's precious to me, Pat, and as far as I know she's never felt like this about anyone.'

'She's precious to me, too, but I respect her judgement. Catherine's never put a foot wrong up to now, and if she's certain in her own mind about this man I think we should leave her alone.'

'I've been counting the piles of votes,' Pamela said, in an excited undertone to Anne. 'And we're right out in front – with twice as many, I'd say.' In the background the long tables were covered in voting slips decanted from the metal ballot-boxes, and the heads of the counters were bent to their task beneath the keen eyes of the party stalwarts.

'Well, I'll believe it when I see it,' Anne said firmly. She had been fond of Pamela ever since she had made her bridesmaid's dress. The girl was a Brenton, and judging by the way she'd handled the big car all day she was certainly her mother's daughter; but today they'd both mucked in together, running up paths, rounding up reluctant voters, ferrying them backwards and forwards from the booth, with Pamela calling her 'Aunt Anne'. Which of course she was, the ways of God being more complicated than a cat's cradle.

The polls had been closed now for more than an hour, and the count was on. 'I'll never survive till the declaration,' Anne said, 'and these shoes are killing me.' She rubbed the toes she had just freed against the other calf, wincing as the circulation returned.

'Dad's certain Frank will win,' Pamela said. 'And he told me to tell you that you'll both be welcome to use the London house until Uncle Frank finds a permanent place there. It's hardly ever used by us, so it'll be nice if you two stay there.'

She had meant to cheer Anne up, but her words had exploded in Anne's head like a bomb: *'Nice if you two stay there.'* You two? Surely no one expected *her* to live in London? Who would take care of the Belgate house and family? And what could she find to do with herself in the heart of a city? She had never thought beyond a first triumphal visit to see Frank installed – she wanted a moleskin coat for that, however they paid for it. But staying there? She couldn't do that in a million years – and yet if she didn't, Frank would be alone in the city subject to all kinds of temptations.

Anne sighed, and eased her foot back into her shoe. Life was like mountain-climbing: you'd no sooner scaled one peak than you saw there was another, bigger one ahead of you.

16

March 1952

'See,' Sammy said, pushing through the office door exuberantly, and waving a sheaf of papers in the direction of Esther's desk. 'Here's the proof of what I've been telling you. I spoke to the Self-Service Development Association and they sent me the latest data. Self-service trading is inevitable, according to this. They've had a fact-finding mission in the States, backed by the National Productivity Council, and it's exciting, Esther – breath-taking, even. Custom-built buildings, new materials for packaging, bright labelling and clear pricing – and everything under the sun on sale. And – wait for it – forget baskets, Esther. We give customers *trolleys* to wheel like prams: no more aching shoulders! How about that?'

'That's a good idea,' Esther said. 'But . . .'

'Never mind "but", my *oytser* – this is the future. No more queues, no more lines of tired, drab women with strained faces, waiting their turn. There are 750,000 stores in Britain: One per sixty of the population. That's all right if people are queuing, but it's far too many for the future. It's already started, Esther: the first self-service store has been open in Britain since 1942. If we don't hurry, we'll be left behind.'

'We are doing it,' Esther protested. 'But cautiously.' She put up a hand and ran it through her hair in desperation.

'Cautiously! Like snails, that's us. Think of the turn-over! The gross margin! Savings on staff, on pre-packing, on volume of sales. We can offer a better deal to the customer. I want to turn our whole chain over to self-service within a year.'

'But what about the small customer?' Esther said. 'The little old lady with a slim purse who likes to take her time?'

Sammy smiled a beatific smile and perched a hip on the edge of her desk. 'It's for the little old ladies with slim purses I'm doing this. Their pound is worth less than half of what it was in 1938. They certainly need time, Esther, and we can offer them all the time in the world. No assistant in front of them demanding to know what they want, no queue behind urging them on. Prices clearly marked, no huge wedges of cheese slapped on the scale so they have to be embarrassed to say "No, that's too big." Nice neat pieces of cheese of every size, so they can pick the bit they want – and all the time in the world to dawdle over the choosing, while the people in a hurry rush past them. We'll be rich, Esther – and we'll be benefactors, too.'

Esther put out a hand to the phone to ring for tea. 'We'll be rich, Sammy, I'm sure of that,' she said drily. 'Because you can sell Christmas to turkeys.'

They pored over the report while they drank their tea, and then Esther glanced at the clock. 'Anne will be getting ready to go to the House of Commons, now.'

'It's a great moment', Sammy said, 'seeing your husband installed as an MP.'

'And Anne's first trip to London, too. She's never been beyond the Cleveland Hills until now.'

As if the mention of the Cleveland Hills and North Yorkshire had triggered his memory, Sammy put out a hand to hers. 'Do you remember Whitby?'

'Yes,' Esther said. 'That was a long time ago.' It was twenty-two years since she had fled to Whitby to give birth to Philip's son, and had handed him over to the doctor there who was to arrange his adoption. Sammy, only a boy then, had been with her on that day, as he had been with her almost every day since. She put her other hand across to cover his and smiled at him. 'You were a good friend to me then.'

'You were brave,' he said. 'Giving up the *boy t'shikl*. Have you . . .?' He hesitated.

'Have I ever regretted it? Not seriously. It was for the best. As long as the boy is happy.'

'He'll be twenty-two now.'

'If he survived the war,' Esther said. 'Still, they hardly bombed Yorkshire so I expect he's OK.'

'And you have Beb,' Sammy said.

'Yes,' Esther said. 'One child doesn't make up for another, but if any child could, it would be Beb. And if we don't get on, he'll be wondering where his mother has got to – so, about the Lane Street store . . .'

But the Lane Street store was never to be discussed. There was a knock at the door and then Howard was entering the room. 'Sammy, I've come to steal my wife for an hour. It's urgent or I wouldn't do it – say you'll let her go.'

The smile on Howard's face told Sammy it was not bad news that had brought Howard. He shook his head ruefully. 'I can't part with her, Howard, not even for an hour – unless, of course, you tell me why I should. I'm consumed with curiosity, so what about a trade?'

'Go and get your coat,' Howard told Esther. 'You can't be let into the secret yet. I'll confer with Sammy while you're gone.'

Howard's secret was a house. 'It's just come on to the market,' he told Esther as they drew up to the door. It was a tall, imposing house with a colonnaded porch and Georgian windows, but there was clematis on the mellow brick walls, and the garden was already alive with crocus and tight-budded daffodils. Arched doorways at either side led in one instance to a gravelled yard with garages, in the other to an orchard beyond.

'I can't believe it's in the heart of town,' Esther said, gazing around her. They were less than a mile from the centre of Sunderland, from Howard's office and the core of the Lanver enterprises.

Inside, she walked from one pleasant room to another, and finally into a gleaming kitchen with red-tiled work surfaces and cheerful primrose walls.

'Like it?' Howard asked.

'I love it . . . but are you *sure*? And what about Beb?'

'We'll telephone him tonight, but my guess is, he'll love it. I spoke to Pamela this morning, and she thinks it's the best idea I've had in years.'

'She'll miss Belgate,' Esther said doubtfully.

'No she won't. Nothing will part Pamela from anything

she cares for, we both know that. Now, do I buy it or don't I? And don't ask me if I'm sure: *I'm* certain!'

'How do I look?' Anne said. She had on the scandalously expensive moleskin coat, bought from the Co-op on tick for forty-seven guineas, and a green velvet hat of Esther's that had cost three guineas at Jane Jones in Holmeside and only been worn once, to a ceremony in Durham Cathedral.

'You look lovely, mam,' Terry said, moving across to tilt the mirror so that her mother could better see herself. They were in the master-bedroom in the Brentons' London house, the traffic a dull roar in the street below, both their hearts hammering at the thought of what lay ahead.

'Is your dad all right?' Anne asked, bending closer to the mirror to wipe the corners of her mouth free of unaccustomed lipstick.

'He's prowling about down there like a caged tiger.' Terry was smiling, and Anne, looking at her daughter, could think only of Stella, whose double Terry was becoming – except that there was no slyness there, and none of the hint of wildness that Stella had always had.

'We'd better get down there, then,' Anne said, gathering up the leather bag and gloves borrowed from Esther for the occasion. They went out on to the wide landing and began to descend the stairs. 'This house is like a hotel, isn't it?' Anne said, awestruck.

'Would you like to live here?' Terry turned in the hall to look back at her mother.

'No, pet, I can honestly say I wouldn't.' Anne's voice was firm. 'There'd be the heating of it for a start. And the carpeting. And God knows what it costs to paper. I'd like a bit more room back home, but you might as well live in a ploughed field as here. It's not cosy, our Terry, and that's a fact.'

'Here you are,' Frank said, appearing from a side room. He wore a new grey suit with a faint red stripe in it, and a white shirt. The red tie with a grey spot, a gift from Gerard, was knotted beneath a face now racked with tension.

'Cheer up,' Anne said. 'It's Parliament you're going to, not the block.'

They climbed into a black cab, summoned by Terry with an aplomb that left her mother speechless, and sat, hands clasped on nervous knees, all the way to Westminster.

'This is Park Lane,' Terry said at one time, and at another: 'And there's the river.' But all Anne could see was Big Ben, somehow smaller than she had imagined and yet more impressive. And then they were piling out, and Frank was going off to meet his sponsors, and someone else was guiding them past the watchful policemen and into the great echoing building that housed the Mother of Parliaments.

'You're not crying, are you, mam?' Terry asked as they took their seats in the gallery.

'No fear,' Anne said fiercely, or as fiercely as she could, for the lump in her throat was threatening to choke her. And then she could see the fair head below her, the grey hairs that mottled it invisible at a distance, and someone was rising to his feet and bowing to the grey-wigged Speaker, and the whole great panoply was unfolding before her, a thousand times more splendid than she had ever imagined.

'That's your father down there,' she said, clutching Terry's arm.

'No,' Terry whispered back, 'it's the member for Belgate, mam, and don't you forget it.'

'Mr Biddle?' Sammy leaned back in his chair, supporting the hand holding the phone on the leather arm, for this might be a long conversation. 'My name is Samuel Lansky, and I was given your name by an associate, Hyman Winter. Yes, that's the one. He tells me you specialize in tracing people.'

He listened to the voice on the other end with one ear, the other cocked in case of Esther's unexpected return. 'No, it's not a debtor I wish to trace, it's a child. Well, he's a man now, but I have only his birth details, and they're sketchy. Whitby, 1930. Is that possible? Good. Well, now, I'll tell you all I know.'

*

Howard was reading when he heard the doorbell ring, and he looked up in surprise. Esther had a key. But it was not Esther whom the parlourmaid ushered in, it was Catherine Hardman, wearing her navy-blue nursing-sister's dress beneath her camel swagger coat.

'Catherine! This is a pleasant surprise! Come in. Can I get you a drink? Do sit down. Esther won't be long, and I know she'll want to see you.'

'That would be nice,' said Catherine, allowing him to help her off with her coat. 'But actually I came to see you. I want your help.'

'You have it,' Howard said. 'You were Rupert's friend, and you're mine. Tell me what you want.'

'It's not for me,' Catherine said. 'Well, in a way it is. But really it's Norman . . .' She had seated herself in a wing chair, and now folded her hands neatly in her lap.

'He's OK, isn't he? Last time I saw him, he said everything was fine. He was hopeful of finding interesting work, and cheerful.'

'He would have been,' she answered – and suddenly Howard remembered Trenchard all those years ago. Trenchard had smiled at him, and assured him all was well, and then had gone home and taken an overdose of laudanum. 'I didn't see his need then,' Howard thought. 'I mustn't miss Norman's need this time.'

'Norman's got an offer of a job,' Catherine continued, 'but it's a dead end, and he knows it. He's frustrated, and miserable, and he sees no future.'

'At least he's free of Edward Fox,' Howard said. 'It's infuriating that he's lost most of his capital but, to be perfectly honest, Catherine, it could have gone badly for him if he hadn't been able to face out Fox's threats.'

'He couldn't've done it without you. That's why Fox backed down – the thought that he was taking the Brentons on as well as his partner.'

'I hope I helped. I'd've done as much for anyone who fell foul of Fox and his tricks. And I felt a certain degree of guilt: I should have done more to put off Norman when he first mentioned going in with Fox. My weakness is a certain degree of vacillation, Catherine. But as far as Norman is concerned, I hope he knows I'll back him in anything he cares to take up.'

'He'd never ask you, though,' Catherine said. 'And apart from the working side of his life, he's lonely.'

'He has you.'

'That's just it.' The words burst from her. 'He could have me, but he won't. He says he's too old. There are twenty years between us: how many years are there between mother and Pat? Or you and Esther?' Suddenly she flushed, thinking she might have gone too far.

'You're right,' Howard said. 'Of course you are. And I do know he cares for you. That meeting, the result of his accident, which brought you two together, was fate in Esther's view.' He stood up and went to take her hand. 'I'm going to pour you a drink, and one for myself, and we'll talk about this a bit more. You are going to cheer up before Esther comes back and accuses me of depressing you. And I will help Norman: I can't promise a proposal of marriage – it's up to you to obtain that. But I can do something about his working life, and I will! And now – let me tell you about the house Esther and I bought today.'

Stella devoured the thin airmail letter again. Terry was in London now, David had joined up, and Gerard was working in Newcastle – only Angela and Bernard were still at home. With her father in London most of the time, the house must be like a morgue. Nearly as bad as this place! She looked across the table at her mother-in-law. God, she was a monstrous size. It was all the pasta and oil – they wallowed in oil. Stella thought longingly of fish and chips from Trembaths: crisp, dry batter, white fish inside. And chips that melted in the mouth. Why had she never appreciated Belgate when it was available?

'Have you seen the time, Estella?' Aunt Raffaela's eyes flicked to the clock and back.

'I'm not blind.'

'You should be working with Mario now.'

'You should be working with Mario now,' Stella repeated, mocking. 'Try telling me something I don't know. He can wait. *So eccome abbastranza!*'

The two older women exchanged glances of despair, but Stella was not to be moved.

'I am tired, *mamma*. Worn out. *Molto* weary! I am fed up with ice-cream. I feel like running away. *Comprendi*? Right now, I want to go back to bed, pull the covers over my head and pretend this is all a bad dream. *Va bene*?'

'You want to stay at home today, with the children?' Her mother-in-law was ready to conciliate.

'No, *mamma*, I don't want to stay at home. *Sono stufo* with home. *Molto stufo*.' She looked at them in exasperation. 'You don't understand do you? Not everyone wants to sit around here, praying and making meat sauce. I want some fun, *divertimento*. *Capisci*? I'm going to go to work now, Raffaela, because I'm scared that if I sit around here I might grow fat and sprout a moustache. But that's the only reason I'm moving: fear! And as for you . . . *si faccia gli affari suoi* . . . if you know *how* to mind your own business. Remember, my dad's an MP: if I was back home I wouldn't be working in an ice-cream parlour. Think on that!'

Stella had wanted to sting them out of their stolidity but it was useless. And among her reproaches was hidden a very real fear: She was twenty-eight. It didn't seem possible, but it was true. She was two years off thirty, and she had never lived. If it hadn't been for Hitler, she might have amounted to something. She might have been a Brenton, with a house at the Scar and a limousine. Whereas in New York, she was nothing but a drudge. If it weren't for Pete, wonderful, slightly crazy Pete, who looked like Marlon Brando and could vault rails on the sidewalk with one hand, she would go crazy. At least she had him to look forward to.

Howard had a nightcap ready when Esther got home.

'Tired?' he asked. She had been entertaining suppliers and talking facts and figures all night.

'A bit.' She looked at him curiously. 'Why?'

'I've got a problem,' Howard said. He told her of Catherine's visit and Stretton's difficulties.

'And I can't offer him a job because that would be too

176

obvious a favour. He'd turn it down, anyway. So what do I do?'

'I wonder,' Esther said slowly. 'I have to talk to Sammy, of course, but . . . we need to delegate now. So why don't we employ him to deal with administrative and personnel matters? We have fifty-two workers now, and soon there'll be more. And there's the buildings, the insurance, the maintenance – if I never have to hear about a faulty down-comer again, it'll be too soon. Besides, I need more time for my family, especially with the move. Stretton could be a gift from Heaven.'

17

March 1953

There was frost on the window-pane of the flat, and Frank
rubbed it away with a finger. Once the goings-on in the
London street had fascinated him. Now, after a year of
living there, it all appeared as unremarkable as any street
in any town. He looked at his watch: five to ten. He'd have
another cup of tea and then get going. As he drank he
riffled through the papers. Stalin's death had certainly
stirred the pot in Russia. Funny to think of old Joe gone –
although by all accounts he had been a bad bugger. Nikita
Kruschev, the new man, was an interesting figure: affable
to look at, of no great intelligence so they said, but shrewd.
He had purged the Ukraine of anti-Stalin elements after the
war, and been rewarded for it. Was he shrewd enough
now to see that co-operation with the West would pay?
Frank put aside the paper and stirred his tea.

If only there'd been a letter from Anne to relieve the
loneliness. Two pages of grumbles would have been better
than nothing. If he were at home now, he'd be down the
pit, probably, having a good crack and a laugh. There was
always someone with a joke in the pit. It was a wonder
where the jokes all came from. He was seized with nostal-
gia, until he shook himself out of it. He missed his wife
and he missed his mates, but he was doing what he'd
always wanted to do and he couldn't have everything. And
he'd made Anne proud. She had sat in the gallery that first
day, done up like a dog's dinner in her moleskin, with one
of Esther's hats on her head, looking like the cat who'd
swallowed the cream. But she'd only been to London once
since: on the day he'd made his maiden speech. He had
urged the Minister to reconsider a pit closure, and had

been conscious of Anne staring round the chamber, defying anyone to interrupt him. She was a wife and a half, and a good mother. Brave as a lion when she lost Joe and had to part with Stella and her bairn. Bairn . . . the boy would be eight now, growing up a little Yankee.

There was a sudden ring at the bell, and when he went to answer he found his daughter, Terry, on his doorstep.

'I've got a day off lectures, dad – so I came over on the off-chance that you might be free, too.'

Frank felt a surge of joy at the sight of her. They hardly ever saw one another in London because of his odd hours and her burden of study. But here she was, fresh as a daisy and looking at him with love. He was a lucky man. All thoughts of duty deserted him. If he had to choose between dry-as-dust speeches in the House, and a day on the river or in the park with Terry, there was no need even to think it over.

'You look lovely,' he said as they walked together to the bus-stop. 'You're not in love, are you?'

'Not me, dad,' she said, laughing at him. 'You're the only man in my life, and that's how I mean it to stay.'

'Ruth – how lovely!' Esther cried in surprise, as Ruth appeared in her office.

'I don't see you often enough,' Ruth said apologetically, taking the chair Esther had pulled out for her. While they waited for coffee to appear they made small talk but Esther could see there was something on Ruth's mind. Not the boy in Israel, surely? She would go to Naomi to talk about that; and, besides, Sammy would have been full of any developments on that front. But something was wrong. There were shadows around Ruth's eyes and the hands knotted in her lap were tense. 'All the same, she's beautiful,' Esther thought, seeing the high cheekbones, the dark eyes beneath thick, straight brows, the short hair that waved either side of a side parting. 'I hope she meets a good man one day. She deserves it.'

A clerk appeared with a tray of coffee and Esther poured it out. 'This is nice,' she said as she resumed her seat.

'Not so nice,' Ruth said, as she picked up her cup. 'I'm worried about Naomi, if you must know.'

'Naomi?' Esther said, surprised. 'Surely she's fine? She is running her home, her children . . .'

'But she has loss of sensation in the fingers of her right hand sometimes, and she rubs her eyes because her sight is blurred, and she complains of stiffness, or that a limb is tired.'

Esther shook her head. 'I've noticed her complaining of a stiffness, and a little blurring of her sight – but all these things are fleeting, Ruth. The next moment she's fine again.'

'That's true.' Ruth leaned forward clenching her hands together. 'But they worry me, even so.'

'You know your trouble?' Esther said. 'You know too much . . . you know these can be symptoms, so you look for them.'

'Perhaps I'm making mountains out of molehills. All the same, Esther, I want you to talk to Sammy, and get Naomi to see a specialist. If my fears are unfounded, let him say so.'

'I see,' Sammy said. 'Well, thank you for telling me. Yes, I'd like it in writing – at your convenience.'

The search for Esther's son, which had gone on for two years, had reached a dead-end. He put down the phone, glad he had not told her what he was doing. At least she wouldn't be disappointed. He was reaching for the mouthpiece of his dictaphone when Esther came into the room.

'Have you got a minute, Sammy?' She looked worried, and he sat up in his chair.

'An hour, for you. What's up?'

She sat down opposite him and drew a breath. 'I've got something to tell you, Sammy. I wish I didn't have to do this but I must. Ruth thinks Naomi is ill.'

Anne sighed and shifted in her seat. Around her the café seethed with gossiping shoppers, but the woman opposite was too wrapped up in her problem to notice.

'And after it rains, Anne, there's fungus on my skirting-board. I've said to Jackie, we'll be plodging one of these days if something isn't done.'

Anne had taken to holding court in Luigi's of late. She sat there, sipping a cup of frothy coffee and listening to petitions. A new house, a job, a prosecution, a matrimonial problem . . . people presented their cases, and, if she thought fit, Anne relayed them to Frank for his intervention.

The woman was still talking. 'I'm not kidding, Anne, we've had more carpets since we've been in that house than you've had hot dinners. Now, if we could get a house up the Parklea estate . . .'

'They're new houses.' Anne was affronted.

'Yes, well, it's about our turn. I've been down the council more times than enough. And then our lad said, "See Annie Maguire. Frank can swing it, if anybody can." And they worked on bank together when they were lads.'

'Frank will only step in if he thinks you're not getting a square deal, Betty. He doesn't do favours, not even for lads he worked with.'

'We're not asking favours, Anne, just our rights.'

When Anne got home, she put her carrier-bag on the table, took off her coat and scarf and made careful notes on Betty's plea. Frank would be home to do his constituency surgery at the week-end, and he'd need to know what was what.

While she set about preparing the vegetables, she reviewed what news she had for him, staring from the window as she did so. The yard was bleak, the back street outside rimmed with frost. Roll on springtime! She began to hum the song that everyone seemed to be singing nowadays – 'She wears red feathers' – and then went into a chorus of 'That doggie in the window', which was daft but catchy.

She had meant to write to Frank last night, but the Fletchers had invited her in to watch their new television set and the night had got lost. Everyone was talking about getting a TV set for the Queen's coronation, but if she got one it would be for a better reason than that. The Queen was a nice girl, but she was the very core of the class

181

system and therefore not to be encouraged. Not that there wasn't something to be said for quality folks. When the Brentons had had the Scar, they had never made an exhibition of themselves. Neither had Esther, when she went there. But the people who had it now, since Esther and Howard had moved to Sunderland, were loud and flashy, zooming through the village in a big American car, flaunting their money – and it was made out of scrap. He was a spiv, and his wife had a bleached head that looked like a dandelion clock. If there had to be gentry, it was better to have the real thing than fakes.

And now old Queen Mary was dead, gone in her sleep like the King, her son. She had been a character and no mistake, never changing her style – 'not in my whole lifetime,' Anne thought, astonished. The long dress, the draped toques, the silver curls, the long coat with the fur collar and a silver-topped cane . . . and a face like a battleship. But that was disrespectful, with the poor old lady dead and gone.

Anne looked at the clock. There was plenty of time to nip down to the church and light a candle for her: she'd been worth that. And the King had died worn-out with work and worry, no two ways about it.

Anne was suddenly seized with pangs of conscience. Frank bore a similar burden now, and she left him alone in London, to look after himself. And yet the thought of going up and down on the train terrified her. She was always afraid she'd forgotten something, and would be stranded in the far-off city without an essential, like a nighty or knickers. She scraped the peelings out of the dish and swilled the water away. If she hurried she could drop Frank a line now and pop it in the post on the way to church. And she'd tell him she'd changed her mind about the telephone. If he wanted it that much, they might as well have it.

Ruth put out an anguished hand. 'I wish it wasn't true, Sammy. But it is.'

Sammy Lansky looked suddenly grey, and his hands

182

trembled until he clamped them together. 'But she sings, she laughs – she is well, Ruth.'

'Part of the time, Sammy. At other times, all is *not* well.'

'Tell me the facts. Esther said you understood it all.'

'Well, I think it may be multiple sclerosis – disseminated sclerosis it's sometimes called. It destroys the protective sheaths which insulate the nerve fibres. We don't know the cause: it may be a virus or it may be the auto-immune mechanism. What's certain is that it's a disease of early adulthood. Naomi is twenty-seven. I don't want to go into all the symptoms now: there's time enough for that later. It's a progressive illness, but there can be remarkable periods of remission. And in some cases, too, the disease takes a milder form.'

'Is there someone we can take her to – an expert?' Sammy asked desperately.

'I'm looking into that, Sam. I'm going to do everything I can, you should know that.'

'Yes,' he said, 'I'm sorry, Ruthie. I know you'll do everything. I don't know what I'd do without you.'

'The same as you'll do with me,' Ruth said, trying to sound brisk. 'You'll cope and you'll cheer us all up. At the moment Naomi's fine. Later on, massage and physiotherapy may help her. I'll make sure any infections are promptly treated. I'm giving her vitamin supplements, but her diet's good so she should be OK there. The important thing is to keep up her morale.'

'She's frightened,' Sammy said and his voice trembled. 'I tried not to see it but it's true.'

'Yes, but she's also brave. Brave for you and for her children. I suggest you go to work now, as though everything is normal. That's what we should all do – act normally.'

Sammy stood up and went to the door, but Ruth saw that he was moving like a man in a dream, and she grieved for him. Sammy Lansky was not used to situations in which he was not in control. He would have to learn to accept – and that would not be easy, as she knew from her own bitter experience.

Sammy went in search of Esther, who had first broken the news to him. 'What am I going to do, Esther?'

'Cope, Sammy. Like you always do.'

'Her illness will get worse, Esther, slowly but surely.'

'You don't know that. I've heard of MS before, and it doesn't always get worse.' Esther wanted to put out her arms and comfort him, but she was uncertain. She had never seen him like this.

'I'm afraid, Esther. I don't think I could live without Naomi. And I can't think of anything to do for her. That's the worst part. Me, Sammy Lansky, tied hand and foot. Where does the fancy car, the money, the security take me now? Nowhere!' He threw up his hands in despair.

'Money means you can take care of her, Sammy. It means you can make sure she gets the best treatment, wherever it's available. You can use it to buy care for your children and help in the house. That's what you can do now: ease things for Naomi.'

'Yes,' he said, suddenly calmer. 'Perhaps we should move to a house on the flat, a bungalow? Except that it would break Papa's heart to leave our house.'

'*Plaplen!*' Esther said. 'Your father is a great brain, Sammy. Never underestimate him. He doesn't like change, that's true – until he sees it is necessary. Then he welcomes it. You tell him your need, and he'll agree all the way. We moved from the Scar, but living here in Sunderland has been good for both Howard and me. And it means I'm nearer to you and Naomi now. It's all working together for good, you'll see. Which doesn't mean that I don't realize the agony you're feeling: it just means I know you'll cope.'

Sammy straightened up and went to find his father.

'So,' Emmanuel Lansky said, when the news was broken, 'this is a great sorrow, Sammy.' His voice was muffled by the hanky he was using ostensibly to blow his nose but in reality to wipe his eyes. 'It's a *she'alah*.'

'Ruth says it may not be all bad . . . and they may make more discoveries about multiple sclerosis yet.'

'Scientists are clever,' Lansky said.

'So, we can hope, Papa?'

'Of course. And she is strong, the little one.'

They were beating the air, and they both knew it. They stayed silent, then, till a log fell in the grate, sending up a shower of sparks.

'I think we should move from here, to an easier house.'

Sammy was holding his breath, but he need not have done so. Esther was right.

'We should build, Samuel. We should design a house around the *girl tschik'l* with everything she needs. I have money . . .'

'Papa, I have more money than I know what to do with.'

'And all out of the £50 I gave to start you off,' his father said wonderingly.

It was a night for truth. 'I had £100, Papa. Esther gave me £50 too.'

'That Esther! It's the first time she goes behind my back!'

'And the last.'

'Yes. Esther does not betray – except when it is necessary to deal with a stubborn old man who doesn't recognize that his son is a business genius.' But the business genius had put his head in his hands to weep, and all his father could do was pat the downbent head and make sure his own tears did not fall upon his son.

18

June 1953

Anne lay contemplating the ceiling, relishing the memory of last night's visit to the cinema. What a picture *Niagara* had been: a murder story, with Joseph Cotton and a new star called Marilyn Monroe, who was the image of Stella. Niagara Falls had been breathtaking; the suspense unbearable. At one stage Anne had forgotten her ice-cream and it had melted in her hand and run down the front of her dress. Still, she couldn't lie here, today of all days. It was Coronation Day, and there was a street party to see to. Frank had turned down his invite to the Abbey in order to preside over Belgate, which was only right and proper when he was its Member of Parliament.

As she washed, she thought about the day ahead. Esther had stunned her the previous week with the gift of a television set. 'You've never let me give you anything, Anne . . . well, not anything much. You know you want to see the Coronation, and I can afford it, so *please* take it, from Howard and me.'

If she'd wanted a television, she'd've rented one, like everyone else was doing, Anne thought. Still, it was a kind gesture. As she went downstairs she was rolling up her sleeves: two hundred kids to cater for, and although she'd have plenty of helpers it would be up to her to keep things moving. She'd been able to do a lot on the phone, though, which was turning out to be more useful than she'd expected.

She was scalding tea when Frank came in. 'That's the tables up, pet. Lily Salter's fastening the paper tablecloths down with drawing-pins, and the cups are coming round from the church.'

She pushed his cup towards him, noticing as she did so how distinguished he looked with his greying temples and his good suit and tie. He was a credit to her, and no mistake – but her mouth curved at the memory of the curly-haired, shabby young lad he'd once been.

He came over to her. 'You've done a grand job . . . all that bunting, and the bells on the lamp-post, and the flags. You must've worked.' Anne tried not to show she was pleased, but he was not finished. 'You do wonders up here, Anne. God knows I miss you when I'm in London . . . if it wasn't for weekends I'd go potty . . . but it's you up here that really keeps the constituency together, and keeps me in touch. No, don't shake your head, I'm serious. There's only one Queen as far as I'm concerned, and she's right here.'

It was too much. Anne had to make a joke of it or cry.

'I'll likely get the crown jewels later on, will I? Now, get out of my way, and let's get on. In case you haven't noticed, Frank, I've got my entire family to cater for – bar our Theresa. Not to mention the whole of Belgate, or that's what it feels like. The government's given us all a pound of sugar and four ounces of cooking fat on top of the rations – a fine party we'd get out of that. It's a good job I've got my contacts or it'd be bread and scrape.'

'If all I hear's true Churchill didn't want the Coronation yet,' Frank said sombrely.

'Why not?' Anne's eyes had widened.

'He thinks we can't afford it – it's costing a million or so and we're on our uppers. According to the Whips he said 'We can't have a Coronation with the bailiffs in.' That's what they're saying he said, any road.'

'I'll bet he said it,' Anne said firmly. 'The Tories've always been killjoys. Thank God he didn't get his way, that's all I can say. Now, will you get out from under my feet and let me get on?'

Sammy Lansky had reacted favourably to Esther's suggestion that they employ Norman Stretton. Their offer to him was generous, and couched in flattering terms. Within weeks he had become indispensable to the company, and when Sammy learned the full extent of Naomi's illness he blessed the day that Stretton had come to help him bear the load.

This morning, almost at crack of dawn, they were inspecting Sammy's new house, rising now from a field at the foot of Tunstall, the hill that brooded over Sunderland. It was to be a long, low house, resembling the house on the Scar, but only one storey high.

'You should be in by the winter,' Stretton said as they climbed down from the scaffolding.

'Not till winter?' Sammy was aghast. 'It's only June now and we're almost up to the windows. And remember, money's no object. Whatever it costs, get the roof on quick.'

Stretton laughed. 'I know, but even after the roof goes on there's the first fixing – floors, door-frames, that sort of thing. The electrician will be in then, too. Then it's the plasterers. Second fixing – doors, skirting-boards, mouldings – then your plumbers come in. After that, it's decorating and measuring up. I'd say, the end of November. But meanwhile there's nothing to stop you ordering carpets and curtains, that sort of thing. Naomi will love that side of it.'

Sammy grinned. 'OK, you know best. I'm an impatient geezer, or so my womenfolk tell me. I should be grown out of it by now. It's just that we need this house so much.'

They walked back to the car. 'I'm off home for the Big Event,' Sammy said. 'I hope you are?'

'Yes.' Stretton was nodding. 'Yes, I'm off too. Can't miss the Coronation.'

But there was an air of resignation about him, a feeling of unease, that set Sammy's antennae quivering. He must remember to ask Esther if there was a mystery, as soon as she came back from London.

A thin drizzle was falling but nobody lining the Mall seemed to mind. Some of them had been there all night, under blankets with spirit-lamps to cheer them. A friendly policeman was proclaiming that at least 30,000 had slept out to secure their places, as Howard and Esther, with Beb between them and Pamela and Theresa Maguire bringing

188

up the rear, managed to find a place with a narrow view of the roadway, lined now with freshly cut red, white and blue flowers. Coronets, roses and banners were strung along the streets, and lions and unicorns perched on slender arches along the Mall.

'I'll lift you up when the time comes,' Howard had promised his son, but he had not bargained for the length or the splendour of a procession escorted by thousands of men at arms. It took nearly an hour to pass any given point, with marching men and women in every kind of uniform from the kilts of Scottish regiments to the battledress of the Home Guard and the green of the Women's Royal Army Corps. There were nine separate parts to the procession; the Lord Mayor; the Prime Minister; the overseas guests, among them the enormous Queen of Tonga, beaming widely as she defied the rain deluging her open carriage. Then came the various members of the royal family; and after them the Golden Coach, drawn by eight Windsor Greys in trappings of crimson and gold. With each special coach, like those of Churchill or the Queen Mother, a cheer went up that sent the London starlings spiralling in terror into the sky.

The Queen's coach had passed and Esther was about to ask what they should do when she felt movement behind her. She turned to see a group of young people pushing their way through the crowd. She was about to rebuke them, but Pamela was smiling broadly and Howard had doffed his hat to the girls. He turned to Esther. 'It's the Colvilles, darling – Lee's boys, and the twins, and Max Dunane's sons. Help me introduce everyone.'

Pamela was kissing the boys and laughing with them, but Terry had lowered her head. Esther moved closer to her, feeling protective towards her niece and conscious of how overwhelming the Dunanes and the Colvilles could be. 'Who are they?' Terry whispered, her eyes slanting towards the boys from under her lashes. Esther mouthed, 'Tell you later,' thinking as she did so what a pretty girl Terry had become; like Stella, but with more character, thank God. She leaned closer to whisper, seeing that Terry was still apprehensive, putting up a hand to wipe her rain-soaked hair from her face.

'Their mother was Pamela's mother's friend – well, she's the mother of some of them, the Colvilles. It's all a bit complicated.'

The Colville girls had noticed Terry now and were trying to be polite. 'It's terribly exciting, isn't it, and this is the place to be. Ma and Pa are in the Abbey, but Ma says you can't see a thing in there.'

Terry's cheeks had coloured but she nodded her head. 'Yes,' she said quietly, 'I expect you're right.' The red-headed Colville – Esther thought it was Cicely, but the girls were so alike it might have been Emma – smiled widely, obviously searching for something else to say. She was saved by a surge in the crowd that carried them off, waving their goodbyes.

The Lanskys were settled around the television set, the children on the hearth-rug, Emmanuel in his high-backed chair, Naomi in the easy chair opposite with Sammy at her side.

'Look at that,' Aaron said as the camera panned over the huge crowd. 'So many people!'

'Your Aunt Esther is in there somewhere,' Naomi said. 'We might even see her.'

'In a coach?' Cecelie's eyes were round.

'Maybe,' Sammy said portentously but Naomi chided him.

'Daddy! Don't tease her. She's in the crowd, *liebchen*, with Beb and his daddy and Pamela. They wanted to see it really happen, in London.'

'Why didn't we go to London?' Aaron sounded mildly cheated.

'We will all go there one day,' Sammy said, and was glad he did not have to meet anyone's eyes, for at that moment the Queen of Tonga rode on to the screen in her carriage, and everyone was mesmerized by the sight.

They had packed out Anne's front room, babies and children on the floor at the front, women sitting on chairs behind them, the men standing at the back, holding pint glasses in their hands and trying to look as though they did this sort of thing every day of their lives.

'It's a pity Queen Mary didn't live to see it,' someone said and there was a chorus of assent.

'Stiff as a poker she was, but a good'un.'

'Not as good as Queen Elizabeth,' Anne said stoutly.

'Which one?'

That was Angela being clever, and Anne gave her a black look before she replied: 'The Queen Mother, cleversides. She'll always be Queen to me . . . to anyone who was in the war.'

'She's lovely,' someone agreed. 'Do you think she'll marry again?'

'She could but she won't.' Anne was definite.

'I think she'll go back to Scotland,' Frank said. 'I hope she doesn't, but I think she will.'

'Sh, Frank, it's getting good now – there's the Golden Coach.' For Anne this was the stuff of fairy-tales. Not even Hollywood could match this glittering panoply, and with her house packed she felt like a Queen herself, mothering Belgate.

She looked around her, marvelling at what had come to pass. She was the wife of the most important man in Belgate, now that Howard and Esther were gone to Sunderland. And she had a phone and a telly, and a flat in London at her beck and call if she wanted it. And her latest acquisition, a two-tier cake-stand, was gracing the centre of the table just like the pictures in *Good Housekeeping* at the doctor's. More important, the cake that crowned it had a real egg in it.

Stella had made sure she would be at home for the great day. 'You won't budge me out on that day,' she told anyone who came within earshot. '*E il mio turno*, matey.' Someone, she thought it was Beatrice, had muttered something like '*troppo a letto*', or words to the effect that she spent too much time in bed, but she had not reacted. They were not a *simpatica* family but no one, *no one*, was stopping her from seeing her Queen crowned. God knows she had to listen to 'America the Beautiful' and 'The Star-Spangled

Banner' every time the clock struck, or so it seemed. Today the Brits were on top, and she was loving it. The film of the coronation had been processed aboard a fast plane so, given the time difference, she would see it on the same day as the rest of her family.

Even in the first rush of enthusiasm about living in America, Stella had felt British. She had not taken out naturalization papers, like some war-brides. Mostly they did it to avoid having to register every year as an alien, and for the sake of their children, but Stella had seen it as too big a step, especially as it necessitated exams and the study of American history. When Mario had suggested it, she had said: *'Va via*, chum. Me stand hand over heart "to pledge allegiance to the flag of the United States"? No way: I'm British, and proud of it.' In fact, as far as Stella could see, as long as she did not renounce her British nationality she had the best of both worlds.

So today she sat in a comfortable glow of patriotic fervour for the country of her birth, a good bottle of wine to hand. She watched the Golden Coach, and the guards, and the glittering pageantry, enthralled but unemotional.

It was the sound of rain drumming on the pavements that started her crying – for England, that far-off country where you could hear bird-song, and rain fell upon your face like a benediction. Suddenly she remembered the day she had first seen Rupert Brenton riding his horse like a Greek god. He had died defending his country – and now his son was growing up to run an ice-cream parlour in down-town New York. As she drank and thought about the unfairness of fate, Stella's sobs grew more and more uncontrolled, until the Dimambro women gathered round her like black crows, united in their concern.

'What's the matter, Estella?' '*Cara* Stella.' Someone – Raffaela – was whispering about pregnancy, as if that would account for everything.

'If I was at home now I'd be out there, dancing in the streets, having fun, getting drunk, going to a party,' Stella thought, and began to wail aloud.

But when her mother-in-law begged to know the cause of her distress she muttered brokenly, '*Mi manca mia madre*

. . . I miss my mother.' It didn't do to tell everyone everything.

The Brenton family sat around the huge Mount Street dining-table and toasted the new Queen, each of them remembering the clear, almost child-like voice: 'Through all my life and with all my heart, I shall strive to be worthy of your trust.'

'Long may she reign,' Howard said. 'We need a monarchy – at least I think so.'

'More and more people don't,' Ralph said. And then, 'I know, dad – we'd've done badly without them in the war!'

'It's true,' Esther said. 'You can mock, but they really did make a difference.'

'Don't start arguing, Ralph darling.' Pamela moved to cut off a potential disagreement. 'Not tonight, anyway. Aunt Lee had another bit of gossip . . .'

'She's a walking *News of the World*,' Noel said.

'Shame on you, Noel.' Esther couldn't resist a gibe. 'Fancy mentioning Aunt Lee in connection with such a common newspaper. Call her *The Times* or *The Telegraph* if you must . . . but *News of the World*? Never! What's the latest?'

'She says it was Queen Mary who spotted that the Queen was a Mountbatten. Apparently Dickie Mountbatten was boasting that it was the Mountbattens who ruled England now, and the old Queen was furious! She told Churchill, and he went through the roof, and told the Queen she was a Windsor, and that's why there was that statement in the spring, about her descendants being Windsors. And when Prince Philip heard it, he said they were treating him like "a bloody amoeba".'

'He's not in an easy position,' Howard said. 'More wine, anyone? Remember, he's lived out in the world, he's used to running his own life. I'm not sure he'll take kindly to being a "consort".'

'Don't be depressing tonight, darling,' Esther said. 'It was so lovely today. I hope they're all going to be happy ever after.'

'You are mushy, Esther,' Noel said kindly, smiling at his stepmother to soften the blow.

'I shall poison your porridge at breakfast,' Esther said and Pamela, wiping her mouth with her napkin, produced another rabbit from the hat.

'Take that back, Noel, and I'll tell you the biggest piece of gossip.'

'If it's about the royal family I'm not interested. Everyone's been on about them all day. If it's someone on TV, now . . .'

'Hush,' Esther said. 'What is it, Pammy? You're looking as though you might burst.'

'It's terribly romantic . . . I've always thought she was lovely and so much personality . . .'

'Who?'

It came as a chorus but Pamela, scenting power, raised her glass and sipped politely.

'I shall come round this table and throttle you, Pams, if you don't speak now,' Ralph said. 'Dad, make her spill it.'

'Ralph, when have I ever been able to make the women in this family do anything? Appeal to her better nature.'

'I would if she had one. Come on, Pam . . . and then we can go through and watch the TV.'

'No. You said I have no better nature so I'll prove you right. Come on, cousin Theresa, let's go upstairs and have some real conversation. And I might – just might – tell *you*.'

As the two girls went out of the room together, Esther couldn't resist a smile, thinking of Anne and all her tirades against the Brentons in the old days. And now Pamela and Terry were thicker than thieves and no one more pleased about it than Anne. Truly, the old order was changing.

19

July 1954

Anne gripped the first ration-book in both hands and twisted it until the paper gave and the whole thing was ripped in two. 'There,' she said with a sigh of satisfaction. 'Now I can really believe the war's over.' She reached for the next book and repeated the process, while Mary Quinnell looked on, smiling.

'I think I'll keep mine,' Mary said. 'Have them framed as a souvenir.'

Anne held a book aloft. 'Souvenir? I wouldn't give them house-room, Mary. When I think of the queuing, the effort, the bloody grovelling I've had to do in the last fourteen years – even when I had the points.'

'I never thought it would drag on this long,' Mary admitted. 'Think of everything that's happened since – I mean, your Stella on the other side of the world and David with BAOR. How is he, by the way?'

'Full of praise for the flaming Germans, Mary – that's how he is. "You should see them mending their war-torn cities, mam," he says. According to him, they're hard-working, church-going and hospitable. Oh, and none of them would hurt a fly. How they managed to gas all the Jews I do not know, seeing as they're all so delicate. And if it's not our David singing their praises, it's Vera Lynn on the wireless with her bloody "Auf Wiedersehn, sweetheart". If the world thinks the Germans have repented, Mary, the world's gone mad.'

'Well,' Mary said tolerantly, 'I expect they've seen the light. They can't all have been bad.'

'No?' Anne tore through the last ration-book and swept the pieces into her outstretched pinafore. 'If you ask me,' she said, as she shook the shreds into the fire, 'we should've atom-bombed the lot of them. I hate the Germans, Mary. And the Japs – but I can forgive them on account of them being heathens and knowing no better.' She glanced at the statue of the Virgin on its plinth on the sideboard. 'Germany's a Christian country. Years of civilization, and they did what they did. The sooner my David's out of there, the better.'

Mary could not resist a dig. 'What if he fraternizes, Anne? You might get yourself a nice *fraülein* for a daughter-in-law.'

Anne's snort of derision was a masterpiece. 'You won't get a rise out of me on that one, Mary. No son of mine'd bring a German home. He'd have more sense – and he'd know I'd kill him if he did.'

Stella's relationship with Pete had ended in acrimony, increasing her discontent with life. And then, returning from a visit to see Joan Crawford at a movie theatre, she had encountered Bud, standing by the door to a basement club. Their eyes had met, his careless at first, and then alive with interest.

'Who do you think you're looking at?' Stella had said aggressively, and, as usual when she set her lip up, it worked like a charm.

He had driven her home in a black Packard with opaque windows. It belonged to his boss, the mysterious Mr Schultz, and smelled of expensive cigars. 'Do you get on with him?' she asked.

'He's a cocksucker,' Bud said cheerfully. 'But he pays good.'

'What do you do for him?' Stella had persisted, but all Bud would answer was, 'Cover his ass.'

As often as she could get away, Stella had rung Bud and then taken the streetcar all the way across town to the West 23rd St ferryslip, well out of the areas of the Dimambro ice-cream parlours. And Bud was always waiting, leaping from the car to fold her into her seat for all the world as if she were royalty. After that they would go to one of Mr Schultz's hotels and Bud would nod to the man at the desk and be handed a key to a room. And sometimes, if Bud couldn't wait, they did it in the back seat of the car.

But her liaison with Bud, at first such a source of excitement, was becoming a little scary. Where did he get his money? Why did he constantly look over his shoulder, as if he expected to be shadowed? Was he a *mascalzone* . . . or something worse? He was avid for sex, which did not displease Stella, but as time went on she became increasingly resentful of his off-hand treatment of her. 'So long, kid,' he would say, easing into his pants with one hand and donning his grey trilby with the other. His high white collar and largely knotted tie were his trade-mark, and the heavy gold rings on almost every finger were an exotic touch that thrilled her. But she was growing tired of the hotel rooms or the back seats of limos. And when she plucked up courage to ask about the future, his answer was 'What's a future?' Fed-up as she was with faithful, spaniel-eyed Mario, the faint aura of the gangster that had attracted her to Bud in the first place was giving way to a distinct whiff of trouble.

The park was lush and green now, the lake like a mill pond, with boats bobbing here and there. 'I like the Serpentine,' Pamela Brenton said. She had volunteered to show London to Gerard Maguire, and she was taking her job seriously.

He looked up at the sky as he walked. 'There's another plane,' he said.

'They come over all the time,' Pamela grinned. 'If you weren't such a hick, you'd take no notice of them.'

'Well, we can't all be sophisticated cosmopolitans,' Gerard said. 'Some of us have to toil up there so that you lot can swan around down here.'

'Not me, mate. I'm not remotely swan-like. I work like a slave, studying law, and as soon as I can I'm coming north. I have to endure a lot of archaic and ridiculous rituals because it's the only way to learn my trade, but as soon as I'm a qualified barrister I'm off.'

'Don't you ever feel like rebelling?' Gerard asked.

'Not really. You wouldn't be much good in court if you

couldn't channel your frustration. There's no point in arguing with a blinkered judge, for instance. I've watched enough cases to know that. You smile and say "Yes, your honour" and "No, your honour" until you can get in front of a jury, and then you let them have it with your arguments.'

'So you're going to secure justice single-handed?' he said mockingly.

'No,' Pamela said carefully. 'But I'm going to try and make things more just.'

'You can't do that in a court-room – you need legislation.' Gerard had turned to gaze out across the lake, and they came to a halt, side by side.

'Then I'll just have to get myself into Parliament and help pass the laws.'

'Wow,' he said, mocking once more. 'Bessie Braddock Brenton, no less. The Tories had better watch out.' But then, thinking he had been mean, he smiled at her. 'You just might do it, you know. I hope you do.'

'Why do you think Labour lost power?' Pamela asked. 'I know some of the reasons: too many controls, the after-effects of war. But you go into things so deeply – what do you think?'

He considered for a while before he spoke. 'The US weren't as forthcoming as they might have been. God knows they were shelling out all round – a sixth of their budget went on overseas aid – but they offered us a loan with too many strings. Our reserves were running out, and Attlee had to take what deal he could get. So our standard of living went down, compared to what Attlee had promised. Add to that the fact that they got the costings of the National Health Service wrong – what did Bevan say? He was appalled by the ceaseless cascade of medicine pouring down British throats? And then a Cold War for which no one had budgeted, *and* a war in Korea. Add to that spiralling taxes – well?'

'It's a wonder Labour held on as long as they did,' Pamela agreed. 'Still, they'll have their chance again. I mean to make sure of it.'

Gerard shook his head. 'You're not supposed to be a socialist, you were born a Tory.'

'You can't be born to a political party,' Pamela said

dogmatically. 'You choose your politics. Don't tell me you're a socialist just because your parents are? How weak!'

'*You* could tell *my* mother you were voting Tory?' he asked quizzically.

'No.' Pamela smiled at the prospect. 'No, I'll grant you it wouldn't be easy. But that's what I love about dad: he's a true-blue Tory, but I've always felt free. And I do so hate the silly rules of class – like this latest tomfoolery about "lavatory paper" being U, and therefore proper; but "toilet-paper" is non-U and therefore common. "Rich" is U, "wealthy" is non-U –'

'"Spectacles" are in and "glasses" are out,' Gerard contributed. '"Wireless" U, "radio" non-U.'

'And don't forget "pudding" and "sweet",' Pamela said.

'"Napkin" and "serviette"?' Which one is it that makes me posh?'

Pamela threw up her hands. 'Buggered if I can remember. And it's all so pointless, when there are more than four million people in this country without a plumbed in bath, thousands without a lavatory, and more than half a million without running water.'

Gerard whistled. 'The lady knows her facts.'

'Yes, I do,' Pamela said briskly. 'Now, what else do you want to see? You've only got two days.'

Ruth removed her glasses and polished them carefully before replacing them and going back to Nathan's letter. '*You would like Rebecca. She was born and raised in Elkosh, which is a small village in Galilee. Her family came from Kurdestan and can scarcely read and write, but Rebecca is bright and will go far. In some ways she reminds me of you – such intelligence and a pretty face –*'

Ruth had been expecting this but still cold fear gripped her. She folded the letter, trying hard to be glad for Nathan. He would marry the girl, probably, and be blessed with children. He didn't actually mention love for Rebecca, who was a fellow-worker in the kibbutz, but no doubt it would come with time.

'Ruth – is that you?' Emmanuel Lansky stood in the

doorway and she saw, with a pang, how frail he was, silhouetted now against the sunshine.

'Papa, come and sit down. Would you like some tea?' She took his arm and helped him lower himself into a chair.

'No thank you, *liebchen*. But if you have time to sit and talk – now, that's a feast.'

'Of course I have.' She sat on a stool at his knee and propped her chin on her hands. 'What do we talk about?'

'Holidays,' Emmanuel said promptly. 'It's time you saw the world.'

'I can't go on holiday, Papa.' Ruth was shocked at the suggestion. 'Not while Naomi needs me.' She couldn't add that she couldn't bear to leave him either, not without telling him how much he had aged.

Lansky tut-tutted. 'We're talking of holidays, Ruth, not emigration. For a week or two, we could manage. And you could see – where would you like to see?'

'Oh, I don't know, Papa. I've seen Scotland and England.'

'Ah,' Lansky said, with his old twinkle, 'what else is left, then?'

'Don't tease me,' she said, laying her head against his hand. 'And don't send me away. I'm happy here, Papa Lansky. And I'll never, ever leave.'

20

April 1955

'You can go in now, Mr Lansky. Your father's quite comfortable.' The nurse looked tired in the grey morning light, and the thick navy cardigan over her white uniform dress could not stop her shivering as they stood outside his father's room.

'You're cold,' Sammy said, instinctively putting a hand to the radiator. It was red hot.

'No,' she said, smiling, 'I'm tired, that's all. Your father's probably going to sleep for a while, and Nurse Pilgrim should be here soon. I'll lie down then. I'll pop to the kitchen and have a cup of tea while you're with your father, but shout straight away if I'm needed.'

Emmanuel Lansky had been ailing for six months, and bedfast for seven weeks, but Sammy could not come to terms with the fact that he was going to lose his father. 'I am not old enough,' his heart told him. 'I need him, I need to know there is a roof on my family. I can make the decisions, earn the money, but always I need to know he is there. God, don't do this to me.' But his head told him that what was happening was inevitable, and as his father grew frailer, Sammy did what he could do to make the old man's last days more comfortable, engaging nurses and specialists and filling the bedroom with devices designed to make life easier.

Patrick Quinnell was still the one medically qualified face Lansky welcomed at his bedside, and he had been a tower of strength to the family. Naomi's illness was at present in remission, and for this Sammy thanked God several times a day. He also gave thanks for his partnership with Esther Brenton. 'I'm not you, Sammy,' she told him when his father's condition grew worse. 'But I'm not half bad at running things, and I'll scream fast enough if there's trouble. You do what you need to do, and leave this ramshackle business of ours to me.'

The 'ramshackle business' was prospering. They had seven self-service stores now, in Middlesborough, Sunderland and Durham, each with cooked-meat counters and produce sections. The old established parts of their business continued to prosper, and the furniture-manufacturing project went from strength to strength.

So Esther, with Howard's active co-operation, shouldered more than her share of responsibility for the time being, and Sammy spent the last precious weeks with his father.

Today he slipped quietly into the room but the figure in the bed was still alert.

'Samuel?'

'Yes, Papa?' He looked down at the man, once so large, now a small, almost fragile figure.

'Is it a nice day?'

'Spring, Papa. A little cold, but there's some sunshine, and all Naomi's bulbs are through. Next week . . .' He thought his voice was going to break, and cleared his throat. 'Next week we'll wrap you up and get you out into the fresh air. You need building up.'

'Sammy, sit down here.'

He sat obediently on the edge of the bed and reached for his father's hand. 'What is it now? So you're going to give me a lecture?'

But whatever his father had wanted to say, he had forgotten it. There was silence for a moment and then the old man spoke again. 'What's in the papers this morning?'

'There are no papers, Papa, remember? The strike's been on for almost two weeks now. But I heard the news on the radio, and nothing bad has happened . . . except a train crash in Mexico, near Guadalajara. And there's going to be a new football competition, a European cup.'

'So, how does my grandson feel about this?'

'You know Aaron and football, Papa. He is agog.'

There was no answer and he thought the old man slept, but after a while the hand in his moved a little.

'I met your mother in Paris, Samuel.'

'I know, Papa.'

'Is it April?'

'Yes, Papa. April the 5th.'

'The blossom will be out in Paris.' A longer silence, and then the slow, deeper breathing that meant sleep.

'Darling, you must be worn out!' Esther hurried down the stairs to the hall, where Pamela was setting down the last of her suitcases and unbuttoning the neck of her coat.

'No, I like the sleeper, and getting out at the station early in the morning. I slept like a log, and they woke me with tea and bikkies. Very nice. I've got heaps to tell you. Any word from Huddle and Co?'

'Yes, Daddy spoke with them yesterday. They're looking forward to seeing you, but you're not to rush.'

Pamela was hoping to practise law in Newcastle, in the chambers of Kenneth Huddle, a leading northern QC, and her meeting with them was vital.

They went into the kitchen when Pamela had discarded her coat. She settled at the table and Esther moved about, preparing breakfast.

'Daddy'll be down in a moment – he's shaving. What will you have? Eggs? Cereal? Or there's bacon . . .'

'Ugh, nothing fried. I'm getting fat.'

Esther looked at her step-daughter. She was more than ever like Diana now, the Diana of thirty years ago driving up to the new house at the Scar. Dark curls framed her face and the well-lashed eyes were alive with curiosity and love of life.

'You're perfect as you are. I'm going to poach you an egg.'

'With soldiers?'

'A battalion of them if that's what you want.'

'OK. Any news from the boys? Where's Beb?'

'Probably still asleep. He's reached the age of indolence now – Daddy will have to drag him from under the covers before he comes down.'

'I can't believe he's eight. Will you send him away to school later on?'

'Not if I can help it. Your father skirts around the subject from time to time, but I remember those ghastly trips we used to make, to see the older boys.' She turned from the stove. 'Actually, it's quite difficult. I *want* to do what's best for Beb . . . I just can't bring myself to believe that going away from your family *is* best for you. You did it: what do you think? I'd really like to know.'

'Hmm . . . it's difficult. I can't honestly say I was unhappy when I was away at school, and they did help keep your nose to the grindstone. But the thought of poor little Beb being packed off is awful! Besides, they're a bastion of class distinction.'

At that moment poor little Beb came into the kitchen with his father, and there was a welter of greetings and kisses. Pamela stood back and surveyed her half-brother.

'What d'you mean by sprouting up like that? You were a shrimp when I went away last time and you're *huge* now. Too much feeding! All that will stop when I'm home.'

'No, it won't,' Beb said confidently. 'You spoil me more than mum.'

'Have you heard that Churchill has finally resigned?' Howard asked as they ate breakfast. 'Anthony Eden takes over, of course. But Churchill isn't leaving the Commons, he'll stay on as a backbencher. Some backbencher! I suppose he had to go . . .' There was regret in Howard's voice as he remembered his own days in the House in the dark years of war.

'I only hope he hasn't kept Eden waiting too long,' Esther said. 'He's been crown prince for such a long time, I wonder if he'll have spent himself. And Churchill won't be an easy act to follow.'

'How's all the family?' asked Pamela, reaching for the honey. 'I hear Lanver has opened yet *another* store. I think you've married a tycoon, daddy.'

'Lanver goes from strength to strength,' Howard agreed. 'And Norman Stretton is a great help, because Esther is running the whole show while old Lansky is so ill.'

'It's not serious, is it?' Pamela asked.

'I'm afraid so,' Esther replied. 'Still, we've got good news about the boys.'

'Tell me,' Pamela said eagerly.

'Ralph is going to Christie's, to their Fine Art department, and Noel is in Compiègne. But they're coming home soon, to see you.'

'I had dinner with Uncle Frank one night,' Pamela said, when the plates had been cleared away.

'What did he have to say?' Howard asked.

'Well, I did most of the talking, I seem to remember. But he was super, as usual. We talked politics.' She laid down her knife and fork. 'Actually, I hope this won't upset either of you – but I'm thinking of joining the Labour Party!'

Frank had heard the news of Churchill's resignation on the terrace of the House of Commons. He liked to stand there, watching traffic in the mighty waterway of the Thames, thinking of the river running to the sea, remembering the tides at Belgate: the black edge of coal dust on the beach, the cry of sea-birds, the wind blowing in from the sea.

He had turned as a fellow Member came through the grey stone doorway and moved towards him. 'The PM's resigned. There's going to be a smooth hand-over to Eden, but after that there'll have to be a general election. So – are you ready for the fray? We'll be going for the Tories over cost of living, of course, and the H-bomb. I hope to God the newspaper strike lasts: an election without the Tory press at our throats – what a prospect!'

'As long as there's not another deadlock. The elections in '50 and '51 were stalemates. Now the Tories are asking for a fresh mandate . . . we'll see if they get it.'

Labour had won the general election of February 1950 but it was the closest result for a hundred years. The following year, in October 1951, power had passed to the Tories also with a slender majority. Anthony Eden would want to consolidate his position with a snap election before the economic climate worsened.

'Do you think Eden will win?' Frank asked. The man shrugged.

'I don't know. Probably. When I think how we gained power in '45, on the crest of a wave, I could weep. We were going to build Jerusalem – I told myself that again and again during the war. And for a while we almost did transform this country. Now we've lost all our momentum. The middle class resists change for the sake of resisting, and our own class isn't as keen on social justice as we believed. Give everybody a house and a job, I thought, and we'll be so bloody happy we won't need electricity – we'll be lit up anyway. Now I see it isn't governments who change things: only society can do that.'

'Cheer up,' Frank said. 'At least we'll all be at home for a week or two, if Eden calls an election. And we'll hardly be back again before it will be the summer recess.'

'You're a proper politician now, Frank – bloody work-shy!'

'It gets us all in the end,' Frank said, but as he turned back to the river he wondered. Was he tired of Westminster? During the election campaign there had been moments when he had imagined no man would ever give up power unless he had to. Now he was not so sure. Politics, like any other job, had its share of tedium and frustration. The salary was amazing, but sometimes he thought longingly of the pit.

Anne finished her prayers and hoisted herself back into the pew. She would have a few minutes peace before she went back to the hurly-burly. There was always someone on at her now, wanting this, wanting that – wanting miracles, most of them. It was an MP's briefcase Frank had, not a magic wand; but when she told them that they looked scandalized.

The church was lovely today, with the sunlight coming in at the windows and spring flowers at the altar. She had given thanks to God for spring, which was only right. She had prayed for Sammy Lansky too: he was a feeling man and would miss his father, especially when his wife had a terrible disease.

She was suddenly filled with gratitude for her own good fortune and a terror that she had taken it too much for granted that sent her back on to her knees.

'Please God, take care of Frank and our Gerard. Keep Stella safe and good. I wish she wasn't so far away but if it's your will, Lord, may your will prevail.' A picture of

Stella formed in Anne's mind. She would be even smarter now, with all that Yankee gloss. Theresa had her looks too: stunning. 'My features, Frank's colouring,' Anne thought with satisfaction. If only Theresa wasn't so far away . . . but you had to move to get on if you had her brains. Who'd've thought her family'd have someone working in a publisher's?

Anne levered herself up again and stepped out of the pew. She bobbed to the altar, and turned for the door, pausing at the feet of St Teresa to say a prayer especially for her daughter, who had been named for that particular saint after all. Thank God she was living near her father, and never made mention of men. London could be a cesspool if you didn't know your way around.

She walked back home, seeing the welcome signs of spring here and there – buds on trees, daffodils poking through railings. There was that indefinable something in the air that meant the winter was over. She let herself into the house, her mouth already watering at the prospect of a cup of tea, bending to retrieve the post from the mat as she did so.

There were four letters for Frank and one addressed to her, a rare occurrence. It bore a US stamp and had come by airmail, but the large, round handwriting was strange to her. She sat down at the kitchen table and opened it up.

'Dear Grandma.' The words sprang out at her. 'Dear Grandma.' She had to turn the page to convince herself of what she already knew. The signature was there: 'Tony'.

She put the letter aside, unread, and went to fill the kettle, her heart hammering against her ribs. He had not forgotten her! The little baby she had mothered and loved had not forgotten her. It would be no thanks to Stella, but what did that matter? He had written to her, his grandma. When the tea was brewed she sat down and devoured the letter – again and again.

Esther was with Norman Stretton, finalizing arrangements for opening a furniture-retail outlet, when Sammy telephoned. 'Patrick is here, Esther, and he says it's only a matter of hours now. So, I won't be coming in. Can you . . .?'

But she was already reaching for her bag and gloves. 'I'm coming, Sammy. I'll be there in twenty minutes.'

As she drove towards Tunstall Hill, Esther's heart was heavy. Thirty years . . . more, thirty-three years . . . since she had thrown herself on Papa Lansky's mercy, and never once had he let her down. She felt an almost unbearable sadness that such a life was coming to a close. But by the time she reached the house, she was outwardly calm: the least she could do for such a friend was to be steadfast at the end.

She joined Sammy at the foot of his father's bed and smiled what reassurance she could. 'Do you want to be alone with him?' she whispered. The old Jew appeared to be sleeping now, but his life was ebbing away.

'No,' Sammy said. 'Don't go.'

They sat on for a while, and then Ruth came into the room. Her face was calm but her eyes, behind her spectacles, were swollen.

'Does Naomi want to come in?' Sammy asked. Ruth shook her head.

'She's decided to stay with the children. We think that's best.'

'It is good that he's dying now, I think,' Sammy said suddenly, and his tone was bitter. 'It's better that he should not see the future.'

Ruth was shocked into silence but Esther spoke out. 'Wrong, Sammy. If you mean what I think you mean, you're wrong. Your father never shirked anything. He hated some things and feared others, but he accepted everything, and he rose above it.'

Sammy glared at her for a second, and then he reached for the thin hand that lay on the coverlet. Ruth went to the other side and did the same. Esther stood at the foot of the bed and watched the great features relax and slip into a semblance of sleep, the lips seeming to smile above the grey beard.

'He's gone,' Ruth said. '*Baruch hashem.*'

*

'Any news?' Catherine asked.

'No.' Stretton's tone was sombre. 'Sammy hasn't been in all day, and Esther went off to be with him at mid-morning. She said it was only a matter of time.'

Catherine had brought salad with her. Now she moved around the kitchen, rinsing, shaking, slicing, making supper. 'What did you think about Churchill going?' She was putting cutlery out as he spoke, her movements precise and her voice calm, but inside she was far from tranquil. Today she had seen a young girl die, victim of a road accident, and it had set her thinking about the futility of her own position. She loved Norman Stretton with all her heart and knew he loved her. But she could see little or no hope of their situation ever changing. They would go on like this, friends and companions – but there would be no commitment, no sex, no children, no chance to face the world and say 'We two are one.' Now she had to decide whether half-a-life with him was better than a life without him, which might be fulfilled and happy but equally might be no life at all. But she had known and enjoyed sexual fulfilment during the war, when everyone lived for the day. Now, she wanted it more than ever, but Norman's notion of honour stood in the way.

'It's sad,' she said but there was something in her voice that told him her mind was not on Churchill.

'What's up?' he said sympathetically and she let her resolve to stay calm melt away.

'Why d'you ask?'

'Because I know you, Catherine.' He had come to stand behind her, putting his arms around her, holding her close, his chin resting on her head. 'Something's wrong. Tell me. Perhaps I can help?'

'We had a death today. A seventeen-year-old girl. I thought we'd save her, but we couldn't. It made me think.'

'What about?' He had moved her round to face him, so that his cheek rested against her hair, her mouth against his shoulder, and somehow it was easier to speak into the tweed of his jacket.

'About us. About what I want, and how short life is, and what is slipping away from us because – because you don't have courage.'

209

She felt him grow tense, then, and wondered if she had gone too far. There was silence for a moment and then he spoke. 'It's not want of courage, Catherine, it's the love I feel for you. I don't want to give you second-best. Can't you understand that?'

'Yes,' she said, suddenly fierce. 'I can understand unselfish love, all right: it's the best kind there is. But you're a fool, Norman Stretton, if you see what we could have as second best. A fool – and that's what I can't and won't forgive you!'

Suddenly he was laughing, leaving her wide-eyed and puzzled. She resembled her mother in looks, he thought, but not in stolid temperament. He clasped her to him, smelling the sweetness of her skin and hair, the faint odour of antiseptic that came with her work. 'If you still want me,' he said at last, 'ancient, damaged goods that I am – you can have me.'

'My God,' Catherine said, and her voice was half a scream. 'My God, I never thought you'd say it!'

Stella glanced sideways at Bud. He was staring straight ahead, his gloved hands clutching the wheel of the black Packard, and there was an air almost of menace about him. She huddled down in her seat, looking out at the brilliantly lit sidewalks. She had not enjoyed tonight. They had gone to a downtown bar and had sat almost in silence. Every time Stella tried to make conversation, she had only received a grunt in reply – until she had protested: 'You don't deserve a girl, Bud, treating me like that.'

He had shrugged. 'So go. Hey, women are like lice, kid. If one leaps off you, another leaps on.' She had put out a hand and struck his arm to remonstrate, but he had not even noticed. Two men had come in then, pushing their hats to the backs of their heads, looking around insolently before crossing to the bar. One bought and paid for drinks, the other leaned on his elbow, surveying the room. He glanced over Stella and then his gaze returned to her.

'He's staring at me,' Stella said, hoping to arouse a spark of jealousy. In the distance the horns were wailing blues music, so loud that she had to lean close to hear his reply.

'Maybe he thinks you have class . . . the English thing.'

Stella would have preened but she wanted more. 'You ought to tell him to stop.'

'They're cops,' he said. 'Leave it.'

'How d'you know?' she asked, curious.

'I know.'

'How?' she persisted.

'God, you're dumb,' Bud had said. 'You got a cute face and legs like the Empire State, but you can't take a telling.' She had noticed his tenseness then, a stillness like a cat.

'I'm getting out of here,' she said but when she would have risen he put out a hand and pinned her arm to the table. She had winced but stayed still, suddenly scared. And then the cops had left the bar, and after a while Bud had shrugged into his black overcoat and they had left, too.

'Where are we going?' she asked now, noticing that the neighbourhood was unfamiliar.

'Somewheres.' They turned a corner and suddenly the car was drawing to a halt. 'Stay here,' Bud said, and opened his door.

'Why, where are you going?' When he had picked her up she had wanted and expected sex but he had said he had no rubbers. She looked to see if there was a drugstore, but the street was dark, only brownstone houses with lighted doorbells and nameplates.

'Stay here,' he said again, fiercely. 'And shut it!'

He closed the door carefully, and she saw him reach inside his coat as though he was checking something inside his jacket. He settled his hat on his head then and moved to one of the doors, reaching to press the bell. She watched, fascinated, as the door opened, but the occupant stayed hidden, and after a moment Bud stepped inside. There was a pause, the door remaining ajar, the street quiet, and then she heard a sudden dull crumping sound, and Bud was re-emerging, moving fast, back to the car and into his seat, slamming the car door.

'What was that?' she said as the car leapt forward and lurched round the corner.

'What?'

'That noise?'

211

'I didn't hear no noise.' She moved in her seat and reached to pat his chest, until she felt the hard bulk that was a gun in a shoulder-holster.

'My God,' she said and then again, 'My God!'

'The man was a scumbag,' Bud said, still staring at the road ahead. 'And you and I have been in the Plaza Hotel on East and 25th for the last two hours.'

He was smiling at her now, as though enjoying a joke, but Stella felt a sudden wetness between her legs and something rising in her throat that tasted like vomit but was really fear.

21

October 1955

The newspapers were full of Princess Margaret's statement about her decision not to marry the divorced Captain Peter Townsend. 'I would like it to be known that I have decided not to marry Group Captain Peter Townsend. I have been aware that subject to renouncing my rights of succession it might have been possible for me to contract a civil marriage, but mindful of the Church's teaching that Christian marriage is indissoluble and conscious of my duty to the Commonwealth, I have resolved to put these considerations above all others.'

'She's done right,' Anne answered. 'All the same – he *is* a war hero, and decorated! It says here that he's too distressed to make a statement. Even though she's a Protestant, she's done the right thing.'

'Very likely,' Frank said. 'Now, if you could turn your attention to someone who *is* getting married, and give my suit a press . . .'

'They were glad you could get up from London today,' Anne said, as the iron slid back and forth. 'It's not everyone that has an MP at their wedding.'

'Catherine *is* me niece, Anne. I was hardly likely to stop away.'

'Well, you know what I mean. I'm sorry for your Mary – her only daughter marrying a man old enough to be her father.'

'He's a good man. I never had a wrong word for Norman Stretton.'

Anne pursed her lips, sighing for the days when there had been oppressive coal-owners, and she was not related to them, and you had been able to have a bloody good

213

grumble. Now people were getting so mixed in together, you didn't know who your enemies were. 'There,' she said. 'Don't put it on till it cools, or it'll crease all over again.'

'Any tea?' Frank asked hopefully.

'I suppose that means you want fresh making. Since you were made an MP you want waiting on hand and foot. If this is what you're like in opposition, God help us when you're the government.'

'Fat chance of that, pet, now the Tories are back with a bigger majority.'

'I hope I'm not going to miss anything good on the telly,' Anne said, anxiously scanning the paper as she waited for the kettle to boil. 'You know, Frank – television's killing the cinema. Half-empty, the Roxy is now. And if it's not a good picture I sit there thinking I could be in me own home watching something good for nothing.'

'What's a good picture?'

'One with a star in. Grace Kelly, or Marilyn Monroe. I never see her but I think of our Stella, Frank. We didn't bring her up right. I get more about the bairns from Mario's letters and photos than I do from hers. And whenever I send something for Anna-Maria, it's him who's got the thank-you letter in the post. We spoiled Stella. But Mario's a good lad. He's got her to settle down, and she's made a gentleman of her son. Tony's letters are lovely.'

For a moment Frank wondered if he should try to bring his wife back to reality about Stella being settled, but in the end he decided against it. She had a smile on her face and they were going to a wedding. Better leave well alone.

'Poor Princess Margaret,' Naomi said. She was sitting in a chair by the window, looking out over the garden while Sammy fastened her shoes for her. 'Thank you, darling.' She had poor co-ordination of her hand movements at the moment, but her face was animated at the thought of Catherine and Norman's wedding. 'So much happiness for some people, none for others.'

'Don't you worry too much about what you read in the newspapers, *liebchen*.' Sammy bent to kiss the crown of her

214

head, holding her face between gentle hands. 'They tell you anything.'

'But Princess Margaret looks so sad, Sammy. That isn't faked.' And indeed the newspaper picture of the Princess, seen through the window of a speeding car, was a vision of despair.

'I'm sorry for that,' Sammy said firmly, 'but it's not our affair. Pray for her . . . but in this house it's time we put sadness behind us.'

The Hebrew word for funeral is *levrayah*, which means accompanying the dead from the moment life expires until the burial, when the body returns to the earth from which it came. Sammy had spent every possible moment with his father until the old Jew was laid to rest in a simple shroud, for in Jewish law all are equal in death. But since then he had concentrated on his young wife, doing everything he could to make her smile. Now, Sammy looked at her and smiled as she sought his approval.

'Do you like my dress? Esther brought me five to choose from, on approval.'

'Do I like the dress? The dress is beautiful, and when my princess is wearing it . . . well! The bride should compete – *folg mir a gang!*'

'You look lovely,' Mary said simply. Catherine sat at her dressing-table, ready now except for the dress and head-dress, looking at her mother through the mirror.

'Cheer up, mam, I know what I'm doing. I love Norman. He's what I want, and it made me forceful until I got him. You worry about us having children – well, if they come along, they'll be icing, but he's the cake. I wish you could see that. I really am very happy, you know.'

There was such conviction in Catherine's voice that Mary's face lightened.

'Don't think we don't like Norman. He's a splendid man . . .'

'But he's over fifty, and he's not a northerner! Mam, it's 1955: I'm thirty-four and I've seen the outside world. Be honest – at my age you'd never been beyond the Cleveland Hills, had you?'

'Yes, I had . . . I'd been to Scarborough!'

'Oh no, the other side of the world! We've changed, mam. Hitler changed us – and the TV. There's no such thing as the boy next door now.'

Catherine went to the window where her spray of pink roses and stephanotis lay. 'Look!' In the heart of the bouquet two pansies nestled.

'Patrick picked them for me this morning. He knew the heart's ease meant a lot to you, because of my dad planting them for you all those years ago – and he thought I'd like to carry them today.'

For a moment Mary had to struggle to compose herself. 'Nice,' she said. 'Very nice.' And then they were taking down the ivory-coloured dress from where it hung on the front of the wardrobe, and she was slipping it over her daughter's head.

'All right?' Catherine asked when it was settled, and Mary had fastened the buttons at the back.

'Lovely! Mind, we'll never hear the last from your Aunt Anne that she didn't get to make your dress.'

'Dress-making's done now, mam – unless you go to Dior or someone.'

'I can remember when there was no dress shops – well, hardly any. Now there's C & A and Marks & Spencer . . .'

'And Dorothy Perkins and Etam. It's the rise of the ready-to-wear. There was an article about it in *Vogue* a while ago.'

'We're lowering our standards, though,' Mary said. 'I would no more have gone out once without a hat and gloves . . .'

'. . . and a handbag and an umbrella – I know. Now, I'm ready. Let's get you sorted out.'

'Nervous?' Howard asked, handing Stretton a glass of wine.

'Petrified. Is that par for the course?'

'Of course . . . however many times you do it!'

'Once will be quite enough for me, thank you. I never thought I'd do it, not once I got to forty.'

'But you'd reckoned without Catherine? I've watched

216

her grow up, and she's as steady as a rock. Once, when they were children playing together, I thought she and Rupert might become fond of one another. But they went their separate ways.'

'Do you often think of Rupert? Forgive me for asking, but when you mentioned him just now you half-smiled . . . as though it was pleasant to remember.'

'It is. And I do think of him – not every day, but something will happen, or I'll see something, and it all comes back. If Rupert had had a child . . . He wrote to me, just before he was killed, saying he had something to tell me, something that had made him very happy; and I wondered then if he and Catherine had met up again. But they hadn't. It was probably some squadron thing. Anyway – time's getting on. Let me fill your glass, and I'll tell you about my daughter, the socialist, who will probably be our first woman Prime Minister.'

They were all there in the church, the Maguires, the Brentons, the Quinnells, and the Lanskys, who were looking a little confused by the unfamiliar surroundings. The priest was smiling benignly, and then the organ pealed out and the bride was coming down the aisle on her stepfather's arm.

Once Patrick had given Catherine away he stepped back beside his wife and squeezed her hand. But Mary was remembering the day she had stood in her tiny miner's cottage with little Catherine in her arms, while her dead husband lay upstairs and Howard Brenton had come stooping through the doorway to bring her comfort. As if he, too, remembered, Howard looked across at her now and smiled, a smile of reassurance that her daughter was moving forward into happiness.

The reception was a mêlée of children – Beb Brenton, the Lansky three, and Ben Quinnell, freed from his page-boy duties, the ring-leader. 'It's a bull-bait, isn't it?' Mary said happily and Anne, beaming as she tucked into her first asparagus roll, agreed. Afterwards she would tell Frank it had been cold and mushy, and she'd never liked brown bread, but on the whole it was an experience not to be missed.

'Of course, our Esther knew about Princess Margaret years ago,' she said. 'Well, being in London so much – and then Howard's connections.' Her eye was caught by the sight of Gerard deep in conversation with Pamela Brenton, and her concentration wavered. Not that Pamela wasn't a nice girl – she was very nice. All the same . . . Anne sighed and looked round for a refill of her wine glass. There was always something to worry about when you had a family. Stella in America, David in the army, Terry in London . . . which was a sink of iniquity and no two ways about it . . . and now Gerard, who had once almost been a priest, sidling up on a Brenton.

'It was a lovely wedding and they'll live happily ever after, but I think these shoes have permanently deformed my feet.' Esther stepped out of her navy court shoes and wiggled her toes.

'Thank goodness we're back in time for television.' Beb was already darting towards the living-room.

'I worry about that boy,' Howard said. 'He'll be square-eyed when he's grown.'

'He wants to be a television announcer,' Esther said sweetly. 'Look on it as training for his chosen profession.'

'Do you want tea?'

'I'd adore a cup. And then let's sit and do nothing for the rest of the day. Pamela won't be in for dinner, by the way. She's gone off with Gerard and Angela, and the others.'

'Gone off to talk to Frank, I should think. I hope she's not making a nuisance of herself.'

'I shouldn't think so. And I don't think this socialist fervour will last.' She giggled. 'I'd love to see Loelia's face if she became a Red and chained herself to something. Wonderful!'

'Loelia's been remarkably quiet lately. Don't raise demons.'

They took their tea into the morning-room and sat in the window seat to look out on the autumnal garden.

'Naomi looked well, I thought.'

'Hmmm.' Esther sounded dubious. 'I think she's in remission at present, but Sammy is coiled like a spring. He covers it up, he jokes as he always did . . . but I think it's breaking his heart.'

'The bride and groom seemed happy enough. I'm not sure Norman has thought through the business of having children, though.'

'I'm quite sure Catherine has thought it through,' said Esther. 'If she means to have children, the matter will be put in hand. Expeditiously.'

'Poor Norman. You make him sound like a victim.'

'Well . . . it's a terribly good way to go, isn't it? Now, pour me another cup of tea and then you can rub my feet. I've lost all feeling in them.'

22

November 1956

'I want us to step up soft goods, Esther. And we need better stock control. Talk to Norman . . . by the way, where is Norman?'

'Telephoning home. Catherine had a pain in the night, and you know what he's like about this baby.'

'I thought it wasn't due till Christmas?'

'That's right – but he's thinking premature today.'

Sammy grimaced. 'I remember the feeling. Now, these soft goods: we should never hold more than two weeks' stock in the warehouse, so as to keep the capital turning over. A warehouse should be a distribution centre, not a store. Who've we got on that at the moment?'

He was destined not to know, for at that moment Norman Stretton came into the office, his normally calm expression replaced by a wide-eyed stare.

'She's having pains now at regular intervals.'

'You should go to her,' Sammy said decisively, abandoning thoughts of work. 'I'll take you in my car.'

'Remember she's a nurse, Norman. She knows what she's doing,' Esther said, but Sammy was already hustling his employee through the door.

'Three times I've lived through this, Norman. Mark those words: "live through". You think the strain will kill you. They give the mother gas and air, but it's the fathers who need the pain-relief . . .'

As their voices died away Esther reached for the phone. The least she could do was let Catherine know she was about to have *two* distracted fathers to cope with.

*

The Lansky children had been presented to their mother for their goodnight kisses. 'I'll be along in a moment to tuck you in,' Sammy said. Naomi lifted a hand and stroked Saul's head. 'Goodnight baby,' she said, her eyes bright. Sammy had noticed lately that she was frequently overcome with emotion. Ruth said it was part of her illness, and he should just accept it, but it was hard.

'Off you go now,' he said to the children. 'I want to talk to mama about something nice.'

'Tell me,' Cecelie said imperiously.

'No, not here. In bed perhaps . . . but not if you don't all scarper. *Vite! Allez!*' When the children had gone, jostling and giggling, through the door, he plumped up Naomi's cushions and sat down on a stool beside her.

'We should have a holiday. Not a little trip to Yarmouth or Southport, but a big holiday.'

'Where to?' Naomi asked.

'Disneyland. Have you read about it? A never-neverland built by Walt Disney near Los Angeles: 17 million dollars, it cost. It has everything – castles, fun-fair rides, rocket-trips to the moon, even. We should go, the children, you, me, and nanny. Ruth too, if she wants to come.'

'I couldn't, Sammy, but you could go . . . you and the children. I'd only hold you back.'

'You say silly things sometimes, Naomi. Without you what sort of a holiday would it be? I have spoken to Ruth, and she says that if we plan it all carefully, you can manage it. She thinks it's a good idea, and she's right. Already your eyes have lit up. This is what you need, a tonic. You sit there and think about it while I go and tuck in your terrible children.' He went off cheerfully enough but both of them knew that talk of foreign holidays was only part of a charade.

Howard and Esther were both ready in plenty of time, terrified lest they be late for Beb's school play and attract attention to themselves. Pamela was meeting them there, straight from her chambers in Newcastle.

'We'll be early if we go now. D'you want a drink?'

Esther was still pondering when the door bell rang. 'I'll get it,' Howard said, and moved towards the hall.

Stretton was on the doorstep, haggard but beaming. 'It's a girl! Seven and a half pounds. Both of them well.'

'Congratulations,' Howard said, drawing Stretton over the step. 'I bet you could do with a drink. Have you let anyone know yet?'

'Mary and Pat Quinnell. I came straight round here.'

'I'll ring Sammy,' Esther said. 'He's been on edge all day, imagining complications. Open some champagne, Howard. We're due at Beb's school later on, Norman, but we've time for a quick drink. Is there anyone else I can ring?'

She went off to make calls, while Howard shepherded Stretton through to the living-room and went in search of champagne. He returned with a tray of glasses, and prised out the cork with a satisfying pop. 'To your daughter,' he said, raising his glass. 'Has she got a name yet?'

'Sara . . . Sara Mary Stretton. I've warned Cathy that the poor child will be called SS, but she likes the name Sara . . . spelled with only an a, by the way, no h.'

'To Sara then . . . and to Catherine.'

It was late when Howard and Esther got to the school hall. 'He'll kill us when we get home,' Esther said as they squeezed along the row to the seats Pamela had kept for them. 'Sorry we're late,' she whispered as she slid into her place. It was only then that she noticed Pamela had an escort: her nephew, Gerard Maguire.

Alone in her kitchen, Anne drank a small sherry to the new baby who had made her a great-aunt. Where did time go? She looked in the mirror over the mantelpiece and found at least one new grey hair. A grandmother and a great-aunt – she'd be on the pension next. She went to the telephone and rang Frank in London to tell him the news, and to bend his ear about some of her worries.

'I want you down those council offices as soon as you get back, Frank. Lay the law down. I've got people on to me day and night. They're at the top of the housing list, some of them, and then they see other people getting the gable ends. It's not good enough. I don't know what this world's coming to, with Teddy boys on every corner, Russia sending in tanks to crush the Hungarians, God forgive them and all the chaos over Suez.'

The world was still reeling from shock at a combined British and French assault on the Canal Zone and the subsequent withdrawal from Egypt. In the world's money-markets the pound was on the run, Commons sittings had been suspended several times, and Frank swore that Tory members had stopped him to express their disgust at the way their government had handled the crisis.

'Well,' he said now at the other end of the line, 'never mind that. What about the family?'

'There's no news of our Stella, and no news is good news. Have you seen our Terry this week?'

Frank had indeed seen Terry, and his daughter's air of isolation had alarmed him: London could be a lonely place. But he played down this angle as he related it to his wife. 'I saw her – but you know girls, always gallivanting, especially when they're pretty.'

When Anne put down the phone, she poured herself another sherry. Please God it wouldn't be history repeating itself, with another daughter picked up by a fancy man and left pregnant. The sherry calmed her: no family could spawn two Stellas. Terry was sensible and a good girl, which was more than Stella had ever been.

She heard a car's engine at the door, and looked at the clock. It couldn't be Bernard – not this early. And David wouldn't come home in a car, even if he had leave.

It was not Angela. Nor was it David. It was Stella and seven pieces of luggage.

'Where's the bairns?' Anne asked when she had got back her breath.

'I've left them behind, mam. Not from choice – Mario wouldn't let them come. I begged him.'

'Did you tell him our Tony wasn't Ricky's?' Anne asked, anguished. 'He'd've let him come then.'

'I did tell him, mam. He only said, "So what?" She didn't add that Mario had said he wouldn't hand over a puppy-

223

dog to her care, never mind two children. Nor that her answer had been, 'Please yourself. It's all the same to me.'

Instead she wiped her eye just a little, and wrung her hands whenever she remembered, and allowed her mother to clutch her to her bosom as the prodigal returned.

BOOK THREE

23

November 1960

Anne gave the sleeve of her moleskin coat one more stroke and sniffed the mothballs attached to the hanger, before putting it back in the wardrobe. It had cost a fortune – a year's wages, once upon a time – and you couldn't be too careful. She went downstairs and drew back the kitchen curtains on another grey day. Still, not long to Christmas when the family would be together again. Not that you could be really happy with all this talk of H bombs and A bombs, massacres in the Congo, and even Clark Gable dead. The latest devil's work was a pill to prevent contraception, which meant sex round the clock for some.

Thinking of sin reminded Anne of Stella. It was four years since she had arrived home, four years of rocketing around dressed up like a dog's dinner, coming home at all hours in great big cars. She had an American drawl which men seemed to find irresistible, but none of them had been moved enough to offer something permanent.

At first Anne had waited for Mario to come hot-foot from the States and reclaim his errant wife. Frank had been more realistic. 'Be honest, Annie – do you blame him for thinking he's well out of it? Our Stella's not cut out for ordinary living. She never was.'

'But he's a good Catholic,' Anne had said as though that made martyrdom a certainty. She had truly believed that Mario would cling to his vows, but he had given in to Stella's constant pleading and divorced her on the grounds of desertion. That had been two years ago, just after Stella had landed herself a job on the cosmetic counter in Dunn's and rented a flat in Sunderland on the strength of it.

Anne lifted the kettle on to the fire and began to set out

her breakfast. It was lonely when Frank was away, now that Stella had her own place and Angela was married. Terry hardly ever came home, from London, and Bernard was still at college, having had to do his National Service first. Gerard was only in Newcastle but it might as well be the moon, and David was back in BAOR after two years at home. So much for having a big family: it all came to nothing in the end.

She was scalding her tea when the post plopped through the letterbox and she hurried to see if any of her children had remembered to write to her.

There were two circulars, a letter for Frank and an airmail from Germany. She picked them all up, together with the *Mirror* and her copy of *Woman's Realm*, and went back to the table. It was lovely to get a letter. Frank used the phone often enough but she had never got used to it, the receiver heavy in her hand and all the irritating little clicks. And there was Esther with an ivory-white telephone in the bedroom, now, and a green one in the hall. She took a sip of her tea and then slit open the airmail envelope.

Dear Mam and Dad, hope this finds you all well. I bet mam's up to the eyes with Christmas. I will be getting leave and hope to be home the 18th. I know this will come as a bit of a shock but I won't be coming home alone. Her name is Ilse, mam, and she is hoping you'll like her, which I do too.

It had come, the thing Anne had dreaded since the day he was first posted. A German wife. A *fraülein* in the family. A picture of the Hitler Youth sprang into Anne's mind: fair and braided and ruthless. She drained her cup and stood up to reach for her scarf and bootees. It was probably too late for praying, but at least she could let off steam.

They had huddled over the books for an hour now, and the office was littered with files and statistics.

'So, Esther,' Sammy said, swinging back on his chair, 'I think we should go public now.'

'Don't do that to the chair, you'll break the legs,' Esther

228

said. 'Why do we need to go public? Things are going well – very well – as we are.'

'Future capital requirements, Esther. Things *are* going well, but expansion doesn't happen to order. It has a pace, a momentum of its own, and when it's ready to go you need the capital to fund it. We've got to talk about it, I know, but in the mean time I suggest we hire a corporation lawyer to get permission for the flotation, the quotation and all the statutory dealings with the Capital Issues Committee. We're worth something in the region of £270,000 now – that's in property, equipment and so on. Goodwill is worth that much again, or more. If we go public we'll need a board of directors, no more Esther and Sammy slogging it out alone. I suggest we ask Howard and Norman to join us. And we'll need a company secretary.'

'You've got this all worked out,' Esther said, outraged.

'Of course I have, my *oytser*. But one lift of my Esther's finger, and it's in the bin.'

'Ha,' Esther said. 'Very funny. Well, I might as well give in now, I suppose.' She smiled. 'I never could resist you, you idiot.'

'So I'm an idiot – the man who got you listed on the Stock Exchange!'

'You haven't done it yet – now get out and let me get some work done.'

When Sammy left she went on a tour of inspection, congratulating managers, meeting new staff, casting an eye over display and stock records. Sammy called them her 'back-slapping' tours, but she knew he approved of them. She was back in her own office and just about to ring for coffee when Sammy's secretary put her head in at the door.

'Mrs Brenton, there's someone asking to see you. She won't give me a reason, except that it's personal. Do you want me to find Selina and ask her to deal with it?'

Esther pulled a face. 'I'm dying for some coffee but . . . if she says it's personal, you'd better show her up. I'll buzz if I want you to get rid of her.'

The woman the secretary ushered in a few moments later was thin and grey-haired, neatly dressed but clutching and unclutching her shabby handbag.

'Sit down,' Esther said. 'What can I do for you?' If the

woman wanted a job, it wouldn't be easy to place her – not at her age which must be at least fifty.

'You're Esther Gulliver, well . . . Brenton, that is.' It wasn't a question but Esther nodded just the same. 'Your dad kept a draper's shop in Belgate.'

'Yes,' Esther said. 'A very long time ago.'

The woman was nodding, too. 'Your mother died and your father kept the shop going . . .'

'My sister helped him,' Esther said. 'I was too young to be of much help. Did you live in Belgate? Did I know you? I'm sorry if I've forgotten . . . but it was a long time ago.'

'I never knew you,' the woman said flatly. 'I'm not here on account of meself. It's Leida – Aleida Barwick. I work with her; well I did. She worked with me on the school dinners.'

Esther was trying to be polite but thirst was overcoming her. 'This Mrs Barwick, is she someone I knew?'

'*Miss* Barwick. I don't think you ever knew her, but your father did.'

'I see,' Esther said slowly, not seeing at all. 'Would you like coffee? I'm dying for some.'

The woman clutched her bag more firmly and shook her head.

'No thank you, I can't stop. I just came to tell you about Leida. She and your dad . . . well, they would have got married if it hadn't been for your sister. She had a terrible tongue, Leida says, and your dad was scared of her. He meant to do right by Leida, but – well, he never got around to it, and then he died. She's never asked anyone for anything. Always worked. But she can't work now, she's ill. She's on the sick, but that doesn't go far.'

So that was it, Esther thought. Someone wanting a hand-out. 'I'm sure I'm very sorry, Miss . . .' There was a ring on the woman's finger. 'Mrs . . . I didn't get your name?'

'Smith. Lilian Smith. Leida was his mistress for four years. She was seventeen when she took up with him and twenty-one when he died. She had a bairn, but he died too, not long after your dad.'

'I'm sorry,' Esther said, 'but I can't believe this.' She felt a faint sweat break out on her brow, and her legs were trembling.

'It's true enough. Leida was a waitress, then a barmaid. Your dad came to the room she had every night till the drink got him. She used to visit his grave regularly. She's got photographs, letters, everything.'

'What do you want of me?' Esther said.

'*I* don't want anything, Mrs Brenton. But by all accounts you're not short of a bob or two – and she was your dad's friend. What might be nothing to you could be a fortune to her.'

Esther pushed forward a piece of paper and pen. 'Give me her name and address. I'm not promising anything but at least I'll make enquiries.' All she wanted was to get the woman out of her office, so that she had time to think! The woman had mentioned her father's grave. There *had* been flowers there once – unexplained flowers.

After Mrs Smith had gone, Esther wondered whether to run to Howard with the revelation, but in the end she went to Sammy.

'I hardly remember your father, Esther,' he said, rocking his chair on to its back legs behind his big desk. 'I only saw him from a distance when Papa took me to Belgate. But I don't think I believe this: it's a con. They know you have money, this business, the Brenton name: they see a chance of gain. That's all. Forget it!'

'I can't forget it, Sammy. I've got to check it out, for the sake of my peace of mind. But I'm not going to tell Anne. She'd go mad!'

'I hope you'll be cautious, Esther. There's been a lot about Lanver in the papers recently, how well we're doing and that sort of thing. I mean, why have these people come forward now?'

'Because the woman's dying, Sammy – that's what's brought it on now. And I don't think it's any big con. I think they're hoping for a few quid . . . the difference between hardship and comfort. I can afford it.'

'You've made up your mind, haven't you? Ah well, don't say I didn't warn you.' He was shaking his head mournfully and lifting his hands in a gesture of dismissal.

'I'm only going to see the woman, Sam. That's all, at this stage. And if she is fooling me she won't get more than a flea in her ear. But I have to go.'

231

'When?'

'Today, I think. There's no point in waiting.'

'And this is the woman who says Sammy Lansky rushes in! Well, all I can say is, I wish you *mazel*.'

It was raining, and the London traffic was swirling around Marble Arch. Theresa Maguire hoisted her bag higher on her shoulder, turned up her collar, and watched for a cruising taxi. She saw one in the throng of cars with its flag down and stepped forward, her arm outstretched. But, as the car pulled into the kerb, a young man in front of her was putting out a hand to the cab-door.

'Excuse me,' Terry said, darting past him.

'Hold on!' He was both startled and affronted. The taxi had come to a halt, and the driver was staring wearily through his windscreen until a decision was made.

'He stopped for me!' Theresa insisted.

'All right.' The red-headed young man was staring at her and she felt herself flush. 'No need to fight over it. I'm going to Regent's Park – is that your direction?'

'Well . . .' She was going to Baker Street. 'OK. I get off before you. We can share it.'

Inside the car she started fishing for her purse, but the man held up a hand.

'Please . . . let me. I'd be paying anyway. And actually, I think we've met before.'

Terry let her lip curl with what she hoped was woman-of-the-world cynicism. 'I don't think so.'

'We have – on Coronation Day. In the Mall. I was with my cousins and my brother and sisters, and weren't you with your aunt, who married my parents' friend, Howard Brenton?'

'I *was* in London for the Coronation with my aunt, Esther Brenton. So you must be . . .?'

'I'm Greville Colville, and you're Theresa Maguire. You see, I've remembered your name.'

He leaned forward and spoke through the half-open glass partition. 'Can you pause at the Portland Hotel? I'm picking up my uncle there.' He sat back in his seat and smiled at Terry. 'He's waiting in the portico, so we won't hold you up. Are you living in London? I know Esther's family comes from Northumberland.'

'Durham,' Terry said firmly. 'You southerners think we're all Geordies. Well, we're not.'

Greville Colville held up his hands in horror. 'Sorry! I didn't mean to offend your patriotism. What are you then, if you're not a Geordie?' But the taxi was pulling in to the entrance of a big hotel and another man, older but red-headed like Greville, was stooping through the door of the cab. He looked at Terry and smiled as Greville moved to a tip-up seat opposite.

'Well,' he said, 'this is a pleasant surprise. I'm Max Dunane. Who are you?'

The long grey car was waiting in the alley when Stella emerged from the staff door. She put up a red-tipped hand to check her upswept hair, and then moved confidently forward as the passenger door swung open.

'Sorry I'm late.' She swung her legs into the car, reflecting how nice her knees looked in the sheer Hint of Smoke stockings.

'Where do you want to go?' Edward Fox let out the clutch and the car purred into the traffic.

'Somewhere nice. Far away.' Stella stretched in her seat like a cat, liking the effect it had upon the driver.

'I thought we might have a night in tonight?' He was not looking in her direction, but he was very aware of her.

'At your place?' she said mockingly.

'No, yours. I thought you might make me a three-course dinner.'

'Only three? I'm not domesticated, Eddy, you know that. Beans on toast, sausage and beans on toast – that's my limit. And I'm hungry.' She glanced sideways at him, seeing the blue-shadowed jowl, the crisp shirt collar, the heavy gold bracelet on one wrist and the diamond-studded signet ring on the other hand. God, he was attractive! 'We could go back to my place later on. For coffee.'

'Proper coffee?'

'*Very* proper coffee,' she said as seductively as she could manage.

'OK, we'll go to Crimdon Hall for a meal. The food's good, and it's off the beaten track. Then we'll come home for afters.'

'"Home"? Are you moving in, like?'

'If you treat me well enough.'

It was dark in the car – no moon, and no street lamps now they were out of the town – and Stella was glad Fox could not see her face. She would have to box clever: give him enough to keep him happy, but not so much that he'd think he could have it for nothing. She wanted marriage, no less: you could be left with nothing if you didn't get your marriage-lines. Getting Mario to divorce her had been difficult, but essential. Edward Fox was going places, going up in the world, and Stella Dimambro was going with him. First, though, she had to get rid of the dumpy little woman with the pepper-and-salt hair who occupied his gorgeous house – but no longer, thank God, his bed.

'Give me a kiss,' she said, as the car drew up at the hotel. And when their lips were locked together, she guided his hand to her breast, covered with a pure silk shirt that had cost her nearly a week's wages. The sooner she had somebody to keep her the better. She didn't mind working on a cosmetic counter, but it was murder on your feet.

Esther did not feel nervous until she raised her hand to the knocker, but at that moment her customary composure deserted her. What did you say to a woman who claimed she had been your father's lover thirty years before? The door opened, and she looked into the face of an old woman, thin, lined and the colour of putty. Only the eyes were alive, and they sparked with an emotion Esther could not quite interpret.

'Come in,' she said, before Esther could speak. 'I know who you are, I've seen you round Sunderland. And Lilian said she'd been to speak to you. She had no call to do that and I've told her so. Still, now you're here . . .' She was not gracious but that reassured Esther. This was not the manner of the con-woman, so for once Sammy was wrong.

They sat in shabby, wooden-armed fireside chairs on

234

either side of a plopping gas fire. Aleida Barwick made no offer of tea, or other comfort.

'I'm not sure why I'm here,' Esther said, loosening her coat. 'Except that your friend aroused my curiosity. I loved my father . . .'

'I know,' the woman interrupted. 'I know *you* loved him. It was your Anne that racked his nerves – she was always on at him. Still it's water under the bridge now.'

'I don't think you're being fair to my sister,' Esther said firmly. 'She had to take on a great deal of responsibility when she was very young.'

'Aye, well, let's not argue. What did you want to know?'

'Your friend said you met my father in a pub . . .' Esther began.

'No. If she said that she was wrong. I met him in Etchell's, the fish restaurant . . . remember? Beside the bus station in Park Lane? I went to work there straight from school. Your dad used to come in every Friday, on the dot of one o'clock. Always polite, he was. It was 1918. I was sixteen and your mam'd just died. We got friendly . . . he used to talk about you and your Anne. "The girls" he called you.' She paused and Esther could see she was remembering.

'He always went to the wholesalers in Sunderland every Friday,' Esther said. 'I remember that.'

'Well,' the woman said, coming back to life, 'at first we just met in the café, and then I got a better job in Lockhart's and he took me out to celebrate. After that . . . He wasn't a bad man, your dad. He didn't force me. It was more me pushing him. I felt sorry for him, and I suppose he was a bit like a father to me. I used to feel safe with him.' Aleida brooded again, and when she looked up her face was bleak. 'He'd've married me when the boy came along, if it hadn't been for your Anne. He was too scared of what she would say.'

'But why?' Esther said, for want of anything better. She could think of seventeen things Anne would have had against the match.

They talked on for a while, the silences in between the reminiscence growing longer and longer, the ticking of the clock more apparent. At last Esther stood up to leave.

235

'Please let me know what I can do for you. Your friend told me you hadn't been well. If some money would help . . .'

'I don't know what Lilian told you,' the woman said firmly, 'but she had no right. I can manage, I haven't got much, but I've always kept meself and I will to the end, now.' Her eyes burned fiercely in her skeletal face.

'All right,' Esther said. 'I can respect that. I've always worked, too, and I like it.' But this woman couldn't work any more. Esther felt a sudden flash of fear at the thought of growing old and helpless. 'Will you tell me if there is ever anything I can do for you? Please?'

'Yes,' Aleida said. 'I will do that.'

It was a concession and Esther smiled her thanks. She wondered for a moment if she should lean forward and kiss the pale cheek, but she didn't dare.

'Goodbye,' she said, turning at the front door. 'I hope we meet again.'

Sammy put the beaker of water close to the edge of the bedside table, and switched off Naomi's bedside lamp. They slept apart now, to make sure she got her rest, but his bed was only an arm's length away and sometimes, in the night, when neither of them could sleep, they would hold hands across the intervening space.

She was asleep and he put out a hand to smooth the hair from her brow and eyes. 'Sleep well, *liebchen*,' he said and bent to kiss her. Her skin was almost transparent now, her face paler than it had ever been, even in those days when she had come, a terrified waif, to seek refuge in his home. But her spirit burned brightly. Sometimes, particularly when her children were around her, he thought her eyes grew bright with tears, but then she would shake her head and the next minute she would be smiling and making fun.

He climbed into his own bed and put out his lamp. He was positioning his pillow for sleep when Naomi spoke.

'Sammy?'

'Darling.' He was alert at once, feeling for the lamp-switch.

'Don't put the light on – I just want to talk.'

Sammy subsided on to his pillow. 'Then talk. I'm listening.'

'It's Ruth. I'm worried about her, Sammy.'

As the room came faintly into view he could see his wife's face in profile against the whiteness of her bed-linen.

'Ruth's fine. She works hard – but that's Ruth.'

'She's sad, Samuel. After Papa died, I thought that was what was wrong, but it's more than that. She reads all the time – books about Israel. And Czechoslovakia – that's Nathan's country.'

He reached across to take and pat his wife's hand. 'Nathan? Nathan went away years ago. She's forgotten Nathan, and so should you. Put it out of your mind and go to sleep.'

24

July 1961

'Laura and the boys went back for the President's inaugur-
ation, of course,' Loelia said. She and Howard were lunching at the Dorchester, and the conversation had turned to
the new President and his wife, whose names seemed to
be on everyone's lips. 'She says Jackie Kennedy is simply
delectable, such a contrast to his sisters, those horsey,
galumphing Kennedy girls. Do you remember them before
the war, Howard? Always smiling, laughing, leaping
around, as though they had St Vitus' Dance. Laura thinks
he's going to be an inspiration, though. She says he's
already transformed Washington.'

'His Peace Corps is rather a good idea,' Howard said.
'It's idealistic, but it could make for co-operation between
the world's young. A thousand eager young American do-
gooders . . .'

'. . . could easily cause World War Three,' Loelia said.
'Still, tell me about the family. How is darling Pammy? We
don't see nearly enough of her in London. Nothing's the
same now, Howard. Verity Charles can't even present her
daughters: that's another tradition gone. Thank heaven
Pamela came out properly. We were so relieved.'

It was there again, the downcast glance that always made
Howard wonder if she knew more than she was saying.

'Loelia . . .' She looked up, startled at his tone, her eyes
flashing a message. *'Be discreet,'* they said. *'Don't make
things uncomfortable.'*

'Loelia . . .' He had gone too far to stop. 'I think we
should acknowledge the truth now, after all this time.
Pamela is not my child, except that we love one another
deeply. Max is her father, and she's your niece. Why don't

we admit it, at least to one another? She's thirty years old now. I think it's time to abandon pretence.'

'You're right, of course.' Loelia had begun to move her heavy rings round and round on her fingers. 'At the time I couldn't . . . daren't . . . admit I knew. As much for Diana's sake as my own.'

A woman in beige slowed her step and nodded graciously. 'Loelia. Lovely to see you.'

'Eithrie . . . how nice. Love to Gregor.'

'After that,' Loelia continued, when the woman was passed, 'well, we had to be discreet for Pamela's sake. Now, I must be honest and say I can't see the point of making it public. There are Max's children to be considered. And what would Esther think?'

'Esther knows. She's known for a long time. So does Pamela. However, I agree with you. If Pamela ever wanted to proclaim her parentage, I wouldn't stop her – but I don't think that will happen.'

Loelia's eyes had flared in alarm at the news that Pamela knew the truth. Now she shook her head. 'No,' she said. 'Poor Max. He has a daughter who isn't his; his wife is, frankly, a burden; and his sons – Gerald actually wants to join the Peace Corps. A boy who could have had a Guards commission for the asking! No, Max hasn't been at all lucky.'

The temptation to talk of poetic justice almost overcame Howard, but in the end his better nature triumphed. 'Shall we order?' he said. 'I think we'll get better food than that time we dined here at the end of the war – do you remember?'

Stella kept arranging and rearranging the lipsticks, aware that the turquoise tubes showed off her perfect cerise nails to advantage. Rich Ruby, Coral Charm, Perfect Pink . . . Across the counter Fox was pretending to choose between phials of perfume.

'Come on,' he said in a low voice, not looking at her in case the floor-walker noticed. 'Come on . . . don't tantalize. Will you be there tonight?'

'I'm sure I don't know. I haven't made any plans.'

'Stella! Please!'

'Oh yes, it's please now, and thank you when you're done. But what about the future, Eddy? That's what I want to know.'

'I'm trying, Stel, but it's not that easy. I'm fond of Florrie. She's my children's mother . . .'

'And I'm your convenience. No thank you.' She raised her voice as the floor-walker drew near. 'Passion Flower is nice . . . woodland tones with a hint of musk. Or you may prefer the French perfumes: Chanel, Guerlain, or the new Dior?'

'Which do you like?' he asked, when the floor-walker was out of earshot.

'Chanel No 5. I love it.'

'Give me the biggest bottle you've got. Gift-wrapped. It's yours if you'll meet me tonight.'

She reached for the largest size of perfume and then looked him squarely in the eye. 'All right, Eddy, I'll be there. But I won't wait forever. And don't give me the "I can't bear to hurt her" routine. You'd strangle your grandmother if it was in the line of business, so getting rid of your wife should be a doddle.'

Anne took off her glasses in the London restaurant and looked at Frank across the top of the menu. 'Have you seen these prices?' She was speaking in a hushed voice, which made her words all the more anguished.

'It's supposed to be a night out, Annie,' Frank said, trying to look unconcerned.

'*Night* out, Frank? At these prices it's more like a week out.'

'Well, just choose what you want.' He was getting irritated, now, as the treat he had planned began to disintegrate. Anne had surrendered her moleskin coat to the waiter with a look that suggested she had imprinted his face in her memory ready for the identity parade. Now she lifted a piece of the cutlery and scrutinized it carefully for traces of grime.

'Come on,' Frank said again, 'what have you chosen?'

'Oh, that's easy. Run your eye down till you find something at a sensible price, and that's what I want.'

He gave up then and, on the waiter's return, ordered for both of them with an aplomb that secretly impressed his wife. 'Do you come here often?' she said suspiciously.

'No,' he said, 'but it's got a good name.'

Anne sniffed. 'Pricey!' She looked around her at the tables filled with fashionable diners, the signed photographs lining the walls, the potted plants in huge containers that filled every niche. 'Pricey!' she said again. 'And hard to keep clean.' This last was in tones of salmonella-tinged gloom. 'Now,' she said, as though the difficulties had been dispensed with, 'when are we going round to our Terry's?'

Frank's swift prayer for rescue was as swiftly answered by the arrival of the soup. He wasn't sure how he was going to handle the thorny question of Terry. She had moved into a flat on her own, and there was a man in the background somewhere. Give Anne five minutes and she would smell trouble. And if she didn't, his own guilty face would probably give it away. He had never laid eyes on the man, and knew nothing about him, in spite of probing. There was a rabbit away somewhere, he was sure of it.

'Nice soup, isn't it?' he said anxiously. Anne leaned towards him and lowered her voice.

'What is it?'

Frank was about to say 'cream of asparagus' when he thought better of it. 'Lentil,' he said instead.

'I thought that's what it was,' Anne said triumphantly. 'It's not bad, at all.'

It was the third time she had visited her father's mistress, and yet Esther felt no greater rapport with the woman than at first. They talked and talked, but there was still an unease between them, a feeling that something dramatic – terrible, even – was constantly about to happen.

'And your sister's man's still in London?'

'Yes. Anne misses him a lot.'

Aleida sniffed her disbelief. 'She always was proud – too

241

big for her boots. I should think it suits her, him going up in the world.'

'She's proud of him, if that's what you mean,' Esther said, her hackles rising at criticism of Anne.

Aleida laughed thinly. 'Don't get on your high horse. I've got no quarrel with you. You were a good bairn; your dad always said that. It was her, your Anne, that crucified him.'

She was about to embark on the oft-told tale of star-crossed lovers parted by an uppity daughter, and Esther stirred uneasily in her chair. 'Tell me about you and dad,' she said hastily. 'I loved my father, but I don't clearly remember how he was with my mother.'

'Oh, he loved her, right enough.' The dark eyes gleamed as Aleida got into her stride. 'She was a lady, according to him. And gentle – never a wrong word. You were like her, he said. Quite serious. Your father was always one for a laugh – '

'My dad?' Esther was incredulous.

'Yes. He loved a yarn and a joke. And he could do all the music-hall songs: "John took me round to see his mother", and "My old man said follow the van". "Only a bird in a gilded cage" was his best one, though.' She cleared her throat and hummed a few bars before a cough rattled in her chest and she had to cease. 'He was a loving man,' she said when she had regained her breath. 'We could've been happy, Sidney and I. And our boy would've lived, if things'd been different. Sidney never knew he had a son – '

It was painful, this re-creation of the past. Esther looked at the clock wondering how soon it would be before she could decently take her leave. All the same, it was amazing to hear this description of her father which bore no relation-ship to the dark-suited, heavy man, always in his cups, that she remembered.

'Kennedy looks good,' Gerard said, 'and he says good things – but I've always had my doubts about him. Too much money, too much razzmatazz. He was behind the Bay of Pigs, depend on it.'

242

They had come out of a meeting in Newcastle where America's disastrous landing in April, at the Bay of Pigs in Cuba, of an armed force determined to overthrow Fidel Castro, had been heatedly discussed.

'You can't be sure of that,' Pamela said. 'I don't think Kennedy would back a hole-and-corner affair like that . . . it's not his style.'

'You're sounding like my mother,' Gerard said. '"He's a good Catholic," she'd say. Which means he's above reproach.'

'You don't talk much about your religion,' Pamela said, 'but you still believe, don't you?'

'Yes. I gave up religion, not God.' Gerard took her arm and pulled her nearer. 'Don't let's talk about complicated things. My head's still reeling from the meeting. So much hot air. But that's politics.'

'You intrigue me, Gerard Maguire. You sit there, like a Buddha, listening. Occasionally you'll come out with a remark that cuts through all the . . . all the . . .'

'Persiflage?' he suggested.

'Waffle. Don't be so intellectually overbearing. D'you want to come back for coffee?'

'One cup. I have to get up in the morning and face forty rebellious teenagers, remember.'

'Poor you. I've only got a judge to face, of course, so there's no comparison.'

'None. The modern teenager is a terrifying beast. There are more than five million of them in this country now, four million of them earning good money – that's a power-block.'

'They only earn good money if they're boys,' Pamela said pointedly. 'And it's women who do all the work.'

Gerard grinned. 'That's because men have superior intellects. I'll tell you what, though, have you watched them rock and roll? The boys standing there trying to look like Elvis Presley, no facial expression, just shuffling their feet underneath their tight blue drainpipes – and the girls whirling round, but no joy in their faces. I can't work them out.'

'That's because you're not with it,' Pamela said, linking her arm in his. 'You're an old square.'

'Yes,' he said gravely.

'You've no objection to that description?'

'None. Come on, I'll race you to the car.'

They joined hands and ran, whooping, along the street of tall, terraced houses, built in Newcastle's heyday, a more graceful age.

'That smells good,' Max Dunane said, wrinkling up his nose as he moved across the tiny kitchen of Terry's flat to take her in his arms.

'Careful,' she said, but made no attempt to wriggle free. She loved to feel desire in him, to know he wasn't tired of her, that he would always be there in her life. He was pulling up a finger now to move the fair hair from her forehead, to trace her straight dark brows, her cheeks, her nose, the outline of her mouth, and once more she gave thanks that her parents had decided to have a night on their own, leaving her free for Max.

'The dinner . . .' she said weakly, but he was already drawing her toward the door to the living-room, and steering her between the chairs and coffee tables to the door to the bedroom.

'Come,' he said, feeling for the lamp without taking his eyes off her face. 'I want *you* to make love to *me* this time.'

Terry smiled and shook her head: even after all his tuition she found it impossible to make the first move. But he wasn't angry with her. He didn't make her feel inadequate or a provincial fool. Instead he was kissing her, unbuttoning her shirt, unzipping her skirt, slipping his fingers into the elastic of her pants to draw them down, laughing softly when they resisted and he had to tug gently until the silk and lace gave way and slid down her thighs.

'Oh Max,' she said. 'Oh darling, darling Max.' For a second, as he entered her, she wondered why, when their love-making was so perfect and his life with Laura was over, he didn't make the break. They could be married then, and have children, and never ever be parted again. But then he was moving inside her, and she forgot everything except the wonder of it all. Until it was over, and he was raising himself in the bed and reaching for his shirt.

244

'Darling – it's a dreadful drag, but I'll have to skip dinner tonight. Some dreary political thing – a dinner party at Lee's. But we both know what I'll be thinking of all through the boring chit-chat. No, don't get up, there's no need for you to stir yet. I'll switch off the cooker as I go.'

25

September 1961

Frank's nose had been buried in the newspaper for half an hour and Anne's temper was growing shorter by the minute. He would be reading about the Berlin Wall, no doubt, the ugly erection thrown up between East and West to stop the flow of Germans who were desperate to escape. Anne was worried about the Wall too, but Parliament's summer recess was drawing to a close and she was eager to talk to Frank before he went back to London.

'Get things in proportion, Anne,' he had told her when she bemoaned the absence this month of a letter from Tony in America. 'Take a look at those pictures, and thank God that you *will* see the lad one day and not a ruddy great wall to stop you.'

It was all very well for him to talk: he hadn't loved Stella's bairn like she had. Nor had he turned a hair about David consorting with the living image of Eva Braun. At least Anne's letter had put a stop to him bringing the faggot home, and now he seldom, if ever, mentioned her; but you could never be sure there wasn't an ember somewhere, even when you'd stamped out a fire. Anne was beginning to dread being alone again: if it hadn't been for that, she would have given Frank the rough edge of her tongue now. As it was, she contented herself with a snort and reopened the subject of their daughters.

'Three girls, Frank – and if it wasn't for our Angela being happily married I'd be tearing out my hair. Look at our Stella, living in a flat in Sunderland. What for, I ask myself, when she has a good home here?'

'Trenchard Street isn't posh enough for her, I expect,' Frank said, shaking out his paper.

246

Privately Anne was fond of the house they had lived in from its building, but it didn't do to appear too contented.

'Well,' she said, 'I've been saying for years that you should have a house better suited to your position, but who listens to me?'

'D'you mean buy a place?' Frank's eyes appeared above the rim of his paper.

'Why not? And don't give me rubbish about capitalism, Frank. From what I can see it doesn't hold other MPs back. Some of them live like lords.'

'That's as maybe, Anne. It doesn't say I have to do it. And have you seen prices lately? They've gone wild.'

It was true. The small suburban house built before the war for £700 was now worth more than £3,000. If it was in a so-called desirable area, you could add another thousand.

Anne sighed and rolled her eyes. 'Why do I bother? Still, to come back to our family, Frank – are you telling me that our Stella's only reason for leaving was snobbery? We both know it wasn't – not that my tongue's hanging out to have her back – I haven't forgotten last time. But I still wonder what she's up to . . . which brings me to our Terry: I want you to find out what's going on, and why we never see her. Why is it always left to me? You're her father and you're in London: find out what's going on down there, and let me know.'

Frank mumbled something she couldn't catch and went on reading. 'And then there's our David – spending half his leaves in Germany,' Anne went on remorselessly. 'What's the attraction there? If he ever mentioned that Ilse, I'd think it was her – but she's gone from his letters, thank God. All the same, something's up. Speak, Frank, for God's sake! No wonder the Tories are in power if the Labour lot's as voluble as you!'

Among the letters in the post at breakfast there was one from Beb. He was settling down at school, playing rugger for the second eleven, and thrilled with his new bike. Esther was still smiling as she slit open the second letter, but her smile quickly faded. It came from Aleida Barwick, and was brief and to the point.

As you'll see from the above, I'm in hospital now. Not long to go, I expect. I've thought a lot since the last time you came to see me, and I want to talk to your sister as I talked to you. I don't want anything from her, just to see her face to face. You can be there as well, if you want to be. I hope you can do this for me, but if not, I will write to her direct. And if that fails, I'll have to look at what other steps I can take.

As she slowly put the letter back into the envelope, Esther felt a knot of unease collect in her stomach. She would have to tell Anne: that was better by far than letting her find out from a stranger. All the same she wasn't looking forward to it.

She decided to get it over before she went in to the office. It wouldn't be any easier if she put it off. As she drove over to Belgate, she tried to find an acceptable form of words, and all the way between the lush late-summer hedgerows she rehearsed it. 'I've got something to tell you, Anne, and you're not going to like it . . .'

But when she got there, Anne gave her no chance to speak. 'Am I glad to see you, our Es! I've just sent Frank off with a flea in his ear.'

'What's he done now?' Esther asked, settling on a chair at the kitchen table.

'It's what he's not done that's the trouble. I'm left to sort this family every time. Our Stella's living like a floozie in Sunderland; our David's up to God knows what in Germany; our Terry's in London with someone called Max, who's not good enough to introduce to her father – I only found out his name when she let it slip on the phone the other night.'

She had been preparing for a constituency meeting, and papers were littered across the kitchen table. Esther made soothing remarks about Terry and accepted a cup of tea, and then, aware that if she waited her nerve would fail, she plunged in. 'I'm afraid I've got something to tell you, Anne – and you're not going to like it.'

Anne was at the sink drying her hands on a tea-towel. Now she raised the towel to her lips in a gesture of fear.

'It's not bad news about the family,' Esther said hastily.

'Well, not the kind of bad news you think. No one's going to die – well, at least, no one you know – '

Anne removed the tea-towel from her mouth. 'Get on with it then,' she said, moving to the table and lowering herself on to a chair.

There was silence for a moment as Esther tried to marshall her words.

'Go on, then,' Anne said again, her heart thumping uncomfortably against her ribs. She had had her troubles with Esther in the past, but blood was blood – and every other person you met nowadays had cancer or TB.

But the news, when it came, was worse than cancer or tuberculosis ever could be. 'What?' she screamed. 'A fancy piece? Me dad? The bugger, the sodden bugger!' There was a pause and then she spoke again. 'It's a bleeding lie. A bleeding, bloody lie!'

'For God's sake hush,' Esther said. 'They don't talk like that down the pit, Anne. And you can take it from me, it *is* true.'

Anne struck her cheek with her clenched fist. 'That's right, Esther, you be sweet and bloody reasonable: leave the fighting to me. My God, the disgrace. What'll we tell our Bernard and our Angela?'

'As little as possible,' Esther said cheerfully. 'Dad's been dead forty years, so I don't suppose it'll be that much of a shock to them. What we have to do is make some decisions. Will you tell Frank?'

'Of course I will,' Anne ground out. 'He's not in any position to be awkward, is he, with a sister that once lived in sin for years? My God, our Esther, my God – what'll happen next?'

'I don't know, Anne. But the thing is this: Aleida wants to see you. She's insistent about it.'

'I'm not going,' Anne said flatly. 'I wouldn't give her the satisfaction of it. She did what she did with dad behind my back. She can stay there.'

'I think you should read her letter,' Esther said, producing it from her bag. 'And I'd humour her if I were you. She hasn't much time left, and we don't want trouble.'

Anne skimmed down the letter and then looked up.

'What does she mean by the last bit – about what else she might do?'

'It's just talk,' Esther said. 'Bluff to get you there. She's a sick woman, Anne. If you saw her, you'd be sorry for her.'

'Never! And I still don't believe it. Dad didn't have it in him, particularly towards the end. She's after money, you mark my words.'

'She's not,' Esther said firmly. 'I offered her money right at the start, and she refused it. If she'd wanted money she wouldn't've waited forty years.'

'We didn't have anything before, Es: there was nothing to get. Now you're well-off, and Frank's a public figure – and she's closing in for the kill.'

'She's dying, Anne. She's not closing in for anything except the end of her life. Say you'll come and see her – just once. It's her dying wish. When you see her, you'll believe her, like I do. Besides, I remember after dad died seeing fresh flowers on his grave. I wondered who put them there – well, it was her.'

'What does she want to meet me for?' Anne asked suspiciously. She chewed her lip. 'All the same – perhaps it'll shut her up. We don't want anything coming out – not now.'

'I needed that,' Esther said, downing the sherry Howard had given her in one gulp. She had driven straight to his office when she left Anne's home, desperate for his calming influence. Now they sat in his oak-panelled office high above Sunderland's traffic and she gave him a word by word account of her visit to her sister.

'Well, I think you were brave even to broach the subject,' he said, when she'd finished. 'How did you begin?'

'She was going on as usual, about all the children being crosses to carry: Stella just being Stella, which is more than enough; David fraternizing with Nazis; how she's longed for Terry to have a man in her life but now that she has this Max that's another catastrophe – anyway, I just sat down and came out with it.'

Howard frowned. 'Max? Did you say Terry had a boyfriend called Max?'

For a moment Esther was puzzled at this diversion but then she smiled. 'It's not likely to be Loelia's Max, darling. Terry's half his age, and doesn't move in his exalted circles.'

But as Howard drove towards Newcastle, where he was lunching with Pamela, he couldn't get Theresa Maguire out of his mind. If, by some mischance, she was involved with Max Dunane, he thought soberly, she wouldn't stand much chance. Diana had been no match for him, and she had been a thousand times more capable of holding her own than a young daughter of the Durham coalfield.

And then he was entering the low-beamed restaurant, and Pamela was rising to kiss him, looking absurdly like her mother in spite of the severe black suit and white silk shirt she wore to her work in the courts.

'This is nice, daddy,' she said when they were seated and sipping a fine dry sherry. 'I don't know why we don't do it more often. Esther must join us next time. Is she well? Pretty busy, I expect?'

'As a matter of fact she has a little worry – or thinks she has. I'll tell you about it in a minute. Let's order now, so that you don't have to hurry back.'

They talked of the law over onion soup and roast beef and vegetables, especially the case of embezzlement Pamela had recently handled well.

'So I said, "Yes, m'lud, but if my client had foresight he wouldn't be in the dock now, would he?" I saw his lips twitch, but of course his face was a study.'

'You love your profession, don't you?' Howard said.

'I do now that I'm past driving offences and petty theft. That was pretty dire. Now that I can defend someone I feel has been unjustly accused, I find it very satisfying. It's a terrible ego trip, the law. If you see me getting above myself give me a swift kick. That's what Gerard has promised to do.'

Howard raised a hand to summon the waiter and then asked the important question. 'Do I detect a romance in this relationship of yours with Maguire? I mean son Maguire, not father, with whom I know you're besotted.'

She threw back her head to laugh and for a moment it was as though Diana was there, sitting opposite him. But when she stopped laughing the eyes fixed on his were calm and serene in a way Diana's eyes had never been.

'I don't know, Dad. That's the honest answer. I like being with Gerard and I think he likes being with me. We're alike . . . I mean we have the same values, the same beliefs. But he's a strange guy. I think I'm down to layer three, but how many more are there to go?' She shrugged.

'Perhaps he still feels he has a vocation?'

'No, I don't think that's it. He just takes his time. I like that. Besides, I'm not too sure I'm ready for long-term romance . . . and take that worried expression off your face. Nothing has scarred me for life, if that's what you're thinking. You and Esther are about the best advertisement for marriage I've seen. Now, if you'll permit me, I'll treat you to this lunch. I'm fearfully well paid, you know . . . it makes me quite ashamed.'

'We'll argue about that later,' Howard said. He was trying to decide whether or not to confide in his daughter. Would she know anything that could help Theresa? He made up his mind suddenly. 'Look, how close are you to Gerard's sister Theresa? How much do you know about her life in London?'

'Not a lot,' Pamela said slowly. 'I see her when I'm down there – and we talk on the phone. Why are you asking?'

'She's involved with a man, apparently.'

'I know there's someone,' Pamela said. 'She's always been cagey about saying who. But so what? She's old enough.'

Howard hesitated. It was not too late to draw back. But Pamela's eyes were on his, demanding answers. 'Esther says his name is Max,' he said, half-apologetically. 'But it couldn't be . . . could it?'

For a moment he thought Pamela had not heard what he had said, and then he saw that the fingers of her right hand had tightened on the tablecloth, drawing it up until her wine glass threatened to topple over.

26

September 1961

They were debating limiting immigration in the House. Frank listened to the impassioned arguments with a heavy heart. At the end of the war there had been an atmosphere of international goodwill, but now everyone seemed to be at everyone else's throat. As far as he could see, the British public had approved of immigration as long as it was their immigration into other lands. Now the situation was reversed: people from the Empire wanted to come into Britain to improve their lot, and the public didn't like it. In 1948 the *Empire Windrush* had brought 500 Jamaicans to Tilbury, and that had proved the start of large-scale immigration from the West Indies. The figures had soared from 2,000 in 1953 to 125,000 last year. Frank was now stoutly resisting calls for a ban on their entry but he mourned the change in public attitudes. Where once they had welcomed newcomers, now they begrudged them houses, jobs – even seats on buses.

He looked across at the government benches. If all reports were true, 'Supermac' – Harold Macmillan, the patrician Prime Minister – was at loggerheads with Selwyn Lloyd, his Chancellor; and with a budget coming in a few weeks that didn't augur well. Frank knew he ought to be glad to hear of Tory disarray, but he was fed up with gloom, wherever it came from.

He was down to speak in a little while, when the subject would be coal-mining, and already his mouth was dry at the prospect. He had never got used to addressing the House. There were so many brilliant speakers there: lawyers, barristers, men who had learned their oratory at Oxford and Cambridge. He was only a miner who had learned to quip in the pit or hold his own at a local party meeting. Nevertheless he meant to have his say.

He looked around him at the surprisingly small chamber, rebuilt at the end of the War and looking engagingly like a chapel. Its smallness had surprised him when first he entered: it was no bigger than a tennis court, its green leather benches accommodating only about 450 of the 650 MPs. There were plenty of spaces today, and only a smattering of press and visitors sat in the galleries above.

The MPs wore dark lounge suits, and the two or three women present stood out like brilliant birds in the dull assembly. 'It should've been Annie here instead of me,' Frank thought and had to suppress a grin. The immigration debate was ending, and Members were standing up and moving out of the Chamber. So coal was less worthy of attention than immigration, was it? Never mind, he would still have his say.

He listened to the Minister's statement; and then the Speaker was catching his eye, 'The Honourable Member for Belgate' was rising to his feet, and a voice, that might be his own, was resounding.

He made a mess of his opening remarks, as he always did when he had to speak in the House, but once he was into his stride he kept his eyes fixed on the government front bench, and the words flowed. 'In this time, Mr Speaker, the years 1947 to date, output in the nation's coalmines has remained almost the same, although manpower has declined from 108,291 in 1947 to 83,654 in 1961. In other words, productivity has improved. Pits have closed and the workforce has co-operated with the closure programme because we are told it is necessary to cut away the unhealthy parts so that the whole may thrive. But there is a limit to how much surgery the patient can stand, and I would like some assurance from the right honourable member opposite that willingness to sacrifice on the miners' part will be matched by willingness on the part of the Coal Board to get off its backside and institute some modern marketing methods to ensure not only the survival of coal but its pre-eminence as a source of energy.'

'Well done,' his neighbour whispered when he sat down,

but Frank had eyes only for the Minister opposite, who could hardly suppress a yawn.

Anne and Stella queued along the counter, choosing pie and chips with watery green peas, and lurid trifles in waxed paper dishes.

'You're still going out with that Fox, then?' Anne said when they were seated.

'Sometimes,' Stella said. 'He's not the only pebble on the beach.' She was grinning like an idiot as she spoke.

'Too many rings around Rosie, Rosie gets no ring at all,' Anne said ominously, but then her fork stopped half-way to her mouth. 'I don't know why I'm talking about marriage . . . you *are* married, in God's eyes.'

'I lived in purgatory over there, mam. Pray and work, work and pray. Land of the free? No one had told the Dimambros. But I'm divorced now, so it's all over, and you might as well face that.'

'Don't you miss your bairns? I don't know how you stand it.' Anne's brow was furrowed, her expression one of misery.

'I'll see them one day,' Stella said airily. 'And they're better off over there. Mario's a good father, I'll say that much for him.'

'To someone else's bairn.' Anne was bitter now.

'Not as far as Mario's concerned. He worships Tony. Tony has a chance to do all right. D'you think I'd've left him there if I'd . . .?'

'Yes,' Anne interrupted, 'I do think you'd've left him, Stella, if you were determined to hop it.'

'Oh well, if you're going to be like that . . .'

They ate in silence for a moment, and then Anne returned to the attack.

'Fox is a married man, our Estelle. There's no future in it. And he's a ruthless sod. If you knew what I know . . .'

Stella was grinning in a cat-who's-got-the-cream-way, and Anne wondered if she should tell her why Fox had been sacked from the Scar. Discretion prevailed. Stella had betrayed a confidence once, telling Frank how Anne had deceived him into marriage, so the less she was told the better. Fox was the type who would sue at the drop of a hat, and Frank couldn't be involved in scandal, being an MP and a public figure.

'Well,' she said, to close the conversation, 'I've had thirty years of purgatory with you so far. I hope the next twenty are going to be better.'

Stella smiled coolly. 'You'll have to wait and see.'

'I'm sorry about this,' Terry said as they squeezed into a booth, holding their glasses of wine carefully so as not to spill them. 'If I'd known you were coming down I'd've made sure I kept lunch-time free – or, better still, we could've had dinner. What are you doing tonight? I've got something on, but I could ditch it . . . it's lovely to see you. How is everyone?'

'Fine, as far as I know,' said Pamela, slipping off her jacket. 'I've been pretty busy, though. I wish we could meet tonight, too, but I've got an important meeting . . . so let's make the most of now. How long did you say you had?'

'Half an hour. So, who starts?'

'Me. My life is gloriously uncomplicated, so it won't take long. I love that shirt, by the way. Is is Liberty's?'

'Yes.' Terry was self-consciously tucking down her collar. 'It was a present, so I'm fond of it.'

'From a man? *The* man, if all I hear is true.'

'What on earth do you mean?' A red flush had risen beneath Terry's pale, fair skin and her hands came down from her collar to form fists. 'There isn't anyone special. I mean – you know London . . . lots of ships that pass in the night. And you know mam and dad. I watch my Ps and Qs . . .' Her words trailed off as Pamela's eyes remained unwaveringly fixed on hers.

Suddenly Pamela reached out and covered Terry's hand with her own.

'Look. I didn't come here today just to see you, I admit that – fond as I am of you. You said I knew your parents. I not only know them, I respect them. As for your brother, I think I'm in love with him. Now, there's a confession for you! So for all those reasons, as well as our friendship, I care about you, Terry.'

Around them the bar throbbed with juke-box music and the laughter of city workers, but neither of the girls heard it. They were locked together in a capsule of emotion, each fearing what the other might say next.

Suddenly Terry's chin came up and she shook her head. 'Listen, this is silly. I know you care about me . . . and we're all dying for you and Gerard to get a move on. So what?'

'So someone put an idea into my mind, Terry . . . an idea so bizarre, so bloody awful, that I got on the first train and came down to make sure it isn't true.'

'What idea?' Terry had recovered her composure, now, and she lifted her glass and took a drink.

'Does the name "Dunane" mean anything to you?'

Terry's eyes closed for an instant and then snapped open, too nonchalantly. 'Weren't they friends of your mother? I've heard Aunty Es talk about them. At least, I think it was Dunane.' But her eyes avoided Pamela's.

'Are you sleeping with my Uncle Max?' It was a direct question, but Pamela already knew the answer and the tone in which she asked it was a weary one. There was no reply and after a moment she spoke again.

'I should've guessed something was up – you've always been so open. Gerry is the only inscrutable member of the Maguire family. If everything had been above board, you'd have told me every tiny detail about him. As it is, you've waffled for the last year. Or is it two? How on earth did you meet him? I hope to God it wasn't through us . . . that would be too awful.'

'You don't understand,' Terry said desperately. 'It's going to be all right in the end. When Max can break free. I love him so much, and she doesn't understand him – she left him in the war, and he was faithful to her all those years. Now he stays just for his sons, until they're established . . .'

'Don't go on,' Pamela interrupted. 'Let me get us both another drink and then I'll tell you one or two things about Max Dunane.' But as she shouldered her way to the bar, Pamela suspected she was wasting her time.

*

'I hate hospitals,' Anne said as they went through the massive doorway and the smell of antiseptic engulfed them. Outside it was still daylight, but the birds were flying back to their nests. 'We won't stay long, will we?'

'I don't suppose so,' Esther said. 'Let's just see how she is and take it from there.'

In the ward corridor they tapped on the door marked 'Sister-in-Charge'.

'Miss Barwick?' the Sister said, rising from her desk. She was small and pretty, and looked too young to be in charge of a ward. 'She's very poorly, I'm afraid. Very poorly indeed. We've screened her. But you can have a minute.'

She preceded them down the ward, and drew aside a screen. 'You've got some visitors, Miss Barwick. That's nice, isn't it? But don't talk too long.'

Inside the screens they seemed to be cut off from the life of the ward. 'Hello,' Esther said. 'I got your letter and I've brought my sister to see you.' The sight of the woman shocked her. She seemed half the size of their last meeting, and the hands that clutched the bedclothes were like claws. But the eyes were the same – alive with determination as she looked past Esther to where Anne stood, clutching her handbag in front of her like a shield.

'Sit down,' Aleida Barwick said, after a moment. 'Near to me. No, you.' It was Anne she wanted in the chair at the bedside, not Esther. 'You're Anne,' she said, and Esther saw her sister swallow and then nod, for once at a loss for words.

'I've wanted to meet you for a long time.' There was venom in her tone that lifted Aleida's head from the pillow. 'We could've been happy, your father and me. But that wouldn't do, would it? You'd rather have seen him dead than happy.'

'We never knew about you,' Esther said helplessly, stepping in for a strangely silent Anne. 'He never told us. How could we have made a difference when we didn't even know?'

'He was afraid to tell you . . . afraid of her and her tongue. "She's only a bairn," I said. "Don't take any notice." But he couldn't face up to her. So we couldn't marry.'

She was spent now, lying back on the pillow exhausted.

Anne cleared her throat. 'Well, all this is as it may be,' she said with uncharacteristic meekness. 'But how do we know you're telling the truth? I'm not denying you might've been friends with dad. He was a gentleman, I'll give him that, and he was polite to everyone. Maybe you just read too much into it? We all do that as time goes on – reminisce, pack it out a bit.' She was getting into her stride now and regaining her composure.

Aleida Barwick raised herself painfully on her pillows, her eyes glittering now that she had been challenged. 'So that's how you're going to take it,' she said. 'It never happened – is that it? Well, let me tell you, madam, it did happen. Sidney loved me. Physically, yes, but we had real love, pleasure in each other's company, laughter, delight in little things. He *was* a gentleman, your dad, in every sense of the word. But he was a good lover. I can see you don't like that – he *loved* me. Whenever he could get away from you and your cruel tongue, we made love. And I had his child. I was proud of that. I loved that boy and I worked for him.' She was panting, and Esther felt a sudden fear. The woman would kill herself if she went on like this.

'Please don't upset yourself. If you say that it was like that, I'm sure it was,' and she flashed a warning look at Anne, daring her to disagree. But nothing would stop Aleida Barwick now. Her voice rose shrilly.

'You killed him, cold-hearted venomous little bitch that you were. You killed him and you ruined my life.'

The Sister's head appeared between the curtains.

'I think you'd better go,' she said firmly to Esther, advancing on the bed. 'It's nice you've seen your friends, isn't it, Miss Barwick? They'll come back tomorrow.'

Esther and Anne stood awkwardly for a moment, and Esther laid a hand on Aleida Barwick's. Then the Sister shepherded them through the screens. In the corridor, she shook her head. 'I'm sorry, but you can see how it is. Poor soul, she's hung on as long as she could.'

Outside the sky was streaked with red and there were no birds left in the sky. Esther was expecting a torrent of recrimination from Anne, but there was not a word except a muttered 'thanks' when she folded her into the car. They were half-way back to Belgate before Anne spoke.

'Do *you* think they loved each other?' she asked.

Esther shut from her mind the memory of her father in that last year, drunken and stumbling. 'I don't think it matters now, Anne. Aleida thinks they did, and we'll never know. But you mustn't take what she said to you to heart. She's been brooding on it all these years, poor thing.'

When Esther had seen her into the house and driven away, Anne scalded a spoon of tea in a mug and sat down with it by the fire. No one had ever looked at her with hatred until tonight. With anger, yes. With exasperation and dislike – but never with hatred. Her mind was seething, but she didn't want to ring Frank. Not yet, not till she had sorted herself out.

She reached for the evening paper and began to leaf through it, hardly seeing the items because the picture in her mind, of a dying woman with hate-filled eyes, was too strong to be overcome.

'I wanted to bring you here because it was one of your mother's favourite places,' Max said as he and Pamela threaded their way towards their table, preceded by the head waiter. 'I was delighted when you telephoned me. Delighted! You know how fond Aunt Lee and I are of you – and the boys, of course. Your mama was our dearest, dearest friend.' They were seated now and he was turning to the attentive head-waiter, whispering, nodding and smiling.

'You'll like this wine: it's Macon Chardonnay, your mother's favourite.'

'You must have wined and dined my mother quite a lot to be so sure of her preferences,' Pamela said.

The barb had not gone home: if anything, Max's face brightened, as he leaned towards her.

'We were very close, Diana and I. It began when we were children. But I never realized how beautiful she was until one day I came home to Scotland Gate and she was there with Loelia. She hadn't been married long. It was like lightning – for both of us, I think.' He was silent for a moment, turning the stem of his glass round between forefinger and thumb, and when he looked up he had an air of determination.

'Actually, Pamela, there's something you should know . . . and I think now is the time to tell you.'

A waiter was placing quail's eggs before them, perfect white ovals in a pink sauce. Pamela looked down at her plate and then up at the man across the table. Around her the dining-room of the mighty Ritz Hotel buzzed with conversation and tinkled with laughter. She put a finger to her mouth, as though considering, and then she spoke.

'I wouldn't bother, Uncle Max. There's nothing you can tell me that I don't already know. You were present at my conception, I believe. You weren't present when I was born, or cried, or fell down or off my pony. You didn't console me when I lost my front teeth, or congratulate me when I passed my piano exams. Dad did all those things. According to Aunt Lee, Aunt Laura is going back to the States and your boys are going with her – but that doesn't mean you can walk into my life and claim me. I'm a big girl. I choose. Dad taught me that: to make choices. It's just one of many things I learned from him. I enjoy life, so I'm grateful for that single, brief contribution you made to my existence. But not grateful enough to spare you much time. In fact, I can feel my train getting steam up in King's Cross right now – so if you'll excuse me, I'll come to the real purpose of this meeting.'

Max Dunane's face was pale beneath the rusty hair, and his green eyes were suddenly wary. 'Pamela . . .' he began, but she held up an imperious hand.

'Please – I asked you to meet me because I have something to tell you. It's about Theresa Maguire. She's my friend, and her parents – her father especially – are people for whom I have the most enormous respect.'

Max had recovered himself a little. 'I know Theresa slightly. She's a friend of Greville's – you must know that.'

'Don't bother to lie,' Pamela said. 'You're using Terry, and we both know it. And I won't stand for it, *Uncle* Max. Do you understand? If you don't give Terry up – give her a convincing excuse, and then keep right away from her *forever* – I will make such trouble as you can't even imagine. I'm your daughter, remember . . . and my mother's daughter, too. My headstrong, beautiful mother who was also used by you. Well, I'm headstrong, and I have just enough of you in me to be a bastard if I have to be. I've had the benefit of being reared by one of the most decent men in the world, so I've turned out to be quite civilized – but it's there, *Uncle* Max, under the skin. I mean to make sure that Terry Maguire breaks free of you. I've talked to her, but she's too helplessly besotted to do anything about it. So it'll have to be you who severs the connection. Do I make myself clear?'

There was no reply, and Pamela repeated her words.

Max Dunane had lifted his glass. Now he drank from it, and then returned it to the table. 'There's little or nothing between me and the Maguire girl,' he said, with forced casualness. 'But if you're going to make such a fuss about it I won't see her again. And Pamela . . .'

She had pushed away her plate. Now she rose to her feet. 'Do enjoy the Chardonnay. And actually, my mother preferred a Puligny Montrachet. I thought you ought to know.'

As she walked from the dining-room her heart was thumping uncomfortably, but she knew with certainty that no case she could ever win in future would be as important as the one in which she had just triumphed.

27

February 1962

Howard and Esther were in London to discuss the refurbishment of the Mount Street house. They had considered giving it up, but decided to hang on to it for a year or two, until it became clear what the children intended to do. The boys had both gone late to university because of doing National Service. Now Ralph was working in the Boston branch of a London auction house, and Noel was settled in France, teaching English in a private school and struggling with his first novel. 'But,' Esther said, 'you can't count on Pamela always staying in the north. In a year or two things will all be clearer. Sell then, if you want to. In the mean time, let's do it up. And I must pay my share.' When Howard agreed, she felt a sense of relief that at least one of Diana's homes would remain theirs, for the time being, anyway.

At first she had been awed by the size of the London house, but now the very magnitude of the task was its charm. She was moving from room to room, considering and sometimes making notes, when she heard the doorbell ring and the lumbering sounds of the daily woman crossing the hall. The visitor was Loelia Colville, dressed in furs, a green pillbox perched on her immaculately coiffured hair.

'Esther! I bumped into Howard in Piccadilly and he said you were here.'

Esther made a mental note to disembowel Howard and waved Loelia through to the drawing-room. 'You'll have some coffee, of course? Excuse me while I speak to Mrs Gray.'

When she returned to the room Loelia was standing at

the fireplace, surveying her surroundings. 'Howard tells me you're going to redecorate all this.'

'Yes,' Esther said. 'It's time for a change.'

'Diana had such perfect taste,' Loelia mused, looking at the grey carpets, the white walls with their now-dated panelling, the reeded screens that divided the room, the ebonized furniture upholstered in grey. It had all been cared for over the long years, but now it looked shabby.

'Yes,' Esther said. She wanted to say 'but it's my turn now', escept that the words wouldn't come. And why should she sound petty and childish simply to counter Loelia? 'Yes,' she said again, 'Diana was talented. I shall simply have to do my best.'

'Of course,' Loelia said. 'You can but try.' Her tone implied it would be an uphill task. 'Diana would have changed it, of course, if it hadn't been for the war.'

'Yes,' Esther agreed. 'The war affected so much.'

'Does your sister still make your clothes?' Loelia asked, as they drank their coffee. 'So clever of her.'

'She really doesn't have time now,' Esther said. 'Her husband is an MP, so she's too busy with constituency affairs.'

'Of course, I remember.' Loelia smote her brow at her own forgetfulness. 'He inherited Howard's seat. How bizarre.'

'Oh, I wouldn't say that. At least we're keeping it in the family,' Esther said cheerfully. 'More coffee?'

They talked about Pamela, then, which was undoubtedly the real reason for Loelia's visit. 'We do so hope she'll come to Valesworth this year when the season's over. I'm very attached to her, Esther. I hope you understand that bond?'

'I do,' Esther said. 'Believe me, I do.' She was thinking of Pamela's account of her meeting with Max. Poor Loelia – if she had hopes of any reconciliation, she would be disappointed.

Loelia returned to the safe topic of fashion then. 'I go to Balmain now. He dresses Marlene Dietrich, you know. And he's safe. None of this H-line, Y-line nonsense of the 'fifties. Occasionally I go to Yves St Laurent. He's settled down so much since his terrible flirtation with short, short skirts. I like his A-line, and he uses the loveliest fabrics.'

She rose to go, full of apologies for her brief visit. 'Do feel free to call on me if you want to confer about the house. Two heads are better than one, and I do so remember Diana's hard work.'

When Loelia had gone Esther stood in the hall and raised her arms above her head in a gesture of frustration. Ask Loelia for advice? *'Fog mir a gang!'* she said aloud.

Later, when she and Howard lunched together, she told him of Loelia's visit. 'She didn't upset you, did she?' he asked.

'No, darling, I'm wise to Loelia. And I'm sorry for her too. She loved Diana, she probably feels guilty about Max's behaviour towards a friend, and the fact that Diana died intensifies that feeling. My presence . . . my obviously happy presence . . . in your life seems to her to obliterate Diana, so she has to fight me. You and I know that Diana is still very much alive – in your heart and in your children. It doesn't trouble me because I know, from my love for Philip, that one love doesn't cast out another. Pamela is another matter. I keep hoping she'll realize Pamela is her own woman now, quite independent of you and me. But I don't think she does. She sees it as a tug of war. She must pull on one end, or we'll wind up with the whole rope. It's sad, and I don't know what to do about it yet, but I'm working on it. If this thing between Pamela and Gerard develops, Pammy will need all the help she can get to fend off the Dunanes.'

He leaned forward to cover her hand with his own. 'How did you get to be so wise?' he said. 'But don't worry about Pamela: she can stand her corner.'

The room was painted a curious shade of beige, and the linoleum that covered the floor was worn and cracked. An electric kettle, in need of cleaning, stood on a side table along with a motley collection of cups and saucers. 'What a dump,' Stella whispered and looked down from her ranch mink jacket to her elegantly shod feet. Fox squeezed her arm, where it was threaded through his.

'Never mind,' he said. 'I'll make it up to you.'

'You sure as hell will,' she said in the Yankee drawl that always amused him.

He shot back an expensive cuff to reveal a gold wristwatch. 'They're taking their time.' But at that moment the registrar came back in with a young clerk, and a cleaner wiping her hands on her hessian apron.

'Right,' he said. 'Miss Blake and Mrs Shotley will be your witnesses. Now, can we get on? I'm running behind.' The next moment, or so it seemed, Stella Dimambro, *née* Maguire, was Mrs Edward Fox. 'I've done it,' she thought, as she lifted her face to be kissed. 'I'll never need to scrimp and scrape again.'

They went from the registry office to the Mowbray Hotel where champagne was waiting on ice in a side room. 'Well, Mrs Fox, what do you want for a wedding present?' he said, as he helped her out of her fur jacket.

He half-expected her to blush and say, 'Now I have you I have everything,' but he should have known better. She ran her hand down her raspberry shift dress and adjusted the little raspberry Jackie Kennedy pillbox hat that perched on her blond head. 'I know exactly what I want, Eddy, darling. I want a great, big house.'

Anne was frying herself a decent tea. Lately she'd got out of the habit of eating a proper meal. It was easier to pick, now she was on her own most of the time. But today she felt like feeding her face: sausage, bacon, black pudding, a mushroom, a tomato, and two sliced left-over taties. Her mouth was watering as she began to shovel the contents of the frying pan on to a warmed plate. A couple of slices of bread turned over in the fat, and she'd have a meal fit for a king . . . or even an overworked MP's wife.

She was turning the second slice when she heard the car at the door and then the patter of high heels on the yard. It couldn't be Esther – she was in London. And Stella would still be at work. It must be Angela.

But the figure that appeared in the doorway was that of her eldest daughter, done up like a dog's dinner in a fur jacket with carnations pinned on it, flashing a ring like a searchlight on her outstretched hand. And behind her, lurking in the doorway, was the figure of Fox, whom Anne did not, could not, and never would, like.

'Mam, I've come to tell you the good news. You haven't lost a daughter, you've just gained a son.'

It was too reminiscent of that other arrival – Stella with Mario, and the bairn on the way. Anne's appetite deserted her. Silently she pressed down on the pedal bin and decanted her plateful of tea into the rubbish. 'Well,' she said when she'd straightened up, 'I hope you're not expecting congratulations.' She looked at Fox. 'You'd better sit down, I suppose.'

For once Edward Fox was taken aback. He had expected not only congratulations but gratitude for having made an honest woman of Stella. After all, he was a hell of a catch. He cleared his throat. 'All right, Mrs Maguire, I'll sit down. Any chance of a cup of tea?'

'In a minute,' Anne said. She motioned Stella to a chair and then sat down herself, facing them. 'Let's get a few things clear,' she said to Fox. 'I wish her dad was here to back me up, but he isn't, so I'll just have to manage on my own. Now, I know you two: never mind the fancy get-ups – I know you. I gave birth to her and she's been a headache ever since. I've known you since you wore a uniform and gaiters up at the Scar. And what I know isn't much to be proud of. One way and another, I reckon you two deserve each other. I won't say it'd be a shame to spoil two families because I'm a Christian and it's your wedding-day. But I will say this to you, our Stella: this is your last chance, as far as I'm concerned. I've had my last shock from you, miss.' She looked at Fox. 'So you'd better get a rein on her, and keep a rein on yourself in future – or you'll both be for it.'

She was spoiling for a fight and would have welcomed an outburst from one or both of them, but as usual Stella took her by surprise.

'Thanks, mam,' she said sweetly. 'I knew you'd be pleased at the news.'

'Try this,' Gerard said, picking a morsel up between chopsticks and lifting it to Pamela's lips.

'Umm – nice. What is it?'

'Pork, I think. The blissful thing about Chinese cooking is you're never sure.'

'You like enigmas, don't you?' Pamela said but he merely smiled in answer.

They were seated in Sunderland's first Chinese restaurant, its tables crowded with enthusiastic diners sampling unusual culinary treats. As they ate she watched him, sometimes catching his eye so that they exchanged smiles and did not look immediately away.

'My God, I love him,' she thought – thinking, too, that although there were elements of Maguire in him, Frank's integrity and Anne's stubbornness, he was really his own man. 'A one-off,' she thought ruefully as they came at last to fragrant China tea. He was not lily-fair like his sisters, nor auburn like David and Bernard. His hair and eyes were darker, more like his mother's colouring, and he had long, slender hands. She shivered, thinking how nice it would be to be held in his arms. All they had now was friendship, and it was ceasing to be quite enough.

'Are you going to stand for the executive?' she asked, to change the flow of her own treacherous thoughts.

'Probably not,' he said. 'At the moment I can't see who else I'd support, but I'm not Labour right-or-wrong like Dad. And you have to admit some of our comrades have a whiff of Big Brother about them.'

'Some of them. It's just bluster, they're good-hearted underneath.'

'Good-hearted . . . but are they good socialists? Do you want a fag?' As they both lit their cigarettes Gerard went on: 'If socialism means anything, it means respect for your fellow-man . . . and woman. So my hackles rise when I hear "We know best," or "It's for their own good".'

'I know what you mean. Dad has a quote from Douglas Jay, who wrote something called *The Socialist Case* before the war, and was pretty sniffy about the man in the street. Or the woman. Dad had one sentence by heart: "For in the case of nutrition and health, just as in education, the gentleman in Whitehall really does know better what is good for people than the people know themselves." There, didn't I remember that well?'

'Clever,' Gerard said.

'As well as beautiful?' She was teasing him, but it was half-serious and they both knew it.

'Passable, for a woman.'

'Thank you for the hyperbole, comrade. And here was me thinking you were a cut above most men. Now I hear a distinct sneer in your voice when you say "woman".'

'This is nice tea,' he said.

'Never mind tea, Gerard Maguire. Pay some attention to me.'

He put out a hand and teased her dark hair out of her eyes. 'Why should I?'

She was tempted to say, 'Because I want you to,' but hurt and pride intervened.

'Why should you, indeed?' she said, with an attempt at flippancy, and then, 'Let's get out of here.'

They were leaving the restaurant when she spoke again and her voice was not quite steady. 'You'd never have made a priest, Maguire. There's not a compassionate bone in your body.'

Gerard waited until they were out in the street, and then he gripped her elbow and steered her almost roughly towards a shop doorway. Pamela half-protested, but went with him just the same. And in the dark recesses of the doorway, with only eyeless fashion models to see, he kissed her without compassion but with a vehemence that left nothing to be desired.

28

November 1962

Esther had chosen pale colours for the Mount Street walls and a patterned carpet that spread, like a flower meadow, throughout the house. When it was finished it was light, airy and spacious, a perfect setting for Diana's furniture and Howard's excellent watercolours – but not a family home. Perhaps Howard was right and they should let it go now, she thought. Perhaps it was time for loyalty to Diana to be laid to rest.

In the fifteen years they'd been married they had used the house several times a year, no more; the children, when they stayed there, must rattle around in it like peas in a drum. 'This is not a house for the 'sixties,' she thought. 'Not for one family, at least.' It was a house for the 'twenties, with servants two a penny, and time to entertain and fill the huge rooms with guests. 'We are rich,' Esther thought, for indeed she was rich in her own right now, thanks to Sammy. 'We are rich, but we are not leisured.' The day of a large rich, leisured class was over.

It was November and London was beginning to hum with the excitement of the festive season. 'I'm going to enjoy this Christmas, with everyone home,' Esther said the following morning. She was lying in bed in their Mount Street bedroom while Howard got dressed, looking out of the window as he did so.

'Yes,' he said. 'It will be nice.' It was a flat statement and his head was bowed over the cufflink he was inserting.

'Darling, you sound jaded.' Esther raised herself on her pillows. 'Are you tired?'

He did look at her, then, and he smiled. 'A bit. Nothing that a trip to the theatre won't cure. I've got to dash: I've got a meeting with the Board of Trade at ten, but I'll be back here on time for lunch.'

As Howard made his way downstairs, he could hear his wife singing as she got ready for her bath. It was half-past eight and he was due at the consultant surgeon's at nine-thirty. 'Don't tell Esther,' he had warned Pat Quinnell when they agreed an appointment should be made. 'We're going to London in any case, to put some final touches to the house. I'd rather she didn't know, because in all probability it's nothing – why cause her concern?'

But as he emerged on to the Mount Street steps, he had a sudden foreboding that, whatever lay ahead of him this morning, it would not be lightly brushed aside.

'You're looking cheerful, Anne,' Mary said, as they settled into their seats either side of the restaurant table. 'Coffee for two please, and cakes,' she told the hovering waitress.

Anne scratched at a faint spot on the cloth and scrutinized the pastry fork.

'H'm', she said dubiously and then, her face clearing, 'I'm still over the moon about Cuba. We could've had another world war, Mary . . . and our David in the front line.'

Two weeks ago the world had held its breath until the United States and Soviet Russia stepped back from the brink. Mr Kruschev had promised to remove Russian missiles from Cuba, and President Kennedy had promised to lift the US blockade of that island. There had been a world-wide sigh of relief and universal acclaim for the young US President. Only Fidel Castro, who had not been consulted by either side, was displeased by the way things had turned out. Anne, who had prayed till her knees were black and blue, regarded the settlement as all her own work, with a little bit of help from God thrown in.

'Speaking of David,' Mary said, 'what happened to his big romance? The German girl you were once so worried about?'

'He finished with her, thank God.' Anne's face was a study in disapproval. 'According to him, she was a cross between Mrs Beeton and Saint Teresa. But I had her marked. He sent us a photo of her, and her eyes were set close together, Mary. You know what that means. Besides, if he was a bit older, if he'd seen what we saw, he'd've known you can't trust a German.'

'He was twelve when the war finished, Anne.'

'Eleven! And I kept the worst of it from my bairns . . . more's the pity.'

'We can't go on blaming the Germans forever. Certainly not new generations. As Pat says, bairns are born innocent.'

'Excuse me, Mary. British bairns well may be, but German bairns are another matter. Now, let it drop. I won't have my morning out spoilt . . . not for a Hun.'

Around them the café hummed with gossip and the tinkling of cups. 'What d'you think about this Marilyn Monroe business?' Mary asked. 'Was it suicide? The papers say one thing one day, another thing the next.'

'I hope not,' Anne said gloomily. 'Suicide's a sin. I cried my eyes out when it came on the TV. She only needed a bit of real love.'

'Yes,' Mary said. 'We all need that. Thank God our Catherine's got a good man.'

'Oh.' Anne was smug as she raised her cup. 'You've decided it's OK now, have you?'

Mary smiled sweetly. 'Would you like the éclair or the cream horn, Anne?'

'Our Stella's still house-hunting,' Anne said when the cream horn was demolished. 'But the big news is . . . I think our Terry's coming home!'

'So we concentrate on large supermarkets,' Sammy said, closing the file and pushing it back towards Stretton. 'The figures are plain, that's the way ahead. Bulk orders for better buying terms, active selling, special offers as traffic-builders for goods with better margins. Special weeks, in-store competitions . . . the sky's the limit.'

'We'll need close stock-control,' Stretton said.

Sammy nodded. 'Automatic invoicing, and streamlining of the warehousing system. But whatever it costs to improve or invent, we still do so much better here.' He

apped the folder. 'I think we should close down or sell all
he peripheral industries, and concentrate on what we
vere originally. We've made money out of furniture,
specially in the early 'fifties, and the other bits and bobs
have paid their way. But this – this can be gigantic,
Norman. So, I'll put it to the board at the next meeting and
presumably they'll agree.'

'When is Esther coming back?' Norman asked as they
moved to the door.

'Tuesday, I think. I hope they're having a good time. She
deserves it. How is your Catherine and the *girl tshik'l*?'

'You shouldn't have asked that, Sam,' Stretton said,
putting down the folders he was carrying. 'I just happen to
have some snaps here . . .'

Howard walked in a daze for a while. The confusion had
begun as soon as the surgeon had faced him across the
desk after the examination was complete. There had been
compassion in the man's face, the sight of which had
confirmed Howard's own pent-up fear.

'There's definitely something there – a tumour in the
region of your colon. I think we should operate as soon as
possible,' the man was saying. 'We'll need to do tests. I
presume you can come in at once?' So he was to be
admitted to a private hospital in a few days' time, days in
which he must break the news to Esther and his children.
'Try not to worry,' the surgeon had said, but he had not
liked meeting Howard's eye, and that was another bad
sign.

He hailed a cab at the end of Wimpole Street and heard
himself say 'Trafalgar Square' to the driver, for no reason
he could summon up. He thought about changing his
request – but where would he go to? Where did he want to
be at this particular moment? The answer was, nowhere.

He alighted at the National Gallery, seeing the students
thronging the steps. Did he want to look at works of art?
He turned away and began to walk aimlessly, first towards
South Africa House, and then past the figure of Nelson on
his column and towards Whitehall.

Clouds were gathering in the sky to obscure the weak

November sun, and Howard felt suddenly chilled. In a month or so it would be Christmas. They would bring the great tree from Norway and raise it in the Square. And after that it would be a new year. He was suddenly conscious of the passage of time – spring, summer, autumn, winter, the years passing, a life rushing by.

He glimpsed Big Ben between buildings as he walked. He had been a Member of Parliament for all those years and never made a mark, except in constituency matters. What had his life been worth, when it came to a statement of profit and loss?

Buses and taxis sped past as he walked down Whitehall between the great, grey-white buildings; and then the Cenotaph was before him, rising from a sea of red poppy wreaths, tribute to the 'glorious dead' of two world wars. He sniffed suddenly, certain he could smell mimosa, remembering the landlady's face when she told him Trenchard was dead. Trenchard, his friend of the trenches, dead in a garret because his country had had no further need of him. And Rupert, born almost as Trenchard died and dead in his turn at twenty-two. Had it been for nothing? All it had produced was an age of fear created by two big power-blocks bent on perfecting their military machines.

The three flags were stirring gently in the breeze as he stood there, his hat in his hand, remembering. The winter trees were bare, except for single leaves here and there clinging to their branches, only to be whirled crackling away at the wind's behest. 'Like our lives,' he thought, and turned heavily for home.

Nathan's old letters were getting worn, creased by constant folding and unfolding. There had been no new letters now for a long time. 'I'm glad,' Ruth told herself fiercely. 'It's what I wanted for him. He's happy – that's all that matters.' But it hurt that he had not written to tell her, if he had met someone else. 'I thought we were close enough for him to let me know it.'

It was growing dark in her room, and she switched on

274

her bedside lamp. Just one more letter and then she must go to Naomi.

Today I went to Yam Kinneret, the Sea of Galilee. There is a settlement there, near a hill called Sussilia. Once upon a time the hills here were covered with trees, but the Turkish occupation did away with most of the forestation. There is a sardine-canning industry here but the lake is supposed to hold more than twenty species of fish. The whole place is so beautiful, Ruth. You must see it one day. I stood on a flower-covered slope, looking across the blue expanse to Mount Hermon. I feel at peace here in Israel, even when we have arguments in the kibbutz general meeting. We're all expected to attend that, and take part in decisions, and it can get heated at times. But we are a family, after all – the first family I've had since I left Czechoslovakia.

Do you still think of Munich? Sometimes I remember my mother's raisin blintzes and her boiled cabbage. Did I tell you boiled cabbage is almost the Czech national dish? Come and cook cabbage for me, Ruth, and see this beautiful country.

Ruth had to stop reading then, before tears overcame her. It would never do for Naomi to know she had been crying. She went to the bathroom before she joined the others and sluiced her face with cold water, but in the mirror her eyes looked back at her, sad and shadowed.

It was dark, now, and she found Naomi sitting in an unlit room, unable to put on the light for herself. 'Naomi?' In the distance was the sound of Sammy playing with the children, clowning until they roared with laughter. A phone rang, and she heard Sammy cross the hall to answer it.

'Don't put on the light,' Naomi said from the depth of her chair. 'Not yet. Come and sit beside me. I love this time, when we are all here, in the home, and the day has gone well.'

Ruth crossed to the hearth and kneeled at her sister's side. 'Yes,' she said. 'It's good to be safe in the home.' Even to her own ears her voice sounded muffled. 'I think

275

I'm getting a cold,' she said, sniffing and reaching for a handkerchief, noticing as she did so the patterns the flames of the fire made, dancing on the ceiling.

'Are you happy, Ruth?'

Here it was, the question she had dreaded. She summoned up her courage and a cheerful voice. 'Of course I am.'

'You don't hear from Nathan any more?'

'Not for a while, no. Well, they have a lot to do there, and not much time for writing letters.'

'Do you mind that, Ruthie?'

'No, not really. He's a friend, and no one likes to lose touch with a friend. But I have other friends.'

In the darkness she heard Naomi sigh. 'Ruth, my arms and legs may let me down. My brain still works.' She was tearful now, her careful control deserting her. 'Why aren't you honest with me? We're sisters. I know you think of Nathan – why pretend otherwise? And I know you dream of Israel. Well, don't you?'

It was too direct a question to permit a lying answer.

'All right, Naomi, I'll tell you – because if I don't, you'll imagine something worse. Nathan and I did once talk about my going to Israel. It's the dream of every good Jew, isn't it? But that's all it is, a dream. Forget it. And forget Nathan. I have.'

The room blazed into light suddenly, as Sammy came in, his face a picture of misery, so that Naomi forgot her own agitation. 'Sammy! What's wrong?'

'It's Howard. He was ringing from London. He's got to have an operation – some internal thing. He's going to tell Esther tonight, but he wanted me to know the facts, in case she turned to us for help.'

'It's serious, isn't it?' Naomi asked, looking from one to another.

'Yes,' Ruth said. 'I know about it, and it's serious. But it's not hopeless. There's a difference.'

They talked for a while, all trying to make conversation, and then Ruth went off to see to the children. Sammy sat down opposite his wife.

'Come here,' Naomi said. 'Oh, how I wish I could come to you . . .' Sammy came then, quickly, and she put weak arms around him. 'This must be faced, Sammy. And now that we speak, *we* have to stop pretending, too. I am not going to get better.' He would have hushed her but she was not to be stayed. 'But neither am I going to slip away the next moment. You live as though there was only today, Sammy, working, planning, struggling . . . anything not to think. But we must think . . . think of what we have together, you, me and our children.'

'I think of that all the time,' Sammy said.

'Good!' Naomi said, leaning back to see him better. 'Because I'm planning to be around still for a very long time.'

Sammy's head drooped as his eyes filled, until at last he looked up and smiled at his wife. 'What a *shlemil*,' he said. 'I cry at the drop of a hat.'

'Only a *shlemil* sometimes,' Naomi said. 'Most of the time, a genius. So tell me, what are we going to do about Ruth? And Esther, too. She must have as much time away from the business as she needs to nurse Howard back to health. I will think of ways to help and . . .'

'I can carry them out,' Sammy said ruefully. 'Of all the women in the world, I picked the slave-driver.'

29

December 1962

'There now . . .' Sammy had reached the light switch, and light flooded the Mount Street hall. 'I could do with a drink, and so could you.' He and Esther had waited at the hospital while Howard's operation was taking place, Sammy having come to London at Naomi's insistence. Howard had recovered from the anaesthetic and was sleeping, and Pamela had elected to stay by her father's side, urging Esther to get some sleep so that she could take over in the morning. Sammy now set her down by the fire, making it up with coal from the scuttle, before he went to the sideboard and poured a generous measure of brandy for each of them.

'Drink up,' he said. 'The worst's over, Esther, but Howard's going to need you in the coming weeks, that's certain. So in a moment, bed. Do you have hot-water bottles in this grand house?'

'In the kitchen,' Esther said. 'Hanging on the larder door. There should be two or three.' He went away, then, and she sat watching the fire, trying not to remember Howard's face, white and thin, wincing occasionally as pain struck him. Or the nurse beside the bed, which was a sign that he was still in danger. Or the tubes taped into his flesh, and the drainage tube that came from under the blankets to the bag hanging from the side of the bed. The smell of pain and death was in her nostrils, the smell of Philip's sickroom, of her father laid out in the bedroom. But Howard was not dead – not yet . . . She managed to set down her glass before sobbing engulfed her. Then Sammy was in the room, tutting, shaking his head, taking her in his arms.

'*Oy vey*, Esther, don't take on so . . . he will be all right hold on to that, as I hold on to my Naomi. You have to hope, Esther.'

'But I'm afraid, Sammy. I'm frightened.' She could hear the scream gathering in her chest, threatening to escape.

'Cry then. If you are frightened, cry.' She laid her head against the smooth cloth of his expensive jacket and wept, remembering as she did so the little boy who had leaped into her life all those years ago. '*So you're the new Shabbos goyah,*' he had said, and had held out his hand. She had been fifteen and he had been thirteen, and he had turned from shaking her hand to beg her father's housekeeper for cookies.

'Oh, Sammy,' she said when at last she had dried her eyes, 'what would I do without you?'

They sat back, sipping their drinks and cheering one another, until at last he looked at the clock and said, sternly, 'Bed!'

But before she went upstairs he had one more story to tell her. 'Do you remember the war? When I went away and you kept saying I was up to something?'

'Yes,' Esther said. 'And you were being a spy and writing postcards to put us off the scent. And getting medals for being deceitful, into the bargain.'

'State secrets,' he said. 'I was on war work. Seriously though, I lay down to sleep one night, and I was so afraid. And then I remembered something I'd heard Churchill say when he spoke to occupied France. He said, "Sleep, to gather strength for the morning. For the morning will surely come." So sleep Esther – and in the morning, I'll bring you a cup of tea in bed.' He kissed her brow, and stood while she mounted the stairs. '*Shalom,*' he said when he turned on the landing, and blew her another kiss with his hand.

Ralph was the first to arrive the following morning, setting down his bags in the hall and straightening to kiss Esther on the cheek. 'How is he? And you? I caught the first possible flight but I wish I could have been with you last night.'

'He's fine, Ralph. I'm going to the hospital now, but

279

Pammy rang me first thing to say the night had gone we
Noel telephoned from Victoria. He should be here an
minute.'

And a few moments later, there he was, looking appr
hensive until he saw Esther was smiling. 'He's OK, ther
Thank God.'

She drew them through to the kitchen, and quelled th
desire to go to Howard there and then. 'It's going to be
pretty long haul. We have to pace ourselves, if we're goin
to be really effective. I'll go to the hospital now; you con
over when you've had a bath and a rest. I know you'll bot
want to see him this morning. After that we'll make a rot
And please look after Pammy when she gets here – she
had a long night.'

The boys were relaxing a little, comforted by the pract
cality of her suggestions, unaware that inside she wa
afraid. Afraid for Howard; even more afraid of having 1
make a life without him. But then she remembered Samm
last night, and his 'gather strength for the morning'. Aft
that, she had slept.

'Sam Lansky's upstairs,' she said. 'Getting a bath, I thinl
He's been here since yesterday morning, and I don't knov
what I'd've done without him. Do make sure he has som
breakfast. I've left everything ready.'

But it was Sammy who took over the chef's role when h
appeared, breaking eggs with one hand, wisecracking a
he did so, filling the kitchen with the nearest thing t
laughter they could muster in the circumstances – so tha
Esther could break away, well satisfied that she was leavin
her family in the best of hands.

It was noon when Sammy pushed open the office door an
advanced on the enquiry desk. 'Mr Lansky for Mr O'Ha
gan,' he said.

'Ah, yes,' the girl said. 'I'll just tell him you're here.'

'Now, Mr Lansky,' O'Hagan said, when Sammy ha
been ushered upstairs and was seated in the client's leathe
chair. 'I understand you want someone traced?'

'I think perhaps what I want is a miracle,' Sammy said
'For reasons I'd like to keep to myself, I can't speak to m

friend – so the only information I have is what I can remember myself, and it's sketchy. It was more than thirty years ago. However, I'm told you're the best in the business, so perhaps you'll give me a miracle. I can afford it, that's one good thing.'

O'Hagan was smiling and tilting back in his chair. 'I like the sound of this,' he said. 'A challenge. Let's see what you've got.'

'I've got a date in 1930, and a place, Whitby, in Yorkshire. A girl called Esther Gulliver gave birth to a child, a boy. The doctor's name was Gilroy and there was a nurse assisting him. I don't remember her name but the pair of them always worked together, so it shouldn't be too hard to find her.'

'How old was the doctor?'

'Oh, forty, forty-five. Why? Ah, yes . . . he's still alive.'

'We hope. But yes, in all probability he is. Go on.'

'The doctor was to arrange the child's adoption – it was a family in the area who couldn't have children, that's what Esther was told. And I can see you're curious, so I'll tell you: I wasn't the father. That's not why I want to trace him. I want to do that because Esther Gulliver is my friend. And I must be honest and tell you that I've tried to trace the boy once before, and they said it couldn't be done.'

The car was long and sleek, and when Anne sat in the front passenger seat she sank down and down into soft leather upholstery.

'It's not like you to be up at the crack of dawn. Where are we going?' she asked, but Stella just shook her head.

'You'll see.' She was wearing trousers in an indecent shade of cream that would show every mark, and a shaggy fur jacket that looked and felt expensive.

'You're sure you've got enough jewellery on?' Anne asked, as Stella's ringed fingers let out the clutch and the car purred into action.

'Nice, aren't they?' Stella said, unperturbed by sarcasm. 'And plenty more where they came from. Eddy says you can't do better than diamonds when it comes to investing. How's me dad, by the way? Still ruling Britain?'

'Your dad's all right, but your Auntie Esther's got trouble. Howard's had half his insides taken out. A major operation, in London. Your dad says he looks like death.'

'Pity,' Stella said, negotiating the Half Moon corner. 'But then he's getting on, isn't he?'

'He's only sixty-six,' Anne said indignantly. 'Not that much older than me and your dad, if it comes to that. And where are we going, Stella? This is not the road to Sunderland.'

'I never said we were going to Sunderland.' She was going to play it out to the last second, the little bitch.

'You don't change,' Anne said wearily. 'You do not change.'

'You can't improve on perfection, mother, so why should I bother?'

Now the car was turning towards the Scar.

'What's this, then?' Anne said as they drove up the hill, and through the gates – and the house, long and white and green-roofed, loomed up before them, its windows sparkling in the winter sunshine.

'You know what it is, mam – it's the old Brenton house. Where you nearly went as a skivvy, as you never tired of telling me. And now it's all mine!'

'Beb!' Esther rose from her seat beside Howard's bed as her son came uncertainly into the room.

'Mum . . . Dad . . .' He was looking at the paraphernalia of post-operative treatment, the trolleys and tubes and suspended bottles of plasma and glucose, and there was horror in his eyes.

'It's all right, darling, Dad's going to be fine.'

'Beb.' Howard's voice was husky and his lips were crusted. Esther dipped a swab into the small bowl of sterilized water and gently wiped his mouth. 'That's better, thank you. Come here, Beb . . . where I can see you.'

The night before his operation, Howard had reproached himself for Beb's birth. 'Perhaps I was too old, Esther. If . . . if I don't live to see him up . . . what will happen?'

She had snapped back at him, angry at his assumption of guilt. 'I was the one who decided to have him, Howard,

282

so if anyone's to blame it's me. And I'm glad I did it. He's had you for fifteen years, and according to the Jesuits, seven years is enough. And he's got much more of you to come.'

She looked at her son as he bent over his father. They were alike, dark and handsome and quiet. But strong, too - for now the boy had recovered his composure.

'I've been thinking an awful lot, dad, about when we're all back to normal at home for Christmas. I think it's time I learned to drive! You did say you'd take me to that old airfield, and ma says I can try in her car at first, it being a banger. So if you'll just get fit . . . I mean, I know it's early days because I'm not tremendously mechanical, but it would be huge fun to make a start . . .'

'Just the right thing to say,' Esther thought, and was suddenly filled with pride that her son was a *mentsh*, and a wise one at that.

Howard's face had brightened. 'I remember when the others were learning – I used to close my eyes at times.'

'They drive terribly well now,' Beb said wistfully.

'So will you.' Howard's mouth had dried again and Esther stepped forward with a swab.

'Thank you,' he said when she was done, and looked at Beb again. 'I wish you'd known Rupert. You'd have liked him.'

'I feel I do know him really.' Beb smiled up at his mother. 'Ma's told me about him, and so have Ralph and Noel. But it's Pammy who knew him best. She took me to Durham Cathedral once, to see the RAF window there. She said Rupert was like the pilot in the stained-glass, very brave and dashing.'

Esther felt her lips tremble and clamped them together. She knew the window Beb had referred to, and had stood beside Howard at its dedication, not long after the war. There, in the glass, were the grey skies of the north above smoking chimneys and the huddled houses of a Durham village, and the towers of the cathedral too. But what held the eye was a young pilot, kneeling on the outspread wings of an eagle, looking up into the skies where angels hovered. And below were the words: '*As birds flying so shall the Lord of Hosts protect Jerusalem*'.

Her eyes met Howard's and she saw that he too wa
remembering that dedication day.

'I think your father ought to sleep now,' she said, an
Beb straightened up.

'OK. Hurry up and come home, dad. I've heaps to te
you, and I'm longing for those driving lessons. Also, m
chess has improved. I'll knock you for six next time w
play.'

30

February 1963

Once more Sam Lansky was meeting with O'Hagan, but this time the setting was an hotel in Robin Hood's Bay, where O'Hagan had been staying to pursue his enquiries in Yorkshire.

'I've found the doctor. Of course, he's retired now. Affable, but not about to betray a professional confidence. The nurse who was midwife died three years ago.'

Sammy groaned, until O'Hagan spoke again.

'It's not all bad news. The birth of Esther Gulliver's son was registered, so I was able to check the birth date. You had it right. Then we checked the court registers for adoption orders that tallied with the statutory period that has to elapse between adoptive parents taking the child and the court making it legally theirs. We found two which tally: the child was a boy with the same birth date, in both cases. We've traced one, but the other died in infancy. You said Esther Gulliver's child was healthy?'

'As far as we knew,' Sammy said, remembering the child in Esther's arms, the steady blue unfocused gaze. 'So there's only the other one?'

'The family and boy moved to York in 1938 – that much we know. We're checking the schools now. His name is Peter Elphinstone. Of course, he may not be the one: the adoption might have taken place outside the jurisdiction of the Whitby court. If so . . .'

'It would be like looking for a needle in a haystack,' Sammy said. 'Well, we'll hope for the best. Keep checking. I'd like to know for certain before I speak to Esther.'

*

Ruth had wheeled Naomi into the garden to see where bulbs were breaking through the frozen earth.

'I love the spring,' Ruth said. 'An English spring. Do you remember when we came? It was summer, but we were so cold.'

'Out of so much misery, good came. Papa loved having us here . . . and Sammy has been happy with me. He has been happy, hasn't he, Ruth?'

'Silly question – you know he has. And Esther has liked being our friend. I worry for Esther . . .'

'How is Howard?'

'As far as we know, the cancerous tissue was removed. But we won't know for sure if he's cured, for a while. He is weak, and not a good patient, I think. Cancer is much like other illnesses, in that the body can react in strange ways – you know that from your own illness. The mind always plays a part. It sounds like witchcraft when you say it, and doctors are wary of making too much of it, but we all know it is true. Believe you will get well, and you frequently do. Give up, and you die. I think it's probably got a sound scientific basis – will-power producing some helpful chemical reaction – but I wouldn't dare to say that to a gathering of my fellow practitioners. So there's hope for Howard, if he fights back. And medicine is making such strides. Last week they transplanted a kidney into a man whose kidneys had failed. Isn't that a miracle? TB and polio have been conquered. There's so much progress.'

They had paused beside a row of green shoots powering upwards from the earth. 'I'll be glad to see the daffodils come out,' Ruth said.

'What about the iris and the cyclamen and the rock rose of Carmel.' Naomi smiled as she spoke, but Ruth frowned.

'What do you mean?'

'They're the flowers of Israel, aren't they?'

'Yes,' Ruth said slowly. 'But why bring them up now?'

'Because I need to talk to you and I want you to listen. We were interrupted last time. This time I mean to finish, and you know it wears me out to shout. But I will if I have to. So, be a good doctor and humour your patient.'

'Speak,' Ruth said airily, but avoiding her sister's gaze. 'Whatever you want, it's yours.'

'Anything?'

'Ah . . . well . . . anything within reason.'

'What I want is reasonable, Ruthie. I want you to tell me the truth. If it were not for me and for this illness, would you and Nathan be together in Israel?'

'No.' Ruth's denial was too quick.

'Ah,' Naomi said. 'So you would. I don't blame you. I have also been reading about this new country, which has a salty sea and a desert and a snow-capped mountain and flowers and forests.'

'Yes,' Ruth said, 'it's beautiful, they say. And I will go there one day, for a holiday. But my place now is here with you and the children and Sammy . . .' Her voice trailed off as she met her sister's quizzical eye, and then rallied. 'Anyway, Nathan doesn't write to me any more, as you know. There hasn't been a letter for months. Perhaps he's married . . .'

'And perhaps he's not,' Naomi said. She was fumbling beneath the blanket that covered her knees and at last her weak hands produced a flimsy air-mail letter. 'This is from Nathan. I stole it from the breakfast table this morning because I wanted you to read it in front of me. If it says Nathan is married, we'll both cry, and then we'll rejoice for him. If it says something else . . . I want to know what it is.'

Ruth took the letter from her sister's hand and opened it with careful fingers that shook slightly. Her face was tense, her lips compressed, and Naomi held her breath for the first hint of expression. Would it be joy or regret?

But when Ruth raised her head there was neither emotion on her face, and her eyes glittered with tears.

'Well?' Naomi said desperately.

'He's well . . .'

'Is he married? Is he getting married?' Naomi's agitation was almost lifting her out of her chair until Ruth began to read aloud.

'*And so, dearest Ruth, I ask you one more time, to come and share this land with me. The world is shrinking. If your sister needs you you can leap on to a fast plane . . .*'

'. . . and be there in minutes!' Naomi finished triumphantly.

'I *couldn't* go,' Ruth said despairingly. 'My place is here.'

'Your place is with Nathan, if he's the man you love. I want you to go to Israel, Ruth – not in spite of me, but *for* me. Sammy talks of travel . . . of Israel sometimes, of Disneyland, of Paris in the spring, and the Lido, and Rome. We know, you and I, that I am not going to leave this house, except perhaps to be wheeled in the sunshine. But you can go for me, Ruth. You can be my eyes and ears, and tell me of Israel and all the world I have never seen. If you stay, you would only be my doctor. So what's Pat Quinnell? But my sister, my friend, can travel. She can fill my head with the wonders of the world.'

'Sammy would never forgive me for going,' Ruth said flatly.

'You leave Sammy to me,' Naomi said confidently. 'He's only a *boy tshik'l*, after all.'

Pamela had wrapped her father up against the February chill and now, arm in arm, they went slowly out to the car.

'Would you take me to Belgate?' he said.

'Belgate? Why there?'

'Meaning there are prettier places? Perhaps. But I'd like to have a look at the old place . . .' He didn't say 'one last time' but it hung in the air.

She drove to the Scar, to a point below the old house from which they could look out over the village, seeing the clustered houses, the roads and railway lines from the pit, and the village green with its war memorial.

'Do you remember the victory bonfire down there?' Howard asked.

'No, I was away at Valesworth, remember? But I remember lots of lovely Guy Fawkes nights here before the war, and after. And Hallowe'en, and Rupert terrifying us all when we played Sardines.'

'Yes, we had some happy times. But now, tell me about this curious relationship of yours with young Maguire.'

'Not so young Maguire, dad . . . he's thirty-five and I'm thirty-three. Can you believe it?'

'No. Nor can I believe that Beb's sixteen. I wonder what he'll do? Follow Esther into the business probably.'

· 'And be a tycoon?' Pamela said thoughtfully. 'I don't think so. He's practical, like Esther, but I don't see him wheeling and dealing. I think he'll be an engineer . . . he's chosen to do maths and physics and chemistry, so you can see which way his mind's working. Whatever he does, he'll be OK. Beb's a happy person, dad. Not everyone is – it's quite an asset.'

'Are you happy, Pammy? Should I ask Maguire about his intentions?'

'Don't you dare! If I'm to die a spinster, I shall do it like Elizabeth I, with dignity. Anyway, I think you might say I have the matter in hand. You concentrate on getting well, and leave the rest to me.'

Sammy looked across the office to where Esther stood at the window, looking out on the winter day. 'Penny for them?' he said.

'Not worth it.' She turned back into the room. 'I'll be glad when the winter's over.'

'You and Howard should go on a cruise. Somewhere warm. I could get brochures for you and fix it all up?'

She smiled at his eagerness to help. 'I know you would, and I'd ask you if Howard could be persuaded.'

'He's still depressed?'

Esther shook her head. 'Not depressed. I think "detached" is a better word for it. As though he's slipping away from me. Oh, I know I have Beb and Pamela and the boys . . . and you and Anne. But I love Howard. I want years and years more with him, but . . . he seems to have given up.'

'Hey, the man's tired. He's had a brush with mortality – that tires you out.'

'If only he'd eat . . . Still, I mustn't go on. It's just that I feel I've lost so much over the years.'

Sammy hunched his shoulders, considering. When at last he spoke his voice was firm. 'I think you'd better sit down, Esther. It's time for confession.' He told her, then, of O'Hagan and the search for her son that might be coming to fruition. 'Have I done wrong?' he said at last, when the tale was told.

'I don't know.' Esther had paled, and her nose looked pinched in her face. 'I'm not sure I could face seeing him now he's a man. And what if he was the child who died? I've often wondered if Philip's frailty would've made a difference to his child's survival.'

'You don't have to meet him, Esther. I just wanted . . .' Sammy hesitated. 'And I'm certain your child survived. I feel it in my bones.'

'I suppose at least I'd know,' Esther said thoughtfully. 'But how could I come face to face with him? If he's happy, I wouldn't want to interfere. Better he doesn't know . . . unless he needs me.'

'It may be better that you don't actually meet him,' Sammy said. 'It could be complicated. We don't know if he knows he's adopted.'

'I would like to know he survived childhood and the war, that he's thrived,' Esther admitted. 'That would do. But finding him – my son – wouldn't make up for losing Howard. Nothing would do that.'

They were debating Europe in the House of Commons, denouncing De Gaulle's blocking of the British application for entry. De Gaulle stood for a close-knit Europe with a Latin slant, undiluted by the touch of the Americans and British, whom he deemed to have humiliated him during the war. Frank was none too keen on Britain's entry into the Common Market, but French ingratitude was hard to bear. 'I lost a son on a French beach-head,' he thought. 'Only to be turned down now.'

As he listened to the speeches, which were mostly so lacklustre that they hardly held the attention, Frank's mind wandered. Anne would be at home now, cooking or knitting, blazing up the fire, drawing a chair to the hearth to toast her feet on the fender. He could be there, too – except that his place was here, his punishment to listen to droning voices long into the night. The trouble with politics was that good men got out of it, and only the dross remained. No, that wasn't fair: there were good men on both sides . . . though Hugh Gaitskell's untimely death had meant a great loss to Labour.

Suddenly he thought of Howard Brenton, sitting here throughout the war and seeing the truly great men in operation: Churchill and Ernest Bevin and Attlee. Where was their like today? Howard Brenton was ill, and a shadow of himself, according to Anne. 'We wronged him,' Frank thought, not for the first time. 'We did what we thought was best, but we robbed him of a grandchild.' Left to himself, he would own up to it – but Anne would never allow it. She would do murder first.

Above Anne, on the screen, Elizabeth Taylor was making love to Rock Hudson, but for once the romance didn't grip her. Tonight she was missing Frank more than usual. If only she were going home to put the pan on the fire, and peel taties and neeps for a stew, ready for his coming home. She had not bargained for the loneliness in the days when getting him elected had been a mission so exciting that it blocked out thought of anything except the polls. 'I'm lonely,' Elizabeth Taylor said, and in the stalls Anne echoed her words. If Frank had been here tonight, he'd've told her not to worry about Terry, who was sitting in night after night, listless and losing her looks, as though her light had been put out. It wasn't natural for a girl of that age to live for her work, whether it was a good job or not. She'd've been better off like Angela, married to a power-loader and already fat with her third bairn.

And Frank'd've been there so she could confess her all-consuming guilt about Howard. Last night she had listened to Esther on the phone: 'He doesn't eat, Anne. There's not a picking on him.' She had promised to make Howard an egg-custard full of goodness and get him some Lourdes water, but it wouldn't go away. Thoughts of her father and Aleida intruded; and of Joe, and the times she had boxed his ears; and of Tony, a dark-eyed boy growing up amid the alien corn. She didn't stay for the B movie, a gangster story with Steve Cochran. There was trouble enough in her own backyard – what did she need with Chicago?

*

Stella and Edward Fox had dined at either end of the lon_
table when first they came to the Scar, sitting solemnl_
while 'the staff', as Stella liked to call them, carried thei_
food between them. But they soon tired of splendour, an_
opted instead for trays on their knees in front of the TV_
What they did not tire of was moving from room to roon_
to revel in their possessions and the changes they ha_
wrought in the house. There was a cocktail bar in ever_
reception room, suspended silk ceilings in the dining-roon_
and lounge, a floor-to-ceiling neon light on the landing_
and wrought-iron-over-glass doors everywhere. 'Sparse_
had been Stella's verdict on what remained of Diana'_
decor, when they took possession. Now the house held n_
trace of its first owners, except when seen from the hill, a_
sunset, when the green roof glowed and the windows . ._
the 'lots and lots of windows' of Diana's dream house . ._
were gold with reflected light.

Tonight Stella had news for Eddy. 'I've had a letter fron_
the States. Mario wants to send Tony over to us.'

'For good?' Fox almost choked on his T-bone steak.

'No, just for a few weeks. He thinks it's time Tony sav_
his mother's home-land. Well, I've told you what Mario'_
like for tradition. If he'd lived a bit more in the present da_
. . .' But she would still have left him, and they both knev_
it.

'I had everything over there,' she went on airily, crushin_
inconvenient memories. 'Everything. And they were_
lovely family – his mother and his aunts adored me. I wa_
waited on hand and foot.'

'Why did you leave then, if it was such a good sittin_
down?' Fox was picking a tooth with an ivory toothpick_
looking at the debris he managed to extract before h_
popped it back into his mouth.

'I've told you: I was homesick. And America's very fast_
Frightening sometimes.' She thought of Bud, and the awfu_
days after the shooting when he had sat in the blac_
Packard outside the brownstone while she feigned illnes_
and hid in her bed. 'I was glad to get out in the end – bu_
it'll be nice to see Tony again.'

'I suppose so,' Fox said grudgingly. 'Any mor_
cauliflower?'

As Stella spooned out more vegetables, she reflected that she had been right not to tell Eddy the truth about Tony's conception. She loved her husband, and he was a good provider — but he'd use anything, if it was to his own advantage. Some secrets were better kept secret forever.

31

May 1963

'Is that everything?' Ruth asked again.

'Yes,' Esther said patiently. 'That's everything.'

They were in the hall of the Lansky house, and Naomi, in her chair, was the only one smiling. Sammy looked downcast, and Esther determinedly cheerful. As for Ruth, she looked . . .

'Like a refugee,' Naomi said suddenly. 'You look exactly like we looked all those years ago, Ruthie. Harassed and weary and scared. Come on, where's your sense of adventure?' Her voice was noticeably weaker, but her smile was still brilliant.

'What do you want?' Sammy said. 'Two choruses of "Hava Nagela"?'

'If it helps,' Naomi said sweetly. 'Now, who will open the door?' The women stayed close together while Sammy loaded the bags, Esther knowing the turmoil under Naomi's cheerful exterior only because her hand was on her friend's shoulder and she could feel the tremor.

In the end the sisters clung to one another, and had to be parted; but it was Ruth who cried, her face pressed to the window of the taxi until it was lost to sight.

Sammy cleared his throat. 'It's a *she'alah*,' he told Esther when they had returned Naomi to the living-room and gone in search of tea. 'She shouldn't leave her sister now. Naomi needs her.'

Esther shook her head. 'Naomi has what she needs. She's cutting Ruth free. You ought to be proud of her, Sammy.'

'I am,' he said shamefacedly. 'Now, get out the cups and

don't be right all the time. In a partner this is not a good trait.'

'Shucks,' Esther said, shaking the caddy spoon like a castanet. 'And to think I never knew.'

'Sit down,' Sammy said, when Esther came into the office. 'I have a little news, and we need to talk.' He opened a folder on his desk. 'My detective has checked out the man I told you about – whose name is Peter, by the way – and he's sent a photograph, taken in the street, of Peter as he was going to his work.'

Esther's hand was shaking as she took the snapshot. If this were not her child, it would mean the child she had made with Philip was now probably dead – had never had a life. She peered at the photograph, wrinkling her brow. 'I don't know, Sammy. I mean, what am I looking for? There's a look of my father about him – at least, I think so. But it's so indistinct. It could be my son, I suppose. What else can I say?'

'Don't panic,' Sammy said, 'or I'll wish I'd left well alone. There's only one thing for it, Esther: we'll have to go to York. If you see him, you'll know – one way or another.'

Esther would have protested that seeing the man would change nothing, that she couldn't leave Howard – not even for a day; but she knew Sammy in this mood. He wouldn't take no for an answer. An hour later they were on the road to York.

'Don't think about it,' Sammy said as he threaded the big car along the road. 'Time enough for that when we get there. Talk about current events – food prices – anything.'

Esther talked obediently about the topic of all-consuming current interest: the Profumo scandal. 'He's the Secretary of State for War, Sammy, and the girl they say he's sleeping with is in cahoots with a Russian. And the Russian's almost certainly a spy, because everyone in that Embassy is up to something!'

'Well, it's tawdry,' Sammy conceded, 'but I don't think it's as important as the papers are making out . . .'

They both knew that the rumours sweeping the country were important, if they were true, but the conversation had to be kept going somehow until the outskirts of York came into view and they could lapse into silence.

'Peter's a partner in his adoptive family's jewellery business,' Sammy said as he parked the car. 'It's an old-established business, and apparently he trained as a silver-smith and loves it, unlike his father, who hated it and became a teacher.'

'The man who took my child was a teacher. The doctor told me that,' Esther thought, but kept it to herself.

The shop, when they found it, was imposing: a mahogany front surrounded plate glass windows with gold-embossed letters proclaiming: 'S. P. Elphinstone and Son.'

'What if he's not here?' Esther whispered as Sammy swept her into the shop.

'Have some faith,' he whispered back and made his way confidently up to the counter. 'I want to see something unusual,' he said firmly, to the young girl there. 'A crafts-man-made piece for my wife. Do you have anyone here who makes to order?'

'Mr Elphinstone does very fine work, sir. Mr Peter Elphinstone. I can see if he's free.'

And then a man was coming in from the workroom behind the shop, smiling at them from a face Esther knew well. It was Philip Broderick's face, the face of the man she had loved, and whose child stood now, tall and strong, in front of her.

'My friend has come to advise me,' Sammy said, squeezing Esther's arm at the elbow to indicate his support. 'I want something made up for my wife. A specially created brooch, I think. She loves pearls – what do you suggest?'

And Esther's son was smiling at her, and pulling at pencil and paper, and she could see that he was indeed a happy man, and all was well.

The news that Tony was coming to Britain sent Anne into a paroxysm of excitement. What would he like to eat? She got an American cook-book from the library and experimented with waffles and syrup, before deciding that she would be better off introducing him to good British food, like Yorkshire pudding and hot pot, which he had once talked about in his letters.

But when the first euphoria wore off and the visit drew near she began to dread his arrival. Would he look at her with cold, distant eyes? After all, he had never seen her, except when he was too young to register. She would be simply a stranger, a foreigner, a funny woman without a trace of transatlantic gloss. She looked at herself in the mirror and was depressed by what she saw. No doubt his American grandma was sloe-eyed and olive-skinned, and all Stella's talk of moustaches was a myth.

But there was a greater fear attached to the boy's appearance in Belgate. Why was he coming now, with Howard Brenton growing frailer and quieter before her very eyes? Was it the hand of God? And if it was, what was she to do about it?

She drained her cup, and stood up to stretch. She methodically wound the clock, turned off the lights, and checked the doors and windows. Then she climbed the stairs, her limbs suddenly like lead. No insomnia tonight! She passed the closed door of Terry's bedroom, hearing one of her daughter's beloved Beatles records, wishing she could have confided in her daughter and knowing she could not, for Terry had a look of misery on her face these days that defied description.

In bed she thought of all the people she knew who were in trouble, a prayer-list that got longer by the hour. She rattled through them until she came to Howard Brenton. Yesterday Esther had cried: it was the first time Anne had seen her cry since she was a bairn. And all the time her own guilt had been gnawing at her, even while she was telling her sister to brace up and all would be well. If Howard died . . . when he died . . . without knowing about Tony, she would be in purgatory for the rest of her life. Not to mention the life to come.

32

June 1963

Britain was buzzing with a row that had erupted after the scandalous revelation that John Profumo, Secretary of State for War, had been lying, after all, when he denied 'impropriety' with the 'model', Christine Keeler.

'This will bring the Tories down,' Frank told Anne on the phone. 'Macmillan was close to tears, according to our Whips. And there's a lot more still to come out.'

Ordinarily Anne would have been cock-a-hoop at the thought of a Tory government's possible downfall, but today it seemed not to matter. She was grieving for her beloved Pope John XXIII, who had lost his painful struggle against cancer. He had been Pope for only five years, and yet the impact the saintly and warm-hearted man had made was enormous. Protestant neighbours offered their condolences in the street, and she heard sobbing in the packed church when they met to pray for the repose of his soul.

One picture in particular recurred in Anne's mind's eye: Pope John walking along the packed cages of an Italian prison and smiling at the villains, who held out their hands to him through the bars, with compassion in his face, and love for the dregs of society. For most of her life, Anne had found it hard to love even ordinary, decent people. Worst of all, she had not only been unloving, she had lied and schemed. Howard Brenton was in London now, for a check-up with the surgeon who had treated him for the same disease that had killed the Pope. Her footsteps were leaden as she went to early mass to ease her troubled conscience.

How many times, in the old days, had she prayed for

Howard Brenton to come to a sticky end? However she had phrased it, that was what she had meant. Now he was ill, and too late she had realized that he was a good man, and was her sister's man to boot. Worst of all – she had kept him from knowing he had a grandson, and now the boy was lost to all of them. It was retribution on her, and well-deserved.

She fell back upon the Our Father, the easiest of prayers to say, but as the words followed one another automatically, her mind raced. If Howard died, she would never be able to look Esther in the face. If Esther ever found out about the boy . . . a trickle of sweat ran down Anne's back although the church was like an ice-box. And what if God decided she had not been punished enough – for her sins were many? What else could he take from her? She shifted on her knees, threading her beads through nervous fingers, thinking of Aleida Barwick's eyes on her from her hospital bed. *'If it hadn't been for you . . .'* The woman had almost spat out the words. And then, when she had died, there had been an opportunity to make amends – but she had refused to join with Esther in sending flowers: *'Don't put my name on the card. She can burn in hell, as far as I'm concerned.'* But had she really ruined her father's life? Caused his drinking? His death?

And then there had been her long-ago deception of Frank. She had been willing to sacrifice her virginity and lie to Frank, just to escape having to bend the knee to the Brentons. The sin of pride. Was there no commandment she had not broken? But worst of all, by far, were the lies she had told over Stella's son. She had banished the child and denied him his birthright – for Howard would have acknowledged the boy but not robbed her of him, she knew that now. 'Forgive me, Father, for I have sinned.'

When at last Anne rose to her feet, she felt a hundred years old. She would have to hurry if she was to get Terry's breakfast ready in time. Her clever daughter, the best of the bunch when it came to brains, was a pale, withdrawn girl since she had come back from London, going from work to bed to work again. 'It's a judgement,' she thought as she came out into the sunlit morning.

Tripping on the kerb on her way home, she stumbled, grazing her hand on the grey stone wall, which gave her at last an excuse to cry.

As soon as she had waved Terry goodbye, she put on her coat and hurried through the Belgate streets towards the Quinnell house and surgery. Frank might not be here, but his sister was there. Perhaps Mary could give her some kind of absolution for a sin she dare not confess to the priest.

She found Mary Quinnell in her kitchen. The smell of proving bread was in the air and Mary was up to the eyes in flour.

'I've got to talk to you, Mary,' she said. 'If I don't talk to someone I'll go mad.'

'What is it?' Mary said, alarmed. 'It can't be that bad, surely?'

'I've done wrong. A lot of times – but one of them is killing me.'

As she poured out the tale of Stella's child by Rupert Brenton, she saw horror dawn in her sister-in-law's eyes. 'Well, what do you think?' she asked desperately, when her tale was told.

'I don't know what I think, to tell the truth, Anne. I can't really take it in. You mean you lied, and kept on lying all those years? And our Frank, too? Whatever was he thinking of?'

'I know we did wrong, Mary.' There was a touch of acid in Anne's voice now. She had not come to have her own disapproval confirmed: she wanted a solution. 'No one's denying we did wrong. The question is, what do we do now?'

'I know what I'd do,' Mary said.

'What?'

'I'd tell Howard Brenton the truth . . . and double-quick, before it's too late.'

'I couldn't tell him, Mary. It'd have to be Frank.'

'Or your Esther? You could tell her, and she could tell him.' It was the perfect solution 'Well, there's the phone,'

300

Mary said. 'Ring her now, before you change your mind.'

'No,' Anne said. 'I'll tell her face to face.'

'There now,' Aaron said, adjusting the footstool on which his mother's feet were resting. Naomi smiled at him and the boy leaned closer so that her limp fingers could touch his arm. 'Are you ready?' he asked, and she nodded. 'Right, then I'll begin.' He unfolded the airmail letter and began to read.

Hello to you all, how I wish you were here now so that I could put my arms around you and hug you. I thought about you all on the journey here and, in between, I worried about the moment when I would step on to Israeli soil, and what Nathan would think of me after so many years apart. As the plane came down I saw Tel Aviv. It is the largest city in Israel and it seemed to stretch forever, along the coastline and as far as the eye could see, Naomi. I wish you could have seen the blue of the sea, not exactly a sapphire, not a turquoise – a blue like no other.

I did not see Nathan at first, but then he was there and he knew me. After all these years, and the lines there must be on my face after so many patients and so much form-filling, he just looked at me and smiled and said, 'Ruth' and I said 'Nathan?' but with a big question-mark because he *has* changed. He is bigger – he has filled out and he is brown with the sun, except in the lines around his eyes which are crinkled up because he laughs all the time. We are to be married in the kibbutz, and I will wear the blue crêpe dress Esther had made for me, and Papa Lansky's pearls. Oh, Naomi, how proud Papa would be of Israel, and the people who are building, and planting, and making the desert bloom. Nathan says I have 'Israeli-fever' and do not see the hard work and the sweat, and that I will get a shock when I do! But all I know is that I thank you with all my heart that I am here with your blessing.

The boy's voice quavered, and when he looked up he saw his mother's eyes were fixed on him. 'It's nice that she's happy,' he said and cleared his throat to continue.

'Anne?' Esther was amazed to see Anne standing at her door, unannounced. 'Come in – there's nothing wrong, is there?'

Anne preceded Esther into the hall, which was filled with the scent of stocks, and then turned to face her.

'I need to talk to you, Esther. By ourselves. Is Howard in?'

'He's in the morning-room – come in here.' She ushered Anne into the study, and closed the door behind them. 'What's wrong?'

'Sit down,' Anne said grimly, and took up a stand by the fireplace.

'For God's sake, Anne – what *is* it? You're frightening me.'

'I've got something to tell you, Esther, and it's terrible. It's not trouble for you – it's something we did. No, *I* did. Frank said all along it was wrong, but I'd made my mind up and so when it all turned sour it was only me to blame.'

'What was it?' Esther said desperately. 'What did you do?'

'Our Stella's bairn, Tony . . . when she fell pregnant and married Mario – well, I suppose some people realized he wasn't the father.'

'I wondered,' Esther said. 'But Mario seemed happy enough to father Tony, so I let it go.'

'Mario knew *he* wasn't the father: he thought it was his friend's bairn. Ricky was killed on D-Day, and Mario, being what he is, stepped in when he saw how Stella was. But Ricky wasn't Tony's father, Esther. Tony is Rupert Brenton's son.'

For a moment there was silence. An uncertain smile came on Esther's face, and then vanished. 'You're joking,' she said at last. 'I mean, you *are* joking?'

'I wish I was,' Anne said miserably. 'I never intended it to turn out like it has. When Stella told me she was pregnant, I made her keep it quiet. She and Rupert were going to get married, and I thought Howard might stop it if he knew. Then, when the lad was killed, I hushed it up again – because I was scared Howard would want the boy, and take him away from her . . . from me. I didn't know him then, Esther: I just thought, "It's the Brentons. They take everything." I never thought Stella would go and marry a Yank. I thought she'd marry some nice Belgate lad –'

' – and you'd keep the child,' Esther said slowly. 'And for that you've lied all these years. Denied Howard his grandchild. My God, Anne, I knew you were ruthless, but I didn't know the half of it. Why have you come clean now?'

'Because I can't stand it any longer,' Anne said, close now to tears. 'It was bad enough before, but now – with Howard held the way he is – I can't stand it. You've got to tell him, Esther!'

'Me! *I'm* not telling him,' Esther said vehemently. 'You've got a cheek to even think I would. Do your own dirty work.'

'I can't, Es. I couldn't face him. But you can tell him – he'll take it from you.'

'I'm glad you think so. I think he'll be devastated, whoever tells him. To find out now, when it could be too late. All those wasted years without his grandson, Anne – how will you pay him back for them?'

Normally Esther would have insisted on running Anne home in her car, but she had made no such offer tonight. She saw her sister over her doorstep without even the offer of a cup of tea, leaving Anne to trudge miserably to the bus-stop and wait there for half an hour until a Belgate bus came along.

In the bus she tried to whip up some indignation to assuage her misery, but it was useless. Esther had been right to tongue-lash her; she would be entitled never to speak to her again. If anyone had done to her and Frank what she'd done to Howard – for a crazy moment Anne wondered whether Joe had a child somewhere, but that couldn't be: Joe had been brought up in a Christian home and wouldn't have got a girl into trouble.

It was a relief to let herself into her own home, and close and bolt the door. The light was on in Terry's room, so she was already in bed. Anne filled the kettle and switched on the radio, but it was only more boring details about the Profumo scandal, which looked likely to go on forever.

She was scalding the tea when she heard the back gate. Who could it be at this hour? If it was a constituent wanting help, they could bugger off. She would do most things to get Frank a vote, but she couldn't sympathize with anyone else tonight. She was too sorry for herself.

Suddenly the door latch was tested. That meant it was family, expecting the door still to be open. Anne hurried to unlock it, expecting to see Angela on the step wanting sugar, or a few potatoes, or just a chat. But it was not Angela on the step, it was David – in civvies, not his army uniform. And behind him was a slip of a blonde girl with a fat little child in her arms.

'Mam?' David was stepping over the threshold, his face earnest. 'Mam, I know it's a shock, but I had to do it now or never. This is Ilse, mam – I told you about her before. We're married, and this is our son. That's why we didn't come home that Christmas – because he was on the way and Ilse was scared.' His mother's unaccustomed silence had suddenly struck home. 'Say something, mam.'

Ordinarily Anne would have launched a tirade of abuse at him, at the German girl, at life in general. But the events of the last few days had weakened her.

'What d'you want me to say, David: "Come in, that's nice, I've got another grandchild. Fancy?"'

'Well – ' He was growing defensive now. 'You could tell Ilse she's welcome.'

For the first time Anne looked properly at the girl. She looked wretched, clutching her child, the pair of them for all the world like refugees. Anne sighed and held out her arms.

'Give me that bairn and get yourself in by the fire, lass. You look perished.'

The child smelled sweet, which was a good sign, and there was no hint of Nazi in his little face. 'What's h called?' she asked, as Ilse settled tentatively into a chair and David took his coat off.

'Joe,' David said. 'We called him Joseph – after our Joe.'

And Anne laid her cheek on the baby's head, and breathed thanks for something given back.

33

June 1963

Esther waited, looking out on the London street, until the consultant came out into the waiting-room.

'He's getting dressed, he won't be long. And don't look so anxious: as far as I can see, the operation was a success. Of course, as I explained before, we can't be sure. Not for years. But, at the moment, all is well. What worries me is your husband's general condition. He's painfully thin, and he's morose, Mrs Brenton. Or is it just today and coming to see me?'

'No, he's like that all the time . . . apathetic, I think I'd call it. He doesn't care about eating. He's not enthusiastic about anything.'

She broke off as Howard appeared, and went forward to take his arm. 'It's good news,' she said, but received only a faint smile and an inclination of the head.

'Howard is lunching with my brother-in-law,' Esther told the surgeon, 'while I do some shopping.' In the end it had been decided that Frank should break the news of the existence of Rupert's son, and the meeting today had been specially arranged. Esther had wondered if it was wise to tell him now, but in the end the fear that time was running out had settled it.

'Ah,' the consultant said. 'A convivial lunch . . . just what the doctor ordered.'

Esther smiled, thinking of her own quiet joy at seeing her son at last, and hoping that for Howard the revelation would bring peace, not anger.

They took a cab to Westminster, where they found Frank waiting, bare-headed in the sunshine. 'You go on to Harrods in the cab, Esther,' Howard said. 'I'd like to take a

306

walk across Westminster Bridge. It was almost the only part of my sojourn in this place that I enjoyed.'

As Esther drove off, she saw that Frank's face was a picture of nervousness. It wouldn't take Howard long to guess something was up.

The two men walked along the busy pavements, until at last they were out on the bridge, the Thames rolling beneath them, the cars speeding along the Embankment.

'How are you?' Frank asked. 'And I don't want the stock reply – I really need to know.'

Something in Frank's voice made Howard pause in his steps. They faced each other, each resting a hand on the parapet. 'I wondered why you suggested this lunch. What is it?'

'It's not bad news,' Frank said quickly. 'Well, not in the way you might think. No one's going to die . . .' He looked at the thin face opposite him and cursed his words. 'You know what I mean. I have something to tell you which is difficult – for me to tell, for you to accept. But I have to tell you. I've wanted to do it for years, and now Anne is making herself ill over it.'

Howard turned to the balustrade of the bridge and put both hands on it for support. He looked down unseeing at the rippling water far below. 'What is it?' he said. 'It's not about Esther?'

'No, it has nothing to do with her. It's . . .' He stopped, lost for words. 'My God, I don't deserve a job like this. Still. You know my girl, Stella, the one who went to America?'

'And is now married to Edward Fox,' Howard said. 'Yes. What has she to do with it?'

'She married a GI, a nice chap. Well, you know about Mario. She never loved him, but she needed a husband. A father for the bairn she was carrying.' Frank had turned to the balustrade too, both men staring downriver as though their lives depended on it. Frank was doggedly determined; Howard was a little embarrassed at this unravelling of another family's secrets.

'The thing is,' Frank said flatly, 'it was – well, it is – your Rupert's child. He and Stella . . . they were both young and it *was* war-time – '

'You mean, Stella had a child by Rupert? But they didn't even know one another! I'd've known, I'm certain. Rupert would've said – '

'It *was* Rupert's child, Howard, believe me. I don't know how we can prove it. There were letters, and that sort of thing.'

'But you knew – and Anne knew. Why didn't you tell me?'

'Don't ask me, Howard. If you knew the times I've wished we had. Anne never reckoned on the child going away. She wanted her grandson to be a Maguire. It nearly killed her when they went to New York, but Stella was married, and headstrong, and it was out of our hands. And it was a long time ago – things were different then. We thought you'd come down with a heavy hand, and we'd lose the child to you.'

'How could you think that of me?'

'Come on, Howard – you were the enemy, then – rich and distant. Be honest, you always had to remind yourself who I was in those days. "It's Maguire, isn't it?" That's what you used to say. I could see it in your eyes: "Oh now, this is one of my workers – who can it be?"'

'It wasn't quite like that,' Howard said miserably, but there was no real conviction in his tone.

'Well, we could rehash the past forever,' Frank said. Far down the river a siren hooted; behind them the traffic roared. 'The point is, what do we do now?'

'I don't know,' Howard said. 'You'll have to give me time. Where is the boy now? Is he one of the children she left in America?'

'Yes. She has a habit of leaving things behind.' It was hard for Frank to be so honest about his daughter, but it was not a time for further dissembling. 'The father – the man Tony thinks is his father – is a good chap. The best. It was his idea . . . well, that's another thing to tell you: the boy's coming over here, very soon. To visit us, and see his roots. His mother's roots, as far as he's concerned.' There was another pause. 'How would you feel about meeting him?'

'Why did you keep this from me?' Howard burst out again. 'All these years!'

'God knows,' Frank said. 'Fear, like I said: you were rich

we were poor. Black and white, it seemed then – well, it did to the womenfolk. And when Stella got wed behind our backs, I had to accept that she had a new man and a new life to make.'

They turned and began to walk on, neither of them hearing the traffic or seeing the birds that whirled above the river. 'Where d'you want to eat?' Frank asked. 'I've booked at Benders, but we don't have to go there.'

'I don't feel like eating, not at the moment. Shall we have a drink?'

A cab came by and they climbed aboard to make for the nearest pub. 'He'll be seventeen,' Howard said, half to himself. 'When does he arrive here?'

'He's here already,' Frank said, looking from the cab window to the face of Big Ben above them. 'At least, he should be by now.'

Anne had had her hair done specially for Tony's arrival. Now she looked at herself in the mirror – was it too 'set'? She put up a hand and ruffled the prim curls a bit. She was his granny, after all, and if half of what Stella had said about the Italian lot was true, she hadn't much competition.

On the table behind her she had laid out the best of her baking. She had tried out a recipe for muffins, which Stella had said Americans ate all the time, but they had turned out a disaster and gone in the bin. He would have to make do with good British girdle-cakes and home-made plum jam, but she had laid on some expensive coffee in case he turned his nose up at tea.

She watched the clock, all the while trying to decide what he'd look like. He had been a bonny baby: her first grandchild, and the best-loved, just as she had loved her Joe, her first-born – not more than the rest, but specially. She looked at the photo of the new baby Joe, now in pride of place on the telly. It was to be hoped Frank was right, and German blood was no different to any other. But Ilse was nipping clean in her habits, which was something.

There was the sound of activity in the backyard, and Anne stood up, her heart thumping uncomfortably under the new acrilan jumper.

The boy whom Stella ushered through the door was a disappointment at first – a man, without a trace of the child she had yearned for all these years. And then he smiled and held out his arms, for all the world like a film-star. 'Come on, grandma,' he said, sounding like an American film-star, too. 'The least you can do is hug me.'

34

August 1963

'Comfortable?' Sammy asked. Naomi smiled at him to show all was well, and he sat down and took up the airmail envelope. 'Now . . . let's see what she has to say this time.'

Last week we went to Jerusalem [Ruth wrote]. As we drove along the Jericho road near the Kidron valley, I saw the walls and towers of Jerusalem float into view. We stopped at the foot of Mount Moriah, where Abraham prepared to sacrifice Isaac – the place David bought from the Jebusites to build an altar. It is a holy place for both Jews and Muslims. Even the Romans built a temple to Zeus here in the 2nd century, after they had destroyed the great temple of Herod.

The golden dome of the Mosque of Omar is dazzling in the sunshine, so dazzling that the Crusaders thought it was Solomon's temple when they took the city and filled the Dome of the Rock with Muslim dead. There has been too much killing in this beautiful land, Naomi. I see the guns and the barricades, even now. All men should be able to live here, to enjoy it and worship in their own way. I don't know how, but we must find a way.

Tell Esther I saw the Garden of Gethsemane at the foot of the Mount of Olives, and said a prayer for her and Howard. I pray for you and Sammy and the children always, and so does Nathan.

'There,' Sammy said when the letter was ended and folded back into its envelope. 'You were right and I was wrong. Ruth is happy, Nathan is happy, and I see from your face that you are bursting with happiness. It was right that it should be so. I should've seen that.'

Naomi smiled. 'You can't be expected to be right every time. And most of the time you're perfect.' She put her left hand to assist her right and raised them slowly to touch his cheek. 'Sometimes I can't believe you're my husband. I love you so.'

Sammy caught her hands and held them palm upwards to be kissed. 'Not half as much as I love you, *liebchen*. I wake up in the night sometimes, and I think what would have happened if Eli Cohen had got things right and delivered us two boys. No Ruth, no Naomi . . . I go cold at the thought of it, believe me.'

'Eli knew what he was doing,' Naomi teased. 'He knew you and Papa Lansky were soft touches. Now, off you go and see to your business. I'm getting my hair done today, so I'll be even more beautiful when you come home.'

'Impossible,' Sammy said.

He was half-way to the door when Naomi's face clouded. 'What if Ruth has children, Sammy? Will I ever see them? And don't say we'd go to Israel.'

'No need,' Sammy said cheerfully. 'Today Esther and I sign contracts for two new supermarkets. I am rich enough to fly Ruth and Nathan and her triplets over here to see you. And if that *shmuck* gives me an argument about being indispensable to Israel, I'll send a task force to replace him. Satisfied?'

'Very,' Naomi said. 'Now go!'

Anne had to be persuaded to get up from her knees that morning. 'You're making too much of it,' Frank said testily. 'If Howard was going to make trouble – and he'd've been entitled – he'd've done it already. He's simply going to meet the boy, that's all.'

'But he won't say anything to Tony?' Anne asked anxiously.

'Well, he *might* say "How do you do, I'm your grandpa" – but I don't suppose he will.'

'It's all very well for you to be sarcastic,' Anne said. 'You don't know how I feel.'

She set out the breakfast things, checking the clock as she did so. 'Our Terry's usually down by now.'

When her daughter came into the kitchen, ten minutes later than usual, there was an air of eagerness about her. 'That's a nice suit,' Anne said, approvingly. 'You haven't worn that before.'

'No,' Terry said. 'I haven't worn it since I came back from London. Actually, I'm going out tonight – that's why I'm a bit dressed up.'

'Going out . . . with someone?' Anne's eyes were pools of curiosity.

'Now don't start making mountains out of molehills. But, yes, I've got a date. A date, mam . . . not an engagement party.'

'Thank God,' Anne thought. Aloud she said, 'Well get that bacon and egg down you before it gets cold.'

She tried to eat her own breakfast, but the food seemed to stick. What would happen at the Scar today, with Stella and Eddy and the boy and Esther and Howard and her and Frank all tossed together? The last time Esther had spoken to her, her eyes had been like two flints in her face, and Anne had avoided Howard since he'd learned the truth. She tried to put it out of her mind by doing chores, but as the clock moved towards eleven-thirty her unease deepened.

'Come on, then,' Frank said when she gave up the struggle. 'Let's get up there and get it over and then we can all settle down.'

But as Anne went up the stairs to dress, she was thinking that perhaps some people were born to trouble, and if so she was certainly one of them.

As they drove towards Belgate Esther looked out at the hedgerows. When she had walked these same roads thirty years ago, the grass had been lush and green, spangled with yellow buttercups and purple vetch and blue scabious and red campion. Most of that had gone with the dominance of the motor car, but the hedges were still there, sturdy and green. She put out a hand and covered Howard's hand, where it rested on his knee. 'All right?'

'I'm fine.'

She looked into his face and saw a calm there, but it was a stony calm that had no hint of serenity in it. For the hundredth time she asked herself how Frank Maguire could have been a party to such a deception. Anne – yes; she had always been able to convince herself that what she wanted to do was the right thing to do. But Frank?

And then it was there, the house she had watched them build on the Scar forty years before, the roof of green Westmorland slate weathered to a softer green – or so it seemed to Esther. So had the blaze of limestone that gave the Scar its name.

'Do you miss this house?' she asked, seeing that Howard too had been staring. The house they lived in now was fine and spacious, but did not possess the grandeur of this place.

'I don't miss it as a house,' Howard said carefully. 'Where we live now has a better feel, it's more of a home.'

'But it brings back memories?'

'Yes,' he said, and Esther let it go because Anne was standing to greet them on the steps, with Frank behind her, and there was such a look of misery on her face that Esther couldn't help feeling sorry for her.

'Auntie Esther!' Stella was a blur of chunky gold jewellery and Chanel perfume. 'And Uncle Howard. Do come in. You'll remember this house – not that we haven't gutted it, really, and started from scratch. You know my husband, Edward, of course. And this is my son, Anthony. Say "hello" to your aunt and uncle, Tony.'

Howard stretched out a hand, seeing a boy, a young man, who was a total stranger and looked foreign to boot.

'Welcome to my home, Howard,' Fox said, shooting out a hand and breaking Howard's concentration.

Esther groaned inwardly. That they should be beholden to Fox, of all people! Still, it would have to be endured. She glanced around the vast hall, seeing Diana's beautiful bare walls covered now with artefacts. And yet the ghost of Diana Brenton lingered there, on the wide staircase.

'Now,' Stella said. 'What will you have to drink? We've got everything, so don't be shy.'

They moved into the living-room, everyone milling

314

around until by a general unspoken consent, Howard found himself at one end of the long room with Stella's son, his grandson, beside him. He could see Diana in the boy, now, but there seemed to be a serenity he had never seen in her . . . or in Rupert. Was this the gift of the American man who had acted as a father to him? In that moment, any idea Howard might have had of reclaiming Tony left him, for the face that confronted him was happy, the eyes were bright with expectation of good things, the mouth kind. Suddenly he remembered Rupert, eager like this in the days before the war. He put out a hand and grasped a nearby chair.

'You've been ill, sir.' The boy sounded concerned. 'But my mom says you're getting better?' The voice was pure New York, and Howard smiled.

'Yes. Forgive me – just for a moment there I felt a little faint. It's been a warm day. You've come a long way to visit us.'

'Yes sir. We've been planning that I should come for some time, but then my grandpop died, and my dad works hard. He has six stores now, so he's got his hands full. Mom says my great-aunt . . .' He hesitated. 'It's Esther, isn't it? Yes, mom says Aunt Esther is in trade, too?'

'Yes,' Howard said. 'She and her partner have a number of big supermarkets and retail outlets. You must have a chat with her before you go back. Perhaps you could come to dinner with us?'

'I'd like that. I hope to see everyone in the family. There are an awful lot of folks, Maguires and Gullivers and . . . you're Brentons. And I want to see a bit of England, if I can. My dad talks about it a lot – his war service, and everything. They were great guys. Were you in the war, sir?'

'Not in that war, Anthony – the war before. But my son was in the last war. In the Royal Air Force.'

'He was killed, wasn't he? A fighter pilot? My grandmother's told me about him. And he had these great names . . .'

'Charles Rupert Neville Brenton. I think you'd've liked him.'

'I'm sure I would. My dad lost buddies in the war. He doesn't forget them.'

Stella came round then, bearing a silver tray of canapés. 'Smoked salmon,' she said. 'And those are cream cheese. Everything all right?'

'Splendid, thank you,' Howard said. Their eyes met, and he saw a flicker of unease in hers before she looked away.

'You'll see some changes here,' she said, as though to cover her confusion.

'Yes.' Howard averted his eyes from the clash of chrome and wrought iron in the corner of the room, topped by bottles of spirits and a silver-plated cocktail-shaker. 'Yes, it was different when I lived here – but that was a long time ago.'

Across the room Anne had relaxed, content, now, that there would be no explosion. She looked around her, seeing her daughter's home for the splendid place it was. All in all, things worked together for good.

'Thank you,' Esther said to Stella, when it was time to go. She had tried to read Howard's expression, to see how he felt about the meeting, but it was enigmatic. She took Anne's arm in the hall and squeezed it to show forgiveness.

'God bless,' Anne said as they kissed before parting. 'I pray for Howard every night. And Naomi Lansky, too.'

Edward and Stella Fox stood on the step to wave good-bye, their arms linked. 'Come any time,' Fox said expansively. 'Any time at all.'

Esther was waiting by the car, but Frank and Howard had wandered across the grass to the spot where they could look down on Belgate.

'It's a funny old place, isn't it?' Frank said, seeing the roof of the Half Moon, the welfare hall, the spires of the churches and the pit heap, neatly tailored by a bulldozer now but brooding over the village still.

'I had a dream for the end of the war,' Howard said. 'I was going to make Belgate a new Jerusalem.' He was picking out the war memorial, imagining the names upon it: Brenton and Maguire and Liddle and Bedell, and all the others.

'Well, it's not Jerusalem,' Frank said, 'but we're getting toward it. I'm proud of it, anyway, and I hope my children are, too. At least the war freed us from the old ties of class and deference.'

It was said without malice and Howard nodded agreement.

'Will your son marry my daughter, do you think?' he asked.

'If she'll have him – and if he's got sense. I'll tell you this though – your Pamela'll be the next MP for Belgate. She's got her head screwed on. And I'll pack it in, sooner rather than later. I miss Durham, and Anne frets a bit.'

'I know how you feel,' Howard said. 'I wouldn't have stayed at Westminster for so long if it hadn't been for the war. But I didn't feel able to go, while England was under threat.'

Frank nodded. 'At least, when I go, I'll be able to say, "No more European wars." We've all learned that lesson.'

'Yes,' Howard said. But some words of Kipling, learned in school and not thought of since, came suddenly into his mind:

As it will be in the future, it was at the birth of man,
There are only four things certain since Social Progress
    began –
That the dog returns to his vomit and the sow returns to
    her mire,
And the burnt fool's bandaged finger goes wobbling
    back to the fire.

Pray God that Frank was right, Howard thought, and that the fools were burned beyond forgetting it. It would be up to the people of the world to maintain the peace, for it was a fiction that governments created society. It was the other way around. Already the two minutes' silence on Armistice Day was gone. In time, would people forget what war had been like?

'What do you think of the boy?' Frank asked, as they turned back to the cars. He was trying to sound nonchalant, but Howard could sense the anxiety within him that things should turn out well.

'He's splendid. A credit to his father . . . to both his fathers.'

'So you won't be telling him the truth?'

'No,' Howard said. 'But I shall hope to see him again from time to time.'

'You will.' Frank sounded confident and Howard smiled as the other man continued: 'America's the place. They've got a good President now . . . John Kennedy has five years in front of him, and more Kennedys to follow, when he stands down.'

'Yes,' Howard said. 'A new generation to carry us forward.' He turned for a last look at Belgate, for he felt a sudden intense pride in the land which bred men like Maguire and women like Esther, his wife. God willing he would see another year, and another, and Anthony would come again, and Beb would grow into manhood.

'Thank you for today,' he said. 'Thank you for everything,' and he held out his hand, retaining Frank's hand long after he should have let it go. He turned at the last to see Rupert's son, in the doorway lifting his hand in farewell.

'Are you all right?' Esther asked anxiously, when he was safe in the car.

Howard looked at his wife, remembering the child she had been when first she came to the Scar, thinking how much more beautiful she had become. He leaned to touch her cheek with his lips. 'I'm fine,' he said. 'And suddenly terribly hungry. Can we go home?'

BY THE SAME AUTHOR

The Beloved People

In the Durham mining village of Belgate, the legacy of World War I has far-reaching consequences for rich and poor, socialist and aristocrat, Jew and gentile alike.

Howard Brenton, heir to the colliery, is back from the trenches with a social conscience, but robbed of the confidence to implement it. His beautiful, aristocratic wife, Diana, turns her back on her dour new world and looks to twenties London for excitement. Meanwhile, miner Frank Maguire and his bitter wife Anne becomed fired by union fervour as they struggle to survive the slump . . .

And don't miss **Strength for the Morning**, the second part in this powerful trilogy.

Remember the Moment

At thirty-two Emma Gaunt is in control of her life. She has wealth and independence and is her lover's boss.

Then a series of unlikely events overturns Emma's well-ordered world. Drawn reluctantly into the heart of her lover's family and into a search for the secret in her mother's past, Emma is forced to question her goals, her beliefs and her role as the 'other woman'.

and

None to Make You Cry
The Stars Burn On
The Anxious Heart
The Land of Lost Content
The Second Wife